ESTHER

ESTHER
ROYAL BEAUTY

A DANGEROUS BEAUTY
NOVEL

ANGELA
HUNT

BETHANY HOUSE PUBLISHERS
a division of Baker Publishing Group

© 2015 by Angela Hunt Communications, Inc.

Published by Bethany House Publishers
11400 Hampshire Avenue South
Bloomington, Minnesota 55438
www.bethanyhouse.com

Bethany House Publishers is a division of
Baker Publishing Group, Grand Rapids, Michigan

Printed in the United States of America

Library of Congress Cataloging-in-Publication Data
Hunt, Angela Elwell.
    Esther : royal beauty / Angela Hunt.
        pages ; cm. — (A dangerous beauty novel)
    Summary: "Based on the biblical account of Esther, this story
imagines the life and passion of this beautiful woman whose courage
and influence impacted history and the fate of her people"—Provided
by publisher.
    ISBN 978-0-7642-1695-4 (softcover)
    1. Esther, Queen of Persia—Fiction. 2. Xerxes I, King of Persia,
519 B.C.–465 B.C. or 464 B.C.—Fiction. 3. Bible. Esther—History
of Biblical events—Fiction. 4. Women in the Bible—Fiction. I. Title.
PS3558.U46747E85 2015
813'.54—dc23   2014031987

This is a work of historical reconstruction; the appearances of certain historical figures
are therefore inevitable. All other characters, however, are products of the author's
imagination, and any resemblance to actual persons, living or dead, is coincidental.

Cover design by Paul Higdon
Cover photography by John Salmon
Interior design by Paul Higdon and LaVonne Downing

Author is represented by Browne & Miller Literary Associates

17 18 19 20 21   7 6 5 4 3 2

Angela Hunt Presents
The DANGEROUS BEAUTY Series

"The Hebrew text has two words that are typically used to describe personal appearance. One, *yapeh*, is rather mild and means 'good looking.' The other, *tob*, when applied to women's looks, conveys sensual appeal. This woman is so beautiful that she arouses the desire of men who see her."

—Sue Poorman Richards and Larry Richards,
authors of *Every Woman in the Bible*

Beauty does not always benefit the woman who possesses it. On occasion it betrays her, and at other times it endangers her, even to the point of death.

These novels—*Esther*, and the upcoming *Bathsheba* and *Delilah*—are the stories of three *tob* women.

The light that lies

In woman's eyes

Has been my heart's undoing.

—Thomas Moore

CHAPTER ONE

HADASSAH

You may think you know me, but how could you? Others have related my story, and most of them paint a pretty picture. But unless a woman is allowed to speak for herself, no one will ever fully understand the events of a lifetime . . . and the secret recesses of a woman's heart.

Growing up, I was and yet was not like any other girl. My family was neither wealthier nor poorer than the families of other children in Susa. The cousins who reared me were neither more nor less loving than the parents of my friends. Staring into the polished bronze circle that served as Miriam's mirror, I knew I was neither more nor less beautiful than the other girls in our Jewish community.

Yet while my playmates cherished their dolls and the grown-ups pined for Jerusalem, I dreamed of being a queen.

Not *the* queen, of course. My ambition was not like that of certain men I would meet later in life, bitter men with ice in their veins.

Being unfamiliar with power, I did not crave it; being adequately fed and clothed, I did not covet wealth.

I wanted to be beautiful. From an early age I had been aware that certain things possessed perfection in their aspects—the arrangement of a vase on a windowsill, translucent clouds scuttling past a round moon on black velvet, a lotus beginning to bloom. On two or three occasions, when my cousin chanced to whisper in his wife's ear, her eyes sparked, a smile molded her cheek into a soft curve, and joy transformed her face into something so attractive that I could not speak.

I loved Miriam and her fleeting loveliness, but I wanted a beauty that would not fade with irritation or illness or the passing of years. And since everyone knew that only the most beautiful women in the world were fit to be kings' wives, I yearned for a queen's abiding beauty and flawlessness.

If I had been born with more attractive features I might not have been so fascinated with outward appearances. As a child, I would stare into the polished bronze and appraise my eyes—too big for my face—and my nose, which flattened into a spear shape whenever I smiled. My teeth were too large, my hair too coarse, my feet too long for my body. Being struck anew by my vast array of imperfections, I would lift my gaze to heaven and ask the Holy One of Israel to grant me beauty, fleeting though the gift may be.

My prayers intensified after I actually glimpsed a queen.

Miriam and I were shopping at the King's Gate bazaar, though I had wanted to stay behind. At eleven, I thought myself old enough to remain home alone, for who would want to bother me? The house I shared with my cousin Mordecai and his wife, Miriam, lay in the center of a street occupied by Jews on every side—merchants, jewelers, lenders, and scribes. Many of our neighbors ran businesses from their courtyards, so if anyone dared molest me, I had only to shout and the curious faces of half a dozen friends would have appeared at the top of our courtyard wall.

I shuffled reluctantly to the bazaar, but the bright sights of the marketplace lifted my spirits. The booths of merchants, farmers, and workmen stretched along both sides of a long street, and hundreds of people crowded the pavement. A girl could find anything at the bazaar, if she had a pocketful of silver talents and time to explore.

Though my pockets were empty, I had time to spare. While Miriam argued with the fruit merchant, I pulled my headscarf forward to shield my face from the sun, then strolled through the crowd and surveyed the wares in each booth.

I glanced across the crowded street, where several of the king's officers labored in a complex known as the King's Gate. The sprawling series of storerooms sat at the base of the royal fortress and next to one of the grand staircases that led up to the king's palace. In those stone warehouses, dozens of scribes and accountants accepted tribute from the citizens of Susa and distributed goods from the king's bounty. Mordecai worked in one of those offices, toiling six out of every seven days for the king. He knew Miriam and I were visiting the bazaar at midday, so I hoped he would step out to greet us.

I smiled as he emerged from a doorway and approached the marketplace. He lifted his head, caught my eye, and acknowledged me with a little wave. He took a step in my direction, but before he could make any forward progress, another man caught him by the sleeve and proceeded to vent his unhappiness about some matter.

Not wishing to interrupt, I made my way back to Miriam and desperately looked for something more interesting than rotting dates. The bazaar seemed especially busy, ripe with sounds, scents, and odd sights. A cacophony of animal noises accompanied the chorus of human voices—braying donkeys, the clip-clop of the occasional horse, the chatter of a caged monkey, and the whining of skinny dogs that scurried underfoot in search of crumbs dropped on the cobblestones. Soldiers from the king's vast army laughed as they shouldered their way through the crowd, leering at any woman bold enough to meet their gaze. Along with the usual merchants hawking their wares, Persian women in bright tunics carried wailing toddlers and tried to bargain with the tradesmen.

Of all the sights in the marketplace, the Persian women and their babies fascinated me most. I loved babies and hoped to have a dozen. The native women of Susa—who had been Elamites before Cyrus the Great made them Persians—were unlike the women from my neighborhood. They seemed freer, happier, and they wore lavish clothing that reflected their delight in vibrant colors, luxurious fabrics, and glittering jewelry.

The Jewish women I knew were not dour—they strove to be beautiful for their husbands—but their tastes were more constrained, as if they feared being too self-indulgent. Sometimes, given our people's tragic history, I wondered if they worried about being too happy. They spoke often of the exile and of our beautiful, ruined Jerusalem. They thanked HaShem that a handful of Jews had rebuilt the temple, but from their conversations I gathered that they considered Zerubbabel's effort a pitiful replacement for Solomon's masterpiece.

Still waiting on Mordecai, I turned to study a man bargaining with a rug merchant in the next booth: the buyer didn't like the color of the carpet spread before him. He spoke with an accent I didn't recognize, but Mordecai would. My cousin met travelers every day, for Susa, like Persia itself, was a stew of nationalities. The Medes and the Persians had conquered the world through assimilation, wielding the sword only long enough to force a rival kingdom's ruler to submit. Unlike the Babylonians who had destroyed our holy city, taken our people captive, and demanded that we worship their graven images, Cyrus the Great and his successors Cambyses and Darius did not force the aliens living within the empire to conform to Persian ways. 'Twas all part of HaShem's plan, Mordecai frequently reminded me, for Adonai himself had elevated Cyrus to liberate us from Babylonian captivity and open the door for some of our people to return to Jerusalem.

Yet not everyone had the means or the inclination to return to a ruined land. Thousands of Jews remained scattered throughout the empire, including our strong community in Susa. Mordecai felt that Adonai wanted us to remain where we were, though he couldn't explain why he felt that way.

As for me, I couldn't imagine living anywhere but Susa. The land was beautiful, the climate comfortable, and the bazaar fascinating. I loved visiting the marketplace and running my hand over rugs and fabrics woven in vibrant colors. I loved the freedom granted to our people, and I especially loved living in the shadow of the royal palace.

Like a dutiful daughter I stood beside Miriam and pretended to listen to her give-and-take with the fruit vendor. But my gaze wandered, and as the glittering curtain of an approaching litter caught my eye, curiosity overpowered my manners.

I couldn't see who rode in the litter, but gold and silver ribbons on the four upright supports fluttered in the slight breeze. No less than eight uniformed guards accompanied the mysterious traveler, four marching in front, two beside, and two behind, each man carrying a spear while a sword swung from his belt. A fifth man—one dressed in a hooded white robe, not the garb of a soldier—walked alongside the carriage and frequently inclined his head toward the curtain as if listening to someone within.

Being a native of the royal city, I often saw fine litters and carriages. But I had never seen anything to rival this entourage, and my curiosity yielded quickly to amazement: what sort of man or woman rode in such luxury and with so many guards? Only someone wealthy and important could command such a conveyance. The occupant might even be a member of one of Persia's seven noble families.

I tugged on Miriam's sleeve, hoping she could provide a clue, but she was too intent on her debate with the seller of dates. So as the litter drew closer, I broke every rule of etiquette she had ever drilled into my head.

If you see a person of high rank, you must lower yourself and get out of the way.

I rose on tiptoe to see better.

If you meet an elder or someone of slightly higher rank, you kiss them on the cheek.

I crept into the clearing that had opened for the approaching guards.

If you meet someone of much higher rank, you prostrate yourself on the ground.

Instead of crouching on the street like everyone else, I remained erect and staring, fascinated by the possibility of a brush with nobility.

Miriam turned and caught me gaping. "Hadassah!"

Her hissed rebuke brought me to my senses. I knelt on the cobblestones and swallowed hard when the litter slowed and stopped in front of me. A thick blanket of quiet fell over the immediate area, silencing the merchants around us. Even the chickens across the way stopped their cackling.

Slowly, I lifted my head to see what damage I'd done.

The slender, beardless man who walked beside the carriage caught my eye, then swiveled his gaze toward Mordecai, who was hurrying toward us. "Good day, my friend," the man in white called, his voice high and reedy. "I hope the gods are treating you well."

My cousin nodded to acknowledge the man's greeting, then moved to stand next to me. "Good day, Harbonah," he said, bobbing in a quick bow. When he straightened, he smiled at the man. "Have you been assigned to another post?"

I stared, my thoughts whirling. Mordecai knew this man? Maybe the conveyance had stopped to salute my cousin and not to rebuke me for my bad manners.

Harbonah laughed. "The king has other eunuchs to attend him, but he insisted that I serve as an escort during outings like this. He is careful to guard his treasures."

This man knew the king? And what was a eunuch?

Like an unsophisticated child, I stared first at my cousin, then at the tall man in the spotless tunic. How did he know Mordecai? His garment was well cut and of fine linen, so he had to be wealthy. So why wasn't he riding in the litter?

I didn't have time to consider the question. At that moment the curtain rustled and a feminine voice filled the silence. "Good morning." A bejeweled hand pushed the iridescent fabric aside to reveal raven hair, wide eyes, high cheekbones, and perfectly sculpted lips. The object of the king's protective attention was the most beautiful woman I had ever seen. She was even more breathtaking than my imagined images of Abraham's Sarah and Jacob's Rachel. . . .

At the sound of her voice, both Miriam and Mordecai knelt on the cobblestones. I remained on my knees, but I still didn't understand why we had to kneel in the middle of a busy bazaar. This woman was probably a concubine, and everyone knew the king had hundreds of them.

I lifted my head in time to see the lovely passenger glance at Miriam, then turn her attention back to Mordecai. "I could not help noticing your daughter—she is quite lovely."

My cousin lifted his head and gave the woman a polite smile. "You are most kind to notice my family. The girl is not my daughter, though my wife and I have raised her as if she were our own. She is my uncle's child, and he died years before your husband ascended the throne."

I blinked. Could my cousin be talking to the *queen*? And could the queen be talking about *me*? Surely not.

I hung my head and wished for invisibility. I had been staring at a royal litter, gaping like an ill-mannered slave at the wife of the most powerful man in the entire world. I ought to eat dirt, I ought to grovel for the rest of my life, I ought to be forced to climb the grand staircase on my knees until they were bleeding and torn—

Before I could declare my willingness to perform a proper penance, the woman spoke again. "She will make someone a fine wife. I have been considering brides for my firstborn, the crown prince. Your daughter could never be a royal wife, but Darius might fancy her as a concubine."

Wonder of all wonders, was she offering me an opportunity to live in the palace? Before I could cast a hopeful glance at Miriam, Mordecai answered in a firm voice: "I am truly sorry, my queen, but my young cousin is soon to be betrothed to a fine man from our neighborhood. I'm sure you understand that these arrangements must be respected."

"Must they?"

I did not dare lift my head, but I couldn't help but hear Miriam's quick intake of breath. From where I knelt I could also see Mordecai's hand, which had clenched tightly behind his back.

Buoyed by hope, I cast a quick glance toward the litter and saw a look of regret flit across the queen's perfect features, then she smiled again. "The man who takes her for a wife will be blessed by the gods—and you may tell him I said so."

She dropped the curtain, cutting off all further conversation. The beardless man, apparently her servant, nodded at Mordecai and called a command to the litter-bearers, who squared their shoulders and moved forward. But my gaze caught the tall man's as he looked back at us, and I couldn't help noticing that a corner of his thin mouth had lifted . . . as if he were silently laughing.

He was probably tickled by the notion that I might be fit for a prince.

Chapter Two
Harbonah

Of course, I wanted to laugh at Mordecai's young cousin when we first met. Though pretty, the girl was so obviously impressed by the queen that she could not possibly have possessed a woman's sophistication or intuition. A more experienced female would not have been awed by Vashti's striking face and sparkling jewels. She would have glimpsed the ambition shimmering in those bright eyes and heard the avarice in her tone. Mordecai's Hadassah had not yet learned, as I had, that a devious and jealous heart lay behind the woman's beauty and ostentatious adornment.

The queen spoke the truth when she remarked upon the girl's comeliness, but I had been struck by the obvious longing in the child's expression. Rarely had I seen such wistfulness in a girl's eyes, and never had I seen it in the eyes of a youngster from Judea.

Experience had taught me that most Judeans kept to themselves, conducting their business within the city without ever becoming a part of it. They worshipped, socialized, and arranged marriages only within the small scope of their community.

I chuckled as I dodged a runaway chicken that darted in front of the queen's litter. Mordecai's pretty ward might be obedient in word and action, but I'd wager a fistful of silver that restlessness stirred in her heart. I might have enjoyed talking with the girl, but given our circumstances I could only smile and wonder at the reason behind her wistful smile.

Did she long for romance? She was old enough to be betrothed, so perhaps her young heart pined for love. Did she long for wealth? Mordecai was not wealthy, yet neither was he impoverished. He had earned a responsible position at the King's Gate, which meant he was well compensated and well respected. He probably lived in a comfortable dwelling within walking distance of the palace, and the closer to the palace, the more luxurious the home. So the young girl had not known poverty in her short life.

I stopped walking as a babbling child broke free from his mother and ran toward me, then nodded in understanding as the mother shouted apologies and gathered up her headstrong son. A sidelong glance at the litter assured me the queen had not noticed the interruption, so Vashti must be deep in thought. A happy coincidence for all.

I resumed my steady pace as my thoughts returned to Mordecai and his lovely little ward. Perhaps the girl felt overprotected. Perhaps the child had heard stories of foreign lands and exotic kingdoms, and perhaps her encounter with the queen had revived buried dreams. She had probably never met anyone from the royal family, and if that were so, I felt pleased to have had something to do with bringing her joy. Few girls of her station would ever have an opportunity to see the queen, and even fewer would have a chance to be acknowledged by the king's wife.

Vashti had been correct about one thing—Mordecai's young cousin possessed a rare loveliness, evident even though her face still bore the soft plumpness of childhood. She would soon blossom into a radiant flower, perhaps one fit for the palace.

I was certain the girl would prove to be exceptional. For I, being a eunuch since boyhood, knew far too much about women.

⊰ ❧ ⊱

I might never have seen Mordecai's wife and ward again, but in the third year of his reign my master decided to hold a banquet unlike any in the history of the world. I smiled when he shared the news and naturally assumed that the burden for planning the celebration would fall on my shoulders.

Later, one of the scribes read the official proclamation to me:

"Saith Xerxes the King: Ahura Mazda, the greatest of the gods—he created me: he made me king: he bestowed upon me this great kingdom, possessed of good horses, possessed of good men.

"By the favor of Ahura Mazda I abolished the Kingdom of Babel and carried away the golden statue of Marduk, the hands of which the king of Babel had to seize on the first day of each year. By the favor of Ahura Mazda I killed the priest who tried to hinder me. By the favor of Ahura Mazda, Babel is no more, and Ahura Mazda has made me king in this earth. Unto Ahura Mazda thus was the desire: he chose me as his man in all the earth."

"Get to the point," I urged the scribe. "I don't need to hear all of that ritual talk."

The scribe shrugged, then moved to a paragraph further down the parchment.

"Saith Xerxes the King: At Susa, built by my father, an excellent feast has been ordered. The rulers of all twenty satraps are to come, all one hundred twenty-seven provincial governors are to come partake of a grand celebration, and all who fought with me at Babel are invited to come partake as well. All noble families of Persia are invited to Susa to enjoy a magnificent feast and the splendor Ahura Mazda has granted to me.

"Thus saith Xerxes the King."

The scribe lowered his parchment. "That's it. The king is giving a feast."

"For every noble, governor, and soldier?" I asked. "From throughout the empire?"

The nerves in my neck tensed when the scribe nodded.

So the king wanted to give a banquet—wonderful. He would realize that someone had to feed and entertain his guests, but he wouldn't give a single thought to the fact that his guests would also need a place to live, bathe, and relax for as long as they remained in Susa. They would come with horses and tents; some of them might bring their families. Somehow Susa, an already crowded city, would have to make room for all of them.

I stifled a groan and went straight to work. Never in the history of the world had a king made so generous an offer, and never in the short history of my life had I faced such an undertaking. I found myself hoping the king would never extend such generosity again.

The king's visitors journeyed from every corner of the empire, and all of them were eager to share in the king's largess. From as far away as India and Ethiopia the provincial governors came, along with every nobleman, soldier, and military officer in each of the twenty satraps. When every structure in Susa bulged with guests, I ordered the king's servants to spread luxurious white tents on the plain to house the late arrivals.

Those of us who served in the palace gritted our teeth, girded our loins, and pasted on polite smiles.

For one hundred eighty days, the king's guests raped the city of

Susa, trampling crops planted outside the city walls, ransacking the bazaar, and foisting unwanted attentions on the wives and daughters of Susa's citizens. These men, whose customs were as foreign as their faces, brawled at night and stayed abed through the morning. In their hosts' homes, they tossed chicken bones out the windows and allowed their horses to defecate in courtyard gardens. They bathed their dogs in lavish fountains and used so much water that several of the city's wells ran dry.

After two weeks, I was sick of our visitors, but the king was far from weary. For defeating a mere handful of rebels in Babylon and Egypt, he had become drunk on the praise of his guests.

For those of us who had not been so richly blessed by Ahura Mazda, the months of the royal banquet were more about exhaustion than celebration.

As the king's chamberlain, I was responsible for making sure every aspect of the feast met with the king's approval. Every morning we who served the royal family rose early to bathe and don white garments before we began to prepare the midday dinner. The gardeners pruned and raked and lit incense to sweeten the air; the cooks slaughtered and salted and baked, desperately trying to remain ahead of the guests' appetites. Slave girls mopped and swept and polished the marble columns and hallways while stoneworkers checked every inch of the glazed brick walls in case one of the revelers had managed to chip a delicate pattern.

I began to resent the feast, because it kept me from the work I enjoyed most—attending to the king's personal needs. Though my king had a host of eunuchs to attend him, I yearned to be the one closest to him and most in tune with his variable emotions. But I found it nearly impossible to serve my king and oversee the mother of all feasts.

When my master took a nap or went out for a ride, I remained in the palace and flew from station to station, ensuring that every

oblem had been considered and prevented. If a slave had
I stepped in to do whatever had to be done: grinding wheat,
a roasted pig for the flustered cook, refreshing a wilted flower
gement, straightening the fluttering banners in the garden, or
ng replacement musicians. The only task I refused was slaugh-
ring animals—I have never been able to stand the sight of blood.

The work was tiring, boring, and thankless, yet I understood
my master's desire to please his people. A king without satisfied
subjects would soon find himself no king at all, so every night I
would retire to a quiet corner of the palace, close my eyes, and try
to imagine what each guest must have seen, heard, and smelled after
they left their animals at the livery and climbed the stairs that led
to Susa's splendid fortress.

From the plain beside the river, the royal mountain was a spec-
tacular sight, rising from the flat earth and dominating the city,
one of several capitals in the Persian Empire. Four grand staircases
led up to the fortress, but visitors on horseback approached from
the Ville Royale, where they crossed a sloping bridge that ended
on a landing that flanked the garden.

Whichever approach the guests chose, they would stroll past
glazed walls decorated with reliefs depicting courtly processions,
the presentation of gifts, and preparations for ceremonies, all designed to remind the visitor that he was about to experience the
full splendor of the king's majesty.

Once the guest had arrived at the top of the royal fortress, he
would find himself in a great hall furnished with benches. Surrounded by gleaming tiled walls, here he would wait until summoned or until a servant arrived to guide him to the proper palace
within the royal compound. A guest would be most likely to be
escorted to the *apadana*, the magnificent columned hall designed
for receiving processions and gifts. This audience hall, built on a
plateau high above the river plain, featured towering columns, each

taller than ten men standing one atop the other. As many as ten thousand guests could mingle in the apadana, though not many of them would be able to catch a glimpse of the king.

If the guest were well-known, respected, or of high rank—a general in the king's army, for instance—he might be escorted to the palace of Xerxes, the king's personal residence. He would walk past dozens of heavily armed guards from the elite corps known as the Immortals, and he would meet with the king either in a reception room or the king's personal chambers.

Other high-ranking guests might have reason to visit the treasury, where priceless objects were catalogued and stored after being presented to the king. Dozens of accountants and scribes worked in the treasury, recording payments and dispensing gifts to those who had earned the king's favor. Other valuable items, most of them given as tribute or collected as spoil from conquered kingdoms, remained in the treasury as a constant reminder of the king's conquests.

Only a fool would approach the palace that housed the king's harem. Guarded and attended by a staff of eunuchs, the high-ranking royal women lived in these apartments, including the king's mother, his queen, and his concubines. These apartments differed from one another in size and luxury according to the occupant's rank.

During the banquet, slaves escorted guests directly to the apadana, which occupied the north side of the fortress and offered access to the exquisite grounds. The visitors began to arrive at midday and mingled in the garden until servants led them to the dining couches scattered throughout the apadana, the gardens, and among the fountains. As they ate, the guests bragged of their exploits in Egypt and Babylon, their encounters growing bloodier and the enemy more threatening with each repetition. The soldiers, generals, and governors participated in a continual game of one-upmanship, stopping only when they neared the king's level; then each man praised the king's military genius, power, and skill

ESTHER
Royal Beauty

until Xerxes approached the pinnacle of greatness occupied by the divine Ahura Mazda.

But my master was no god, and I suspected that he often doubted his own suitability for the throne. During the banquet, he continually referred to his father, the great Darius, as if emphasizing their relationship to legitimize his leadership. "By the favor of Ahura Mazda," he would say as each night's revelry drew to a close, "Darius the king, my father, did much good. And by the favor of Ahura Mazda, I will also add to that work and build more. May Ahura Mazda, together with the gods, protect me and my kingdom."

I knew, though few others did, that while the guests laughed and exchanged stories in the gardens, the king held secret meetings with his generals in his private quarters. Eager to avenge his father's only defeat, the king was designing a military campaign against a western nation. His victory in Babylon had been little more than a suppression of rebels, and he knew it. He wanted new territory, and he had turned his gaze upon Greece.

The vast majority of military men at the banquet had no idea they were being fattened like pigs for slaughter. As the sun dipped toward the western horizon, the generals emerged from the meetings and slaves carried trays of food through the crowd, allowing each guest to take whatever he liked. During the meal, servants hovered near with rhytons molded in the shapes of winged lions, many of pure gold. These vessels held the kingdom's finest wine, and slaves stood ready to pour whenever the king raised his glass. No one drank unless the king did, and though some may have quietly grumbled about the king's restraint, I felt grateful for my master's self-control. These were soldiers, after all, so they should be men of discipline.

As the guests ate their fill, slaves lit oil lamps suspended in the trees, and evening crept over the garden. Musicians strummed the lute and lyre while the royal concubines walked throughout the crowd, exuding a feminine loveliness that charmed and fascinated the men in attendance. Not a man present, however, would have dared to touch one of the king's women.

After a suitable interval, the curtains around the king's private enclosure dropped softly to the floor, creating a wall between my master and his guests. The one thousand Immortals assigned to guard the king shifted their positions in order to escort him to his bedchamber.

Our banquet guests recognized their cue to depart.

My fellow slaves and I stood with hands clasped as they bundled the remnants of their feast and headed toward the stairs, some leaning on each other, others accidentally dropping the food intended to sustain them during their stay in Susa. Even though the king discouraged drunkenness during the banquet, his men were not so temperate when away from the royal presence. As I watched one bleary-eyed captain take a long drink on a bottle he'd hidden in his tunic, I marveled that such an army had been able to crush a revolt.

But they had been sober in battle. I knew I should not resent this feast, their reward for valor and victory.

But I did.

⌘

After six full months of feasting and drinking, the soldiers, commanders, generals, and governors gathered their servants, piled their pilfered treasures into carriages and chariots, and followed the king's highways back to their distant homes. While I knew they would never forget this experience, I fervently hoped I would.

Then the king decided to host *another* banquet.

I was not with my master when he made the decision, so the announcement reached me through Memucan, the eldest of the seven vice-regents who advised the king on matters of law and policy. "The people of Susa have been sorely abused by the king's former guests," Memucan explained in the hushed tone suitable for speaking to a slave. "So to placate the populace, he will give another banquet to rival the first."

Tension ratcheted up my nerves. "Surely not for another six months."

"For seven days," Memucan replied. "For the next week we will feast as before, but without restriction as to the wine. As a special dispensation to his put-upon people, no servant is to refuse a guest if he asks for more wine, and no one is to compel a guest to drink. Furthermore, all the citizens of Susa are invited, including the women, who will be entertained by the queen in her chambers. The people have borne much for the sake of the king's graciousness; now they will be rewarded for their hospitality, grudging though it may have been."

Knowing we had to work or face the lash, we slaves set to work again. We replaced faded hangings, polished gold and silver goblets, cleaned silver couches, and refilled silken cushions.

"For all the people of Susa," one servant remarked as he hauled a pile of soiled pillows away, "except those who serve in the palace. When will the king give a feast for us?"

I caught him by the arm and gave him a stern look. "You feast in the king's palace every day, so hold your tongue lest someone chop it off. Your duty is to obey and remember that you could be outside planting crops."

"Like that'd be so terrible," the slave grumbled, shifting his burden to his hip. "Fresh air, the freedom to move about and keep a woman in a hut—that wouldn't be such a bad life. But what would a eunuch know about it?"

I stepped back, repulsed by the derision in his tone. I might have given him a snappish reply, but his words had transported me to a distant place, a vault filled with violent memories I had locked away and sworn never to release.

I knew what he meant because I had once been free. But I had also known starvation and poverty. And I had not always been a eunuch.

CHAPTER THREE

HADASSAH

MIRIAM WAS FINGERING THE DELICATE FRINGE on the border of a rug when I spotted Parysatis in her father's booth across the bazaar. My friend waved, then tilted her head in a small gesture that clearly said *get over here.*

I glanced at Miriam. While she and Mordecai did not keep to themselves as much as some of our neighbors, I knew they would be disappointed if I spent too much time with a girl who didn't know a forbidden food from an acceptable one. Parysatis was as Persian as the carpet beneath Miriam's hand, and she probably worshipped Ahura Mazda, Mithras, or no god at all. But we didn't talk about gods when we were together, and sometimes a girl needed to talk to another girl. . . .

"I'll be back soon," I told Miriam, squeezing her elbow. "I'm going to see Parysatis."

Miriam looked across the road, bewilderment and concern in her eyes. "You're going alone?"

"Parysatis is with her older brother. We'll be perfectly safe."

"Hadassah, I don't think—"

I didn't wait to hear the rest. Miriam was as soft as a feather bed, and I had always been able to work around her gentle protestations. And we *would* be safe, for Babar, Parysatis's handsome brother, had proved himself worthy of a name that meant *tiger*. At eighteen, he seemed to prowl through the marketplace, his muscles gleaming as he glanced left and right for anyone who might dare challenge his skill with a sword and spear.

Babar barely glanced at me as I hurried over and slipped my arm through Parysatis's, but I felt the touch of his gaze like a current on my skin. "I got away," I told Parysatis. "It's so good to see you."

"And you." Parysatis leaned into me as a sister might, then glanced across the road at Miriam. "I don't understand why she's so protective. You're thirteen, practically a grown woman."

"She's old-fashioned."

"And so much older than you. How did you end up with your cousins, anyway?"

I shrugged and ran my fingertips over a bolt of blue silk. "My grandfather, Shimei, had two sons, Jair and Abihail. Jair had a son, Mordecai, and many years later he sired Abihail. The younger son was my father."

"Did you ever know him?" When I shook my head, Parysatis's eyes softened. "I can't imagine not knowing my father. Every day he comes home and asks what I would like him to bring me from the bazaar. But if Mordecai does this for you—"

Again I shrugged, implying that Mordecai asked me the same daily question, when in truth he rarely asked if I wanted anything. When not working on the king's accounts, Mordecai spent his time studying Torah or in prayer. Our home was comfortable, not elaborate, and if my cousin had extra money, he was more likely to give it to the poor than to buy some frippery for the house.

Parysatis's father, however, lived for art, beauty, and music. The aromatic perfume of myrrh filled my head every time I visited their luxurious home, and I could have spent hours examining the vases, statues, carvings, and artworks without seeing everything. Every wall, floor, fountain, and furnishing in the silk merchant's dwelling had been designed to delight the senses, and I drank them in until I felt drunk on beauty. I loved hearing the silk merchant talk about the foreign lands where so many of his exquisite pieces originated. I would have given anything to be able to visit those exotic locations.

But even as I reveled in the stimulating aromas, the amazing sights, and the musical splash of the fountains, I could almost see Miriam shaking her head in mournful reproach. "You are too charmed by the world, Hadassah," she would say. "This place is not our home. Do not let yourself be blinded by trinkets."

But what was wrong with having nice things? Parysatis had everything a young girl could want—lovely garments, a maidservant, fine jewelry, and the most exquisitely wrought sandals. Her family kept horses at a stable near the river, and she could take a guest out riding whenever she wanted. Though Mordecai would probably say that my friend had been spoiled, Parysatis had never been anything but kind to me. She never criticized, never made me feel guilty for enjoying myself, and never asked why my guardians were so dour.

Not even now.

"I saw him earlier today." She pinched my arm in an overflow of excitement. "He was at the stable where my father keeps our horses."

"Who?" I asked, though I knew perfectly well whom she meant.

"Mushka." She breathed the name. "And he looked so handsome on his stallion! My father says he is destined to grow up to be a very important man. I only wish I could know that I am destined to become his wife."

I resisted the urge to roll my eyes. Parysatis was in love with the king's seventeen-year-old nephew. The young man *was* handsome, but Mordecai said Mushka spent far too much time in the pursuit of pleasure. If the boy really wanted to learn how to help his royal uncle, he should take a post in the military or the treasury and not spend his time splashing silver around at the bazaar.

I, on the other hand, felt my heart turn over whenever Parysatis's brother entered the room. I tried to pretend he meant nothing to me, but Babar was the most beautiful youth I'd ever seen.

"So." Parysatis ran her palm over a lovely selection of silk, then held it up to her cheek and grinned at me. "Have you heard the amazing news?"

I hesitated, not wanting to appear completely ignorant. "The news about silk?"

She tipped her head back and released a charming, musical laugh. "The royal banquet, you silly. The feast for *us*."

My heart did a double beat. "Us?" The word came out in a squeak. "As in you and me?"

"As in you and me and your family and my family and all the citizens of Susa. My father learned the details last night. Apparently the king intends to reward us for our patience with his soldiers. He is giving a banquet to honor every citizen of Susa, from the noblest family to the most common. Father says our banquet will be every bit as grand and glorious as the feast for the king's army. And Mushka is certain to be present!"

Stunned speechless, I shifted my gaze to the wide bowl of sky overhead. I had dreamed of visiting the palace ever since meeting the queen, but in my daydreams I was a grown woman and I climbed the steps to the palace with a wealthy and well-bred husband at my side. My dream self wore a long silk gown with dozens of delicate pleats, and my hair was laced with gold cords and pinned up in a riot of curls. My beautiful jewelry gleamed in the sun—gifts from my husband, who bore a striking resemblance to Babar—including a richly decorated necklace, a carved gold bracelet, and a pair of shimmering earrings. In that imagined moment, I felt I could finally be called *beautiful*. . . .

But if Parysatis was telling the truth, I would be visiting the palace soon. I wouldn't be nearly as striking as I'd hoped to be, but I would happily trade my daydream for this incredible reality.

"Are you sure your father's information can be trusted?" I pinched the plump flesh of her upper arm. "Because if you're teasing—"

She pulled away from me, laughing. "I'm not teasing, I promise. So ask your cousin Mordecai for a new gown because you're going to need one. Something regal, something silk and—" she winked—"something expensive. With all of Susa present, you'll want to stand out."

I snorted softly. In the company of so many wealthy and noblewomen, a simple Jewish girl was far more likely to fade into the background.

⚬⚬⚬

Parysatis had spoken the truth. The next day a royal herald stood at the top of the great staircase and announced the banquet for the citizens of Susa, while mounted couriers carried the proclamation to distant points of the city. Women buzzed with the news as they filled their jars at the well, and patrons crowded the silk merchants' shops from the time they opened for trading until the time they blew out their lamps.

Miriam, however, insisted she did not want a new dress, and I didn't need one.

I couldn't have been more horrified if she'd said she planned to attend the royal banquet in sackcloth.

"But Miriam! Every woman in the city will be wearing her best on each of the seven days. You need several new dresses and so do I."

She shook her head. "We shall wear what we have and be happy.

Women should be modest, Hadassah, and not overly concerned with outward beauty. Sarah was beautiful, yes, but her beauty was rooted in her kind and gentle spirit."

"But—" I wanted to argue that I was young, I wasn't yet married, and surely we should want to look our best for a king we respected. But for each of my points, Miriam would have an effective counterpoint. She would say the young should be protected, I would be betrothed soon enough, and I should live to please Adonai and not a pagan king.

I knew exactly what she'd say and didn't particularly want to hear any of her reasons.

So I decided to carry my request to Mordecai. Though the man had a will of iron, if I approached him with a note of pleading in my voice and a pitiable expression on my face, Mordecai's iron could be softened. I always felt a little guilty after manipulating him so obviously, but he was intelligent enough to see through my wiles. And as long as he was willing to grant me a favor . . .

Knowing that Mordecai would soon appear, I waited outside our courtyard as the sun began to set behind the royal fortress. His bushy brow rose when he saw me standing outside the gate.

"Hadassah." A note of rebuke underlined his voice. "A young woman should not stand idly in the street."

"I was waiting for you." I smiled and let him lead me into the courtyard. "I'm sure you've heard about the upcoming banquet."

"I have." He closed the gate behind us and turned, the suggestion of a smile playing around the corners of his mouth. "And I'm sure you'll agree that the three of us should stay home."

I gaped at him, momentarily bewildered by the absurd idea that he might not want to attend. "But—but it's a gift! To thank us for housing those soldiers."

"I hardly think that allowing three men to sleep in our courtyard deserves such generosity."

"But to refuse the invitation would be an insult to the king, would it not?"

His eyes sank into nets of wrinkles as his smile deepened. "Are you worried the king might be offended by the absence of an aging accountant and a thirteen-year-old girl? But that is not why you waited for me. Along with my assurance that we will attend the banquet, what do you need?"

I drew a deep breath, utterly relieved. "Parysatis says she's wearing a new dress every night, and her father has commissioned special jewelry in honor of the occasion. I wouldn't ask for so much, but a new gown would be nice. I want this banquet to be something I will never forget. Soon I will be married and then I will become a mother and have many little ones. Considering that I will spend my days chasing children and keeping house, this banquet might be the high point of my life."

His heavy brows furrowed. "You think your life will amount to so little?"

I sighed, not understanding why he couldn't see the obvious. What other fate could possibly await a girl like me?

"Never usurp the right of the Almighty to plan your future," he said, his dark eyes intent on my face. "HaShem is always at work, even when you can't see Him."

I wanted to cry out in frustration, but a display of temper would never influence Mordecai to act in my favor. My cousin remained silent, his eyes probing mine as if he would discover the motivation for my request. Then he gave me a small smile. "I happen to know a man whose wife is a skilled dressmaker. Tomorrow I will ask if she has time to make another gown before the banquet."

I clapped in victory. "Thank you, cousin! Thank you!"

He looked at me in patient amusement, then shook his head and went inside the house, leaving me to dance in the courtyard alone.

CHAPTER FOUR
HARBONAH

BY THE TIME THE FIRST CITIZEN OF SUSA ARRIVED on the inaugural day of the king's banquet, fresh white cotton curtains canopied the garden, providing shade from the bright winter sun. Beneath the canopies, blue silk banners fluttered from silver rods, tied by purple cords of fine linen. The apadana's towering columns gleamed with a fresh coat of oil, and the marble tile shone beneath our sandals. The intricate mosaic flooring of malachite, marble, onyx, and mother-of-pearl moved more than one guest to stop in his tracks and gape at the heretofore unimagined majesty of the king's palace.

I mopped my damp forehead with a square of spotless linen and tucked it into a pocket of my tunic. We had worked through the night to make certain everything would be ready for the residents of Susa, and by some miracle we had finished our cleaning, baking, polishing, steaming, and roasting. If any element was missing—in truth, I clung to the hope that the king's guests could not miss what they had never seen.

Never before in the history of the Medes and the Persians—perhaps in the history of the world—had a king thrown open the doors of his palace and invited everyone outside his walls to partake of his hospitality. As slaves escorted the male citizens of Susa, both lowly and great, to dining couches in the garden, female servants led the guests' wives and daughters to similar accommodations in the queen's palace. Knowing that women were fascinated by the living quarters of other women, I had suggested the king ask Queen Vashti to give the women a tour of her rooms after the feast. She had balked—no surprise there—but when I reminded her that Hatakh, the queen's chamberlain, would handle all the details, she relented.

Still, the queen was not happy about the king's grand gesture. She had given birth to my master's third son only a few months before, and though she did not have to tend or nurse the infant, she often cited the birth as an excuse for not appearing at various royal functions. On this occasion, however, the king had insisted that she play her part.

I was standing near the western staircase and observing the guests' arrival when I spotted Mordecai with his wife and charming ward. The accountant wore his usual austere tunic, adorned only with a light fringe at the bottom, but both women wore beautiful gowns. The girl's, I noticed, had been cut in the latest fashion, close fitting through the body with long, flaring sleeves. Both Mordecai's wife and ward wore silk scarves over their hair, a modest and traditional accessory.

I lifted my hand and caught the accountant's gaze. "I am happy to see you, my friend. Welcome to the king's house."

Mordecai and his wife responded with the perfunctory nod I received from most people, but the girl fairly glowed at my words.

And since I had a soft spot for that delightful creature, I acted on
an impulse.

"Ladies—" I bowed to them—"may I escort you to the queen's
garden? She is waiting to delight and entertain you."

Mordecai's wife frowned, obviously uncomfortable with the situation, but the girl's lips parted in a gasp of eagerness. Yes, this one
yearned for a taste of the life she would never find among her fellow
Judeans. If the others in the Jewish district were as hardworking,
sober, and taciturn as Mordecai, I doubted they ever indulged in
the sort of feasting they would enjoy at the queen's banquet.

Mordecai's hand caught his wife's wrist before I could lead the
women away. "Be wary." He kept his voice low. "I will attempt to
leave as soon as I can make a discreet exit. We need not stay late
every night."

The girl's face crumpled with disappointment. "Cousin, this is
a celebration!"

"What have we to celebrate here?" Mordecai's mouth took on an
unpleasant twist. "We will enjoy the king's hospitality for a while
and then we will go. We need not remain here all night."

As the young woman's lower lip edged forward in a pout, I lifted
my hand to smother a smile. The Persians had made sure I would
never father a child, but I had grown up serving royal children, so
I recognized youthful displeasure when I saw it.

My friend Mordecai was likely to have an unhappy walk home.

CHAPTER FIVE

HARBONAH

FOR SEVEN DAYS THE CITIZENS OF SUSA feasted and drank at the king's table. Food streamed from the kitchen on hundreds of platters, while wine flowed like water from golden vessels. The king observed everything from the shelter of his private tent, the queen tolerated her role as hostess, and the king's nephew Mushka played the fool, entertaining the male guests with ribald jokes and crude imitations of oblivious wealthy merchants and Persian nobles who passed by his table.

When the sixth day of feasting had ended, I stood at the balcony and looked over the streets of Susa, watching the unfortunate results of the king's liberality. Only a few guests made it home that first night without mishap, for nearly every man who'd indulged in the king's wine either stumbled or vomited or made a fool of himself on the journey. The people managed the king's generosity better on the second and third nights, and guests left the palace on the fourth and fifth nights in relative sobriety. But the collective self-control slipped on the sixth night, as if every man feared he'd never be offered a cup of wine again.

I dreaded the seventh and final night.

Everyone seemed to understand that my master's generosity would be a once-in-a-lifetime occasion. Never again would events align in the same pattern; never again would the king's wine flow without restriction.

I saw resolution in the determined faces of the early arrivals— they had come to gorge themselves. Men greeted me with hungry eyes, many of them admitting they had not yet broken their fast in order to leave room in their bellies for the king's delicacies. The women wore brighter colors and more numerous jewels than on previous days, and many of them twittered with anticipation, eagerly awaiting whatever entertainment the queen had arranged for this last day of the royal feast.

Mordecai's family proved to be an exception. They arrived later than most of the guests, and as they reached the top of the western staircase Mordecai caught my sleeve. "I am glad to see you, Harbonah," he said, motioning toward an alcove where we could talk privately. "And as much as I would hate to insult the king's hospitality, my family and I must depart before sunset. If you could seat me toward the back of the garden so that I can slip out unobserved . . ."

That's when I realized that Mordecai was maintaining a secret.

"Tell me." A smile curved my lips. "Do your overseers at the King's Gate know you are a Jew?"

He might have been surprised that a eunuch could be so perceptive, but Mordecai was nearly as skilled as I at concealing his emotions. His brow flickered; then he tipped his head back and looked at me. "Does my being a Jew affect my work?"

I shrugged. "I have never heard anything but good reports about your service for the king."

"Does my being a Jew matter to you?"

"No more than my being a eunuch seems to matter to you."

A muscle quivered at Mordecai's jaw, and he shook his head. "I am sorry for the injustice that has brought you to this place. But I will always see you as a friend."

"As I see you, truly. And as the king sees you. My master knows his empire is composed of many tribes and kingdoms. He is tolerant and expects others to be tolerant, as well."

Mordecai nodded slowly. "And yet . . . people fear those who are not like themselves. And fear spawns persecution. We saw it in Judea; we saw it in Babylon." He seemed preoccupied for a moment, as if troubling memories had suddenly overshadowed his awareness of our conversation. Finally, he looked up. "For reasons you may not understand, I am not at peace about announcing my heritage in this place. I will not deny it, but neither will I announce it."

"Yet you have no reason to fear." Aware that we might be over-heard, I glanced quickly left and right, then pulled Mordecai deeper into the alcove. "The great Cyrus liberated your people! He gave them permission to return to Judea and even restored the sacred objects that had been stolen by the Babylonians—"

"Of course," Mordecai interrupted, his voice smooth. "He did so because Adonai compelled him to act on our behalf. But this king—"

"Has my master not been good to you?"

Mordecai tilted his head and weighed me with a critical squint. "I can see that you admire him. I do too in some respects. I am pleased to work in his treasury. But do you not recall the occasion when he received a letter from the enemies of Israel? He did not respond favorably to my people that day. Indeed, he condemned them."

I stammered, searching my memory until the recollection emerged. Not long after my master ascended to the throne, a group of Judean Samaritans had attempted to terrorize the returning

Jews and stop their efforts to rebuild the city walls. They wrote my master, charging the Judeans with rebuilding a "rebellious and wicked city." They warned that the Jews, if successful in finishing the city walls, would refuse to pay tribute or taxes, thus reducing the royal revenue. They had ended their letter with a stern warning: "If this city is rebuilt and the walls are finished, you will soon lose possession of all territories beyond the river."

Though previous Persian kings had supported the Jews in Judea, my master determined to research the matter for himself. He had the letter translated from the Aramaic and searched the royal archives for confirmation of the Samaritans' story. After finding proof that Jerusalem had indeed been a rebellious city ruled by powerful kings, he sent the plaintiffs a terse reply: "So now, order that these men stop work and that this city not be rebuilt until I order it. Take care not to neglect your duty; otherwise the harm may increase, to the damage of the king."

The king discussed the correspondence with his vice-regents, and I had been privy to the conversation.

Reluctantly, I met Mordecai's eye. "My master did not condemn the Jews. He merely stopped the work."

"But he didn't support them, as had his father and Cyrus before him. So my fellow Jews and I have decided to quietly remain in Susa. When the ground beneath a man's feet is uncertain, he does well to tread lightly."

I gazed at the accountant, surprised and intrigued by his reasoning. I had known Mordecai only as an accountant who kept records, recorded tributes, sealed and sent correspondence. Our encounters had convinced me he was intelligent and diligent, yet I had never really seen the man behind the desk.

What I saw that night, however, met with my approval.

I bent my head in genuine respect. "I see no need to ever identify you as anyone other than Mordecai, an excellent accountant in the king's service. Persia is an amalgamation of many peoples and many customs. My master has always exulted in the great variety of his empire."

Mordecai nodded, then clapped me on the shoulder, a surprising gesture from one usually so reserved. "Thank you. And if you will seat me in the shadows, I will be able to collect my family before sunset. We do not travel on the seventh day."

I blinked, not understanding, but his request could be accomplished easily enough. "I will not only seat you in the shadows," I said, walking him back to where the women waited, "but I will do the same for your women."

Mordecai and his wife smiled in approval, but when I glanced at the girl I saw disappointment in her eyes.

⁓⁂⁓

During the seventh feast I went through the motions of service and dreamed of again enjoying a normal life in the palace. Though one could argue that no life in the palace was "normal," how luxurious it would be to wake without worrying about the thousands of guests expected for dinner. How marvelous to rub my hand over a throat not swollen from shouting orders to foolish slaves who didn't know silk from linen.

Time crawled on its hands and knees during that final banquet, the hours stretching themselves thin as the wine flowed freely and the crowd grew more raucous. I picked up a golden vessel of sweet wine and carried it through the garden, refilling rhytons while the musicians played and the concubines twirled among the trees. Most of the men had finished with the main courses, stuffing themselves with venison, horse, beef, and pork. Others were still eating, enjoying the sweet baked apples wrapped in pastry, a delicacy the cooks had worked all afternoon to prepare. Throughout the banquet, the guests' golden goblets—no two of which were alike—rose frequently, along with shouts of praise to the king.

I expected the king to be sober and satisfied, perhaps even weary, but as I approached the curtained dais I saw he was in rare high spirits. Apparently delighted to realize that the work of celebrating his army and his citizenry was nearly done, he appeared flushed from inebriation and contentment. He reclined on his gold couch, surrounded by his vice-regents—the nobles Carshena, Shethar, Admatha, Tarshish, Meres, Marsena, and Memucan. These advisors had also been feasting for six months and one week, yet none of them seemed as drunk as my master. Perhaps they had learned the importance of keeping their wits about them while dining with the king.

I shifted the flagon to my pouring hand and approached the royal party. Catching my gaze, the king lifted his rhyton, then glanced at Memucan, the eldest and most trusted member of the inner circle. "I have heard," the king drawled, "that you have taken a new wife."

Memucan nodded. "Yes, my king, I have. A lovely girl from Assyria. She's one—" he hiccupped—"of the most beautiful women I have ever seen."

The king's eyes narrowed. "Were the women of Persia not good enough for you?"

Memucan flushed, undoubtedly realizing what he had implied. For the vice-regent to insinuate that his wife was more beautiful than any Persian woman was to imply that his woman was more beautiful than even the queen—

A muscle in Memucan's jaw flexed, and he shook his head so forcefully I feared he would hurt himself. "Forgive me, my king, I meant nothing by my thoughtless remark. Of course my wife is not the most beautiful woman in Persia or even in the palace. She is the most beautiful I have ever seen because I, being a common man, have not had an opportunity to closely observe the queen or the royal daughters or any of the lovely concubines who grace your presence. Not that I require such an occasion. I am content with my own wife."

"You've never been near the queen?" My master sat up and looked around the circle of counselors. "Have any of you ever been close enough to speak to my wife?"

I stepped back, flagon in hand, and watched as the counselors stared at each other, all seven of them dumbstruck. Vashti had given birth to the king's third son only a few months before, so she had been absent from court for some time. But while all of them had *seen* Vashti before her pregnancy, few would have had occasion to speak with her. No man, however, wanted to report a private conversation, for who could know what a drunken king was thinking?

They waited, each man terrified, until the king looked directly at Carshena, the youngest. "Surely you have been close enough to appreciate the queen's beauty."

"I have, my king, but only for an instant. Yet I did not see her, because I fell prostrate as she passed by." The young man bowed his head, then lifted his gaze. "Still, I am certain that a lovelier woman is not to be found in all the empire."

The king grunted, then allowed his gaze to drift over the hundreds of male guests lolling on the couches in the apadana and the garden beyond. "*They* haven't seen Vashti," he murmured. "They live in this city, they have eaten my food for a week, yet they do not appreciate the greatest treasure I possess. They have no idea that my consort is the fairest woman in all creation."

I took another step back and would have retreated, but the solidity of a marble column blocked my way. An ill wind had begun to blow through the king's mind; I recognized the signs. My master was brilliant, charming, and gracious when he chose to be, but a darkness often descended upon him, a bleak mood brought on by an excess of wine and always accompanied by thoughts of women.

I noticed his lowered brow, recognized the smirk twisting his upper lip, and sensed the disaster about to befall us.

"Biztha," the king roared, setting his rhyton down with such force that red wine spilled on the tray. "You and your fellows go to the queen's palace and fetch Vashti to me. She should come at once, wearing the royal crown, so she will look like the queen of the king who rules the world."

Biztha, one of the eunuchs who guarded the king inside the palace, stepped forward, but he went pale at the king's order. I trembled for him—Vashti was a proud woman, and she had been asked to host a banquet and conduct a tour for the women of Susa. She had reluctantly agreed, but this would undoubtedly be too much. She had frustrated the king before, and unless she was in an uncommonly agreeable mood, she would frustrate him again tonight.

The seven eunuchs who guarded the king filed into double lines and strode out of the chamber. I slinked away from the royal presence, then ran to intercept Biztha in the hallway.

He halted as soon as he saw me.

"What should I do?" He shook his hands as if he would shake off the king's order. "The queen will not want to be summoned, not when she has guests. Every woman in Susa is watching her tonight—will she leave them in order to obey the king?"

"I don't think she will," I answered truthfully. "But you have not been charged with compelling her, so summon her as the king ordered, and let her answer speak for her. You can do nothing else."

My stomach tightened into a knot as Biztha hurried after the other eunuchs in the march toward the queen's palace. "Please," I begged whatever gods might be listening, "please put the queen in an amiable mood."

Compelled by curiosity, I followed the king's eunuchs to the garden where the queen was entertaining the women of Susa. Even before I entered, I could hear the gentle buzz of feminine voices and smell sweet incense. Behind the vine-covered wall, the wealthiest of Susa's families were enjoying a festive occasion with the poorest—truly a once-in-a-lifetime event. This should have been the grandest night of a week-long affair.

But an intuition warned me that Susa's feast would not end on a positive note.

I slipped into the queen's garden through a low door in the stone wall. Crouching beneath a spreading ligustrum tree, I could see the queen reclining alone on a golden couch beneath a white pavilion. Other couches had been spread throughout the garden, the area lit by soft lamps. Wine had been served at this banquet too, but the women had not drunk nearly as much as the men. Their kohl-lined eyes shone above bright smiles, yet no one in my hearing slurred her words or laughed too loudly.

In the center pavilion, watching with the expression of a proud mother, Vashti appeared to be enjoying herself. From the safety of her couch, she called to guests who sat close by. As I stood and crept forward, remaining in the shadows, I recognized one of the women near the queen: Parmys, the lovely woman who had married Masistes, the king's brother. Their teenaged daughter, Artaynta, sat beside Parmys, and both of them seemed at ease with the queen.

I could only hope that Biztha would feel as relaxed when he relayed the king's message.

I had nearly reached the queen when Biztha and his companions entered through a guarded gate and marched immediately to the pavilion.

"Begging your pardon, my queen." Biztha dropped to one knee. "But the king commands that you present yourself at the men's banquet. He would like you to come immediately, wearing your crown."

Vashti stiffened as soon as she heard the words *present yourself,* but she held her tongue until Biztha completed his speech. Then she arched a brow, shook her head slightly, and smiled at two women sitting just beyond the edge of the pavilion. "See how my husband bellows? He has had too much to drink; they all have, I'm sure. So he expects me to rise, leave my guests, and hurry over there to be ogled like some sort of concubine."

She offered honeyed, smooth words, but her dark brows rushed together as she met Biztha's gaze. "Tell your master I cannot come. I have guests of my own, and I must attend to them."

"But my queen—"

"Tell him I will not come." She spoke now in a voice of iron. "No woman abandons the banquet she has agreed to host. And no woman, especially not a queen, obeys the order of a drunken fool."

Biztha stood, his arms trembling at his side. "Won't you reconsider?"

"I will not." Her words were clipped and final. "Tell our king that I will speak to him later. But I am remaining here."

Biztha went a shade paler as he bowed again, turned, and led his company of eunuchs away through the garden gate.

Still hidden among the shrubs, I inhaled deeply and rubbed my chin, uncertain of what I should do next. The success of these banquets was my responsibility, but what could I do if the king and queen chose to argue in the midst of the festivities? Given time and opportunity, I could soothe the king, but I didn't think anyone had ever managed to soothe Vashti.

I sighed and braced myself to endure whatever would come next. Such was the life of a slave—like dogs, we bore kicks we did not deserve and harsh words we had not earned. And when we did accomplish something noteworthy, we stood back and watched our masters accept the praise.

As I turned to slip away, I spotted Mordecai's wife and ward near a flowering hedge. A roasted shoat lay untouched on a platter between them, and their glasses appeared nearly full. They were both staring toward the white pavilion, apparently fascinated with the drama playing out before their eyes. Miriam, who might have understood the undercurrents eddying between a husband and wife, wore a troubled expression, but the girl's eyes had gone wide with wonder.

Clearly she didn't realize that the evening had been a disaster.

I shook my head and crept back through the gardener's entrance. News of Vashti's impertinent response would be all over Susa by morning, and on its way to the far-flung satraps by tomorrow evening. The response would be mixed, but one thing was certain: after this report, some people would begin to question whether my master had the strength of will to rule his father's kingdom.

If a man could not command his own wife, how could he hope to control an empire?

⁓✲⁓

By running through an alley, splashing through a fountain, and making use of a secret passage between the harem and the king's residence, I managed to arrive at the king's tent before the eunuchs returned with the queen's reply. With an ease born of practice, I picked up a golden pitcher and began filling glasses, relieved that no one in the king's party seemed to have noticed my absence. Then again, who notices a slave?

When he and his cohorts returned, Biztha had the good sense to step forward and whisper the queen's response to a guard, who then relayed it to the royal ear. The area beneath the white canopy swelled with silence as the king reflected on his wife's answer to his summons. Then his face went pale except for deep red patches that flared over his angular cheekbones. He stood so suddenly that his guests startled, and then he left the tent and stalked into his chamber, leaving his counselors bewildered.

The vice-regents drew together like frightened children, undoubtedly wondering how they should respond. Shethar, who could barely speak without coughing, wanted to retreat and leave the king alone, but Carshena pointed out that abandoning the king might be interpreted as indifference or disrespect. So one by one, they girded up their courage and stood. The eldest, Memucan, looked at me, then jerked his thumb toward the hall. "You, chamberlain—will you lead the way?"

I lowered my pitcher, bowed to Memucan, and escorted the king's counselors past three guard stations to a private chamber, where the king paced in erratic circles, his hands locked behind his back.

Once they were all inside, I counted heads to make certain we had lost no one along the way. All seven men were considered friends of the king, so my master would do well to heed their advice. They knew every jot and tittle of Persian law, including what a king could and could not do.

"She refused to come!" the king roared, his nostrils flaring as he faced his vice-regents. "What can I do to make her regret this?"

The room filled with a quiet so thick that the only sound was the heavy rasp of Shethar's congested breathing. But Marsena looked at the king with an expression that could only be described as reproachful, and I knew my master would not want to earn the older man's disapproval.

Regaining a measure of control, the king dropped into a chair and rephrased the question: "According to the law, what should we do to Queen Vashti, since she did not obey the order conveyed by my officers?"

The vice-regents stared at each other, silently passing the responsibility of an answer down the line. Finally, wise Memucan spoke in a slow and deliberate voice. "Vashti the queen has wronged not only the king, but all the officials and all the peoples in all the provinces of the king. If this act of the queen's becomes known to all the women, they will start showing disrespect toward their own husbands. They will say, 'The king ordered Vashti the queen to be brought before him, but she would not come.'"

"The women of Susa are already saying it," the king muttered. "They were witnesses to her treachery."

Memucan lifted a hand in silent agreement. "Moreover, the noble ladies of Persia and Media who hear of the queen's conduct will mention it to all the king's officials, which will bring about no end of disrespect and discord in the empire. So if it pleases his majesty, let him issue a royal decree—and let it be written as one of the laws of the Persians and Medes, which are irrevocable—that Vashti is never again to be admitted into the presence of the king, and that the king give her royal position to someone better than she. When the edict made by the king is proclaimed throughout the length and breadth of the empire, then all wives will honor and respect their husbands, whether great or small."

The king stopped fidgeting as anger began to leave his face. "That is sound advice. If Vashti is going to behave like a common woman, let her be one. I have given her honor, I have elevated her above all others, and she is the mother of the crown prince. As such she has been esteemed above all other women in my empire, but if she wants to behave like a concubine, a concubine is what she shall be."

At my listening post near the doorway, I lifted a brow. The king might think he was demoting Vashti to the lowest position in the harem, but as the mother of the king's oldest son, she would always have power in the palace. She would still reign in the women's quarters.

My master looked around the half circle of sages. "Has anyone a better idea?"

I knew no one would speak. No one would dare suggest that Vashti be executed—as mother of the crown prince and two other sons, the idea was unthinkable. And she could not be given to another man. Once a woman had slept with the king, no other man would dare touch her. The act—the symbolism—would be tantamount to treason.

"Very well." The king drew a long breath, then turned and gestured to me. "Eunuch, summon a scribe. Let letters be sent to all the royal provinces, to each province in its own script and to each people in their own language: every man shall be master in his own house and say whatever he pleases."

I left the king's residence and hurried to fetch a scribe, breaking into a run as I skimmed the stairs nearest the King's Gate. Nothing in the world traveled faster than the Persian couriers and the royal post. Along the imperial roads, men and horses stood ready for action at all times; a man and a horse for each station until the king's edict reached the farthest point of the empire. Neither snow, nor rain, nor heat, nor darkness would prevent the couriers from covering their assigned route in the quickest possible time.

Whether by post or signals beamed by light and mirrors, within only a few days the entire empire would learn of Vashti's disobedience, demotion, and disgrace.

I reached the King's Gate. I called out the king's order and watched three scribes spill out of their small offices, boxes and parchments under their arms. And as I caught my breath and watched them hurry up the stairs to the king's council room, I wondered what would become of our former queen.

The king might strip her of her position, but he could never strip away the power of her influence.

CHAPTER SIX

HADASSAH

QUEEN VASHTI'S REFUSAL TO GO TO THE KING ignited a firestorm of gossip in Susa. Rumors drifted through the air like smoke, some saying Vashti would be executed, others that she would be exiled to India. Still others insisting that nothing would change, that Vashti would remain in the palace with her servants and her three sons. The youngest was still a baby, so who would be so heartless as to separate a baby from its mother?

No one mentioned what I later learned about life in the harem: few royal concubines actually nursed or cared for their babies, for the infants were handed over to wet nurses immediately after their births.

When I asked Mordecai about the queen's fate, he simply shrugged. "Vashti will be queen no longer," he said, "but women like her always seem to land on their feet."

I gasped, amazed that he spoke of Vashti as if she were an ordinary person. "Surely someone so beautiful—"

"But the edict," Miriam interrupted. "I understand the king issued an edict after the banquet."

Mordecai smiled. "The king's edict stated that a man is to be the ruler in his own home. So I ask you, wife—has anything changed? Women will continue to call their husbands 'lord' while making all his decisions for him."

Miriam lifted her gaze to the ceiling, huffed softly beneath her breath, and went back to kneading her bread.

I didn't know what had happened to the queen, but I enjoyed speculating with Parysatis. We would meet at the well or in the bazaar, and after I managed to slip away from Miriam, Parysatis and I would walk arm in arm and talk about the king, the queen, and who we wanted to marry when we were older.

Parysatis wanted to marry a man from one of the seven noble Persian families, because members of the nobility were always received at court. "Just think, one of my daughters might marry the king's son," she went on, her voice soft and dreamy. "I would be invited to travel with the royal household, summering in one palace, wintering in another."

"You *are* a dreamer," I teased, lightly pinching her arm. But I didn't tell her that I had been dreaming too, yet not so much of kings and palaces. Lately I had been dreaming of Babar, Parysatis's handsome brother. He frequently walked with us through the bazaar, and though he caught the eye of many a young woman, he seemed to smile most often at *me*.

Had my uneven appearance finally begun to look at least presentable? Could he possibly love me? Could he find the courage to approach Mordecai to ask about marrying me?

I dreamed of walking arm in arm with Babar, of breakfasting with him, and resting my head on his shoulder, but when I tried to imagine him approaching Mordecai, my daydreams came to an abrupt halt. As valiantly as I tried to imagine a situation where

Mordecai might be indebted to Babar—if, for instance, the young man saved me from a runaway carriage on a busy street—I could not imagine a situation dire enough for Mordecai to agree that I should marry a non-Jew.

Those of us who worshipped Adonai, the one true God, were not allowed to marry anyone who did not believe. We could trade with Gentiles, laugh with them and talk with them, but we could not marry them. Some of our people had broken this law, Mordecai told me, and HaShem was not pleased. If we married people who followed false gods, we would undoubtedly pick up some of their detestable practices. We would find ourselves slipping away from the one true God, and the scattered nation of Israel would become polluted.

Yet when I dreamed of kissing Babar, religious purity was the furthest thing from my mind.

I knew I'd have to be married someday, but every day I avoided the marriage canopy was another day I was free to dream of Babar. Every older Jewish girl I knew had been betrothed as she approached maturity, so I couldn't think of any acceptable objection when Mordecai and Miriam asked if I might consider Binyamin, son of Kidon, to be my future husband. Binyamin and I had known each other since childhood, but we rarely spoke. When our community gathered to worship on the Sabbath, I would glance across the space separating the men from the women and find him staring at me. He would look away quickly, a blush tinting his pale face, and I wondered what sort of man he would become. Would he become a merchant like his father? Or would he serve as an accountant like Mordecai? Would he be loud and rowdy like our rabbi? Or would he be like Miriam, gentle yet capable of shouting in a whisper?

I often caught Miriam watching me the way a cook watches a pot over the fire. When I began to bleed in a woman's monthly cycles, she showed me how to care for myself during the time of uncleanness and taught me about the *mikvah*, the bath that would restore me once my bleeding had stopped.

"Soon—" she smiled at me through sentimental tears— "Binyamin's father will send someone to negotiate the bride price and the dowry." She sighed. "You will make a beautiful bride, Hadassah. Like the myrtle you were named for, you will prosper and flower in this land of exile."

Beautiful? She exaggerated, but she loved me, and love made allowances for imperfections.

I smiled at her, but I remained in no hurry to marry. As the only child in Mordecai's household, I had benefited from the attention of two doting adults who could not believe that Adonai had entrusted them with a baby. Aware of their delight, and grateful for it, as a girl I sat by Mordecai's side and learned—an education that would have been denied me if Mordecai had sons to teach.

My cousin taught me Torah. He also taught me about the history of our people and about the sins that had caused us to be exiled from our beloved land. I learned about my royal heritage: Mordecai and I, descended from the tribe of Binyamin, could count King Saul among our forefathers. Because we had also descended from the tribe of Judah, we were part of the royal line of David, a line that would one day produce the promised Messiah. I enjoyed talking about David and his many exploits, but Mordecai's thoughts seemed to center on Saul. He would often shake his head and murmur that Saul's impatience and pride had brought about his downfall.

One afternoon, when I had lingered at the bazaar instead of going straight home as instructed, my cousin sat me down and illustrated my error with a story: "When Adonai told Saul to attack the people of Amalek and completely destroy everything, Saul promised to obey. But he did not keep his word. He destroyed the people, but spared Agag the king, as well as sheep and cattle and other goods.

He destroyed what was worthless, but spared what was valuable, and thus incurred the wrath of Adonai."

I blinked up at him, unable to understand what a long-dead ancestor had to do with my lingering in town.

"Samuel the prophet," Mordecai went on, "reminded Saul that Adonai does not take pleasure in burnt offerings and sacrifices, but in obedience. For rebellion is like the sin of sorcery, and stubbornness like the crime of idolatry. Because Saul rejected the word of Adonai, Adonai rejected Saul as king."

Mordecai's gaze drifted to some distant field of vision as he finished my lesson: "Adonai warned that if we did not drive out the inhabitants of the land He gave us, those we allowed to remain would become thorns in our eyes and stings in our sides—and He would do to us what He had intended to do to them. And that is exactly what He did."

I sat still for a long moment, soberly reflecting on my lesson: *do not disobey.* I inscribed that law on my heart, for I hated disappointing Mordecai even more than I hated the idea of sinning against Adonai.

Though my cousin had a tendency to lecture, I loved spending time with him. As we walked together through the narrow streets of Susa, I realized that Mordecai was highly respected by Jews and Persians alike. Medes, Elamites, Babylonians, Assyrians, and Egyptians greeted him with the honor due a learned man, while our fellow Jews greeted him with the respect due a *tzaddik*, a righteous man.

As a child, I often asked Mordecai what he did when he wasn't at home with me and Miriam. He replied that he worked for the king. When I asked what he did for the king, Mordecai would smile and ruffle my hair, saying some things were too difficult for me to grasp.

But when I grew older, and my cousin saw that I yearned to

understand the world outside our courtyard, he explained that he was one of many accountants who kept records for the king. Every item brought to the palace as tribute, and every allotment of grain, food, or materials dispensed to a citizen, had to be measured, valued, and recorded. And while an honest man did not grow wealthy working for the king, Mordecai said that one could always accumulate the wealth of a good reputation. "And that, Hadassah," he'd say, patting my cheek, "is worth more than all the riches in the king's treasury."

I may never be certain, but I believe Mordecai purposely delayed telling Binyamin's father that I had flowered into a woman. Perhaps he thought me too young for marriage; perhaps he and Miriam wanted to enjoy being parents for a few more months. Whatever the reason, as I entered my fourteenth year I remained in my childhood home, helping Miriam run the household even as I looked forward to evenings when I could sit and learn by Mordecai's side.

By that time, however, I had stopped asking about the kings of Israel and had begun to ask about the kings of Persia. I learned that HaShem had judged Israel and sent our people into exile in Babylon, where many of our young men were castrated and forced to serve a pagan king. One of these youths, Daniel, rose to a position of leadership in the government by interpreting dreams by the power of Adonai. From reading the word of the Lord as revealed to the prophet Jeremiah, Daniel learned that Jerusalem would lie desolate for seventy years. He also learned that great Babylon was about to fall, and it did, the night Darius the Mede captured Belshazzar's kingdom.

As the Persian Empire swallowed up Babylon, Cyrus the Great issued a proclamation allowing the children of Israel to return to Judea, just as the prophet Isaiah had predicted. Not all of us chose to go home, however. Mordecai's people traveled to Susa, where they settled into homes and occupations that would benefit their families and the tolerant Persian Empire. They still kept the Law, but they did so quietly and kept to themselves as much as possible.

The great king Cyrus was followed by Cambyses II, then by Darius the Great, our present king's father. These Persian rulers had accomplished so many magnificent feats and built such amazing palaces that I imagined them as super-humans. Though they did not worship Adonai, I thought their hearts must sincerely follow truth. Why else would Adonai have told Isaiah to call Cyrus His "anointed one"? And if Adonai could use Cyrus, perhaps He could work a miracle for me and use Babar. . . .

Whenever I spoke of the Persian kings in glowing terms, Mordecai cautioned me against becoming infatuated with people who did not worship HaShem. But King Xerxes's royal banquet for all the citizens of Susa had left a deep impression on my young imagination, and even Vashti's abrupt demotion had done little to dispel the romantic haze that enveloped my memory of the event.

Any nation that could produce Cyrus, I told myself, could produce any number of kings and noblemen who would do good and honor the people who honored Adonai.

CHAPTER SEVEN

HARBONAH

MY KING SET ASIDE HIS QUEEN during the third year of his reign, but in subsequent months he had little time to mourn her loss. Confident after quashing rebellions in Egypt and Babylon, he turned his thoughts to the trophy he coveted most: Greece.

My master might never have admitted the truth to his generals, but I understood why he desired Greece so earnestly. His father, the great Darius, had experienced only one military loss: the battle of Marathon, where seven thousand Greeks defeated Darius's army of more than thirty thousand. That loss loomed over the great Darius's career, the one blot upon a spotless record.

I had come to Darius's palace as a ten-year-old, and even then I had noticed how nine-year-old Xerxes yearned for his royal father's approval. Working in the shadows as a fly swatter, an errand boy, and a cook's boy, I watched the young prince grow up in his powerful father's shadow. I saw him skillfully wield bow and sword and spear in an effort to win his father's admiration.

At twenty, I was given to the crown prince, so I was with my master when Darius named his twenty-one-year-old son viceroy to Babylon. I rejoiced with my master when he obeyed his father's wishes and married Vashti that same year.

But on the day my master's first son was born, I shared his outrage and frustration. On the day he should have been elated over the birth of a future crown prince, my master's joy was swallowed up by the news that his father, the invincible Darius, had been crushed at Marathon.

Four years later, when my master ascended to the throne, I knew he would never feel equal to the task of ruling the empire unless he could avenge his father's loss. My king wanted to control Greece, but he especially wanted to annihilate the Greeks at Marathon.

After the king's celebratory banquets in Susa, my master's life filled with preparation for a military campaign. The royal treasury stockpiled grain and weapons, generals conscripted slaves for the army, and captains hired mercenaries as mounted swordsmen. Those who had chosen to serve in the Persian army trained hard, hoping to become one of the king's hand-picked Immortals.

So my king's thoughts turned toward war, not love, and he did not particularly pine for Vashti.

I was not keen on the idea of accompanying my king to yet another war, but I had no choice. I could, however, be grateful that the odds of my standing on an actual battlefield were slim, as my master planned to direct, not fight in, the battle ahead.

After months of preparation, most of the royal household trekked toward Greece. Though we traveled with dozens of the king's concubines, we left his former wife, children, and a skeleton crew of slaves behind to oversee the fortress in Susa.

We would not return until the seventh year of my master's reign.

CHAPTER EIGHT

HADASSAH

WE DIDN'T HEAR MUCH about the king's activities during the months of preparation for his military campaign, but we certainly saw the results of his labor. Regular shipments of food, horses, slaves, and weapons arrived at a depot near the royal fortress, transported on wagons from all over the empire. Hardly a week went by that we didn't glimpse foreigners entering the city, most of them speaking languages I'd never heard. During the hours of early evening we could climb onto our rooftops, gaze out across the plain, and see the glimmer of the soldiers' campfires. Thousands of tents dotted the flatland, occupied by slaves, mercenary soldiers, and the king's Immortals. Every day they trained in the hot sun, and every night they wandered through the bazaar searching for amusement.

Though Parysatis and I were only girls, we couldn't help getting caught up in the fever of war—the city was infected with it. Our devotion to the army only increased when Babar joined the army as an officer. Parysatis pretended that her brother's position was no great honor, but one day I saw him riding a fine horse next to Mushka, nephew to the king.

I clutched at my throat, amazed to see him in such royal company. The realization that I knew a man who rode only an arm's length from a man who knew the king left me breathless.

Parysatis and I took pride in our loyalty and did whatever we could to aid the king's military effort. We bought silk in the king's colors and wore our blue and gold dresses whenever we thought the army might march in or out for a training exercise. We cheered for the soldiers as they practiced maneuvers on the field; we stood by the city gates and offered dippers of cool water when the weary Immortals entered Susa. Of all the king's men, they were the most impressive—ten thousand highly trained fighters, their beards curled and oiled, their long hair gathered at their necks. They wore brightly colored garments, gold earrings and golden chains, carrying their spears in their right hands, with their bows and quivers hanging from their left shoulders. Rumor had it that if one Immortal fell, another would immediately rise up to take his place, so they were, in truth, an immortal company.

When the commanders and generals stood before a gathering of Susa's citizens to proclaim that the king would soon ride off to extend the glory of Persia and bring liberty to the citizens of Greece, we listened and wept, realizing that some of the men might not return from battle. The thought of beautiful Babar lying dead on some patch of foreign soil tortured my sleep, but Parysatis told me not to worry. "He will not do much fighting," she said, shrugging. "Mushka has asked him to serve as a messenger for the king."

The news left me wide-eyed with astonishment and joy. Not only would Babar be safe, but he would spend hours in the presence of the king himself.

The preparation for war awakened a passionate patriotism within my heart, but Mordecai and Miriam only shook their heads when I reported on the progress of the campaign.

"We are citizens of Persia, yes, but this is not our home," Mordecai reminded me more than once. "We are children of Abraham. We are of Israel."

I nodded, but in those days Israel felt more like a concept than a reality, my Jewish friends only a collection of dour, stodgy friends who insisted on tradition above all else.

Nothing short of dire illness could have prevented me from watching the great caravan assemble on the plain. With Parysatis by my side, we sat on a step of the grand staircase and stared at the pageantry of war on full display—bright colors, horses, men, and wagons clad in gleaming metal armor, flashing weapons, and heavily muscled men. The army had been divided into divisions, and for seven days a different division departed for the battlefield. I had never seen anything like it in all my fourteen years.

When the last group of horses disappeared over the horizon, I clutched at my throat, drowning in a flood of adolescent devotion. Those strong warriors, riding off to face noble death—such unbelievable bravery! Such honorable hearts!

Mordecai and Miriam must have sighed in relief when I came home, exhausted, and told them the army had departed. The whirlwind of activity surrounding the royal fortress vanished with them, leaving Parysatis and me bereft and bored.

CHAPTER NINE

HARBONAH

I KNOW NOTHING OF THE ART OF WAR, but my uneducated eye convinced me of my master's conviction that quantity must defeat quality. I found myself traveling in the midst of a huge army, probably the largest ever assembled, while a navy of over a thousand ships sailed parallel to our land route. By placing his faith in intimidating numbers, my master forgot the lesson his father learned at Marathon: the swift little bee can defeat the ponderous lion.

Though I have often prayed to forget that long, arduous journey, my memory has not dulled over time. Most of the king's troops traveled on foot along the Royal Road that stretched from Susa to Sardis while the king and his generals rode in magnificent carriages. The procession was so gigantic that a family seeing us approach on the first day of the week would not see the end of our convoy until sunset of the seventh day. Our men, cattle, and horses drained so many wells and small creeks along the route that those unfortunate enough to live on the king's highway had to find alternate sources of water.

I worried about the thirsty slaves traveling at the rear of our company, but my master seemed not to care about anything but forward progress.

I had never seen the man so possessed. His eyes held a light that burned like a flame. He slept restlessly, even after enjoying the company of a concubine, and frequently woke before sunrise, eager to break camp and move ahead.

Once we reached Sardis, only the Aegean Sea stood between us and Greece. But too many miles of water separated us, so we turned north, toward the Black Sea, where only a narrow strait blocked our passage.

My master called a halt when we reached the Hellespont, a channel so narrow we could see the opposite shore. The king consulted with his engineers, who theorized that it would be possible to build a bridge using the ships of the royal navy. The king then ordered hundreds of ships into the channel, and the engineers tied them together with ropes. My master believed he had solved the problem, but the gods who rule the wind and waves were not on our side. Before even a single soldier could cross, a sudden storm destroyed the bridge, snapping the ropes as if they were threads.

I have never seen the king so enraged, his eyes so black and dazzling with fury. As I stood trembling at his side, terrified that his anger would turn toward those closest to him, my master ordered that the waters of the sea be whipped and branded with red-hot irons. His troops hesitated only a moment, then leapt to obey, flinging iron fetters onto the roiling waters and stabbing the surface with hot irons. The sea responded with steam and hissing, as if it understood that it was being punished.

"Oh, vile waterway!" the men chanted as they disciplined the treacherous waters. "Xerxes lays on you this punishment because you have offended him, though he has done you no wrong! The great king will cross you even without your permission, for you are a treacherous and foul river!"

I watched, aghast, for I had never seen any Persian treat a river with such disdain. Persians revered their rivers, for flowing water is a source of life, and in all my travels with the king's household I had never seen a servant so much as wash his hands in a river lest he befoul it. Yet before my disbelieving eyes, Persian warriors and befuddled mercenaries up and down the shoreline expended their frustration on the waterway.

Why didn't they strike at the wind, which had been just as traitorous as the river?

At that moment, in a flash that was barely comprehendible, I realized that my master was not well. Though his muscles gleamed beneath his tunic, though he rarely coughed and never fainted, though he walked with an air of authority and commanded instant obedience, no man punished the river unless he was confused or tormented by an evil spirit. His men knew this too, and though they obeyed him, their wild grins and exaggerated gestures only served to emphasize the absurdity of his command.

Apparently the scourging of the sea did not satisfy the king's need to vent his frustration. He summoned the engineers who created the floating bridge; when they stood before him, shamefaced and cringing, he ordered their execution. The hapless builders, most of them weeping like women, were impaled on stakes outside the camp.

I watched, my flesh crawling beneath my white slave's tunic, as my master called for a second corps of engineers. When no one volunteered, he called for the assistants of the men he had executed and placed them in charge of building a second bridge. More than one tanned face went pale at the assignment, but oil lamps burned in their tents throughout the night.

The next morning the assistants offered a second plan: they

would build two bridges, one for the soldiers and another, farther downstream, for the livestock. They would use thicker ropes to lash the ships together. And as an extra precaution, they would build large windlasses on shore, a winch at each end of the floating bridge to keep the ropes taut.

Knowing their lives were at stake, the engineers labored for weeks, carefully positioning the boats, lashing the vessels together, and securing the ropes with the windlasses. When the bridge finally floated in its place, the engineers strengthened the structure by placing embankments of timber, stone, and packed earth across the ships' decks. I could barely believe my eyes when a veritable road rose from the sea.

And then we crossed.

My master's army marched through Greece, intent upon reaching Athens, the city that had dispatched its men to Marathon to defeat Darius. Fortunately, we did not encounter hostility along the way. Every city we encountered en route submitted, offering my king food and hospitality, content to let him pass through the land until he reached his destination. Every night we feasted on the best Grecian culture had to offer, and every morning our troops gathered up items of value and we moved on.

I felt a little guilty about stripping the populace as we traversed the land, but the practical aspect of my nature reminded me that we had left the people alive and unharmed. If they had resisted, their cities would be corpse-filled ruins, and their children would be marching away with nooses around their necks and fetters on their wrists. . . .

The thought nudged a memory from the dark recesses of my mind. I had once marched along an unending road with my hands tied. My wrists still bore scars where the rope had chafed the skin away, and my neck would never be smooth and unmarked.

But an orphan slave had few prospects, and I had been more fortunate than most.

CHAPTER TEN

HADASSAH

WITHOUT THE KING, Susa seemed like a body without an energizing spirit. The royal complex still glistened in the slanting rays of a sunset, but the aura of the palace had faded. Men still climbed the gleaming staircases to conduct business in the king's name, but they climbed without urgency and walked without trepidation. Mordecai often came home early, stating that his office had no visitors. The lines in his forehead relaxed, and he smiled more than usual.

Life without the king might be easier for Mordecai, but for me, Susa had become a dull no-man's-land. Without the influx of foreign visitors, Susa closed her shutters and drew inward. Many merchants left the bazaar or closed up their shops. The talented men and women who worked silver, brass, and gold in the Valley of the Artists moved away, in search of other wealthy settlements whose residents could afford the luxury of art. Even shepherds moved their flocks farther south, where the grass hadn't been torn and trampled by wagons and cattle.

I remained at home, helping Miriam, working in her garden, milking the goat. Mordecai said nothing about my marriage, and I didn't mention the topic. Life with Binyamin would probably be even duller than life with Mordecai and Miriam, so I resolved to remain quiet and content. And bored.

As I entered my fifteenth year, I wondered if life—and the king— would ever return to Susa.

We heard rumors from the battlefield, of course, as riders from the royal post circulated reports to the governors of the satrapies. We heard about our great king beating the sea into submission at Hellespont; we heard about his amazing victories over Greek cities in the north. We heard that the thunderous approach of his army so frightened rulers that they threw open their city gates and welcomed him, declaring themselves his slaves to avoid facing his sword.

Merchants in the bazaar draped blue and gold banners over their canopies, proudly displaying the king's colors. Others emphasized their loyalty to the army, loudly proclaiming that they had donated so many baskets of fruit, so many yards of silk, or so many chickens.

One morning I left Miriam with the weaver and saw Parysatis walking near another booth. Instead of calling to her, I threaded my way through the crowd, intending to tap her shoulder and surprise her. But before I could catch up, I saw my friend glance over her shoulder and dart down an alley and then run between two brick buildings.

I stared after her, perplexed. She hadn't seen me, so this couldn't be a game. So why was she behaving like a furtive thief?

I followed to the opening of the alley and saw her at a distance. She walked quickly, her head down and a covered basket on her arm. Intrigued, I followed, but caution stilled my lips.

At the end of the alley, Parysatis turned, leaving my sight, so I quickened my steps until I came to the end of the alley and stood in a patch of sunlight. A pile of rotting fruit stood in a corner, emitting an odor that nearly made me sick. Parysatis was kneeling beside it, talking to someone who remained hidden from view.

Concerned for my friend's safety, I stepped forward. "Parysatis!"

She turned, color flooding her face. "Hadassah! You shouldn't be here."

"So why are *you* here?"

She stood and turned, shielding whomever crouched behind her. "I'm making a delivery, that's all. Come, let me walk you back to the bazaar."

Terrified for her, I pulled away from Parysatis's outstretched arm and spied a man on the ground, her basket on his lap. The man's dark hair was matted and dirty, his hands covered in filth. I had seen beggars who looked like this, but my friend had never shown any interest in beggars.

"Who is this?" The question slipped from my lips before I could stop it, and the man's head lifted at the sound of my voice. For an instant I stared at the familiar face; then my heart thudded. "Babar! Are you hurt? Were you wounded in battle?"

I wanted to push Parysatis out of the way and kneel beside him, cleanse his wounds, do whatever was necessary to restore him to health, but something like a wry smile snaked across his lips. "Greetings, Hadassah. It is good to see you."

I stared in disbelief. "You're not wounded?"

"He's not wounded; he's hungry." Parysatis crossed her arms and turned to regard her brother. "He says he's not going back to the king."

"Not going back? I still don't understand why he's here."

"I don't care if I ever see the king again." Babar's gaze strafed my face, and then he took a loaf from Parysatis's basket and tore at it with his teeth.

"Please, Hadassah." Parysatis pulled at my arm. "Please, we must go. You cannot tell anyone that you have seen him; you must not speak of this."

"But—" I waved at the distant city gates through which Babar had ridden away months before. "He is a friend of Mushka, and Mushka is the king's nephew. Why is Babar here? Who would ever want to leave the king?"

"After being around the mighty Xerxes, I can't understand why anyone would want to be near him." Babar looked up at me, the whites of his eyes gleaming in the shadows cast by the heaps of garbage. "The king is a madman, and anyone who chooses to serve in his presence is a fool."

I stepped back, repulsed by Babar's description of the king and horrified by the depths to which he had fallen. How could I have imagined myself married to this creature? To a man who did not honor and respect my king? To a *deserter*?

"He says the king is not to be trusted." Parysatis tugged at my arm as her words flowed in a steady stream. "He fears for his life, Hadassah. The king executes anyone who displeases him, even if they have done nothing wrong. He has already killed three messengers who brought him bad news, so Babar was terrified he'd be next."

"All soldiers risk their lives," I replied, my voice cold in my ears. "Why should Babar be an exception?"

"He doesn't consider himself an exception—"

"All soldiers," Babar interrupted, "risk their lives in battle, but I found my life at risk simply by being in the king's presence. He is unpredictable and capricious. He is dangerous, an adder with a swift and deadly bite."

"He is not; he could not be." I drew myself up to my full height, convinced that Babar lied to disguise his own cowardice. "My cousin works for him, and Mordecai is the steadiest, wisest man I know. He would tell me if the king were anything but brave. You have fled from battle only because you are afraid."

"Hadassah, please." Tears streaked Parysatis's face; her distress— or her shame—was genuine.

"I'll go." I turned to leave. "And I won't say anything, but not for your sake, Babar. I will remain silent because I do not want to shame Parysatis, whose brother is a coward."

My friend burst into tears as I slipped my arm around her shoulders and led her from the place.

"He's wrong, you know," I told her as we walked back to the bazaar. "The king is a great man, and your brother is the fool. Everyone adores our king, and how could so many people be wrong?"

"I know you must be right," she replied, swiping her face with her sleeve. "And I know Babar has done wrong. But what can he do? He can't go back to the war and he can't go home. Father would kill him for running away, and the king would execute him for desertion."

"Babar has made his decision, so now he must live with it," I said, squeezing her shoulder. I felt great compassion for my best friend, but as we walked through the alley, I wondered how I could have ever imagined myself in love with a man who could be so rash and reckless.

⟶✥⟵

"Do you think the king will return soon?" I asked Mordecai one night after the evening meal. "Will he hold another banquet to celebrate his victories? Surely he will, don't you think?"

Mordecai looked at me, weariness and wariness mingling in his eyes. "It's not my place to read the future, child," he said, dropping one hand to my shoulder. "And your destiny has nothing to do with that pagan palace on the hill. We must think about your future, and that means your betrothal."

I fell silent, knowing what would surely come next. Mordecai and Miriam had successfully postponed the necessity of my marriage for several years, but time was slipping away from us. If a betrothal wasn't soon arranged, people would begin to wonder if something was wrong with me.

Maybe they wondered already.

Miriam cleared the table, then sat directly across from me. "You know we only want the best for you, Hadassah. You have been the light of our lives—" her eyes filled with tears—"and we will hate to see you go. But the time must come when a woman leaves her home and makes a new home for her husband and children."

I squirmed under her sentimental gaze and looked away, though tears stung my own eyes. She was right, and I had been foolish to hope that I could eventually persuade Mordecai to allow me to marry Babar. Mordecai knew best, and without him and Miriam, only Adonai knew what might have become of me. But they had taken me in, and blessed me with so much love. . . .

Someone rattled the gate outside. I pushed myself up from the table, about to see who was there, but Mordecai held out a restraining hand. "Sit," he said, a thick note in his voice. "Let me go."

He wanted to answer the door?

I watched him leave, then looked at Miriam. "Are you expecting someone?"

She said nothing, but sank back onto the bench, keeping her gaze trained on the doorway.

A moment later, Mordecai returned with three men. I recognized Elihu, our rabbi, Kidon, and Binyamin. One glance at the latter told me all I needed to know.

"Miriam, Hadassah," Mordecai began, looking at each of us in turn, "you know these men."

Miriam and I bowed our heads and smiled while Mordecai

escorted his guests into the room and gestured for them to sit on the cushioned benches by the fire pit.

"Kidon," Mordecai continued, looking at me, "would like to arrange a betrothal between you and his eldest son, Binyamin. He has brought the *shitre erusin*, written by the rabbi, to make sure everything is as it should be."

I looked at the rolled parchment in Kidon's hand—the bride contract. While I had been enjoying the life in the aura reflected from the royal family, Mordecai and Kidon had been planning my future.

Mine and Binyamin's.

For the first time, I looked directly at the young man who would be my husband. Binyamin was my age, a bit taller than me, and pleasant-looking. His eyes held neither snap nor twinkle, but neither did they flash in anger—at least they never had in my presence, and I had known him since childhood. He had the look of a man who would pass quietly through life, doing his duty, maintaining the traditions, and obeying the Law. He was not the man I would have chosen, but neither was he the sort I would automatically refuse.

I swallowed hard and forced a smile.

"Hadassah." Binyamin stood and slid a small wooden box from beneath his arm. "I have brought this for you as the *mohar*. Our fathers have agreed that it is suitable."

Despite my disinclination toward marriage, I leaned forward to see what was in the box. Apparently encouraged by my interest, Binyamin blushed and lifted the lid.

Inside was a gold necklace, fashioned with care, and a pendant holding a blood-red ruby. The piece was lovely, exquisitely crafted, and obviously of great value. Even Parysatis would have been impressed.

"You are most generous." I hesitated, knowing that accepting the gift meant I accepted his offer. "Did you make the necklace yourself?"

"I did." Binyamin smiled, waking the dimple in his cheek. "I wanted to make you something no one else had."

"And so you have." I glanced at Miriam, hoping she would suggest a way to postpone this decision, but her watery eyes held nothing but loving approval. She wanted me to marry this boy. So did Mordecai. So did Kidon, and so did the rabbi.

What could I say against so many?

I closed my eyes, silently saying farewell to my dreams and fantasies. Despite my close friendship with Parysatis, I was not a Persian girl. I was not able to wheedle favors out of my father, nor could I continue to dream about noblemen and palaces and beauty befitting a queen. Mordecai would cast me off before he would allow me to deny my people and marry a Persian.

So if I wanted children and to maintain peace in my family, Binyamin should be my husband.

When I opened my eyes, my thoughts had crystallized into hard reality. I forced another smile, then accepted the box and the young man who offered it. "Thank you."

My future husband stood before me, waiting in silence, until his father nudged him. Then Binyamin remembered himself and handed the bride contract to Mordecai. "I want you to know I have done everything possible to protect her," he said. "If something happens to me, she will never be left without property. I have promised not to make her leave Susa, if she does not want to go, or to exchange a good house for a bad house. Within the year, after I have prepared a home for us, I will come to take her as my bride according to the Law of Moses and Isra'el. I promise to please, honor, nourish, and care for her, as is the manner of the men of Isra'el."

Mordecai smiled. "Tell her that."

Blushing even more deeply, Binyamin pivoted and offered me

the *shitre erusin*. I accepted it, then handed it to Mordecai, where it belonged.

The older men laughed at this display of nerves, and then Mordecai picked up a charred stick to sign the document. Binyamin's father followed suit, and just like that, I was practically married. But not to Babar. Never to him.

"Elihu and I are witnesses." Mordecai folded the contract. "Hadassah will remain with us for another year while Binyamin prepares their future home. She will wait until he comes to escort her to the marriage feast." He turned to me, a strange light shining in his eyes. "From this moment, you shall consider Binyamin your husband in all manner except that which leads to children. Do you understand?"

I nodded, bereft of speech. I had known this moment was coming and I did not doubt Mordecai's wisdom, but the full realization of my future left me dry-mouthed and dazed.

A year from now I would be living in my own home, hauling my own water, cooking for my own husband. I would have to obey him, respect him, sleep with him. I would be expected to give him children and devote myself to them for the rest of my life.

My carefree days with Parysatis were numbered.

CHAPTER ELEVEN
HARBONAH

MY MASTER AND HIS ARMY MET NO OPPOSITION until we reached Thermopylae, a settlement only three days' journey from Athens. The surrounding area was nearly deserted, but an army of eight thousand Greeks had reinforced an ancient wall, blocking a narrow road that snaked between towering cliffs and the sea. Xerxes scoffed when he learned that only eight thousand would stand against his vast army, but he had us make camp and wait on our navy, which was soon due to arrive with provisions.

While we waited, he sent his nephew Mushka to carry a message to the Greeks: "King Xerxes of Persia orders you to surrender your weapons, retreat to your native lands, and become his allies. In return, he will reward you with more and better lands than you now possess."

The response was not long in coming. Before the sun set, Mushka returned with an answer: "If we are to be your allies," some confident Greek had written, "we will need our weapons. If we resist you, we will also need our weapons. As for the better lands you promise, our fathers taught us to gain land by means of courage, not cowardice."

"Fools!" the king roared, tossing the message aside. "They will die where they stand!"

I was certain the king was right, yet I had to admire the pluck of the few Greeks who had answered so smartly. What sort of people were these? Hadn't they heard that my master ruled the entire civilized world?

We waited two days, then three, the king's patience thinning as the hours dragged by. Because we expected our ships to arrive at any moment, no one had rationed our supplies. Food and water were scarce, and the king knew he had to act if he wanted to preserve morale and keep his army strong.

On the fourth day, he assembled his front line of foot soldiers, composed mostly of foreign slaves. This motley crew charged the ancient wall, but were cut down by Greek spearmen before ever scaling it. Discouraged but undaunted, the king sent in a second line, a corps of skilled mercenaries. They charged the wall with a great deal more skill and valor, but they died as readily as the slaves.

His eyes narrowing, my master called for his Immortals, ten thousand strong. Courageous, armored, and seemingly invincible, they charged the moldering wall with swords and spears, sliding in the blood of fallen comrades as the sea thundered in their ears.

But the Immortals proved to be as vulnerable as the slaves and mercenaries. From a golden throne high upon a hill, my king watched as the cocksure Greeks forced his legendary army to retreat. The next morning the king sent the Immortals forward again, and again they suffered heavy losses.

As the Immortals bandaged their wounds and counted their dead, a messenger arrived in a small ship. He prostrated himself before the king and reluctantly reported that two hundred royal warships had been lost in a fierce storm.

My master bristled with indignation, and for a moment I wondered if he would again send his army to scourge and curse the sea. One of the king's counselors managed to escort the messenger away before the king turned his anger on the bearer of bad news, but I feared what might happen next. He could execute his generals, his mercenaries, or his horses; only the gods knew whom the king might hold responsible. . . .

Fortunately, a disturbance at the edge of the tent caught our attention. A guard shouldered his way through the attendants, leading a stranger by the arm. "A Greek," the guard said simply, "with news for the king."

The Greek prostrated himself before our king. Through an interpreter, he said that he knew of a secret trail through the woods, a trail that would allow the king to reach the enemy camp without having to scale the wall on the road. He would be happy to show the king a path that would enable our troops to get around the wall and surround the Greeks. He expected nothing for this information, but hoped for his life.

My king leapt from this golden throne, granted the man safe passage, and stalked out to speak to his generals. As the traitorous Greek led the way, we moved out the next day, quietly climbing the mountain trail under cover of heavy timber. At one point we could look down and see the small Greek camp behind the old wall.

A surprise attack would have wiped out the Greek defenders, but an army as large as ours could not move unnoticed through an area, no matter how thick the woods. As we made our way over the rocky terrain, most of the Greek forces fled the area below, leaving a band of only three hundred to defend Thermopylae. Intent upon proving themselves in this attack, the vengeful Immortals slaughtered all three hundred Greeks and opened the road to Athens.

Over the course of several days, my master destroyed that city, though it had been largely deserted. He ordered his men to burn and ransack at will, and the soldiers did not hesitate to release their pent-up frustration at the delay in their victory. From his tent, my master looked out across the smoldering settlement and smiled, knowing he had finally avenged his father's defeat.

He had only one other goal, and it was personal: to continue on to Salamis and capture the refugee Athenians. He intended to lead them to Susa in chains, then set them to work as slaves.

And so we marched toward Salamis, a small island off the coast of Athens. We needed the port at that city because our soldiers were hungry and our ships full of food. Three hundred Greek vessels had anchored off Salamis, but seven hundred Persian warships were sailing toward that tiny island.

In hindsight, I realized that my master should have been content with his revenge and gone home. He should have rested, knowing that he had restored his father's honor and proven Persia's strength and might.

But because he wanted to decimate his enemy, whatever gods there be acted to teach him a lesson. Once again we encountered a bottleneck, and once again the great lion was undone by a small stinging bee.

Watching from his golden war throne on a high hill near Athens, my king sent a wave of warships into the straits around Salamis. From our vantage point it appeared as though the Greek vessels had decided to flee. But after we had gone deeper into the straits, they turned to attack, ramming our ships and leaving us with little room to maneuver. As Greek soldiers boarded our vessels with flaming torches, my master's error became apparent—his navy was trapped like flies in a bottle.

Our wounded ships—disabled, burning, and sinking—blocked the approach of reinforcements, and by day's end I knew victory would not be ours. My king was so disheartened that the next morning he and his servants boarded a ship and sailed back to Persia, leaving General Mardonius in charge of the army. Mardonius had but one order: fight his way home.

I sailed away with my master, of course, and as we loaded men and materials onto the ship that would carry us from the carnage, I looked out over our abandoned camp near Athens. Scattered over the rocky ground lay excessive riches, chests of silver talents that would have served as wages for our warriors, the adornments of many a man of high rank, golden goblets, silver bridles, tents with silk flags and golden ropes, gleaming chariots resting askew on the ground and loaded with treasure. The sight of so much glittering waste hurt my eyes, but I found it far more painful to look back at the harbor. The choppy waters outside Salamis churned with bloated bodies, planks, flaccid sails, and so many overturned ships that a man could almost travel from ship to shore by stepping on battle debris.

Late that night, when most of the sailors were sleeping in their hammocks, my master left his cabin and went up on deck. He stood at the rail, moodily watching the sea. His guards stood to one side, and I waited behind him—close enough to be of use, but far enough to be unobtrusive.

I can't say exactly what my master was thinking, but I sensed the darkness that engulfed him. The illness or evil spirit had returned and confused my master's mind. He wore an expression of mute wretchedness, and I found myself pitying the most powerful man in the world.

To whom do you turn when your generals have scattered for fear of royal retribution? In whom can you confide when no one dares meet your gaze?

I spread my feet, balancing on the gently bobbing deck of the rushing ship. The sea whispered in my ear, the black night caressed me with a damp hand, and I felt myself getting drowsy—

But then the king turned to look at me, and my heart stopped. "Folly," he said simply, then waited as if expecting a reply.

What could I say? I nodded out of sheer instinct, for a slave must agree at all times, and that response seemed to satisfy him. He turned back toward the sea, and we remained on the deck for another quarter of an hour, but he did not speak again.

A few months later, the Persian army met defeat on a plain near Plataea, an area northwest of Athens. The splendid Greek campaign was over, thousands of men had been slaughtered, and the empire had not gained even an acre of new territory.

From my discreet post I studied the king's face as he received the dire news. On the day he assumed his father's throne, he had taken the name Xsaya-rsan because it meant *ruling over heroes*, a name incompatible with defeat. But defeat had confronted him in Greece, and my master did not know how to deal with an unpleasant reality.

And *this* reality gnawed at him.

A king of the Medes and Persians had failed to extend the empire. Months of preparation and toil, along with tons of gold and silver had been wasted. Valiant and loyal Persian soldiers had given their lives for nothing.

The defeat needled my master during daylight hours and haunted him during the night, compelling him to thrash and groan in his sleep.

His appetite waned until he grew thin before my eyes. Streaks of gray appeared in his hair and beard. His temper shortened, as did his patience. Musicians and actors who had amused him for years brought him no joy, neither did hunting or riding. He had always liked the company of his young nephew, but he did not send for Mushka. He spent many quiet hours in his chamber, and I alone knew that he spent those hours lying flat on his back while he stared at the ceiling.

I saw what no one else did. Because he could not express his shame or regret, I bore those emotions for him. And I have recorded these things, because the world should know that he did not bear loss easily.

As I sat in my discreet corner with an eye turned to the couch where my master lay silent, I felt the weight of his inherited burden: for over fifty years a line of legendary kings had ruled the vast kingdom of the Medes and the Persians. My master had been the first to experience such an appalling failure.

Like a looming shadow, we both felt the spirit of the great Darius disapproving from the tomb.

Chapter Twelve
HADASSAH

AFTER ACCEPTING BINYAMIN'S BRIDE CONTRACT, I began to dream about my wedding. Wrapped in the shades of night, I would see myself working in the kitchen with Miriam, preparing dinner for Mordecai. My fingers trembled as I lowered a loaf of bread to the table because Binyamin had told me to be ready. I didn't know exactly when he would come, but Miriam and I had spent the day preparing for his arrival. I bathed that morning and then dressed in a new tunic. As a final touch, I put on the traditional bridal headdress trimmed with gold coins.

A bridal chest filled with wedding garments waited by the door.

I carried a platter of fruit and cheese to the table and froze as I heard noise from the street. A great many people were coming, and they were shouting in celebration. This could only be a wedding party.

"Mordecai, Miriam!" Binyamin shouted from outside, his voice stronger and deeper than I had ever heard it. "I have come for my bride!"

Quickly, lest the crowd become boisterous, Miriam helped me with the finishing touches—a pair of new sandals, a finely stitched mantle, a veil of sheer silk. I paused to look in the bronze mirror—had I finally become as beautiful as brides are supposed to be? I saw only a slim figure beneath a veil from which two anxious eyes peered back at me.

Sighing, I took a moment to give Miriam a quick hug, then opened the door to greet my husband. "I am ready."

I gripped the hand extended to me and walked rapidly through the courtyard and into the street. At the head of the joyful procession, I walked with my betrothed to the home he had prepared. For some inexplicable reason we walked not toward Kidon's house, but toward the royal fortress. I wondered if Binyamin had taken a job at the King's Gate. Then we were standing beneath a wedding canopy while the rabbi read the traditional blessing: "Our sister, may you increase to thousands upon thousands, and may your offspring possess the gates of their enemies."

Someone shouted with joy while my bridegroom tugged on my hand, leading me to a banquet where food had been piled upon groaning tables. I sat beside him and ate and drank and smiled at those who lifted their cups to celebrate my happiness.

Then my groom stood and lifted me, carrying me away from the table and toward the bridal chamber. I trembled in his strong arms, but tried to smile and be brave. When he lowered me to the bridal bed, I finally looked into his face—and screamed.

The face wasn't Binyamin's.

Chapter Thirteen
HARBONAH

LIKE A BEATEN DOG, my master chose to lick his wounds in a solitary den. He could have directed his court to join him at any of the royal capitals—Babylon, Susa, Ecbatana, Pasargadae, or Persepolis—but after the defeat at Salamis, the royal entourage traveled to Sardis, a quiet city conquered by Cyrus generations before. Vashti had not gone with us to Greece, but she traveled to Sardis with the rest of the concubines and children. I wondered if the king would relent and summon her to his chamber, but my master seemed determined to obey his own royal edict. Not only did he not summon Vashti, he did not allow her to appear at court. She spent her days in the harem with her children, and whether she enjoyed that duty, I cannot say.

As our sojourn beneath blue skies and sunny weather extended through weeks and months, I soon realized why my master did not seem to miss the woman who had once thoroughly occupied his mind and heart. As part of the royal family and the king's army, the king's younger brother Masistes remained with us, accompanied by his beautiful wife, Parmys, and teenaged daughter, Artaynta.

With no queen to direct the court's social activities, Parmys blossomed in the light of the king's attention. My master frequently invented tasks for Masistes, sending him on journeys to visit the governor of one satrap or another. While his brother was away, the king privately entertained his sister-in-law and niece.

The first time he asked me to arrange a private dinner, I knew the king had decided to seek solace in a woman's love. Unfortunately, the woman he set his affections on was his brother's wife. He did his best to charm the lovely Parmys, offering her jewels and gowns and slaves, but she remained steadfast and faithful to her absent husband.

While the king offered himself and his kingdom to his sister-in-law, I watched from the shadows and clenched my hands, frustrated at my master's weakness. Why would a king with so many concubines pine for a woman he should not have?

The attempt to win Parmys's love might have continued for months, but the king's wounded spirit needed gratification. When the woman would not submit to him, I feared his mood might grow darker than it had been at Salamis, but then the king surprised everyone by arranging a marriage between ten-year-old Crown Prince Darius and Parmys's daughter, Artaynta.

As I witnessed the wedding ceremony, I wondered if I judged my royal master too harshly. Had his attentions toward Parmys been something other than seduction? Being a eunuch, I had no experience with such things. Perhaps I had misread his gestures and his words. Perhaps he had only intended to arrange a fruitful marriage between his son and her daughter.

Artaynta moved into the king's house to be near her child-husband, but those of us who padded through those marble hall-

ways after dark stumbled over myriad secrets. We learned who
sleeps where.

So I knew when and where the king managed to seduce his pretty
daughter-in-law. And in the jolt of that realization I understood
that he had not arranged his son's marriage out of loving concern
for his son. He had married the prince to Parmys's pretty daughter
so that he could seduce the girl and strike at the woman who had
spurned his advances.

In that instant of comprehension, nausea rippled like a slippery
eel through my gut.

Slaves are not supposed to exhibit feelings, and eunuchs are assumed to have none. But though my body has been mutilated and
some natural desires suppressed, my heart still beat with feeling
and my brain still reasoned. I spent more hours with my king than
any living man, and I understood him better than he understood
himself. I loved him—not with lustful feeling, nor with brotherly
compassion. I loved him because I understood him, and because
I have known him since childhood. I loved him because I saw the
seeds of greatness in him.

I loved him because I hoped his greatness would overcome the
weaknesses that caused him to stumble.

I did not understand his compulsion to seduce women—after
all, at thirty-eight my master ought to have mastered his lustful
impulses—and I wondered if the defeat at Salamis had created a
hunger in him, a yearning to steal what he could not otherwise
gain. An endeavor in which he might finally feel successful.

The king's foolish affair might have come to nothing but for
three unexpected developments: first, Vashti, languishing in her
isolation, took it upon herself to weave a varicolored cloak for the
king. Whether she sought to reacquire her position or assure him of
her love, I cannot say. But she used the finest threads and the most
lustrous colors, creating a garment worthy of a royal conqueror.

Since she could not personally present it to him, she ordered one of the eunuchs to deliver it.

If she'd sent the cloak in the midst of the war preparations, I daresay the king would have thoughtlessly set it aside or given it to one of his vice-regents. But flush with the foolishness of a man caught up in a new infatuation, my master put on the garment and preened before a polished sheet of bronze, imagining how his new love would appreciate his fine appearance.

The gods frowned on us the day Artaynta awoke in the king's bed and saw her king shining in his new cloak like some sort of majestic bird. Later that morning, as the king held her and whispered renewed declarations of love, he asked her to divulge her heart's desire so he could fulfill it. Being a silly girl in mind and heart, Artaynta asked for the cloak she'd seen him wearing.

If I had been present at the time, I would have done my best to warn the girl about the taboo pertaining to the king's royal robes. A king's garment was more than mere clothing—the superstitious Persians believed that a royal robe possessed magical power, conferring royalty upon its wearers. He or she who asked to wear something the king had worn *could* be asking for the right to the throne . . . and the first thing a usurper would do was don the garment of the fallen king.

But foolish girls and unsteady kings did not think clearly. My master, having given his word, felt he had to give the cloak to Artaynta. Then the silly girl was unwise enough to wear it at court.

Vashti was not present, of course, but everyone who saw the girl realized that her relationship with the king had become far more intimate than father and daughter-in-law. Many quietly took offense for the cuckolded crown prince and for Masistes, who had been conveniently kept away from court. I don't know who told Vashti about the incident, but it could have been anyone who knew of her hard work on the beautiful garment.

Wings of shadowy foreboding brushed my spirit when the news of the king's affair became public, but days passed and nothing happened. I told myself nothing would come of the king's foolishness; after all, he had pushed Vashti away and perhaps she had learned her lesson. I even managed to convince myself that Artaynta was a blessing from the gods, for she had been able to dispel the brooding cloud that had engulfed the king since his defeat in Greece.

And then we commemorated the king's birthday. The event, one of the most important of the year, was traditionally celebrated with members from the noble families of Persia, and the king's court was open to any nobleman or noblewoman who wanted to attend. At the feast, any guest could approach the king and ask for a gift, knowing he would be honor-bound to grant the petitioner's request.

The day began happily enough. I woke with a smile and went to work on preparations for the feast. Finally the meal was ready, the pavilion decorated, the slaves at their stations.

The guests began to fill the great hall at Sardis, and then I saw Vashti.

I stood as if rooted to the floor. Our former queen had apparently been waiting for the birthday feast. She no longer wore a crown, but she would always be a daughter of a noble family, so the king would not send her away.

She sat with members of her family and said little while other guests went forward to ask for their gifts—a ham, a golden goblet, permission to plant a vineyard on royal property—and then she stood and approached the dais where the king reclined behind a gauze curtain.

The room stilled as the beautiful former queen moved forward with long, purposeful strides.

I found it hard to breathe as Vashti's painted eyes scanned the gathering, then fixed on her husband. "Life, health, and prosperity to you, my king," she said, her voice throaty and intimate. "I have only one request: to be able to do as I wish with your brother's wife."

In the center of my back, a single drop of sweat traced the ladder of my spine. What was Vashti thinking? My thoughts raced, putting events of the past few weeks together, fitting one to the other, until I formed the picture that must have influenced this bizarre request. Vashti had learned about Artaynta wearing her cloak, and the former queen understood the full significance of symbolic actions. By allowing the girl to wear his cloak, my master had implied that he had given or would share the throne with Artaynta, further implying that he might place her children on the throne, passing over the princes he'd had with Vashti. . . .

Now Vashti was determined to create a symbol of her own.

The other servants and I watched, stunned, as a look of sick realization twisted the king's face. "What is this untoward thing you ask?" he said after a full minute of silence. He lowered his voice. "The lady is innocent of the matter."

Standing in a hidden alcove, I closed my eyes. The king might be impulsive, but he was no fool, and his statement revealed that he fully understood Vashti's motivation. But the woman would not be deterred.

"You are compelled by the law," she insisted, coming a half step closer. "It is impossible that anyone who makes a request before the king at a royal feast should not obtain it."

The king sat up, rested his elbow on his bent knee, and looked around as if he would find an answer to his dilemma on his couch or dining tray. But all he saw was me.

He gestured me closer, and I obeyed.

"Eunuch." He bent closer, so the lady could not hear our conversation. "Run at once to fetch my brother, and tell him this: 'Masistes, you are my brother, and in addition you are a man of worth. So I say to you, live no longer with the wife you now live with, but I will give you instead my daughter. Live with her as your wife, but the wife you now have, do not keep, for it does not seem good to me that you should keep her.'"

I blinked at the unusual message.

"Hurry!" the king commanded, and away I flew.

Masistes's royal apartment was not far from the great hall, and he willingly allowed me into his chamber. Upon hearing the king's message, however, he frowned. "Will you give the king my reply?"

I nodded.

"Tell him that I find his suggestion unprofitable. Why should I send away a wife who has given me sons, who have grown up to be fine young men? And daughters, one of whom you yourself took as a wife for your son. O king, I think it is a very great matter that I am judged worthy of your daughter, but nevertheless, I will neither take your daughter nor give up my wife. Do not force me to do such a thing, and for your daughter another husband will be found who is not at all inferior to me. I pray thee, let me still live with my own wife."

I memorized Masistes's answer and ran back to the great hall.

I wish I could say that nothing had happened in my absence, but apparently Vashti had used the time to send the king's spearmen to fetch Parmys. That lady stood between the king on his dais and the former queen on the floor. The innocent woman's eyes were wide with confusion and fear, and they went wider still when a swordsman stepped forward to do Vashti's bidding.

I saw movement in my peripheral vision and turned to see a pale and shaking Artaynta fall to her knees before the king's couch, begging him through tears not to harm her mother.

But tradition and the immutable law of the Medes and the Persians had tied his hands.

The swordsman withdrew his blade as the entire court watched in horrified silence.

Words fail me. I cannot write the horrible details of what my eyes beheld, but I can testify that the beautiful Vashti took the sword and began to mutilate an innocent woman, choosing to strike at Artaynta through her precious mother.

When Masistes's wife had lost her breasts, ears, lips, nose, and tongue, Vashti calmly asked for a carriage to send the wounded woman home.

Parmys died a few hours later.

During the mutilation, my master lowered his gaze, unable to watch the carnage. In the furrows of that troubled brow I saw the old darkness approaching and knew nothing good could come of the day's events.

Within a few weeks, I was proved right. Masistes attempted to travel to Bactria to stir up a rebellion against the king, but my master had guessed what his younger brother would do. Before the wronged husband, his sons, and his supporters could depart for Bactria, my master arranged to have the entire caravan ambushed and murdered.

The brooding spirit settled over him again.

⚓

The heavy cloud that descended over my master at his birthday dinner did not dissipate for weeks. He kept to himself, spent hours in his chamber, slept far more than usual, and ate as though he were trying to fill a bottomless gorge. An aura of despair radiated from his pale countenance like some dark moon, and anguish shaped his face into valleys and pouches of flesh that suggested illness or extreme age.

He did not send for his counselors, his concubines, or for Artaynta—indeed, I did not think he ever wanted to see his daughter-in-law again. I spent more time with him than usual, preparing

his meals, freshening his linens, and setting out his clothing. But
the king did not speak to me and 'twas not my place to ask him
about anything other than his daily plans. I yearned to know what
troubled his heart, for then I could better serve him, but the king
allowed me no glimpses into his thoughts.

After a month of this troubling behavior, my master asked me
to send for his vice-regents. When they arrived, my master stood,
gripped the edges of his robe, and announced that we would travel
back to Susa.

The vice-regents looked at one another, obviously surprised by
this sudden development, but the news cheered me. My king was
no longer lost in despair. He had suffered humiliation and defeat,
but he was still the most powerful man in the world.

When the vice-regents had gone, the king sat on the edge of his
bed and stared at nothing. For a long while he seemed to wear his
face like a mask. Then he frowned in a way that made me wonder
if he was trying to remember something or struggling to forget.

"We must move forward," he said.

I stepped into his sight line in case he meant the words for me.
"Yes, my king."

He did not speak again.

The next day, the royal household prepared to return to Susa.

I was surprised by the destination, for Persian kings traditionally
moved between cities according to the season—the summer months
were best enjoyed in Ecbatana, high on the plateau and encircled
by towering mountains. Winter was most tolerable in the warm
climate of Babylon, and spring was best enjoyed in Susa, on the edge
of the plain. Previous kings had established palaces throughout the
empire, and each residence had unique features to recommend it.

But Darius had spent a great deal of time and effort developing
Susa, so perhaps my king wanted to soothe his spirit in a place
where he felt his father's presence. Whatever his reasons, we packed

the royal family's belongings and traveled the Royal Road through Cappadocia, Assyria, and Babylonia.

Throughout the long journey, I examined my master, searching for some proof that his spirit had been completely restored. But though the king had roused himself from his lethargy, he remained withdrawn. He did not travel on horseback as was his usual habit, but secluded himself inside a royal carriage, where he stared out the windows and conversed only with his thoughts.

An outside observer might not have noticed anything amiss with my master. As was the custom for Persian monarchs, at every stop along our journey we met with people who brought tribute to the king. Receiving their gifts was the king's duty, as was his giving them something in return. Each guest shared a meal with us, and for each dinner the cooks slaughtered one thousand animals, including horses, camels, oxen, asses, deer, birds, Arabian ostriches, and geese. Slaves served moderate portions to each member of the king's household and every guest, but the greater part of the food was carried into the camp for the Immortals who guarded the king.

Our procession was neither small nor swift. Over two hundred of the king's relatives attended him on the journey, traveling before and behind and on his right and left. Thirty thousand foot soldiers followed the king's family, accompanied by four hundred royal horses. Next in line was a golden chariot occupied by Atossa, the king's mother, and Vashti, mother of the crown prince. A sizable group of handmaids from the queen mother's household followed on horseback. They were trailed by fifteen carriages filled with the king's children, their governesses, and a sizable group of eunuchs, without whom the harem could not function.

Behind the royal children rode nearly four hundred of the king's concubines, all of them regally dressed. They were followed by a corps of archers who guarded the six hundred mules and three hundred camels necessary to carry the king's money. A detachment of friends of the king followed the treasury, and scores of canteen servants followed the king's friends. A company of foot soldiers and their officers brought up the rear.

Our party might have been large, but it was not inefficient. Of the concubines, 329 played musical instruments and were often pressed into service during dinner. Many of the eunuchs were tasked with weaving floral chaplets, while 277 were caterers, 29 kettle tenders, 13 pudding makers, 17 bartenders, 70 wine clarifiers, and 40 perfume makers.

Each day the front-runners halted when the sun began to tilt toward the horizon. Slaves first erected the king's white tent so that the luxurious dwelling would be completely set up by the time the king arrived. My master and I immediately went inside, along with the king's bodyguards, the vice-regents, and several scribes. While the rest of the servants assembled their tents or prepared the evening meal, the king accepted tribute and gifts from subjects who lived in the vicinity.

And while the king met his subjects, rode with his Immortals, and sat with his vice-regents, I observed him as studiously as possible.

Why? Because my duty required me to anticipate and meet his needs before he realized he lacked anything. And because I had grown attached to the man and wanted him to succeed.

I also watched my master closely because I had grown concerned for his son, the crown prince. Young Darius spent very little time with his father, and I worried that his mother had poisoned him against the king. Patricide was not unknown in the history of Persian royalty, and if one day the young man's mind bent toward treason, he would only have to gather supporters and seize his father's throne.

Already I had heard rumblings from discontents. Not only did they complain about the expense of a war without victory, some said the king had committed a grievous wrong against his son by giving him a bride and then using the girl for his own pleasure. No one in the royal household could forget the horrible mutilation of Artaynta's innocent mother, and many felt Vashti would be justified in turning the son against his father.

So I worried.

If I could have carved out a time when father and son could ride together in a chariot, I would have arranged it. If I could have given the king and the prince an opportunity for a private dinner, I would have cooked the meal myself. If I could have convinced the king to go to his son and apologize for his misdeeds, I would have risked the attempt because my king's own life depended on the outcome.

I did not fault him for losing the war against Greece. But he had been a fool to engage in an affair that led to disastrous consequences.

Still . . . one could not change the past. Furthermore, the king's word, once given, could not be altered or denied. Such was the inflexible law of the Medes and the Persians.

And such was the king I served.

Chapter Fourteen

HADASSAH

REALIZING THAT THE PATH OF MY LIFE had been irrevocably fixed, I grew resigned to marrying Binyamin. I told myself I would grow fond of him in time, and fondness would surely turn to love. Miriam assured me that I would love whomever I chose to make precious to me, and that through caring for Binyamin, he would become more precious than life itself.

After saying these words, she glanced over at the fire, where Mordecai sat squinting at a scroll. Though Miriam could no longer be called beautiful, at that moment her cheeks flushed and a sparkle lit her eyes. Comeliness returned to her face, and I realized that love had brought it back.

"May it be so," I murmured, thinking of Binyamin. May my eyes shine when I am old and worn out. . . .

The days of waiting melted into weeks, and weeks into months as spring flowered into summer. Mordecai kept busy with his work, while Miriam continued to take care of the house, though she began to leave more of her responsibilities to me. At first I chafed at the extra work, and then I realized she was trying to prepare me for the life that would soon be mine.

I was standing at the well, holding an empty jug on my hip, when Devorah, a woman from our neighborhood, came huffing up the hill, her face flushed and perspiring. "Hadassah! You are needed at home." She narrowed her eyes as if I had lingered by the well to escape my chores. "Miriam is ill."

I should have dropped my jug and run home, but the woman's chiding tone irritated me. "What's wrong?" I asked, imagining that Miriam had twisted her ankle again. "I haven't drawn the water yet."

"Leave your jar." Devorah's gaze met mine, and her burning eyes held me still. "And pray that you make it home before your cousin departs this life."

I stared. Surely the woman wasn't serious. Miriam had been fine when I saw her last; she sent me to the well and asked me to stop by the bazaar to see if any figs were available. Miriam was never ill—clumsy, yes, especially lately, but she had never taken to her bed, not for a single day. . . .

I left my jar and sprinted home, my tunic flapping around my ankles and kicking up dust. I burst through the courtyard gate and entered the house, narrowly avoiding a chicken that had stopped to scratch the earthen floor. "Miriam!"

"Over here, Hadassah."

The voice wasn't Miriam's. I spotted my cousin in a dark corner, lying on her straw-filled mattress. Mikhal, another neighbor, bent over her, holding an oil lamp aloft as she examined Miriam's lined face.

I sank to a low stool, reeling with confusion. Half of Miriam's face was composed in gentle lines, as if she were resting, but the other half had been pulled downward by some invisible hand. I had seen unbaked clay figurines droop in the same way when sprinkled with water, but I had never expected to see such an expression on Miriam's face.

I tugged on Mikhal's sleeve. "What's wrong?"

Mikhal shook her head, then used a soft cloth to wipe a string of spittle from Miriam's mouth. "She was fine," Mikhal said, the sound of tears in her voice. "She was in the courtyard, talking to me over the wall, and suddenly she said something foolish. I laughed and asked what she meant, and she simply looked at me, her eyes confused. I reached for her, but she fell. By the time I ran around the wall, she was—" Mikhal pointed to Miriam's distorted face—"like this. I have sent for a physician, but I don't know if he will be able to help."

"And Mordecai?" I glanced toward the doorway, hoping my cousin had somehow intuited this tragedy and come rushing home. "Did you send word to the King's Gate?"

A frown filled the space between Mikhal's brows. "I had no one to send. I sent Devorah to get you, and Rachel to get the doctor. Who could I send to the King's Gate?"

I covered my mouth, horrified by the sight of Miriam's mangled countenance. What was I supposed to do?

"Your place is here." As if to emphasize her point, Mikhal placed the damp cloth in my palm, then guided my hand toward my cousin's cheek. "You should care for her now. She has done so much for you."

I knew she was right. I stood on trembling legs and approached the bed, then knelt by Miriam's side. I tentatively brushed the corner of her mouth and looked into the one open eye.

And gasped.

The black pupil, usually so perfectly round in its band of brown, had spattered within its orb. It stared at me, open and unmoving. I didn't need a physician to tell me Miriam was dead.

Something erupted from within me. I tried to clamp my mouth

shut to stifle a cry, but I began to sob in a high, helpless hacking sound. I threw my arms around Miriam and hugged her as if I could hold her spirit in its place.

While I wept, Mikhal squeezed my shoulder.

"She is gone," the woman said, releasing a heavy sigh. "The grave has taken her. See? No breathing, not anymore. We will have to wash and wrap her for burial. Pull yourself together, Hadassah. First we work, then we mourn."

I sat up, hot spurts of loss and love rolling down my face. I never knew my father, and I was a baby when my mother died. I had known loss, but I never felt real grief until that moment.

I stood, trying to control myself, but my lip wobbled and my eyes leaked in spite of my intentions. I wanted to prove to Mikhal and Devorah that I was capable of handling whatever life might throw at me, but I couldn't handle this.

I wiped my face on my veil and took a long, slow breath.

Death had come to our home like an unwelcome guest. Just this morning Miriam had been living, breathing, and working, yet a few hours later she lay still and damaged. And we would have to bury her quickly, so we would need more women to prepare the body.

And someone had to tell Mordecai. I lifted my head and glanced around. Devorah had taken a bowl and gone outside, presumably in search of water, and Mikhal was cutting the tunic from Miriam's body. I would help them, I would, but I had to do something first.

Forgetting everything else, I spun away from Mikhal and Devorah and ran toward the royal fortress.

⊱⋅⋆⋅⊰

Mordecai briefly entered the house to view his beloved Miriam, then retired to the courtyard with the rabbi, as was proper for any man who did not wish to be ceremonially defiled. I joined the women who had washed my cousin's body, dressed her in a simple garment, and laid her out on the table. Now they were sprinkling her remains with spices to disguise the smell of death. Because the day was neither a holy day nor the Sabbath, we would bury her before sunset.

I sat on a stool at my cousin's feet, marveling at their yellowed color even as I struggled to breathe. The air in the house seemed thick with the heaviness of grief.

"The Persians do not understand why we take such pains with the body," Mikhal said, lowering her voice as if she feared someone might overhear. "But I have seen what they do when someone dies. After cutting themselves and weeping, they carry their dead out to the fields and leave them to the vultures. Later, they go back and bury the bones." She shuddered. "I cannot believe they think their practice respectful."

"They do not know any better," Devorah said, speaking in the same low tones. She unrolled a strip of cloth beneath Miriam's jaw and tied it at the top of my cousin's head, effectively closing the mouth. "In this land where a man may worship whatever god he chooses, nothing is holy. No one respects the laws of any god."

"But we know better." Mikhal placed a clean square of woven cloth over Miriam's face, then looked directly at me. "Aye, Hadassah?"

Her question jolted me back to reality. My thoughts had wandered as I imagined Parysatis caring for the body of her dead mother. Would she really carry the remains out into the fields? Would she and Babar dump their beloved mother on the ground like garbage?

"The mourners have arrived." Another neighbor, a woman I had often seen with Miriam, entered the house, dragging a wooden bier behind her. "And so has this. Mordecai rented it from the carpenter."

Mikhal tilted her head and regarded the bier with suspicion. "Altogether plain, isn't it?"

"Mordecai knows best." The woman left the bier on the floor and regarded our handiwork. "As one who moves so freely among the people of Susa, perhaps Mordecai doesn't want to emphasize the differences in our customs."

The women sighed, then drew closer to the table where Miriam lay on a length of fine linen. Accompanied by the cries and ululations of the mourners outside, the women lifted the remaining length of cloth and pulled it over Miriam's frame, tucking the edges beneath the body. When they had finished, they looked at me. "Have you anything to add, Hadassah?"

I drew a breath, but couldn't speak over the lump in my throat.

"That's all right." Mikhal gave me the first smile I'd received since learning the awful news. "Death comes as a shock to one so young, but now you are the woman of the house. How old are you?"

"Sixteen," I managed to whisper.

"More than ready for a husband, then, so prepare yourself. With Miriam gone, you need to move to your own home with your own husband. This is the way of all living things."

I bowed my head as the hard hand of guilt smacked me. Mordecai had been so patient with me. He had stalled my impatient husband-to-be and diplomatically convinced Binyamin's father that I needed more time with my family. But with half my family gone, how could he continue to delay the inevitable?

I stood, knowing that I was not only about to bury the only mother I had ever known, but a life of uncommon freedom and opportunity. Binyamin would soon come to make me his wife, and I had no more excuses.

CHAPTER FIFTEEN

HARBONAH

I DON'T KNOW WHAT THE KING EXPECTED TO FIND on our arrival at Susa—memories of a happier time, perhaps? But as the royal household settled into one of the grandest palaces in all creation, my master's spirits did not improve. He maintained the appearance of normality—hunting, riding, watching athletic contests on the training field—but I felt as though his heart had left us. After sunset, when most of the royal household settled down to sleep, he would rise and wander in the royal gardens, his head down and his hands locked behind his back.

After about a week, I had an epiphany: my master had roused himself enough to make the journey back to Susa, but apparently he had not found what he sought in this gilded palace. Susa held no memories of war or Artaynta, so the influence here could not be negative. What pleasant memories had he expected to find?

I could come up with only one answer: the companionship of a loving wife. He and Vashti had been happy here, rejoicing in their close relationship and the birth of three sons. The former queen might be prideful, scheming, and cruel, but she had been a friend to my master. They had conversed as equals, and though she shared his body with hundreds of concubines, Vashti never had to share his heart. No one—not even Artaynta—had met the king as an equal in nobility, courage, and cunning.

So . . . the king needed another companion. Someone with Vashti's virtues but none of her vices. Someone who could approach the king on equal footing, but who would not wield royal authority with malice.

Though I knew how my master might heal his heartache, what right had I to make a suggestion? I was a slave, a blank wall, a pair of hands and feet. My duty was to be silent and respectful, helpful but not obvious. But still . . .

I knew my master could be made whole again. He only needed a push in the right direction. But if I were to supply the push, I needed the perfect opportunity, an occasion in which my master would be willing to see and hear me.

One afternoon my listless king lifted his head and addressed the air, ignoring the dozen or so servants in the room. "I cannot find happiness here," he said simply. "And I can't help thinking of the day I banished Vashti from my presence. Though I can't forget the awful things she has done, perhaps she is not entirely to blame. I am not free of guilt regarding her actions, and I regret—"

I stepped forward before the king could finish his confession. "My lord the king, a thousand pardons for my impertinence." I lowered my forehead to the floor and waited for his response.

In the stretching silence I heard the breathless shock of the other servants. They had stopped moving, and I could feel the pressure of their eyes on the back of my skull.

"Rise, eunuch," the king said, his voice free of rancor. "You have something to tell me?"

I closed my eyes and exhaled in relief, then pushed myself to an upright position. "Thank you, my good master. I have watched your struggles, and you should not suffer one day more. You know the solution, my king, the answer that will not force you to violate the unbreakable law of the Medes and the Persians."

The empty air between us vibrated, the silence filling with tension.

My king turned his head into the hard light of the sun, and I saw that all traces of youth had fled from his face. "I know the answer?"

"You do." I flushed beneath his intense scrutiny. "You need a queen worthy of you. Let a search be made for young, beautiful women. The king should appoint officials in all the provinces of the empire to gather all the attractive women to the house for the harem, in Susa the capital. They should be put under the care of Hegai, the king's officer in charge of the harem, and he should give them the cosmetics or whatever they require. Then the girl who seems best to the king should become queen instead of Vashti."

The king's eyes narrowed, and for an instant I feared I would not be forgiven for speaking. My idea was unconventional, maybe even crazy, but something had to be done.

But an empire-wide search? The vice-regents would despise the idea, because it would deprive their daughters of an opportunity to marry a king. For generations, Persian rulers had chosen wives from the daughters of one of seven noble families—after a bloody revolt, the resolution had been established by the nobles themselves. Requiring that the king choose a wife from among their households served to establish the legitimacy of the kingship—and guaranteed that they would remain close to the seat of power.

But my master had already met that requirement, for Vashti had been the daughter of Otanes, one of the leading Persian nobles.

So why shouldn't my king search for a new wife from among the commoners of his empire? This one would not be so prideful that she would disdain and disobey her husband and king.

The king inclined his head, a slow smile lifting the corners of his mouth. "Let it be so," he said, his voice resonating with a vigor I had not heard in months. "Let the edict be published, and let the search begin."

CHAPTER SIXTEEN

HADASSAH

I HEARD THE NEWS AT THE WELL, the center of our little Jewish neighborhood. The woman who had greeted us with the story seemed to think the decree an elaborate joke, but when one of the king's courtiers rode by with a sealed scroll beneath his arm, we wondered if the report might be true.

Did the king really want to marry an ordinary girl?

After Babar left Susa for parts unknown, Parysatis and I had renewed our friendship. Though a shadow would cross her face at any thought or mention of her brother, she had finally reached a place where she could be happy again. Like me, she'd been thrilled to see the city come back to life with the king's return. The streets once again streamed with soldiers and courtiers, and Parysatis and I kept craning our necks for some glimpse of a royal litter.

I couldn't help feeling grateful that she hadn't believed Babar's ridiculous stories about the king. After all, one only had to look at the king—prosperous and adored—to know that Babar had been lying. The royal household of Persia deserved to be praised and lauded.

Yet in those days I didn't find as much joy in girlish gossip about royalty and the nobility. I had become too well acquainted with reality, and I found it difficult to escape into fantasy when a new and more somber life would be mine within a few weeks.

I hurried to the bazaar where I knew I'd find Parysatis working in her father's silk shop. I wasn't surprised to learn that she'd already heard the rumor.

"Can you imagine?" Parysatis sighed, wrapping her arms around the basket she carried. "To live in the palace! To eat whatever you wanted, whenever you wanted it. To have servants and beautiful gowns and drink from golden goblets, none of them ever like the one before it—"

"You'd have to marry the king," I pointed out. "And isn't he old?"

"He's not so old," she argued. "I've seen him riding across the plain, and he looked quite handsome on his horse. He rode straight and tall, not hunched over."

"Would you really like to be queen?" I stared at her, unable to believe what I was hearing. "I know he was out of his mind, but perhaps Babar had a point. Even Mordecai says that court can be a treacherous place."

"Listen to you." Her brows drew downward. "A year ago you were dreaming about our handsome king yourself. You defended his honor in front of Babar."

I blew out a breath, conceding her point. "A lot has changed in the past year."

"And have you changed so much? I still adore Mushka, but if the king needs a new queen, why shouldn't it be me?"

Her question hung on the air, silently accenting the rift that had developed between us. Parysatis was still the spoiled daughter of a

rich merchant who would marry her off to the highest bidder, but
I was no longer a carefree girl. I had lost Miriam and surrendered
my youthful dreams of travel and adventure. Now when I caught a
glimpse of my reflection in a bowl or brass, I saw the tired mother
I would become.

I offered Parysatis a weary smile. "I shouldn't waste my time
thinking about foolish things. I will be married soon."

"You shouldn't talk like you're an old woman." Parysatis brushed
off my comment and exhaled a happy sigh. "Living in the palace
would be wonderful. If you were chosen for the harem, everyone
would know you were one of the most beautiful girls in the entire
world—"

"Hush, will you?" An older woman stepped out from behind a
bolt of silk and glared at us. "Have you no sense? No one would
know you were beautiful, because no one would know you at
all. You'd be swallowed up by the seraglio and forgotten by your
friends. If you're thinking such a life is a dream come true, think
again."

She tucked the end of a length of silk around the bolt. "I've
seen beautiful women arrive in caravans from the east, destined
for a life in the harem. They will have nothing to call their own,
nothing. Yes, they live in a palace, but with hundreds of women
to choose from, do you think the king would even remember
your name? Living in a pretty palace might appeal to you now,
but you'd think differently if you'd ever done it. Now get back
to your home and get a veil to cover your face. If you're smart,
you'll think twice about showing yourself in public until all this
foolishness is over."

I glanced around, searching for a way to escape. This woman
might be speaking nonsense, but something in her eyes made me
wonder if she'd lived the life she was describing.

Still, why should I worry about the king's proclamation? No one was going to search for royal concubines in my neighborhood, and I was about as likely to live in the palace as to grow another head.

Obedient Jewish girls simply did not have to worry about such things.

⌃❦⌃

I had planned to prepare a simple meal for Mordecai, Binyamin, and his father, when I found Mordecai pacing back and forth in our courtyard, his hands locked behind his back.

The tight lines of his face relaxed when he saw me. "Come in at once," he said, hurrying to undo the latch of the gate.

When I was safely within our walls, he turned me to face him. "I wish I could keep you safe," he said, his voice low and tense, "but the king's edict will affect everyone in the empire."

"Not me." Surprised by his concern, I sank to the garden bench and folded my arms. "I am not the kind of girl they will be searching for."

Mordecai put on the look of a man who has just been knocked down by a charging goat. "Hadassah, have you not seen yourself? You are a beautiful woman."

"Cousin, I am not."

"You are. And I'd be foolish to think no one has noticed you. Someone will turn you in; they will come for you within the week."

I resisted the urge to imitate Miriam and shake my finger at him. "I think you're wrong, but the answer is simple. I am betrothed, so why not go ahead with the wedding? The king would not be interested in a married woman."

Mordecai cast me a sharp look. "Do you think the king cares if a maid is married or not? The edict calls for beautiful young women, Hadassah, not beautiful *unmarried girls*. And what of Binyamin? It would be far more painful for him to take you as his bride and then have you stolen away. What if you were with child when the king's men took you? No, you cannot be married until the king's latest folly has run its course."

I leaned against the courtyard wall, amazed that Mordecai would give the royal edict serious consideration. "The king can't possibly hope to gather all the beautiful young women in the empire. No one will even notice me, and if they do, they'll not want me. I am too—"

I was about to say *Jewish*, meaning that I was too modest and old-fashioned to excite the attention of a Persian nobleman, but Mordecai interrupted. "Hadassah, listen to me. Every man in Susa will look at you and think of the king's edict. They will dream of a handsome reward for bringing you to the palace. So you shall remain indoors until the king has found his next queen."

I leaned forward, flustered by his stubbornness. "I can't stay indoors. I have work to do, water to fetch, and a goat to milk—"

"If you must go outside, you will wear a veil. Cover your face. Do not wear a belt around your tunic, lest they see your slender form. Disguise yourself from head to toe."

I gave him an exaggerated frown, but Mordecai was not in the mood for joking.

"I don't understand why you're so concerned," I began again. "When King David's servants announced a search for a beautiful maiden to warm his bed, every father in the kingdom hoped his daughter would win the privilege. How is this proclamation any different from that one?"

Mordecai blinked hard, as if astounded by my ignorance. "When David Hamelech's servants sought a virgin for him, everyone understood that only one maiden would be chosen—and those who were not chosen would suffer no abuse. Those fathers would have their daughters returned, pure and unspoiled. But this king intends to take every girl to his bed before choosing a queen, and no parent, not even parents of Egyptians and Assyrians and Babylonians will be pleased to have their daughters used and discarded in such a fashion."

"Cousin—"

"And—" he stepped toward me and grabbed my hands—"if they do take you, Hadassah, you must be careful. You must never reveal who your people are."

I stared at him, baffled. "What do you mean?"

"If you do not speak of your people, perhaps the king will think you are ashamed of your common roots. That you are not fit to be a queen."

"I'm *not* fit to be a queen."

"You are, child. Your roots are as royal as Xerxes's, for you are a descendant of Saul, the first king of Israel. But do not speak of this; let everyone believe that yours was a humble birth." He hesitated, but I saw thought working in his eyes. "If you do not divulge your heritage, every group may assume you are one of theirs. They will all claim you and love you."

And he used to rebuke *me* for living in a fantasy world?

Weary of the conversation, I blew out a deep breath. "I don't believe you have any reason to warn me of such things."

"You must not tell them you are Jewish. You must not use your true name, lest they guess your ancestry."

"Why?" I grabbed his hand and held it, insisting on an answer. "Why must I pretend to be other than who I am?"

Mordecai turned his face to mine as his eyes softened with seriousness. "We do not know what this king thinks of the Jews, and we dare not assume he thinks well of our people. So promise me, Hadassah—do not speak your Hebrew name to anyone in the palace, and do not tell anyone you are a child of Abraham."

I looked at him—so earnest, frightened, and loving—and I squeezed his hand. "I am touched by your concern, cousin, but you need not worry on my account. I am safe in your care, as I have been since my mother died. Do not worry about me. All will be well."

Mordecai nodded, then tugged at his beard. "I trust Adonai to make it so, but still . . ." He shook his head and released my hand, then went inside the house.

❦

Within two weeks, the men in my life had settled the details of my marriage. Binyamin's father met Mordecai at the King's Gate, and over a table at the bazaar they worked out the details of my wedding and the marriage feast. Our ceremony would not be traditional, for neither the wedding nor the feast would take place in Susa. Mordecai, the closest person in the world to me, would not even be present.

He shared the details when he returned home. "Everything has been arranged," he said, his eyes weary as he gazed at me over the small lamp burning in the center of our table. "Marriage may not save you from the king's edict, but it will get you out of Susa. Though copies of the king's proclamation have been distributed throughout the empire, I don't believe the king's agents will look for potential queens in the rubble of Jerusalem. You and Binyamin will go there. You will be married in the temple and start a family in the land Adonai promised to Israel."

I blinked back sudden tears. "You are sending me away?"

The thin line of his mouth clamped tight as he tugged on his beard. "The time comes when a woman shall leave her father and mother—" his voice broke, but he cleared his throat and continued—"and be joined to her husband. Tomorrow, as soon as Binyamin and Kidon have finished packing, you will journey to Jerusalem with your betrothed."

"Without you?"

I felt the weight of his gaze, as dark and soft as the river at dawn. "I will give you my blessing before you go."

I sat back as dozens of emotions stirred in my breast. I had no choice but to obey, but I didn't want to leave the only home I'd ever known, and I didn't want to travel to Jerusalem. From what I'd heard, the city was little more than a collection of ruins with a perfunctory temple. Jerusalem had never been home to me, and I did not share Mordecai's love for the place.

Why should I leave Susa? I was a child of Persia. I had spent my entire life in the shadow of the king's fortress. My friends lived here. Leaving Susa would mean leaving everything I held dear, and for what? The king was no more likely to choose a Jewish girl than he was to marry his horse.

Why did Mordecai think I would be thrilled to live in a decimated city?

I studied my guardian as he stood and moved to the window. The setting sun gilded his face with yellow light as I drank him in, determined to memorize every detail of his countenance. Tomorrow we would say our farewells for the last time.

As much as I loved Mordecai and appreciated all he had done for me, we were completely different people. He liked Persia and loved Jerusalem; I loved Persia and felt almost nothing for the holy city. Mordecai had spent most of his life in Susa, but his eyes lit with an inner glow when he spoke of the City of David. In the quiet of the night he would sing of Zion, songs that filled the darkness with sorrow and longing: "If I forget you, Jerusalem, may my right hand wither away! May my tongue stick to the roof of my mouth if I fail to remember you, if I fail to count Jerusalem the greatest of all my joys."

I lit up when thinking about Persia and its colorful people. I dreamed of the royal family, my friend Parysatis, and her renegade brother.

Mordecai had to know how much Persia meant to me . . . just as I knew he thought my affections were misplaced.

Is *that* why he wanted to send me away?

Later that night, as I lay on my pallet and silently wiped tears away, I tried to envision Jerusalem as a holy, shining city.

But visions of King Xerxes's bright and dazzling palace kept intruding.

CHAPTER SEVENTEEN

HARBONAH

A MONTH AFTER THE KING'S CALL for beautiful young women went out, I began to regret ever suggesting the idea. My master expected me to oversee the gathering of the virgins, which meant I was required to spend far more time in the harem than I wanted to. I had grown up among the royal women and was glad to be rid of them when appointed to serve my master.

Those who castrated me as a youth ensured that I would forever be well-suited for working with females, but I found the king's women catty, boring, and irritating. Too many of them were obsessed with their looks and trivial details, too few truly cared about the king. The royal women also tended to be snappish and jealous, even using eunuchs in their schemes against one another, so I was grateful that Hegai, chamberlain of the palace of the women, would bear much of this latest burden.

Envoys began to arrive a few days after the king's proclamation was issued, and guards brought the virgins—many of whom had been taken against their will—to Hegai and me for evaluation. If we—two beardless eunuchs with good eyes and not an iota of lust between us—found the women worthy of the king's attention, they were taken to the palace of the virgins, whether they were strictly virgins or not. If they did not win our approval, they were told to make their way back to their fathers or husbands. "Since beauty is a matter of perspective," I had earlier warned the king, "we must release those who are unacceptable. We don't want every young woman in the empire lazing about in the harem."

Laughing, my master said he trusted my sense of beauty, and with a clap on my shoulder he went on his way.

Now Hegai and I stood at the southern staircase of the royal fortress, the culmination of a long road that led from the Valley of the Artists. A walled carriage approached, and from within it we could hear shouts and furious pounding on the walls.

"Oh my." Beside me, Hegai went a shade paler. "Sl-slave traders."

I shifted and eyed the vehicle. Slave traders hunted humans the way some men trapped wild game, enjoying the thrill of the hunt as much as the bounty paid for a fine catch. We had encountered several slavers in the last few days—men who usually sought runaway slaves or escaped prisoners now made it their business to scour the king's highways for beautiful virgins.

I didn't know how or where these men hunted, and I didn't care much for their specimens. Though great beauty could hide behind a layer of filth, the women from the plains tended to be beefy, bandy-legged, and lacking a full complement of teeth. I had yet to accept a single offering from a slave hunter, but since the king had authorized an empire-wide search, I had no choice but to consider every female presented at the palace.

"Don't worry," I told Hegai. "If they have brought another load of farmers' daughters, we can simply turn them away."

The carriage rolled up to the stone platform where we stood, and a grinning guard climbed down from his perch and went around to open the side door. "Bet you've never seen anything like these wenches," he said, displaying a gap where a front tooth should be.

I stepped forward to acknowledge the delivery. "Where did you find these girls?"

"Road to Babylon," the guard answered, pulling the bolt free of its hasp. "Some of them Babylonian beauties, at least one an Elamite. All of them fit to be queen."

Hegai shot me a sharp look, then pursed his lips and turned his attention to the carriage. I sighed and tried not to appear too stern as the guard pulled the first girl from the confines of the convey-ance. She was a barefoot Bedouin, her hair a wild tangle about her face. The second girl was a wasp-thin creature who appeared to be from one of the local tribes. The third girl outweighed Hegai, and the fourth could have easily beaten me in a wrestling match. The fifth, however, possessed a comely form, and her face—

I blinked as the features of the fifth captive came into focus. This was no farm girl, no Bedouin, and no warrior woman. Unless my eyes deceived me, the pale virgin who trembled on the pavement was Mordecai's daughter, Hadassah. Like the others, her face was streaked with dirt and her hands were bound. But unlike the oth-ers, her beauty shone through the grime on her face like a lantern in the night.

I felt Hegai stiffen beside me. "Wh-wh-what's this?" he stuttered, his voice thick. "A diamond amid the d-d-dreck."

"Quiet," I whispered, then shot him a look that said I'd explain later.

Thrusting my hands behind my back, I walked to the first woman and asked her name. She told me and I promptly forgot it, but I repeated the experience with the second, third, and fourth girls until I stood before my friend's ward.

Our eyes caught and held. For a moment I feared she didn't remember me, but then a flicker of recognition lit her eyes. "Fear not," I murmured, pitching my voice to reach her ear and no one else's. Then, raising my voice for all to hear, I asked her name.

She lifted her brown eyes and cast me a brief look of helpless appeal. "My name is Esther."

The name was Persian, not Jewish, and it meant *star*.

"Have you a father or mother in Susa?" I asked carefully.

"Neither." Steadily, she held my gaze. "I am an orphan."

I lifted a brow. She must have had a good reason for concealing her link to Mordecai, so I decided to guard her secret. Later I would ask if she wanted me to send word to her cousin.

I turned, bringing my hand to my chin as if I were considering the merits of all the women before me, but my mind whirled with thoughts of the accountant. Should I hide this girl and return her to her guardian? If I did, she would still be at risk, and would probably end up here yet again. And if the slaver spoke truly about finding these girls on the road to Babylon, Mordecai had already tried to send her away. . . .

I stepped back and surveyed the line of women one final time, then turned to the slave trader. "Thank you for bringing these women to the king. I have decided to return all of them to you—all but the last. That one we'll keep."

The man protested, extolling his fine taste in females, but I cut him off by placing three pieces of silver on his palm. "I trust this will cover your expenses. Thank you for your effort on the king's behalf."

While the guard tugged at the rope linking the remaining captives, I pulled a knife from my belt and cut Mordecai's daughter free. I then gestured to Hegai, who stepped forward, curiosity shining in his eyes. "Hegai, I entrust Esther into your hands. Take good care of her, will you? I have a particular interest in her welfare."

While Hegai's forehead knit in puzzlement, I cut the cord that bound Hadassah's wrists and promised I would try to find her later. I wanted to know how she had come to be caught in a slave trader's dragnet, and how she had been separated from Mordecai. But because she had not volunteered any information, I would not ask these questions in public.

CHAPTER EIGHTEEN
HADASSAH

WITHOUT SPEAKING, I followed the short, bald man in the white tunic, keeping my eyes low even as my heart twisted. Once, during what now seemed like a foolish childhood, I had yearned to walk the polished halls of the king's palace and dreamed of exploring its winding passageways. Now I found myself stumbling along one of those hallways, and all I wanted to do was weep.

The day before I had packed my bridal chest and placed it in the courtyard, then knelt at Mordecai's feet while he placed his hands on my head. "May Adonai watch between me and you when we are apart from each other," he said, reciting the blessing Laban had said to Jacob as the two men parted company. "Go in peace, my daughter."

A short time later, Kidon and Binyamin approached our house, leading three horses, a donkey, and a mule. The donkey carried water and other provisions for our journey, so Binyamin strapped my wedding chest to the mule. Then he helped me mount a pretty little mare that reminded me of Parysatis's horse.

I smiled through tears and managed a little wave as we urged our mounts forward. Mordecai stood at our gate, clasping the edges of his robe, his face stiffly arranged in a proud smile.

But as we rode away, I could almost hear the clean, snapping sound of breaking hearts—mine and Mordecai's. With Miriam in the grave and me on my way to Jerusalem, Mordecai would now be alone. No longer a young man, he would have only his work, a few friends, and his God to fill his days.

I should have been a happy bride, but sadness pooled in my heart as we approached the gates of Susa, a heavy grief that not even my groom's eager smile could lighten.

Because safety lay in numbers, we were supposed to join a larger caravan at the Tigris River. But scarcely had we left Susa when our small party was surrounded by sword-wielding ruffians on swift, long-legged horses. Binyamin and his father tried to reason with the men, protesting that we carried few valuables, but the rogues did not seem interested in treasure. As two of them wordlessly threatened Kidon and Binyamin with spears, a third man urged his horse toward me, his sword flashing in the dim light of dusk.

Emboldened by some foolish sense of protectiveness, Binyamin kicked his mount, but his guard caught the mare's bridle and slashed Binyamin with a sword. When my betrothed fell from his saddle, Kidon cried out and dismounted, collapsing at Binyamin's side as though he would be happy to die with his son. I watched in silent horror, not speaking even when the third man snatched the reins from my hands. I gripped the saddle, about to slip off and run for my life, but when one of the men stood over Binyamin, lifted his spear, and looked pointedly at me, I thought I knew what they wanted—a woman to hold for ransom. "Don't!" I cried. "I'll go with you, but don't hurt these men. Please—I won't cause any trouble."

The rogue with the spear looked at the man next to me, then glanced back at Binyamin, who was bleeding profusely from a slice on his arm. Satisfied that he wouldn't die from his wound, I released my grip on my saddle and slumped in a posture of submission. Laughing, the man moved his horse next to mine, wrapped an arm about my waist, and pulled me from my mare. Though everything in me wanted to kick and scream, I couldn't fight as long as Binyamin and Kidon were at risk.

So I did nothing as my captor drew me onto his saddle and pulled my hands around his chest. With my cheek pressed against his back, he bound my wrists together and spurred his horse. We rode off at a gallop, followed by his two companions.

I turned my head, wanting to be sure the men had left Binyamin and his father alive. I saw them struggle to their feet as their horses, donkey, and the mule stood nearby. Would they continue on to Jerusalem or return to Susa? I had no idea, but I bitterly regretted the pain my presence had caused them.

I closed my eyes as guilt smothered me with its hot hand. Neither Binyamin nor his father had wanted to leave Susa; they had done so on my account. And what had been the result? Disaster. These men would probably contact them later and demand a fee neither Binyamin nor his father could afford. When Binyamin did not pay, these men would doubtless sell me into slavery, or, if I proved troublesome, kill me outright.

Tears seeped from beneath my eyelids as I imagined Mordecai's reaction to this terrible news. He would feel even guiltier than I felt, because the journey to Jerusalem had been his idea.

We rode through the sunset and into the night, and then my captors met a group of other ruffians behind a ridge. A carriage waited there, and from behind its wooden walls I heard other female cries. My captor cut me free and pulled me from his horse, then shoved me into the conveyance. The other girls regarded me sul-

ESTHER
Royal Beauty

lenly, and when they did speak, I learned that they had been held in the sweltering wagon without food or water for hours.

What sort of kidnappers were these? The girls with me did not look like they came from wealthy families or even city dwellers. So perhaps I was mistaken about my captors' intentions. . . .

I peered through slits in the wooden walls. The men outside wore the turbans and scarves of desert nomads, a people I did not know. Their language was foreign to my ears, not Persian, Akkadian, or Hebrew.

But why were they capturing young girls? I knew Persia had a thriving slave trade, but Persian slaves were nearly always the people of conquered kingdoms. And who would dare conduct such a criminal raid so close to one of the king's capital cities? Once released, a captive would only have to go to the King's Gate and explain what had happened. She would set the king's justice upon those who had interfered with safe passage on the king's highway.

Unless . . . these men were gathering women for the king.

Cold, clear reality swept over me in a terrible wave, one so powerful that it stole my breath. These men weren't gathering servants for the slave market. Mordecai was right—the king's dragnet had become more aggressive and far-reaching than I had ever imagined it could.

Swallowing hard, I slid down the wall and stared at the shadowy forms across from me. I didn't know where or how they were picked up, but at least I realized why we had been thrust together. Mordecai had understood the danger better than I had, but I don't think he ever imagined that a young woman could be plucked from the Royal Road.

The next morning, when the driver turned the horses toward the east, I watched the sunrise through slits in the wooden walls and surmised that we were heading back to the city of my birth. Once there, I would do my best to contact Mordecai.

Overcome by sorrow and guilt, I lowered my head into my
hands and wept.

❦

"Welcome to the royal fortress at Susa." Harbonah, the tall,
beardless eunuch I had met years before, stood on a marble dais
and regarded the gathering of girls with wide, impassive eyes. He
had not changed much since the day I met him in the bazaar, and I
wondered what, if anything, he remembered about me. One thing
was certain—he did remember my connection with Mordecai. I'd
seen recognition in his eyes when he singled me out from the other
women in the slave trader's carriage, and that look was enough to
calm the trembling that rose from my core.

This man knew Mordecai, so to him, at least, I would not be an
anonymous, throwaway female. At least one man in the palace knew
that I was precious to someone. Trusting in that hope, I found the
strength to calm my pounding heart, lift my head, and dry my tears.

Harbonah stood in the center of a rectangular area furnished
with several couches and large cushions for the floor, many of
which were occupied by young women about my age. Trays of
fruit and goblets of wine had been stationed around the room, and
silent slaves stood against the walls, feathered fans in their hands.
Moving their fans up and down in a steady rhythm, they kept the
flies and the heat at bay. Beyond this space, in an open courtyard,
other girls lounged on cushions and laughed, apparently at ease.
They must have been among the first women to arrive. I doubted
we would be the last.

Frightened and intimidated by our luxurious surroundings, we
newcomers remained silent, but occasionally I glimpsed a timid
smile pass from one stranger to another. Most of us appeared overwhelmed, and I wondered what sort of situations my companions

had come from. Had they surrendered willingly to the king's invitation? Or had they been snatched, as I had, by furious force?

"I am Harbonah," the eunuch continued, "and I have the privilege of serving as your king's chamberlain. This—" he gestured to a shorter man dressed in a similar white tunic—"is Hegai, and he is in charge of the palace of the virgins. His primary duty is to make sure you are fully prepared for your night with the king—and that means he is required to see that you are at your most beautiful, most charming, and most eager to please our royal master. I can tell from looking at you—" his eyes narrowed in a critical squint—"that his job will not be an easy one. You have come from all over the empire, and some of you still have sand between your toes. But never fear, ladies, over the next twelve months Hegai will transform you into the kind of woman the king appreciates."

We girls looked at each other when he paused, each of us wondering what her neighbor would look like after a full year of a eunuch's specialized training. The girl closest to me had skin as black as a midnight sky, with wide, dark eyes, a graceful frame, and a long, slender neck. She was lovely in a way I could never be, and I wondered if she would be our next queen. I thought her the most fascinating person in the room, but who could say what sort of woman the king favored?

Only the eunuchs. They were the key to success in this place, the key to escape.

"You will live here," Harbonah went on, "and you are not to step out of this area for any reason until you are called to the king's chamber. You are now his property, so you are not to flaunt your beauty in front of other men unless commanded to do so. Other men may be allowed to view the king's treasures, but some royal possessions are reserved for the king alone. You are among those other possessions."

My heart constricted at being called a "possession." The children of Israel had been slaves in Egypt and Babylon, and Mordecai would not want to know that I had stumbled into slavery, as well. He had taught me to be an independent thinker, restraining my thoughts only where the Law of Moses demanded that I rein them in. I had been encouraged to read, to study the Law, poetry, and the history of our people. I knew Adonai created man first and woman after, and I also knew our people were never to sell one another into slavery. . . .

Yet here I was, the *possession* of a Persian king. Oh, Mordecai! How could Adonai allow this, a situation that would undoubtedly break the heart of one of his most devout and dutiful servants?

"As part of the royal harem," Harbonah continued, "you should know who the other women are in case you happen to encounter one of them. The highest-ranking woman in the palace now is the king's mother, Atossa. If you should see her, you should prostrate yourself immediately and remain silent unless she addresses you directly. She is to be obeyed without question and shown due deference. She reigns in any chamber she enters and is subject only to the king."

Harbonah arched a brow and looked around the room as if expecting one of us to argue the point, but no one said a word.

"The second-highest rank would be that of queen, but that position has been vacant for several years. One of you may well become queen, and if the gods smile on you in this way, you will be subject only to the king. Do I make myself clear?"

Again he looked around the room, but no one had the courage to utter a peep. I shifted my gaze to Hegai, the shorter man who would be in charge of our house. Why wasn't he delivering this speech?

"The king has other women," Harbonah went on, "but they are concubines kept for his pleasure. Many were gifts from visiting nobles. After your night with the king, you will find yourself living among them in a section of the harem ruled by Shaashgaz. You will be able to live a long and happy life as a concubine, and as the king prospers, so shall you. Beg your gods to bless the king, for he is your protector and lord. He may call for you from time to time; you may even bear a son or daughter for him. If it is a male child, do your best to raise the prince to follow truth and integrity, and he may become a man of power and influence in the empire. The king gives important positions to family members who please him and prove themselves capable."

Harbonah peered at us again. "You will each be given a set of rooms, your home for the next year or so. You will also be given handmaids to serve you. You need worry about nothing. Have you any questions for me before Hegai assigns your living quarters?"

I glanced around, for a question had occurred to me, yet no one else seemed inclined to ask anything. After a prolonged moment, I lifted my hand.

The eunuch's eyes flashed in my direction. "Yes?"

"I beg your pardon, sir, but as you listed the royal women, you seemed to forget someone."

His forehead wrinkled. "I don't know who—"

"Our former queen, sir. Where does Vashti fall in the ranking?"

Harbonah flushed as an uncomfortable silence filled the room and the wide-eyed fly swatters stopped moving their fans. "Um . . ." He cleared his throat. "The woman known as Vashti is queen no longer. But she is the mother of our crown prince, so until the king has another heir, she will be accorded honor in the palace. She is still of high rank."

"So . . . do we bow if we meet her?"

Harbonah tilted his head, leading me to believe no one had ever asked the question. "You do not have to prostrate yourself—she is only one of the king's women. But you should treat her with respect. And caution."

What did he mean? I shot a questioning look to the girl next to me, but her forehead was so wrinkled with puzzlement that I wondered if she understood anything. What if she'd come from one of the outlying satraps and didn't even speak the king's language?

I caught her eye and smiled, giving her an unspoken promise: I would be her friend, and we would help each other through this ordeal.

And after my year of preparation was finished, and after I'd spent my night with the king, maybe Hegai and Harbonah would help me find my way home.

Chapter Nineteen
HARBONAH

To single out Hadassah in front of all the other women might have stirred up jealousy, so I did not speak to her right away. But as soon as I finished addressing the harem's most recent arrivals, I left the girls in Hegai's care and went in search of Mordecai. I found him at his usual station, standing behind a tall desk, his eyes intent on the ciphers pressed into the clay form before him.

I had not seen my friend in several months, and it seemed to me the accountant had aged considerably since we last met. Anxiety and grief had etched new lines upon his face, and loss shadowed his dark eyes. Were these changes due to the strain of grieving for his wife or missing his adopted daughter?

This interview would require my talents for tact and discretion. I didn't know when the man had last seen his Hadassah, or how she came to be in a slave trader's wagon.

"Warmest greetings, Mordecai."

He looked up, startled, then a small smile split his graying beard. "Harbonah! How good of you to come see me."

He stepped out from behind his desk, threw his arms around my shoulders, and kissed me on both cheeks, honoring me with the greeting one man gives an equal. "Come, let us sit and talk for a moment." He led the way toward a bench by a cold fire pit. "We have much to discuss, as I haven't seen you since your return from Sardis."

I took the seat he offered and smiled, not sure how to proceed. "I hope," I began, "this day finds you well."

Mordecai sat too, bracing himself with his hands on his knees. "Miriam died, as you may have heard," he said, staring straight ahead, "and two days ago I sent Hadassah away with her betrothed and his father. They will be married in Jerusalem, and they will make the city of David their home."

So he didn't know. I swallowed hard. "Mordecai, I have news about your daughter."

Reluctantly, he met my gaze, his lower lip trembling at something he must have seen in my eyes. "You have heard something about Hadassah?"

"I am sorry to be the one to tell you." I bit my lip, wishing I could soften the blow. "I saw your Hadassah yesterday when she was delivered into Hegai's custody by a pair of slave traders. I didn't know anything about a wedding, but I know where she is now. She is in the king's harem, in the palace of the virgins."

Mordecai lifted his chin and met my gaze straight on. "Impossible. You must be mistaken. What of her betrothed and his father? They were with her; they were to guard her on the journey—"

"I know nothing of them, and I have not had an opportunity to speak to the girl. But you can take comfort in knowing that Hegai is a friend and your daughter has already won his admiration. He plans to give her the best rooms in the harem, the best of everything. She will lack for nothing."

"Except . . . her freedom." Mordecai closed his eyes, opened his mouth, his expression that of a man who had been pushed beyond the bounds of human endurance. For a long moment neither of us spoke. Then a shadow flickered over Mordecai's face. He bowed his head, pounded his breast, and released an eerie cry that sliced across my soul like a keen-edged blade.

The other men working in the room halted and turned toward Mordecai, horror on their faces.

"I had hoped to get her safely away from the king," Mordecai finally said, his voice breaking. "I knew she was beautiful and bright, but I hoped a marriage in faraway Jerusalem might save her from this fate. She did not want to be married in such a hurry, but she agreed because she is obedient and because she knew it was for the best. And now my precious Hadassah is captive in a pagan king's palace while her betrothed—"

He looked at me, fresh alarm on his face. "Do you know what happened to Binyamin and his father?"

I shook my head. "Slave traders can be ruthless," I warned, speaking gently because I knew my words would not be easy to hear. "They have been rounding up women of all sorts, knowing they will be paid if they bring an acceptable maiden to the palace. If your daughter's defenders resisted, I would not hold much hope for their survival."

"Binyamin and his father were scholars, not warriors." Mordecai's eyes glistened with pain. "I doubt they fought at all, but one can never be sure with young men in love."

He stared at nothing a moment more; then he scooped up a handful of old ashes from the fire pit. He slowly poured them over his head, then leaned forward again. "I had better organize a search party. If they were injured, they may need my help."

I nodded my agreement as I helped the grieving man to his feet. "One more thing." I maintained a tight grip on his arm. "Hadassah has called herself Esther. I assumed she had good reasons for maintaining her privacy."

A certain intentness filled the accountant's eyes, and then he offered me a brief smile. "She is a clever girl. A good girl, and wise. She has done exactly what I asked her to do."

"Disguise herself?" My thoughts whirled, searching for a logical reason. "Why would you ask her to do that?"

Mordecai's dark eyes glittered above his graying beard. "Because we are Jews. And this king cannot be trusted."

I released him. And as much as I wanted to defend my beloved master, I knew I could not.

⁓⚘⁓

Nearly a week passed before I had an opportunity to check on Hadassah, and even then I worried that I might cause trouble by seeking her out. Many a servant, indeed, many a free man, had been undone by harem gossip, so I resolved to do nothing that might injure Hadassah, Hegai, or myself. Life was too short and the alternative far too unpleasant to risk anything that might arouse a royal temper.

On the pretext of needing to ask Hegai's opinion about a seating arrangement, I made my way to the palace of the virgins and found my friend standing in a doorway. I tapped him on the shoulder, then peered past him into the large courtyard, where another eunuch was demonstrating the proper way to braid hair. "See any good prospects, my friend?"

Hegai lifted his gaze to the ceiling and sighed. "Never have I been more c-c-convinced that beauty is not all a man requires in a d-d-desirable woman. Every virgin in yonder room has a pleasant f-f-face, but nearly half don't speak Persian and another half are as g-g-graceless as oxen." He paused to take a deep breath, apparently exhausted by the effort of stringing so many thoughts together. "We have collected c-c-comely girls from everywhere, but n-n-none of them are ready to s-s-speak to the king, let alone share his b-b-bed."

I dropped my hand to his shoulder, silently showing appreciation for the report. Rarely did Hegai speak so many words at once.

"Surely—" I paused to seek the most delicate phrase—"surely not much is expected of a woman who provides only an evening's entertainment?"

Hegai dipped his head and gave me a skeptical look. "The king wants a w-w-wife. And she must follow V-V-Vashti."

"And that will not be easy." I chuckled. "So you must not only make these girls beautiful, you must make them witty and clever."

"If only . . . I could." Hegai shook his head. "Some of them . . . are s-s-stupid. But—" his broad face cracked into a smile for the first time—"I have a favorite. And she is s-s-smart."

I smiled, knowing full well whose name I would hear. "Care to share the identity of this young woman?"

"It is . . . Esther, the one who came . . . with the f-f-farm girls. I have assigned her . . . s-s-seven attendants and arranged . . . special foods because she doesn't eat p-p-pork or shellfish. Whatever she wants . . . I'll get." He turned, resting an appraising eye on me. "I think . . . you sh-sh-should tell me."

"Tell you what?"

"About her. You know s-s-something."

I put on a shocked expression. "What makes you think I know anything at all? You heard her say she was an orphan."

Hegai harrumphed. "Am I supposed to . . . b-b-believe . . . she was born in the desert? No, this rose was c-c-c-cultivated. And you . . . . know her."

I opened my mouth to protest again, but Hegai lifted his hand to stop me. "K-k-keep your secrets, then. But my efforts and my l-l-life . . . will depend . . . on . . . that girl."

He didn't have to say anything else. Hegai and I had been friends since arriving at the palace together. I knew how to read his silences and the gaps between his words. I knew the horrors that darkened his nightmares just as he knew mine.

And since the idea to audition virgins had originated with me, Hegai and I both knew that our lives depended upon the success of these girls, and one in particular.

CHAPTER TWENTY
HADASSAH

I GLANCED TOWARD THE DOORWAY and felt my heart warm when I spotted Harbonah with Hegai. The two were chatting in a friendly manner, so they had to be well acquainted. And since Harbonah knew Mordecai, Hegai was another link in the chain that led to the only family I had left. I needed to keep those links in place, for they would be my way home.

The tall eunuch must have felt the pressure of my gaze, because he looked up, caught my eye, and nodded in a wordless greeting. Or did his nod convey something more? I hoped—with all my soul, I *prayed*—that he had told Mordecai where I was.

My heart ached at the thought of Mordecai's despair. He had done his best to keep me safe, and for what? He had prayed for my safety, yet his prayers had gone unanswered. Despite Mordecai's efforts to remain righteous and faithful in a pagan king's city, Adonai had failed my cousin. I could almost believe that HaShem had abandoned us, but so long as Mordecai believed, I could not abandon my faith. Faith and family were the cords that bound us together.

"And you see," the teaching eunuch said, using his long-fingered hands to demonstrate techniques of hair curling and arrangement, "a six-strand plait creates a lovely basket on the head. Does anyone want to try it?"

Sighing, I rested my cheek on my palm and dreamed of home. If Miriam were alive, at this hour she would be baking bread. She would send me to the well for fresh water or tell me to make sure the glazed jar contained enough oil. Mordecai would be walking home by this time, reflecting on his work, perhaps adding numbers in his head or rehearsing the report he would give to his supervisor. . . .

"You there—sleepy girl."

I blinked as the lecturing eunuch pointed a long finger at me.

"Don't touch your face with your hands or you'll pull your skin into wrinkles. Do you want to be droopy and lined before you've spent even an hour with the king? Of course not. So you must keep your hands away from your face at all times, understand?"

I nodded, embarrassed, and kept my head down for several minutes after he returned to his demonstration.

"Don't worry about him." Artystone, the girl sitting next to me, smiled and lowered her voice. "He's a fussy one, but he has no real power. The only important man here—besides the king—is Hegai. He decides *who* goes to the king, *when* a girl goes to the king, and what she *wears* when she goes to the king. If you want access to the best gowns, jewels, and hairdresser, you'll want to cozy up to Hegai."

I shifted my gaze to the short, bald man who stood in the doorway. Our stuttering guardian had escorted me to the harem on the day of my arrival, and he had gently washed my chafed wrists and applied salve to my broken skin. He'd also given me a suite of nice rooms and assigned seven handmaids to be my attendants. He had assured me, blushing, that those seven girls were the most skilled and discreet maids in the harem.

But because he was a friend of Harbonah's, I would have liked him if he hadn't done any of those things.

I smiled at Artystone. "How long have you been here?"

A faint glint of humor shone in her eyes. "I was one of the first to arrive. My father brought me, and now my entire family waits for word that I've been crowned queen." She hugged her bent knees. "I don't know how to tell them that I'm about as likely to become queen as to sprout wings and fly away. I figure the best I can hope for is to have a royal baby. If I bear a son, I might at least be given better quarters in the harem. But queen? I'm not the type and I never will be."

I swallowed hard, remembering how Mordecai had declared that the king's virgins would be used and discarded. "If you're not chosen as queen . . . wouldn't you want to go home?"

She leaned back as if to see me better, then laughed so loudly that the lecturing eunuch stopped and glared in our direction.

The teacher—I didn't catch his name—looked so much like the others I would have known him for a eunuch from fifty paces away. Since arriving in the harem, I had noticed that the palace eunuchs held certain characteristics in common. Most had smooth faces and rounded figures, soft in the hips and belly. Many were tall and lanky, with voices as high-pitched as a child's. Unless they chose to shave their heads, their skulls were capped with tresses as thick and shiny as mine. Many of the old ones had developed prominent humps on their backs, yet because they projected certain aspects of femininity, several of the eunuchs could honestly be called beautiful.

When the scowling hairdresser finally resumed his teaching, Artystone leaned closer to me. "You can forget about ever going home. No woman who has slept with the king can ever sleep with anyone else—unless he dies and the next ruler marries you to keep the royal connections in place. You belong to the king now, as do I, and we can do nothing about it. The only way out of the harem is on a burial bier."

She spoke so casually, so smoothly, that her words didn't immediately register. When they did, the shock of defeat held me immobile.

No way out?

I swallowed, realizing why Mordecai had worked so diligently to keep me from this fate. I had dreamed of visiting the palace and meeting the king, and I had even dreamed of marrying a prince. Even since being caught by the slave traders, I had entertained the hazy idea I would be auditioned in the king's bed, rejected, and then allowed to go home—a cruel fate, certainly, but not one without hope.

In my innocence I had no idea what being the king's woman entailed.

A memory reared its head—the woman at the bazaar, the know-it-all who scolded me and Parysatis for dreaming of a life in the harem. We paid her no mind, believing her to be old and bitter, but she had given us the unvarnished truth.

Persia might offer its subjects a great deal of personal and religious freedom, but I was a woman, and women belonged to their men. And I, along with dozens of other girls, had become one of the king's women.

For the rest of our lives, we would never belong to anyone else.

◈

After two weeks of living in the harem, I knew that whatever traces of beauty I'd possessed were gone. My smile had become as cold and lonely as my heart, and my eyes had reddened from fits of frustrated weeping. When not required to attend a class on dancing, music, or cosmetics, I retreated to the garden where I could weep undisturbed and relive my precious memories.

Leaving Susa had been difficult, but I had hoped for a husband's love to console me. Now I lived in the world's grandest palace, yet I sobbed inconsolably at the thought of never seeing Mordecai again.

I was sitting in an alcove built into the garden wall when Harbonah walked along the path with Hegai. After a brief conversation, the shorter man left Harbonah. The tall eunuch turned in my direction.

"I thought you might like to know," he said, walking toward me with his hands clasped behind his back, "that a certain accountant from the King's Gate walks along the courtyard wall every afternoon. He seems to be in deep contemplation. Perhaps he is concerned about a family member. Perhaps he would like to know how she is faring."

The eunuch spoke these words calmly, without meeting my gaze. I glanced around, thinking he might be addressing someone else, but no one else was there. I couldn't be mistaken—he had to be talking to me.

I looked at him, confused. "What good does it do me to know this? We are kept under guard, and cannot roam where we choose."

His broad mouth curled into a smile as his eyes met mine. "You need not go outside the harem. On the other side of this wall a walking path offers a most inspiring view of the distant mountains. My friend Mordecai walks the path every day."

I brought my hand to my lips. "My cousin is . . . that close?"

"Only a few feet away, child."

Hope fluttered in my breast like a startled bird, then I sighed. "This is a high wall, sir, and the stone is thick. Since I can't see through these rocks, how will I know when my cousin is near?"

The eunuch chuckled. "My friend walks the path at midday, when the sun is directly overhead. An alcove much like this one has been cut into the south end of this wall. If you were to rest there and sing quietly, I am sure you would be overheard on the walkway. Since the heat is strong at midday, not many other girls will venture into the garden. Not many men choose to walk in the midday heat, either."

I smiled as the ice around my heart began to melt. "You are a friend to me, Harbonah, as well as to my cousin. Tomorrow I will sit in that alcove, and I will sing in the hope that I will be heard."

The eunuch nodded, then glanced at the sky. "Why wait? The sun is nearly at its zenith."

Overcome with the hope that I might be able to speak to Mordecai right away, I thanked the eunuch and hurried toward the south wall. I found the alcove and sat on the marble bench, concentrating to hear the sound of footfalls on the path beyond. I could hear nothing but the rustle of a nesting bird and the gurgle of a fountain, but hadn't Harbonah suggested that I sing? I would, but if I sang a familiar song, another girl might assume she was free to join in. So I would not sing in Persian. I would sing a tune Mordecai knew. . . .

My tongue picked up the haunting melody as easily as if I'd heard it the night before.

"They will come and sing on the heights of Zion," I sang in Hebrew, "streaming to the goodness of Adonai, to the grain, the wine, the olive oil, and the young of the flock and the herd. They themselves will be like a well-watered garden, never to languish again. Then the virgin will dance for joy, young men and old men together; for I will turn their mourning into joy, comfort and gladden them after their sorrow."

"Hadassah?"

The sound of my Hebrew name felt as sweet as a cool mountain breeze.

"Mordecai!" My pulse quickened as my eyes filled with tears. "I thought I would never hear your voice again!"

"Are you well, my daughter?"

"I am very well, cousin. Since coming to the palace, I have been treated with the greatest kindness. But Binyamin and his father—"

"I have seen them, and they have recovered from the attack. They are going on to Jerusalem, so they have agreed to break your marriage contract."

"Oh." I brought my hand to my mouth, my throat aching with regret. Even though I hadn't been excited about marrying Binyamin, Mordecai's news still stung. If Binyamin had found me so easy to forget, the king would barely even note my presence.

"You must put that sorrow behind you, daughter. You are in danger here, and you must be ever on your guard."

I blinked, trying to comprehend what I was hearing. Mordecai sounded tense and worried, but why? I had already resigned myself to being a concubine, and though this wasn't the life I would have chosen, I didn't think it deserved to be called *dangerous*.

"You must not worry about me, cousin. You should eat well and get your rest. Do not let your fears keep you awake."

I heard his deep chuckle and could almost see him absently tugging on his beard. "It is good to hear your voice. I will rest easier knowing you are well. If you need anything, you have but to let me know. If you need something immediately, speak to Hegai. He knows Harbonah, and Harbonah is a friend."

"I should have known you'd find a way to check on me." I hesitated, searching for words that would adequately describe the glorious joy that had flooded my heart. "I will live for the day when I see you again, cousin, whether in this life or the next."

I thought he would respond with the same sentiment, but instead he said, "Go in peace, Hadassah. May HaShem watch over you until we speak again."

Chapter Twenty-One

HARBONAH

FOLLOWING IN THE TRADITION OF HIS FATHER and other kings before him, when balmy spring surrendered to summer the king and his household packed their belongings and moved to the palace at Ecbatana. Usually I made the trip with a light heart, much preferring the northern palace's weather and locale, but that year I left reluctantly. I had developed a real affection and sense of responsibility for Mordecai's young ward, and I hated to leave her behind.

At least I would not leave her alone—Mordecai spoke to the girl every day but on his Sabbath, and Hegai would remain behind to oversee the palace of the virgins.

My place was with my master.

Though I had a thousand details to oversee as we prepared for the journey, I did not worry about my friend Mordecai. Since he had found a way to communicate with Hadassah, I knew he would be available to provide counsel should she become depressed or discouraged.

But why should she be discouraged? No virgin in the harem was more pampered than Esther. As Hegai's favorite, she enjoyed the best of everything. As Mordecai's ward, she would never be alone. Her unseen guardian would always be available to comfort, counsel, educate, and correct—in the unlikely event that she needed correction.

As the royal party began the trek over the mountains, I set my concerns about the harem aside and began to concentrate on my king. The idea of crowning a new queen had brightened his mood while we remained in Susa, but we left the virgins behind. With no hope for a consort's comfort and companionship in the near future, the king's dark mood returned.

Not even our arrival at Ecbatana cheered him. The summer palace was situated by a river and located on an elevated plateau, where the air was cool and thin. The impressive Zagros Mountains overlooked the city, with Mount Alvand towering over us with its snowcapped heights. An otherworldly sense of calm dominated the settlement, despite the capital's torrid and bloody history.

The summer palace held deep personal significance for my master. His father, the great Darius, had overcome a rival here, executing the traitor Phraortes atop the city wall in full view of the public. Darius preserved his legacy with that act, and I knew my master could not gaze upon the city wall without remembering that he would have no empire if not for his father's valor. The older people in Ecbatana remembered as well, and expected to see the same power and authority in Darius's son.

I could only hope that my king would accept the memory as a challenge. With the memory of his failure in Greece still fresh in his thoughts, my master did not need another taunting reminder of his father's success.

The palace at Ecbatana was a marvel, equally as beautiful as the compound at Susa. Seven concentric walls enclosed the king's house and gleamed in the slanting sunlight, its high battlements plated with gold and silver. The river ran deep and fast at the west side, providing life and security to those who dwelled inside the walls. Deep within the secure fortress lay the royal treasury, and deeper still lay the king's residence.

I hoped the change of scenery would do my master good, but after our arrival he retired to his rooms and went straight to bed. He stayed abed for days, waking only to relieve himself and eat a bit of fruit or meat. His dark mood deepened with every passing day, and more than once I found myself wishing that he had allowed Vashti to accompany her children. Though she was never again to sit beside him as queen, I could have arranged a chance meeting in a hallway or antechamber. . . .

In truth, no woman had ever delighted my king like Vashti. With a tongue as sharp as a serpent's tooth, she had a gift for cutting to the heart of a matter. Her beautiful eyes saw through the facades of smiling sycophants, and her ears caught rumors long before they surfaced to do damage. Though her obstinacy had resulted in her downfall, I think the king would have enjoyed being with someone who saw him not as a king, but as a man in need of a soul mate.

I hesitate to write of these things because I am a slave. I have no right to exhibit even a sliver of pride, but I am sure there were occasions when the king considered me a friend. Not because I had done anything to be worthy of his notice, but because I was a stable fixture in his life. I had seen him at his best and at his worst. I had seen him hearty and ill, cheerful and disagreeable, in love and lonely.

Lonely is the word that best describes my king that summer. My royal master longed for someone in whom he could confide, yet no confidant could be found in Ecbatana—or at least none that was worthy of a king. Even his nephew Mushka, who had always delighted him, left my disgruntled master murmuring about the extreme foolishness of restless young men.

After realizing that our beautiful surroundings had done nothing to improve my master's mood or his health, one evening I gathered my courage and suggested we return to Susa early, before autumn advanced. "The plain is so lovely in the cooler months," I said, pretending to talk to myself as I removed his royal cloak and prepared him for bed. "The king has always enjoyed looking across the plain at the river."

The king grunted an inadvertent reply, then lifted his head and looked around his chamber. Recognizing his thoughtful mood, I stepped away, content to let him explore whatever thoughts lay on his mind. He settled onto his bed, punched his pillow, then rested his head on one arm and stared out the balcony of his chamber.

"Eunuch, look at this," he finally said, lifting one arm to indicate the elaborate columns around his bed. "The finest artisans in all the world wrought this chamber for my father, but what pleasure can a weary man find in it? A life without joy is no life at all."

I pressed my lips together and waited. I would have remained silent, but then he turned and met my gaze. "I did wrong to set Vashti aside," he said, his voice flat and matter-of-fact. "And now I must take a new queen, but I do not think I will find Vashti's equal. She was more royal than anyone I know."

I drew a deep breath, not sure how to answer. I did not want to criticize the former queen, for she was still the mother of the crown prince, but neither did I want to criticize the king's decision.

"I am sure your majesty will do the right thing," I finally said, offering a safe and cowardly answer. "My king has great wisdom."

"Your king has wise counselors." My master turned back toward the balcony and peered into the darkness. "My father often said I should be more decisive, that I lived too much in my thoughts. But

ANGELA
HUNT

I never know how to choose the right thing, so my counselors give me wisdom . . . or at least the appearance of sagacity."

I bowed my head and said nothing, for my master was speaking as if to an intimate. What I heard could never be repeated outside the king's bedchamber and was probably best forgotten.

"Tomorrow we shall make immediate plans to return to Susa," my master said, abruptly punching his pillow again. "Have my generals plot a swift track over the mountains. I would like to be home before the snow makes travel impossible."

I pressed my hands together, bowed, and backed out of the room, turning only when I had stepped between the guards in the outer hall.

I had been successful. We would return to Susa immediately, and that fair city and its warmer climate should do much to ease the king's melancholy. He could ride out on a hunt or watch the soldiers train on the open plain. He could take his sons riding by the river.

And if the city failed to lift the dark cloud around him, my master might call for an evening's entertainment and I would recommend Hegai and his palace of the virgins. Scores of beautiful young women waited there, and any of them would make a better queen than the selfish, scheming Vashti.

I had a good feeling about one girl in particular.

CHAPTER TWENTY-TWO

HADASSAH

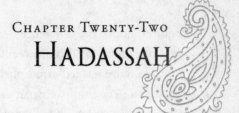

As girls, Parysatis and I had often remarked about the discernible difference in the city's atmosphere when the king was away from his palace. We groaned about how boring and dull Susa was without him, but that difference was magnified a hundredfold when one lived in the royal fortress. When I entered the palace, the harem buzzed with activity, and every slave walked with a brisk step, never lingering for more than a moment in any one spot. But once the king and his household departed, an air of somnolence descended over the place.

Those of us who had been gathered into the complex reserved for virgins grew sluggish and lazy in the heat. We were still fed choice foods (Artystone claimed the eunuchs were fattening us like lambs for the slaughter) and given our beauty treatments: each morning we bathed in waters laced with myrrh, and each evening our handmaids massaged perfumed oils into our skin. I had already begun to notice the difference—when I removed my tunic each night, the fabric smelled of sweet flowers.

In the more relaxed atmosphere of the hot summer, we were allowed to sleep until we woke naturally, and nap in the late afternoons. I spent long hours lying in my chamber, staring at the painted ceiling and wondering how I had come to be in that place. I certainly had no choice in the matter, but what choices did any woman have in her life? Whether we were betrothed and married to friends of the family or sold into slavery or sent to a king's palace, what did it matter? We had no control over our fate.

Yet we were not the only powerless beings in the palace. One afternoon I stood at the gate to our building and saw a line of shackled boys arriving with a caravan. Stick thin, barely clad, covered in scabs and grime, they stood silently, the fight gone out of them. These lads, the oldest of whom was probably no more than ten or eleven, were directed to another building where they would live until ready to serve the king.

I looked over and caught Hegai's eye—he had seen the boys, too. "Will they be slaves?" I asked.

Hegai opened his mouth to speak, then clamped his mouth shut and nodded.

"Will they be eunuchs?" I asked, more carefully.

Hegai turned away, but a moment later he turned toward me again. His eyes brimmed with tears as he answered: "Y-y-yes. They will be c-c-castrated within the week."

I gave him what I hoped was a sympathetic smile and reconsidered my fate. The king controlled everything in the palace, including our right to lie with a man we loved and create children. We virgins were not the only people who'd had the king's will forced upon us, but I felt far more fortunate than those captive boys.

With the king away, Hegai allowed us to wander throughout the fortress so long as we promised not to draw attention to ourselves.

Like surreptitious ghosts we slipped out of the harem at night to tiptoe over the marble floors and stare at the towering columns, marveling at their colorful designs. I ran my fingers over glazed tiles arranged into intricate figures of lions and horses and marveled at the luxury of my king's palace.

I had never seen such beautiful images, not even in Parysatis's home. Mordecai and Miriam had simple tastes and bare walls, but amazing art covered nearly every object in the palace. Walls, ceilings, columns, floors—colors blazed from every surface and shone in the slanting rays of the sun. Fountains bubbled up in the most unexpected locations, and the shrubs in the garden hung low with huge blossoms. I loved walking in the garden adjacent to the apadana and breathing in the scents of so many flowers. A shame, really, that the king chose to be away during the most beautiful growing season.

Sometimes I felt almost guilty for being so pampered. Mordecai talked as though I were being held prisoner, and while I was not free to leave the royal palace, no one asked me to do anything but submit to my lessons, ointments, and garment fittings.

When we weren't eating, resting, or exploring, we attended lessons under Hegai. The little eunuch did not seem to enjoy speaking about intimate topics, but he had grown up in the harem and knew everything we would need to learn.

Such as how to walk so that our hips swayed from side to side. "Like a b-b-beguiling pendulum," he said, waving a silk scarf back and forth like a cattail blowing in the wind. "The king's view of your backside should be gr-gr-graceful and f-f-feminine, hypnotic."

His advice confused me. When we were summoned to the king's chamber, weren't we supposed to immediately prostrate ourselves? And when he dismissed us, weren't we supposed to back out of the room, head down, eyes averted, until the guards closed the door? If so, how would the king ever have an opportunity to glimpse anyone's backside?

I wanted to ask my question aloud, but Hegai had said nothing about the span of time between our entrance and our exit, so perhaps some occasion in the gap might require walking away from the king. If he took one look at my face and pronounced me unattractive, perhaps I might be allowed to turn and slink away from his harsh disapproval . . . or maybe not.

An Ionian beauty fluttered her fingers to catch Hegai's attention. "What are we supposed to do with the king other than . . ." She rolled her eyes in a coy gesture and tugged at her long hair. "Are we supposed to talk to him?"

"And what would you t-t-talk about?" Hegai shook his head. "Would you tell him how to run the k-k-kingdom? Would you give him advice on the r-r-royal children?"

Obviously sensing Hegai's discomfort, another eunuch stepped up to finish the answer. "You forget, girl, that you will be talking to the most powerful man in the world. You could not possibly say anything he would find interesting or useful, so keep your lovely lips clamped together. You are there to please him. If he wants music, play the harp. If he wants song, sing for him. If he wants to be touched, touch him as he directs. But do *not* talk to him. The royal ear must not be distracted or disturbed by one so young, and a female at that."

I cocked an eyebrow, annoyed by the eunuch's advice. Mordecai was a wise man of some importance, yet he had never hesitated to talk with me. He had listened respectfully to my thoughts even when he considered them foolish, and then he had asked questions to make me think more deeply about my opinions. Though sometimes he talked about concepts and beliefs I didn't understand, he had never told me to be quiet or shamed me for my ignorance.

Perhaps the king would like to know about the homes from whence we had come, or the plans we had made before his summons interrupted our lives.

I looked around the airy chamber and saw young girls from all over the Persian Empire. None of us had ever been in a situation even remotely like this, but under Hegai's tutelage we had formed a bond. Nearly all of us had come to believe that our situation, though not of our choosing, was a step up in the world. If the king had not decided to choose another queen, we would probably be married to whomever our fathers chose. We would be eking out an existence far more difficult than the one we enjoyed in the harem. To the world we were anonymous females, but we knew each other.

And in our hearts we cherished one unspoken hope: that the king would remember our names.

One afternoon Hegai plucked my sleeve and pulled me from a group of girls who were painting one another's faces. Artystone had applied cosmetics only to the right side of my face, and Hegai blinked at me in confusion until I picked up a towel and scrubbed some of the powdered malachite from my eyelids. "Sorry," I said, blushing. "We didn't think we'd be interrupted."

Instead of answering, Hegai took a half step back and looked me over, his bright eyes drinking me in from head to toe. "G-g-good," he said, more to himself than to me. "Even with the messy c-c-cosmetics, g-g-good."

I squinted at him, unable to understand what he meant. "May I do something for you, Hegai?"

For the first time that day, he lifted his head and looked directly into my eyes. "The k-k-king is returning early this year."

My stomach tightened. "He's coming soon?"

"Advance r-r-riders arrived this morning, s-s-so we expect the king within days."

An invisible cord pulled my shoulder blades together. "You don't have to remind me to be more circumspect when the king is in residence. I know we won't be able to leave the harem."

"Not here to r-r-remind you." An odd look settled over Hegai's face. "I want you to see H-H-Humusi. Today."

I turned to look at Artystone, but she had quietly slipped away. "I don't believe I've met anyone by that name."

Hegai shook his head. "Sh-sh-she lives in the palace of the c-c-concubines. She belonged to the present king's f-f-father."

Though she had outlived her master, she would reside in the harem until she died. I pressed my lips together, aware that my destiny had just unfolded before my eyes. Hegai might as well have said, *And you, Esther, will languish with Humusi until you shrivel up and waste away. . . .*

A lump rose in my throat. Did Hegai think me so unlikely to please the king that he would send me to live with the concubines now? Was this his way of preparing me for rejection?

Did he know I secretly dreamed of wearing a crown?

I swallowed hard. "Are you sending me to live in the house of the concubines?"

The little man's face rippled with anguish. "By all the g-g-gods, you misunderstand. I am sending you to H-H-Humusi because she knows what a w-w-woman must do to please a man." A furious blush glowed on the little eunuch's cheekbones. "She knows things I will never know. B-b-but you need to know them, t-t-too."

I lowered my gaze, embarrassed for both of us.

"I have asked H-H-Humusi to meet you in the harem garden. Your time is coming."

"My time?" I asked even though my racing blood had already intuited the answer.

"I want you to entertain the k-k-king on his first night at h-h-home."

❦

After repairing my makeup, I went at once to find the old concubine, my head filling with imaginings as I walked. Would she be beautiful or an ancient crone? Would she be slender, or would she have grown fat after a lifetime of luxury and fine foods?

I hurried through the columned hallway, feeling small as I slipped from shadow to shadow. The harem garden lay beyond the hallway, and I could see a blur of green in the distance. I smiled as I kept my steps to a steady pace. Though I had spent hours in the room where Hegai taught his lessons, all my most important communications had taken place in the garden. I spoke with Mordecai in the garden. When Harbonah wished to give me an important message, he always guided me to the garden, where we could speak more freely than in the enclosed spaces of the harem. And now an old woman would teach me about men . . . in the garden.

A chorus of twittering birds heralded my entrance to the rectangular space, but in scanning the shrubs, fountains, and trees I saw no woman, aged or otherwise. I walked slowly over the north-south pathway, not wanting to startle one so advanced in years, and passed several tall cypress trees without glimpsing anyone. A rectangular pool, reflecting the sky like a silver mirror, lay parallel to the path I walked.

As I neared the three-quarter point of the path, I came upon the pavilion at the intersection of the east-west walkway. Beneath the shelter of the gleaming structure, I saw a woman wreathed in colorful veils. She wore a long garment that covered her arms, and a sheer veil concealed her face. Her hands rested upon a carved walking stick, and though she must have heard my approach, she did not look in my direction.

I stepped closer. "Be well . . . Humusi?"

Slowly, she turned her head, and through the sheer veil I saw a flash of the same head-to-toe glance Hegai had given me earlier. "You must be Esther."

"I am."

"Sit, please." She nodded at the open space on the curved bench. I sank gratefully onto it, hoping this interview would be quick and to the point.

"Go ahead." She lifted her veil. "Look me over and tell me what you see."

I had not wanted to stare, but I was curious about what the years ahead held for an aging concubine. Grateful for the frank and open invitation, I studied her, knowing that I might well be looking into my future.

I was startled to realize that the woman could not yet be forty. Laugh lines radiated from the corners of her dark eyes like cracks, and her teeth, even and white, contrasted beautifully with her olive skin. Traces of humor lay around her mouth, and wisdom shone in the eyes that smiled at me.

Darius's favorite concubine was still a remarkably beautiful woman.

"Hegai has high hopes for you," she said, her eyes sparkling with spirit.

I lowered my head, uncomfortable with the compliment. "I will try to please him, but I can only do what I can do. Either the king will like me or he won't."

"And that's where you are wrong, my child." She leaned toward me and looked up into my eyes. "I have seen many beautiful girls come into the harem, yet the king forgets most of them by the next morning. Women are different in many ways, but basically we are the same: we have two arms, two legs, two breasts, two eyes, two lips, two ears. We are a vessel for a man's pleasure and a nest for his unborn children. But if you would be called into the king's presence a second and a third time, you must be a shelter for the king's heart."

I stared in silence, stunned by her words. From Hegai's manner I had expected a lesson on how to give a man physical pleasure, but Humusi was talking about a man's heart. I wanted to believe my king had a noble and generous heart, but Babar had not thought so. . . .

"I do not think," I said, stammering, "that a powerful king, a man full grown, will want to entrust his heart to one so young."

"And since when do you know so much about kings?" She laughed softly, her eyes dancing inside her veil. "When the king is alone with you he will be, at times, a man, a boy, and a baby. He will be at his most vulnerable with you if he trusts you, and if you would love him well, you will teach him to trust you." She smiled, and her gaze drifted off to some invisible territory I could not even imagine. "I have never met the son, but I knew the father, and I have seen him weep when hurt. But I never spoke of his tears until today, and I only speak of them now because Hegai believes you are special."

My heart pounded as her lips curved in a rueful smile. "When you go to the king, do whatever he asks, but never forget that he is a powerful man, and men who command others need a woman to admire and respect them. So listen, little Esther, and hear what is on his heart. Hold it securely and do not share it with anyone. And then, if you can find it in your heart to do so, love him for the man he is and the man he could be. Expect greatness of him. And then, perhaps, he will find it in himself."

"And if he doesn't?"

"Love him anyway."

Grateful for this surprising advice, I smiled at her and kissed her on the cheek. "I do not know what will happen when I go to the king. But I promise I will not forget what you have shared with me today."

CHAPTER TWENTY-THREE

HADASSAH

TWO DAYS LATER I STOOD AT THE EDGE of the apadana, staring north, the direction from which the king's caravan must come. The mountains stood like sentinels in the distance, their jagged surfaces already dusted with white.

"It is a good thing the king arrives before the frost," said a familiar voice behind me. I turned and saw Harbonah, his weathered face scanning the mountain range.

I clapped, delighted and relieved to see Mordecai's old friend. "Harbonah! When did you arrive?"

"Not long ago." He lowered his gaze and smiled. "I rode ahead to see to the preparations for the king's arrival. I've just come from the harem. The king will want a warm body in his bed tonight, and I understand that body will be yours."

"Ah. You have spoken to Hegai." I turned back toward the horizon, not wanting the eunuch to see the emotions tugging at my face. "Will the king arrive soon?"

"Later this afternoon. Definitely before sunset."

"I wish I could know if our meeting will . . . go well. If he will like me." I gripped the stone railing to steady my nerves and tried to shift the conversation away from talk of my first encounter with the king. "Tell me, Harbonah, how *you* came to the palace."

He cleared his throat. "The story is long, and certain to bore you."

"I won't be bored." I tossed a quick smile over my shoulder. "And I need something . . . to keep my mind off tonight. To keep me from being nervous."

From the corner of my eye I saw him approach the railing, though he remained a respectful distance away.

"I was born in a little village," he said, his eyes scanning the landscape, "and my parents died of a fever. I might have been set to work in the fields, but the governor of Assyria gathered up five hundred orphan boys, many from my village, all of us between ten and twelve years of age. We were marched for miles, then put in wagons and brought to Susa, along with a thousand talents of silver, as a gift for Darius, the present king's father."

I looked at him, searching for signs of resentment in his expression, but I saw no trace of bitterness. "We have something in common, then," I said. "I, too, arrived at the king's palace in a wagon."

He chuckled. "Our arrivals may have been similar, but our training was not. You have spent a year in the harem—I was dragged to the ironworker and mutilated." He hesitated, and his voice had thickened by the time he spoke again. "That day I prayed for death."

I hung my head, simultaneously ashamed and embarrassed. I could not look at him, but after a moment I heard a wry smile in his voice. "I am sorry to mention such an indelicate subject . . . but you did ask."

"I never—I never thought about such things before coming to the palace."

"You thought eunuchs were born as sexless creatures? You are young, so I suppose you don't know how cruel the world can be. But generations ago some ancient ruler noticed that after being castrated, unruly horses ceased biting, bulls gave up their disobedience, and dogs ceased to abandon their masters while remaining ever faithful and strong for the hunt. So castration, he reasoned, must surely affect men in the same way—they will be more obedient and less unruly, but no less devoted or courageous."

I gripped the stone railing and gasped. "I am afraid I have lived a sheltered life."

"You have." Harbonah crossed his arms, then leaned on the railing, still maintaining a sizable gap between us. "Persian palaces are filled with eunuchs because kings believe no one can be more trustworthy than a man who has no one else to love. And because kings are never more vulnerable than when eating, drinking, washing, or sleeping, eunuchs are employed to guard and serve in the most intimate capacities. So that is what I do. I have served our king since boyhood. We have grown up together, but while my master has grown strong, I have grown . . . old."

I shuddered in regret for having invited such a story and for what had been done to Harbonah. When I found my voice again, I lifted my chin and turned to meet his gaze. "So . . . do you serve the king out of love? Or have you reason to resent him for your fate?"

He smiled, sunlight glimmering over his narrow face as he turned toward the eastern horizon. "I do not resent our king. What happened to me as a child was regrettable, but if I had remained in my village, I would have died from starvation within the year. Instead I was brought to Susa, where I have risen to a place where I am trusted by the king of all the earth. I have suffered, yes, but I have also overcome."

He looked directly at me then, and in the cloud-softened sunlight his features were so graceful, so symmetrical, that any more delicacy would have made him every bit as beautiful as the harem virgins. "And I do love our king. Not in the way a woman loves him, but as one who cares for him from sunrise to sunrise. He has become the center of my world, so how can I help loving him? I rise when he wakes at night. Nearly every thought centers on what he might need in the next hour, the next day, the next week. My life is entwined with his—and now I wonder if yours will be, as well."

I drew a deep breath, grateful that the conversation had moved to the present day. "I have heard that the king is . . . frightening. But you would tell me if he were, wouldn't you?"

Harbonah's jaw flexed. "He is frightening only to those who have reason to fear him."

I smiled in relief. "Tell me—what is he like? As a man?"

The eunuch's sandals scuffed the tile as he shifted his weight. "Who can really know a king? Everyone around him is out to gain something; his nobles say what they think the king wants to hear. The king behaves the way he thinks people want him to behave. To his warriors he is strong and mighty; to his people he is regal and imposing. To his servants he is brusque; to his concubines he is virile and proficient. To the Immortals he is the chief soldier; to the seven vice-regents he is the epitome of what a Persian king should be. Vashti knew him as well as anyone, but she will never enter his bedchamber again."

He looked at me, his brow wrinkling as something moved in his eyes. "I wonder what you will be to him, my young friend."

I swallowed hard and thought of what Humusi had told me. "I will be . . . if he will let me, I will be a shelter for his heart."

Harbonah did not respond, but his wide mouth curled in a one-sided smile before he turned and moved away.

With a flurry of trumpets and the rumble of hooves, the royal caravan approached Susa. The other girls and I hurried back to the palace of the virgins lest we be found wandering in the hallways. Several of us gathered in the garden, and Artystone was brave enough to stand in the clasped hands of another girl in an effort to climb up and peer over the wall.

"Do you think?" another girl whispered. "Do you think the king will be too tired to call for a woman tonight?"

"The king has been traveling for days," Artystone answered, lifting her chin. "Surely he has become accustomed to the pace of the journey."

"And he is the *king*," another girl stressed. "He cannot tire like ordinary men."

I pressed my lips together and stared at the ground, knowing that if the king *did* ask for a woman, Hegai would send me. After sleeping with the king, I would go to the palace of the concubines, overseen by Shaashgaz, another eunuch in the king's service. I would not see these girls again until they too had slept with the king and joined the concubines . . . in the house of the anonymous and deflowered.

"A concubine will not visit the king's chamber again," Hegai once informed us, "unless he was especially pleased with her and summoned her by name."

If our future depended upon an aging king's memory, maybe Hegai should write our names on our foreheads before sending us into the royal bedchamber.

The chatter around me silenced as the eunuch rounded a pillar and discovered us in the garden. He glared at Artystone, still peering over the wall, and when she jumped down, he lifted the other girl's reddened hands and made quiet *tsk*ing sounds. "You will ruin your s-s-skin," he said, his voice high and soft. "You should think b-b-before you d-d-do these things."

The girls backed away, then Hegai's gaze fell on me. "Esther." His eyes lit with anticipation. "C-c-come with me."

Questions rose in a sibilant chorus around me: "Has the king returned?" "Has he sent word?" "Is she the one for tonight?"

As I followed the eunuch, warm palms brushed my arms—gentle touches of envy, encouragement, and disbelief. Hegai led the way up the stairs, then took my arm and patted my hand. My maids stood waiting on the landing, smiling as if I were a bride about to meet her groom.

"You will be fine." Hulta slipped her arm around my shoulders. "The king will love you."

Would he? Or would I be one of a thousand other pretty girls who had filled his bed for an hour or so?

As my maids and I followed the eunuch, I couldn't help feeling grateful that I hadn't known about the king's homecoming when I spoke with Mordecai earlier in the day. He would not have been pleased to learn I was about to lose my virginity. He had grown complacent in the king's absence and was probably hoping Xerxes would remain at Ecbatana forever. . . .

Hegai led my entourage to a special robing room, where hundreds of silken gowns, wigs, and veils were piled in baskets, overflowing in sumptuous disarray. Against the back wall, gold and silver jewelry spilled from an immense chest.

"Ch-ch-choose what you will." Hegai gestured toward the treasures of the harem. "Each g-g-girl is allowed to determine what will make her most b-b-beautiful."

I stepped back, overwhelmed by the number of choices. "I cannot. Please, Hegai, choose for me."

The eunuch blinked, then moved forward and rubbed his hands, a delighted smile splitting his face. "I have waited years for s-s-such an opportunity." He gestured toward a pile of tunics and sent one of my maids scrambling in that direction. "Over there, the sleeveless gowns."

My maid pulled out two garments, one scarlet and one purple, but Hegai shook his head. "Not for Esther, our virginal star. Stars are b-b-bright and b-b-brilliant. They are pure. The white gown, please, from that c-c-corner."

The maid pulled out a shimmering silk gown, a one-shouldered design I had never seen before. She brought it to Hegai, who held the fabric up to my skin and nodded in satisfaction. "This one." He handed the garment off to my dressing maid. "And as for j-j-jewelry . . ."

He ran his finger through a tray of gold chains, silver ropes, mounted gems and precious stones, then chose two clear diamonds, each suspended from a fine golden chain. "These earrings." He handed them to another maid. "And n-n-nothing around her neck. Let n-n-nothing stand between the k-k-king and her sweetness."

"What about her hair?" The maid behind me unpinned the braided knot at my neck and pulled it loose. "Should I plait it or curl it or—"

"B-b-brush it," Hegai said, stepping back. "Brush it until it sh-sh-shines, and then do n-n-nothing. Let it be a r-r-river of black s-s-silk." He smiled, his teeth gleaming in the gathering dusk. "Our king will think a g-g-goddess has d-d-deigned to visit his ch-ch-chamber."

I sighed, wanting to ask if the eunuch made these elaborate pronouncements every time he sent a virgin to the king, but then decided to hold my tongue. If my tutor wanted to carry on over a favorite pupil, who was I to deny him this joy? He had showered me with unmerited kindness, so the least I could do was let him take pleasure in his task.

"All right, g-g-girls." Hegai stepped back. "Begin your w-w-work."

One of the maids playfully pushed me down on a stool, then all seven of my girls commenced with their preparations: one brushed my hair, two massaged fragrant oil into my skin, another smoothed my feet with a pumice stone. Yet another girl sat across from me and applied kohl to my eyes and color to my lips. Behind me, two other maids put a pot of water on the fire to steam the wrinkles from my gown.

When they had finished with their tasks, I stood and walked to the bronze mirror against the wall. I wore golden sandals and a one-shouldered garment of white silk. Diamonds the size of walnuts dangled from my earlobes.

"B-b-beautiful," breathed Hegai.

"Really?" I tilted my head, studying my reflection. "I am not—"

Hegai answered so confidently that he didn't stutter: "You are perfection."

Perhaps he was right. Over the years, I had grown into my too-large eyes, my face had filled in to frame my nose, and my body had lengthened to better suit my feet. Oil had softened my hair, perfume had sweetened my skin, and the eunuchs' lessons had calmed my impetuous spirit.

We waited. Hegai ordered a tray of food that I gave to my maids, for I was too nervous to eat. I dared not step outside lest the wind muss my hair, and I dared not lie down lest I wrinkle my gown. So I sat on a stool while my maids laughed and ate with Hegai, who kept venturing into the hall to see if a message had come from the king.

A short while after sunset, as the palace settled down to rest, a group of eunuchs approached the robing room, and Hegai entrusted me to their care.

And so I was delivered to King Xerxes's bedchamber at Susa in Tevet, the tenth month, during the seventh year of his reign.

A squad of seven silent eunuchs escorted me out of the harem, through straight corridors and twisting paths, up stairs and over marble patios. Finally we approached what I assumed to be the king's private residence. A company of Immortals stood outside, with armed men guarding three separate doorways. Though they had sworn to be vigilant and alert for danger, the guards stared at me with weary, bored expressions, reducing me to complete insignificance. How could I have ever hoped to be anything more than an anonymous girl who existed to pleasure the king?

I lowered my gaze as a blush seared my cheeks. With the extravagant imagination of girlhood I had dared to dream of being queen, and under Hegai's tutelage something in me had begun to hope the king would at least remember my name. But because so many beautiful girls competed for the same prize, I knew I'd been a fool to dream of anything.

I daresay every girl in the harem secretly wished to become one of his favorites, guaranteeing that he would send for her a time or two. If we were ever to experience love, affection, or motherhood, it would have to come from our relationship with the king.

One of the eunuchs murmured something to the burliest guard. After raking me with his eyes, the man stood aside and allowed the two of us to enter. My heart trembled within me as we passed through the doorway, but instead of entering a room, I found myself following the eunuch through a hallway so narrow that two men could not walk abreast in the space. Wondering if the design had something to do with security, I followed the eunuch so closely that I didn't see the serving girl until the eunuch turned and flattened himself against the wall, allowing the slave to slip by. She must not have expected to see anyone else, because she ran straight into me, spilling her tray with a most alarming noise.

The slave girl stood in transfixed horror, her hands pressed to her cheeks as she surveyed the remains of fruit, meat sauce, and poached pears on my spotless gown and the marble floor. She whispered something in a foreign tongue, probably an oath, but I shook my head, knelt, and began to pick up the gold dinnerware.

"Don't worry," I murmured, reaching for a still-spinning bowl. "I'm sure this sort of thing happens every now and then."

The girl dropped in front of me, tears forming in her eyes as she ran her palm over the polished tiles, desperately attempting to wipe gravy from the floor.

The eunuch bent toward me, his face tight with stress, his eyes blazing. "Get *up*, girl! Turn away this instant and run back to the harem. Hegai must send someone else. The king won't be happy about the delay, but I will not present him with a mess like—"

The eunuch fell silent as a shadow loomed over our small huddle. I looked up, my blood curdling with dread, and saw Harbonah's narrow face.

"The king will receive you now," he said, looking directly at me. Though his lips did not curve, I thought his eyes flickered with the faint beginnings of a smile.

CHAPTER TWENTY-FOUR

HARBONAH

SOMETHING IN ME PITIED MORDECAI'S little Hadassah the
night she entered the king's chamber, but something else in me
wanted to laugh aloud. My weary master had been standing near
the interior passageway as Biztha and the girl approached. When
the eunuch moved aside for the departing slave girl, the king and
I saw everything—the clumsy slave, the nervous virgin, and the
resultant mess.

But what Biztha and Hadassah did not see was my master's
expression. Instead of hardening in anger at their clumsiness, his
haggard face softened at the sight of that beautiful young woman
on her knees. "Look yonder, eunuch," he said, his voice barely
reaching my ear. "Have you ever seen one of our noble families'
daughters bend to help a slave?"

I replied with a quiet grunt, knowing he needed no other response.

Then, suspecting that Biztha would hurry to send the sullied virgin out of the room, the king looked at me. "That girl is not to leave, do you understand? Set out a robe for her at once."

Struggling to keep an exultant smile from my face, I first ran to my flustered friend. I told Biztha that the king was ready to receive the virgin, then waved the frightened kitchen slave away.

Biztha, red-faced and trembling, crept out of the hallway and into the king's bedchamber. "Your majesty, the lowliest of all your servants does sincerely apologize—"

The king, who had wandered to a wide window overlooking the river, did not even turn. "Who has Hegai sent tonight?"

"A most lovely young woman, my king. He calls her Esther."

"Where did he find this beauty?"

"Susa, my king. She is from Susa."

At that point, the king turned. Biztha stepped aside, revealing the pale young woman with waist-length brown hair, wide eyes, a lovely face, and a gravy-spattered gown.

My master took the virgin's measure with one glance, his eyes widened with appreciation, and his jaw flexed as he tried to restrain himself.

But my master had never been able to restrain his emotions for long. After a momentary valiant effort, he burst out laughing.

And then, to Biztha's obvious horror, the girl laughed, too.

Chapter Twenty-Five
HADASSAH

I DON'T KNOW WHY I LAUGHED. Maybe as a release of pent-up nervousness, or perhaps because the king's laughter proved infectious.

Maybe I laughed because tears might have ruined his mood.

All I know is that when he laughed, I joined in, and I laughed even harder when I saw Biztha's stunned expression. He must have thought the king and I had been affected by some sort of sorcery, or that the stress of the encounter had caused me to lose my wits.

In any case, the eunuch backed out of the chamber as swiftly as he could, head bowed, feet shuffling as he closed the doors behind him.

I stopped laughing when I heard the doors come together, shutting out the world and confining me with the king who held my life and my future in his hands.

I lifted my hand to wipe a tear of mirth from my eye, then lowered myself to the floor in proper obeisance. Crouching there, my nose pressed to the polished marble, I wondered if I should have kept silent. He was a king, after all, and I but one of his most lowly subjects.

"Rise and come closer," the king said, gesturing for me to step away from the entrance. "Let me see what damage has been done."

A wave of relief lifted me and carried me into his presence. He wasn't evaluating my beauty or my grace; apparently he simply wanted to see my gown.

I moved a few steps closer, then halted and peered at the stain on my bodice. "It isn't too—oh!" I fell silent, forgetting that I wasn't supposed to speak unless asked a direct question. I bit my lip and peered at him, but he didn't seem to be angry. "May I—may I speak, my king?"

He granted me a forgiving smile. "Please do."

"The stain isn't too terrible—a soak in cool water should make things right. Miriam taught me how to wash away worse messes than this."

"And who is Miriam?"

"My—the woman who took care of me as a child."

The king tilted his head, then walked to his couch and sank onto it. "Why didn't your parents take care of you?"

"I was an orphan. My father died before I was born, and my mother did not survive childbirth."

"So you were raised by strangers?"

"No, sir—by cousins. They were very kind to me."

"But they used you as a servant? Made you do the cleaning?"

"We all worked, sir, at daily chores. Whatever had to be done, someone had to do it."

"Your family had no slaves?"

"We never saw the need, my king. We worked together."

The king stretched out in a languid pose, resting his elbow on the arm of the couch. "I must thank you, little one. Virgins are brought here to entertain me, but you entertained me more than most before Hegai left my chamber."

Uncertain of his meaning, I gave him a wavering smile. Had I already fulfilled my purpose?

Apparently not. He lifted his chin and folded his hands. "I'm sure Hegai told me your name, but I've already forgotten it."

"Esther, my king."

"The name suits you. Do you sing, Esther?"

"Not very well, sir."

"Do you dance?"

"A little."

"A little, she says. Then we shall not bother with dancing. What have you planned for my entertainment, little Esther?"

"I thought—"

I hesitated when a servant entered from another passageway. I did not notice his face because he carried a gorgeous robe of deep purple silk, a luxurious garment that looked as though it would wrap around me twice.

"For you. Esther." The king gestured to the eunuch, whom I recognized as Harbonah when I finally looked up. "Take off that sullied gown and give it to my servant. Put on the robe. I will wait for you on the balcony."

I lifted a brow as the king stood and left the room, granting me a measure of privacy. Harbonah turned away, one hand extended as he waited for the soiled gown.

I undid the belt and the shoulder strap, then stepped out of the silky puddle at my feet. I took the purple robe from Harbonah's arm, wrapped myself in it, and tied it with the belt. Then I picked up the stained gown and handed it to Harbonah.

"Thank you," I whispered.

He glanced back and caught my gaze. "Congratulations." He spoke in a faint whisper. "You are the first to make the king laugh right away."

I wasn't sure my misstep qualified for congratulations, but as the eunuch walked off, I drew a deep breath and wondered what the rest of the night would bring. I had either made a good start or ruined my life altogether.

I walked toward the patio, my heart braced to pass the next few hours as stoically as possible. I had already ruined my appearance, broken royal protocol, and proved that I would never be as dignified as Vashti. Surely I had done all the damage a girl could do in the space of half an hour, so why should I worry about the rest of the evening?

"My king," I called, my fears falling away, "you asked how I planned to entertain you? I thought we might talk before you took me to bed."

Chapter Twenty-Six

HARBONAH

As usual, I entered the royal bedchamber about an hour before dawn to lead the king's concubine away. I had pulled many women out of the massive bed—some who would become the king's favorites, and some who proved to be so completely forgettable that they remained in the palace of the concubines for the rest of their lives. Some woke easily and followed me without question, while others ignored my tapping on their shoulders. Those I had to grip firmly and pull, even though their resistance sometimes woke my royal master. But the king and I had an understanding. He wanted the women gone when he woke, so if a concubine proved reluctant to leave his bed, he would roll over and pretend to sleep through the unruly exit.

When the woman returned to the harem, she was free to share whatever she wanted to share with her fellow concubines. As a youngster, I spent a fair portion of my day working in the harem, so I knew what passed for entertainment in that place. Some of the women spoke of their hours with the king in glowing terms, crediting him with the strength of a lion and the ardor of a stag in rut. Others responded to queries with a coy smile, as if their experience were too sacred to frame in words. No one spoke ill of the king, for in the harem any disloyal comment or insinuation might be repeated until it reached unforgiving ears.

I smiled as I passed the spot where the kitchen slave had spilled my master's dinner tray. What would Mordecai's innocent Hadassah say about her night with the king? She was one of the gentlest and most pliant women in the house of the virgins, and I shuddered to think that the king might have handled her roughly. A young woman like Hadassah should be treated with delicacy. . . .

I approached with the stealth of a cat, so that my sandaled feet made no sound on the tiled floor. Moonlight streamed through the open balcony, spangling the marble floor with silver. Through the gauzy bed curtain I saw the king sprawled over the mattress, one leg extended toward the foot of the bed, the other bent to support the small woman who lay curled beneath his arm. A gnat of worry pestered me—had he been too rough with her? This king could be erratic in his moods, and for all I knew he might treat an intelligent woman like he treated intelligent men—as though they were enemies to be conquered. Hadassah deserved a better fate.

I tiptoed to the side of the bed, pulled back the curtain, and peered at the girl's sleeping face. Then I drew a breath and poked her upper arm.

Her eyelids flew open. She blinked at the sight of me standing before her, then nodded when I held my finger to my lips. The king's silk robe lay on the floor like a dark stain, so I grabbed it, held it up, and averted my eyes as she slipped into it.

When she had wrapped the robe around herself, I shifted to peer at the king's face. My master lay with his mouth agape, his beard dark against his pillow, his skin as pale as stone in the moonlight. Not a muscle flickered. He was sleeping deeply, a good sign.

I motioned for Hadassah to follow, then led her out of the king's bedchamber and into his dressing room. "Here," I whispered, offering her a plain tunic. "Do not wear the king's garment outside this room. That could lead to trouble."

She lifted a brow and took the gown I offered. "Is the king possessive of his robes?"

"It's not the king I worry about," I replied, thinking of Vashti and her palace spies. "It's the symbolism. Wearing the king's robe in public is improper for a concubine, no matter how lovely she is." I tapped my lips, abruptly returning to the present. "So—did you enjoy your night with my master?"

She looked at me, her eyes wide and dark, and then a slow smile blossomed across her face. "Shouldn't you be asking if he enjoyed his night with me? That's why I'm here, isn't it? For his pleasure?"

I shrugged off her question. "Well?"

"I don't know what he thought of me or my company." She tightened the belt at her waist. "And I don't know if he'll ever call for me again."

Her indirect answers began to annoy me. "Any girl could say the same thing. But you, Hadassah, are not just any girl. What did you think of my master?"

In response, the young woman I had thought completely open and honest laid her finger across her smiling lips and walked toward the door, leaving me to follow like a shadow.

❧

My master did not send for a virgin the night after Hadassah's turn in the royal bedchamber, yet none of us were surprised. The man might be a king, but he was also forty and had just returned from an arduous journey. Not every man wanted a woman every night.

But at the conclusion of the next day, when Hegai entered to ask what sort of woman the king might desire, my king sat upright, smiled broadly, and asked for Esther.

Hegai blinked in pleased surprise. "The maid who visited you two nights ago?"

"Has your memory slipped so soon?" The king smiled. "Yes, bring me Esther. And you, eunuch—" he swiveled to face me—"do not spirit her away in the middle of the night. For once, I would like to wake with the woman who has shared my sleeping hours."

Hegai and I bowed, then gave each other knowing looks and hastened to do the king's will. Hegai hurried to prepare Esther for another royal appointment while I hurried to arrange a gathering of the vice-regents. The king had not yet announced his intentions, but I knew him like no one else. I suspected that soon he would want to address his counselors about a matter of some importance.

I was right.

The next morning, a few hours after Hadassah had returned to the harem to change her clothing and reapply her makeup, she appeared at the back of the royal audience hall. Flanked by the two eunuchs I sent to escort her, she walked through the assembled vice-regents and members of the nobility. She appeared young and small, like a child creeping past giants, and seemed to tremble as she walked past the hulking guards. Yet every man present gazed at her in awe, impressed by her gentleness and fragile beauty.

The counselors and nobles murmured to each other, wondering who she was, because the king had made no mention of her to anyone but Hegai and me. Yet onward came this slip of a girl, no older than sixteen, walking past burly men who could snap her neck with one twist.

Approaching the king without permission meant death, which

ANGELA
HUNT

usually occurred without hesitation or explanation. If the king did not immediately extend his scepter to pardon the interloper, the Immortals around the throne would draw their swords to execute swift and final judgment . . . unless the guards at the door managed to spear the offender first.

But my master smiled as the girl he knew as Esther came down the long aisle that bisected the audience hall. And as she glided toward the dais where he sat upon his throne, he not only held out his scepter, but stood and walked down the ivory-clad steps to greet her.

Mordecai's brave ward seemed to collapse when she reached the throne. She bent to prostrate herself, then stretched her arms toward the man who held her life in his hands.

"Behold, counselors and noble friends," the king said, lifting her from where she knelt. "By the favor of Ahura Mazda, on this day I have chosen this woman to be my queen."

Mushka, the king's nephew, stood close enough that I heard his reaction: "If only I had seen her first. What I wouldn't give to bed a woman like that."

Thankfully, the king did not hear his nephew's brash comment. The room broke into furious buzzing as eunuchs, officers, and counselors craned their necks and marveled at the pale beauty and grace of the young woman gripping the king's hand. This one had not entered the great hall like Vashti, with an uplifted chin and mincing step. This girl would never stiffen her spine in defiance of the king.

I folded my hands and smiled, quietly delighted by the rampant speculation humming around me.

"Who is she? Where did she come from?"

"Is she Persian?"

"She must be Egyptian. Look at her eyes."

"She is small of stature; she has to be from Babylon."

"Raven hair—a Macedonian beauty. But whose daughter is she?"

The king offered no answers, and Esther uttered not a word, but shyly dipped her chin and looked around the great hall as though amazed to find herself amid such majesty and splendor.

The speculation about Mordecai's ward only increased when my master held a banquet for his officials, governors, and even the palace servants. He decreed a holiday for the provinces, liberally gifting his subjects with a day free from forced labor. In Susa, he freely distributed gifts from his treasury, all to honor the quiet girl who sat on a couch beside him during the generous feast.

I couldn't help comparing this occasion with a previous feast—this one was lavish, but the food and decor were appropriate for the occasion and not designed for ostentation. The wine flowed a little less freely at Esther's banquet, the decorations were more in keeping with good taste, and the king was in a far better mood.

Perhaps this banquet would erase the memory of that other disaster . . . and Esther would overshadow Vashti. For my master's sake, I fervently hoped she would.

In the midst of the festivities I looked for Mordecai, who should have been celebrating by his ward's side. When I found him sitting with a group of accountants and scribes from the King's Gate, I realized he had chosen to remain anonymous. Because Mordecai, being Jewish, lived among other Jews and did not mingle among the Persian nobility, I doubted anyone else knew of his relationship with our young queen.

But even from where I stood, I could see the glow of concern in his dark eyes. Upon reflection, I realized he had probably not spoken to his ward since Hadassah had moved to the palace of the concubines. Had the king's announcement caught him by surprise?

I finally caught my friend in the garden, where guests wandered freely after partaking of the delicious meal. "Be well, Mordecai!"

I called, hoping to find him in high spirits. "Congratulations are most certainly in order."

The sharp look he gave me put an immediate damper on my mood. He pulled on my sleeve, drawing me apart from the crowd, then looked at me with blazing eyes. "Congratulations are certainly *not* in order. A woman who should have been married to a kinsman has been ripped from her family, imprisoned in a palace, and had her virginity stolen by a man more than twenty years her senior," he said, his voice breaking. I blinked, stunned to see the glimmer of tears in his eyes. "Can you give me a single reason why I should celebrate this turn of events? Or why I should be happy for the girl I have loved as a daughter?"

"I, well—" I looked away, unable to bear the man's probing gaze. "It may be a small comfort, but she does seem happy. I can promise she will be well cared for. I wasn't surprised when the king chose her. Everyone who meets our queen adores her."

"I have been worried sick about her." Mordecai continued as if he hadn't heard me. "She hasn't come to the garden wall in several days. It's not like her to keep things from me."

"She is no longer a girl." I tempered my voice with discretion. "In appearance and manner she has become a desirable woman, and she has been with the king. She may not want to share every detail of that experience with you—or anyone else."

Mordecai blinked as if he had just learned that his ward had been sold into slavery. He closed his eyes and groaned. I don't think he'd ever envisioned his Hadassah as a mature woman, and he hadn't seen her in over a year. He didn't know how lovely, how *desirable* she had become.

"I grieve for the righteous woman she could have been." Mordecai ran his hand over his face, then looked at me with regret in his eyes. "I can obey Xerxes as my king, but he is not the sort of man I would ever want my daughter to wed. He is not worthy of her."

I glanced around, worried that my friend might be overheard. "You can't believe every rumor you hear." I lowered my voice. "And you should be more discreet. Even the garden hedges conceal spying eyes and listening ears. Hundreds of people live within these walls, and hundreds of plots along with them."

"So why should I rejoice that Hadassah lives here, too? With an unpredictable king and a murderous former queen?"

I closed my eyes, realizing that Mordecai had undoubtedly heard the story about Vashti's bloody request at the king's birthday banquet. Everyone who worked on the royal mount probably knew the tale, for servants liked to talk . . . and so did noblemen and their ladies. My new queen had probably heard the story, though I wasn't sure if she would believe it.

"Hadassah is different." I softened my voice to a more gentle tone. "And I am watching out for her. I can promise you she will be safe. I will do everything within my power to make certain of it."

"And therein lies the problem." Mordecai met my gaze as he laid bare the reality before us. "Because your power, great as it is, is not enough to ensure that the king will never tire of her. So thank you, Harbonah, but do not congratulate me on one of the darkest days of my life."

A dozen emotions swirled in my heart as I watched him trudge away, but chief among them was gratitude . . . that Esther the queen had not glimpsed her kinsman's haggard face.

Chapter Twenty-Seven
Hadassah

Queen Esther.

I repeated the stranger's name, slowly, trying it on for size. The name didn't seem to fit; like a baggy cloak, it hung over me and weighed heavily upon my shoulders.

Yet that's who I had become. Over the past year, Hadassah, the girl who dreamed of princes and palaces, had become Esther, a virgin in the king's house. And now, the queen.

Truth to tell, though Parysatis and I daydreamed about our handsome king and life at the palace, I never expected to even walk these halls, much less wear a crown. Some part of me felt that the throne still belonged to Vashti, and living in the harem had done nothing to eradicate that feeling. Even in the palace of the virgins, we could sense the former queen's presence, and though she rarely left her quarters, we saw the evidence of her power by the way servants scurried at the rumor of her approach and the awe with which the eunuchs pronounced her name.

And . . . there were stories. We had all heard them, for the eunuchs in the house of the virgins loved to gossip. Hegai himself told us of Vashti's horrific revenge upon the girl who won the king's affection in Salamis. Hegai stuttered worse than usual during the retelling, and his face grew pale beneath its tan. Clearly he considered Vashti dangerous, and he ended his story by thanking Ahura Mazda that he worked in the house of the virgins and not the house of the concubines.

I did not believe the story. I could not accept that the beautiful woman I'd met could be capable of such bloody cruelty. Surely the story had become embellished during the passing months, and who could blame Vashti for being upset with the man who had spurned her? Not only had the king removed her from the throne, but he had married her eldest son to a girl he wanted in his own bed.

No, I did not believe the eunuch's tale. Vashti might have been angry, but she had reason to be. And the king had behaved badly because the war ended badly. And who was I—or anyone else—to judge him?

Vashti was still the mother of the king's three eldest sons. Unless I had a baby boy, Vashti's son Darius would one day be king, and she would be the Queen Mother, one of the most powerful women in the empire.

Until then, I would wear the crown.

When the king declared he would make me queen, I felt an icy finger touch the base of my spine. For over a year, I had been an anonymous virgin, unknown by everyone but Hegai and the other girls. But now the king knew my name, and he seemed determined that everyone else should know it, too.

Fear blew down the back of my neck. As queen, I would be horribly alone, elevated and exposed.

During my brief time in the palace of the concubines I heard others talk about their night with the king. Some of the stories made

me blush, but later I remembered those conversations and wondered
if those women had lied. If not, their nights with the king had been
nothing like mine. The king had not behaved like a mythical god;
he had treated me with kindness and gentleness. Moreover, he had
looked into my eyes with genuine *interest*, as if he cared about the
girl who lived inside the smoothed and perfumed body.

The morning after, when Harbonah quietly asked how I had
fared, I finally gave him a truthful answer: "We ate grapes, we
drank wine, we talked for a long time. Then he took me to his bed
and told me he would be as gentle as possible. I thanked him, and
afterward we fell asleep. The next thing I knew, you were jabbing
my arm."

I gave Harbonah the facts about what we did, but I could not
tell him about how I'd been changed. How at first I felt foolish and
tongue-tied, a simple girl sitting on the same couch as the king of
kings, but the man's dark eyes were kind and snapped with laughter
when I told him stories I'd heard from girls at the bazaar. He asked
about my life outside the harem; I told him about growing up as an
orphan and living with my cousins. I told him—after some hesitation—about being engaged to a family friend, and how we'd been
stopped on the road by slave traders, who were taking captives by
force. The king's expression darkened at this, and I hoped he would
put a stop to the practice. Though I had not been eager to marry
Binyamin, I never wanted to see him hurt.

Then the king began to ask more personal questions. Again I
felt awkward and shy, because how could I give a witty answer to
such simple and direct queries? He asked what sort of flowers and
foods I liked; I told him. He asked if I had brothers or sisters; I told
him no. He asked if I had dreams . . . and my tongue failed me.

Guilt ran through my veins as Mordecai's teachings echoed in my
ears. I knew this was the moment when a good Jewish girl would say
she dreamed of returning to Jerusalem and of one day welcoming

the Messiah, but in truth I *didn't* dream of those things. I dreamed of seeing the world outside Susa. I dreamed of standing on one of the Zagros Mountains, of riding across the plain and dipping my toes into the great sea. I wanted to sail on a boat. I wanted to care for my own horse and know that it loved me. I wanted to do all the things I had read about others doing, and I wanted to do all those things before life forced me to grow old.

Before I knew it, my pliant tongue spilled my secrets into the room. Like irretrievable feathers flying from a ripped pillowcase, they fluttered throughout the chamber and made the king smile . . . when I had hoped to please him in a far different way.

When I had emptied my head of my ridiculous notions, I pressed my hands to my lips and froze, horrified by my impudence. Surely this would be the moment the king sent me away or had me whipped for impertinence. I should have said that I dreamed of meeting the king, and of the honor of being his concubine. . . .

But my king listened . . . and laughed. And the sound of his laughter was so unexpectedly warm that I stared at him, my eyes widening at the sight of mirth on his face.

"You . . . are . . . so—" He forced the words out between spasms of laughter.

Foolish? Audacious? Silly? I braced myself for the consequences of my outspokenness.

"Lovable," he finished, his smile softening. His gaze traveled over my face and searched my eyes, and then his hand found and held mine. "My little adventurer, could you be happy in a king's bed?"

My mind shifted to everything the eunuchs had told us about royal protocol and the act of love. We were not to refute the king, not to argue, and only to speak if he asked us to respond—

But my mind couldn't come up with any answer other than words both true and naive. "I don't know, my king. But I am usually happy by nature."

He laughed again and drew me into his arms. I went stiffly at first, then remembered Hegai's advice to relax. The king's kisses were the first my lips had ever received, his eyes the first ever to bore so closely into mine. I responded cautiously, then the part of me that yearned for adventure flared to life, and I met the king's ardor with an inquisitive passion of my own.

Later, when we lay together and the king had buried his face in my shoulder, his beard tickling the skin at my neck, I remained quite still and tried to sort through the tumultuous emotions raging in my heart. Was this love? It certainly must be part of love, for such things were reserved for men and the women who belonged to them. I wanted to love my king, but I couldn't seem to merge the king who ruled an empire with the dark-eyed man who looked at me with such desire that my heart leapt. . . .

I shared none of those thoughts with Harbonah. I simply followed him to another area within the harem, where I was introduced to Shaashgaz, the eunuch in charge of the concubines. Then, scarcely before my maids and I had grown accustomed to our new quarters, the king sent for me again . . . and announced that I would be his queen.

∼❦∼

Immediately following our wedding banquet, the king had two of his officers escort me to the queen's palace, a lavish suite that had belonged to Vashti. I entered the spacious chambers cautiously, as if the disgraced queen might be hiding behind a marble pillar, but Harbonah and another eunuch were the only people waiting in the luxurious space. Both men prostrated themselves as I approached.

"Greetings, my queen."

I couldn't stand to see my friend on the floor. "Please, Harbonah. Get up."

He stood, but then he wagged his finger at me. "Do not ever do that again, not with anyone. When servants and subjects make obeisance to you, accept it graciously."

"But I'm just—"

"You are queen, due to the king's insight and generosity. If you belittle that position by telling servants to get up from the floor, you are lowering your royal station and making the king's gift appear common. And I know you wouldn't want to do that."

Hearing the warning in his voice, I nodded, though I knew I would always find it difficult to watch people grovel at my feet. I sprang from more humble roots than many of the nobles who had bowed before me at the wedding feast, but Harbonah was correct—for some inexplicable reason, the king had elevated me, and I had to accept his will. No matter how uncomfortable I felt.

I forced a smile. "As always, I will try to follow your advice."

"Then you will do well." Harbonah smiled, then gestured to the unusually heavy eunuch at his side. "This, my queen, is Hatakh, who will be your chief attendant. He reports to no one but you—and the king, of course."

Knowing that Hatakh and I would need to become friends, I turned my brightest smile on the eunuch. "So you have been chosen to tend to a woefully inexperienced girl. I hope you will be happy in my service."

He pressed his hand to his chest and gazed at me as if dazzled. "My queen, it is my honor to serve you. I would move heaven and earth to fulfill your slightest wish."

"I doubt I will wish for anything so extravagant." I clasped my hands together and glanced around. "So this is the queen's palace?"

"Your home now," Harbonah answered. "But you'll be pleased to know that all the royal palaces have similar quarters for the queen—the queen's palace in Ecbatana is particularly beautiful."

My heart fluttered with yet another sudden realization. "I will be traveling to Ecbatana?"

"Of course. The queen goes wherever the king goes, and the king travels frequently to maintain order in his empire."

I would be able to travel! Somehow I restrained myself from flying to the open balcony that faced the mountains. One day, perhaps soon, I would journey over those rocky cliffs and experience whatever lay on the other side. I would visit cities and kingdoms I could barely pronounce, and in each of them I would be free to explore, with no one to restrain my wanderings. . . .

I closed my eyes as my heart sang with delight. Had the king known I would react with such enthusiasm? Was this why he singled me out from so many other beautiful girls?

"My queen?"

For a moment, I didn't realize Hatakh was speaking. "Yes?"

"Would you like me to show you around? The rooms have been empty for four years, but two days ago the king asked us to refurbish them. I decorated your chambers myself, and I hope you will find the furnishings to your taste."

I bit my lip, curbing the smile that threatened to break out on my face. As soon as two days ago? Had the king chosen me after our first night together?

I followed Hatakh as he led me through a procession of rooms, each more beautiful than the last. We had entered through the great hall, where the queen received visitors, and passed through another lavish space with inlaid mosaic floors and towering marble columns. The walls, covered with glazed brick arranged in patterns to represent mounted horsemen, seemed to joust and jump in the fading light of sunset.

From the lavish public rooms, Hatakh led me through several smaller chambers for the use of my handmaids. The girls had already arrived, and they abruptly stopped giggling when I crossed the threshold.

Remembering Harbonah's advice, I smiled and told them I would depend on them to help me be a good queen. "I know I could not have pleased the king without you," I said, thinking of the hours they had slathered me with lotions and perfumes and hot wax, "so I will continue to depend on your help. If you need anything, please don't hesitate to come to me. The king has chosen to make me your queen, but I would like to remain your friend."

The girls bowed as Hatakh led me away. We then entered the queen's bedchamber.

I don't know what the room looked like when Vashti lived in it, but I had never seen a more beautiful space. The walls, of a white marble veined with golden flecks, shimmered in the canted rays of the afternoon sun, and columns of pink stone rose from the floor to support a ceiling that had been painted in the gentle colors of a rose garden. Sheer curtains divided the room into sections—one for a dressing area, another for bathing, and another for the application of cosmetics. Curtains also surrounded the bed, but they had been pulled back to reveal the most luxurious linens I had ever seen.

"This is too much!" The words sprang from my tongue before I could think to restrain myself. "Truly, Hatakh, these fabrics ought to be used for something finer than bed coverings."

The eunuch shook his head. "The king delights to share the wealth of his empire with those he loves, and he would not have his queen sleeping on sackcloth. This is yours, and if you desire anything else, you have but to ask. Whatever you need, whatever you want, I am here to serve you."

I sank onto a small upholstered stool and felt the rich texture of tapestry beneath my hand. In all my girlish imagination, I had never imagined such riches in one chamber. Though I hadn't thought of my friends from our Jewish community in months, I had a sudden impulse to find them and invite them to my bedchamber—they would have to see it to believe it.

"And now, my queen," Hatakh said, stepping back and gesturing to a gilded doorway, "an audience awaits you in the garden."

My heart leapt into my throat. I hadn't prepared to see anyone. If these were counselors or even household staff, I knew less than they did about being a queen. Panic-stricken, I turned to Harbonah. "Who's out there?"

His reserved expression relaxed. "The king's children, my queen. Thirty-three of them."

Children?

Summoning a smile, I rose and moved to the doorway Hatakh had indicated. A short walk through an elaborately decorated passageway led into a rectangular garden of clipped shrubs and fruit trees arranged around a long reflecting pool. Beyond a particularly thick shrub, I heard hushed whisperings.

I hurried forward, and the moment I turned the corner, a noisy chorus of "Welcome, Queen Esther" greeted me. As one, the children prostrated themselves on the flagstones, a half circle of squirming bodies and disobedient heads that kept rising in order to peek at me.

My heart overflowed with happiness. I had always wanted a sibling, and later I had dreamed of a house filled with children. How wonderful that marriage to the king had brought me a garden brimming with youngsters.

I sighed, then swiped a tear of joy from my lower lashes. "Rise, please," I begged them, reaching out to the closest child. "I am so happy to meet all of you. Would you please come and tell me your names?"

They rushed forward, surrounding me, but another eunuch, clearly their tutor, restored order by clapping. He ordered them to approach me by rank and birth order, beginning with the crown prince and his brothers.

The children shuffled into a single line, headed by a handsome boy. I recognized the eyes immediately—they were replicas of the dark orbs that had shone only inches from mine the previous night. "I am Darius." The boy stepped forward. "I am the son of the king and his true queen, Vashti."

I caught my breath as a flesh-and-blood character from Hegai's story looked up into my eyes. If the eunuch spoke the truth, this was the prince my king had married to his own lover, Artaynta. I glanced at Harbonah. How was I supposed to handle this child? Did I ask about his wife? Did I even acknowledge her existence, since she had fallen out of favor? Did she still live in the harem, or did she still . . . live?

"Thank you, Prince Darius," the tutor called, providing me with a means of escape. "I will speak to you later about how to show proper respect for your father's queen."

My heart was still pounding when a second boy moved forward and bowed stiffly. "I am Hystaspes, second son born to the king and his queen Vashti."

I nodded and forced a smile. Either Vashti had put her sons up to these awkward introductions, or they were formed of the same mettle as their mother.

A third boy, a more compact copy of the first two, walked up. "I'm Artaxerxes." He peered up at me through bangs that nearly covered his eyes. "I'm this many." He held up five fingers and gave me a smile that nearly swept me off my feet. This darling child, at least, had a gentle heart.

"Wonderful to meet you, Artaxerxes." I bent and braced my hands on my knees. "I hope we shall be very good friends."

The boy grinned at me, then shuffled off to rejoin his brothers. I watched him go, realizing he had been a mere babe in arms at the time of the king's first banquet. Unlike his brothers, he hadn't been old enough to feel the sting of humiliation when the king moved Vashti and her children out of the queen's palace.

I cut my calculations short and returned to my task. Thirty other children still waited to greet me, the sons and daughters of concubines. All of them charmed me, even those who were too young to walk, but I came away determined to fulfill three important resolutions: first, as the king's wife, I would do everything in my power to influence Vashti's sons. They would benefit from their father's strength, but they did not need their mother's thirst for blood. Such a combination in a king could result in the destruction of the empire.

Second, I would never forget that I was one of many women who shared the king's bed.

And third, though the king had honored me and placed a crown upon my head, I could never take my position for granted. He had already deposed one queen; he could easily set aside another.

If I did not honor and obey him, I might find myself anonymous and forgotten in the harem.

During the early months of my marriage, I was as happy as any woman has a right to be. Though I no longer enjoyed the companionship of my friends in the house of the virgins, I drew closer to the seven handmaids who had been with me since my arrival at the palace. I gave them pet names to remind me of my Jewish upbringing, and each time I called for one of them, memories of Mordecai and Miriam flooded back to my heart.

The bossiest of the maids reminded me of Sunday, our workday after the Sabbath, so I named her Hulta. Rokita was as light and fair as the sky overhead, so I named her after the Hebrew word for *firmament*, created on the second day. Genunita specialized in cosmetics and lotions made from plants, so I named her after the Hebrew word for *garden*, created on the third day. Nehorita I named after the Hebrew word for *luminous*, for HaShem made the moon and the sun on the fourth day. On the fifth day of creation our world saw the first animals, so I named my fifth maid Ruhshita, for *movement*. Hurfita was as soft and sweet as a *ewelamb*, created on the sixth day. Finally, I named Regoita after the word for *rest*—our duty on the seventh day.

My days were mine to fill as I pleased, and in the early months of our marriage the king often invited me to join him in his throne room. I did so eagerly at first, happy to sit by his side and learn more about the man I called husband. The king spent most of his time hearing the petitions of visiting nobles, governors of the provinces, and emissaries to the various satraps. Occasionally he entertained nobles and members of various trade expeditions. Most of these hours were pleasant, both for me and my king.

But occasionally I saw and heard things that chilled my blood.

One morning a casual air filled the audience hall. Several of the nobles and vice-regents were mingling in the center of the great hall as the king spoke to one of his generals. They had lowered their voices to discuss the defense of a border at one of the outposts, and I had completely lost interest in the conversation.

But a stirring at the entrance to the throne room caught my attention. I looked up and saw a man approaching, a gutted deer slung over his shoulder. A pair of guards stepped forward to detain him, but the man pushed through, smiling and cocksure as he stalked forward.

As he passed the guards, his features came into full view and I gasped. Mushka. The youth who had so charmed me and Parysatis in our younger years had matured into a powerful man. He strode forward, blood and gore dripping from the animal on his shoulder, but nothing in his appearance appealed to me. He moved with a certain arrogance, and his attitude spoke of disrespect for his royal uncle.

Nevertheless, Mushka strode into the throne room as though certain of his king's tolerance and forgiveness. Every eye in the hall widened at his approach, then heads shifted toward the throne, where the king was still conversing with his general. The two Immortals who stood before the throne stepped forward and drew their swords, but hesitated.

"Uncle!" Grinning, Mushka slung the bloody doe onto the floor. "Look what the hunter has won!"

My husband looked up, and in that instant I saw the king replace the doting uncle. What happened away from the throne room had little to do with what was allowed to happen within it, and no one, not even a favorite relative, could jauntily stroll into the royal audience hall and demand the king's attention.

The king turned his face away, and in that gesture I read the man's fate. The two Immortals closest to the throne stepped forward, swords in hand, and cut Mushka down before he could draw breath to protest.

I gasped and covered my eyes, unable to bear the sight of such violence. When I was finally able to look, members of the king's guard were carrying the body away. A lone guard carried Mushka's head by its hair, leaving bright spatters of blood over the mosaic tiles.

According to Persian law, no one, not even a king, could execute a man for a single offense, but any person approaching the king without permission was assumed to have murder on his mind. The guards, therefore, struck without hesitation.

After that, I did not visit the throne room unless the king expressly asked me to appear at court.

CHAPTER TWENTY-EIGHT

HADASSAH

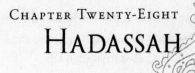

As the night exhaled spring perfume, I snuggled closer to the warmth of my husband's body. The king snored softly and drew me closer, gentle and sweet even in sleep.

I sighed and brushed his arm with my fingertips, then smiled as a realization struck me: I had fallen in love with the man who commanded me to marry him. Before meeting the king, I never understood what love entailed—I understood infatuation, for what young girl couldn't identify with the intense yearning and erratic pulse of young love—but I never fully comprehended the relationship between Miriam and Mordecai. Their love was an almost tangible connection, anyone could feel the bond between them, but I had no idea how to form that kind of attachment to someone else.

When I had protested that I did not love Binyamin as a wife should, both Mordecai and Miriam assured me that my love for him would grow as naturally as a flower reaches for the sun. But because I had known Binyamin since childhood, I imagined that married love would be akin to the love a sister feels for a brother.

I had never imagined this.

I smiled and ran my fingertips over the wiry dark hairs along my husband's arm.

What I felt for my husband the king was far more vital than anything I could feel for a brother. The urge to have his lips on mine was so strong I often had my handmaids dress me hours before I expected his summons. I paced in my chamber, so eager to see him that I practically flew to the door when the eunuchs arrived to escort me to his presence.

The rumors I had heard, the old stories that filled me with dread and anxiety, vanished in the warmth of my husband's smile. How could the man who laughed at my silly stories ever execute an innocent? How could the man who called me his tiny angel be ruthless or cruel? How could the man who slumbered in my arms be impulsive or bloodthirsty?

In truth, I saw my husband as a great king, a kind man, and a vibrant lover. He smiled when I entered the room; he ordered everyone else away and led me to his banqueting table, where we fed each other from fruit trays and drank sweet wine. With great concern he asked how I had spent my day; with equal concern I asked if he had any news he wanted to share with me.

He never did, but I never expected him to ask my opinion, for what did I know of empires?

Then he would ask if I was happy, and with a heart full of love I would answer *yes*.

He would hand me a scroll, a collection of love poetry or a romantic story, and I would sit at his feet and read to him. But before I finished, my husband the king would gather me into his arms and carry me to his bed. There I finally understood the passion in the *Shir-Hashirim*, the sacred scrolls written by Solomon, the son of David:

As the king reclines at table,
My nard gives forth its perfume:
To me the man I love is a sachet of myrrh
Lodged between my breasts;
To me the man I love is a spray of henna flowers
In the vineyards of Ein-Gedi . . .
Sustain me with raisins, refresh me with apples, for I am
   sick with love.
I wish his left arm were under my head,
And his right arm around me.

As the long night faded into morning, the sunrise bringing my husband to wakefulness, I would press my ear to his chest to hear the strong beat of his heart.

A brave heart.

A loyal heart.

A king's heart.

And when he was fully awake, my husband would kiss me again as my eyes filled with tears at the thought of parting from him.

But I had to leave him, for he had an empire to oversee, and I had to return to my handmaids for a day of lotions and dressmaking and hairdressing.

Parysatis, I thought one morning as I walked back to the queen's palace, would be sick with envy if she could see me now. But Mordecai would not approve of my lifestyle, for I had thoroughly and unabashedly given my love to a man who neither knew nor respected the God of my fathers.

My mouth twisted at the thought of my long-neglected cousin. I had not been to the harem garden in weeks, though I was certain Mordecai still walked outside the wall every day. He was not the sort to forget a promise, even though he might have wondered if I had forgotten him.

He walked that path to keep me safe, but when lying in my husband's arms I had no need of a defender. I belonged to my beloved and he to me, and no one could touch me. No one would dare.

Especially since I carried a secret.

For the past two months, my body had not bled in its regular cycle. My handmaids were atwitter with the possibility that I carried a new crown prince, and I had caught them whispering about the possibility that Vashti might finally be stripped of all pretensions to power. I did not dare speculate about the future, but happily sat in the garden and watched the royal children at play, imagining my own child among the mix.

What might my son look like? He would have his father's strong chin, of course, and I hoped he would inherit the king's tall frame. He would be strong, dark-haired and dark-eyed, with shapely arms and olive skin. He would be the perfect little prince.

The king would want him to be fit and powerful, but I would be content if he were endowed with a quiet spirit and a kind heart. The king had exhibited nothing but tenderness toward me, though I knew he could be ruthless when he had to be. I would never forget what happened to Mushka.

I understood that a king could not rule so vast an empire with nothing but gentleness. Iron undergirded my husband's velvet hand, or he would not have deposed Vashti and made me queen. Power lay in his fist, or he could not have avenged his father's defeat in Greece.

I could only hope I would never feel the weighty force of his disapproval.

My husband expected his children to be strong, as well. While watching a group of eunuchs tutor the king's sons, I saw that the princes were expected to be proficient in archery, spear throwing, and horsemanship. When not exercising their bodies, their tutors drilled them about how to prevent evil, behave with good morals, and follow the truth. But what truth did they follow?

As I listened to the tutors discuss truth as though it were a tangible essence to be discovered and grasped, I found myself missing Mordecai. He found Truth in the word of Adonai, and I had never met anyone so wise. More than anything, I yearned for my son—or daughter—to benefit from my cousin's teaching.

I once asked Mordecai how he came to know so much. Instead of answering, he bent to pick up a scroll. His hands caressed the leather straps with reverent tenderness as he met my gaze. "The Tehillim," he said simply, unrolling the scroll. Then, holding the scroll in a golden orb of lamplight, he began to read:

> "How I love your *Torah*!
> I meditate on it all day.
> I am wiser than my foes,
> because your *mitzvot* are mine forever.
> I have more understanding than all my teachers,
> because I meditate on your instruction.
> I understand more than my elders,
> because I keep your precepts.
> I keep my feet from every evil way,
> in order to observe your word.
> I don't turn away from your rulings,
> because you have instructed me.
> How sweet to my tongue is your promise,
> Truly sweeter than honey in my mouth!
> From your precepts I gain understanding;
> This is why I hate every false way."

Mordecai lowered the scroll and looked at me with patient love shining in his eyes. "Do you see, Hadassah?"

I bit my lip, understanding but not particularly liking what I understood. "You are wise because you read the holy scrolls." *All the time.*

He smiled. "If you want wisdom, daughter, know this: Torah is a lamp for your foot and a light on your path."

I nodded, then pretended to hear Miriam calling me to help with the evening meal. And as I walked away, I heard Mordecai sigh.

Later, I had told myself. When I had married and begun to raise a family, I would listen to my husband read Torah and become one of the wise old women everyone respected. Until then, I had dreams to cherish and ideas to explore.

But as I considered a long and luxurious life with my royal husband, I found myself longing for the sight of Mordecai reading a Torah scroll by lamplight.

⁓✻⁓

Why does love move into a barren heart and furnish its home with fear? Love came to me unexpectedly, but with its attendant joys I discovered unimagined sources of dread. Light and happiness surrounded me when I basked in the king's presence, but away from him, shadows colored my thoughts and darkened my imaginings.

Do we fear because we think ourselves unworthy of happiness? Do we dread the inevitable day when death must bring an end to earthly delights? Or does love awaken such pleasures that ordinary life feels empty without them?

When my heart first awakened to love, I had no answers. What I did have was a small but persistent conviction that such joy could not last forever.

One afternoon, while still cocooned in the afterglow from a night spent in my husband's embrace, I sent Hatakh to invite the royal children to visit the queen's garden. I did not expect them to love me as well as they loved their mothers, but I hoped to be a good influence and encourage the king to show them a father's affection.

Weeks before, I had been astounded to learn that childhood in the Persian royal family was nothing like the life I had enjoyed with Mordecai and Miriam. I remember being loved by both my cousins, but when I asked if the king might join us in the garden, Hatakh explained that Persian fathers did not want to even *see* their sons until the children had passed their fifth year.

I blinked in utter amazement. "Why not?"

The eunuch lifted one shoulder in a shrug. "This is done so that if the child dies young, the father will not be afflicted by its loss. But the fathers *do* love their children. The greatest proof of manly excellence is to father many sons."

So though my beloved husband had many children older than five, he rarely spent time with them. When one evening I delicately asked if he would like to invite the crown prince to dine with us, he gazed at me as if I'd demanded that he snuff out the moon. "Why would we want to do that?"

Flustered by the sharp edge in his voice, I flushed and quickly retreated. "I thought you might enjoy his company. But if you would rather have a quiet evening, forgive me."

He glared down the length of his nose, but something in my expression must have smothered his irritation. "You shouldn't worry about the crown prince or his brothers." His eyes softened as he reached for my hand. "You are too sweet to become involved with rough boys. Leave them to their mother."

At this reference to Vashti, I pressed my lips together and resolved not to say another word about the princes.

Though I had lived in the former queen's chambers for some months, I still felt her presence in those rooms. She had slept in the columned bed, walked through the private garden, and run her hands along the tiled walls. Though Hatakh had changed the draperies, linens, and artwork, Vashti's voice seemed to echo in the high-ceilinged rooms. One of the gardeners remarked that she had planted the pear trees at the edge of the balcony. After that, I knew I would never enjoy pears again.

I'm not sure why my stomach knotted at any mention of the former queen—she could not usurp my position, for Persian law decreed that she would never again wear the crown. But at the height of her power everyone in Susa had adored her legendary beauty. Even I had not been immune—I could not forget our chance meeting in the bazaar and how the perfection of her features had snatched my breath away.

What if the king couldn't forget her, either?

I slept and woke in the queen's palace like an impostor who expects to be unmasked and evicted at any moment. My anxiety grew from a niggling apprehension to a near constant dread.

Mordecai had asked me to keep my heritage a secret because he thought the king might not trust Jews. What would my loving husband do, then, if he discovered he'd married a daughter of Jacob? What would he do if he learned the child growing in my womb was descended from Saul, the first king of Israel?

I thought about going to Hatakh with my concerns, but he would probably think me foolish. I considered calling for Harbonah, who seemed to know everything about everyone in the palace, but his willingness to speak openly with me made me wonder if he would speak as openly with the king. If so, what was to keep him from revealing the very things I wanted to keep secret?

As the days passed, I tamped down my fears and tried to be a good wife and a dutiful queen. And though I didn't understand the king's reluctance to spend time with his children, I yearned to help them in a way their tutors and even their mothers could not: I wanted them to learn what I had learned at Mordecai's knee. Though I wasn't sure how to do that without revealing my heritage, I decided to make an attempt.

So I invited them to join me in the queen's garden.

The children soon began to arrive, accompanied by their mothers or eunuchs who served the harem. I greeted everyone with a smile and suggested the children play among the hedges while we waited for the others to arrive. Because I was not ready to reveal my barely visible pregnancy, my handmaids had dressed me in a flowing shift of white linen, leaving my hair to hang free around my shoulders. Not wanting to intimidate the little ones, I was glad I looked, as one of my handmaids said, "almost like a child" myself.

I spotted Hatakh counting the youngsters. When he had finished, he looked at me and grimaced. "Only three of the king's offspring are not here."

I suspected which three were missing, but I had to be sure. "Who has not yet arrived?"

"The sons of Vashti, my lady. The crown prince and his brothers."

I drew a deep breath to quell my irritation, then smiled. "Then we shall play without them. Maybe next time they'll beg their mother to come."

Hatakh, who could not understand why anyone would want children underfoot, watched in bewilderment as I stood on a marble step of the portico and clapped. "Children! Come here, please."

Those who were old enough to walk hurried forward, then prostrated themselves. "Thank you, now get up," I said, embarrassed to see so many little rear ends wavering before me. "Please, this is a time to play. You don't have to lower yourself every time you approach."

A little boy in the front of the group lifted his head and squinted at me. "But you're the queen."

"This is true, yes. But when I'm in the garden with you, I will be your friend. And today I'd like to teach you a new game."

The brave lad in front rose to his knees. "Do we ride horses?"

"No horses."

"Do we need spears?"

"No spears, I'm afraid. We only need ourselves."

More heads popped up, and puzzled looks appeared on the faces of the concubines who held their toddlers. "Even the little ones can play," I said, smiling at the women, "but you bigger children must be careful not to knock them down. Understand?"

The children rose slowly as I walked into the midst of them. Soon one of my children would be among this group, and he or she would have the kind of family I had always wanted. Mordecai used to tell me that the Jewish community was all the family I needed, but *this* is what I longed for, the shiny-faced joy of little ones who did not have to worry about running on the Sabbath or eating a forbidden food at the bazaar. . . .

"This team—" I gestured to the group on my right—"will hold hands and form a line. You will be the army of Saul, a fierce king. And this team—" I gestured to the group on my left—"will hold hands in a line and be the army of the Philistines, a fierce people. And the Philistines will say, 'By right or by might, send David to fight!'"

The children shuffled about in confusion, but the eunuchs helped them form two lines, one facing the other. Then the Philistines halfheartedly shouted the challenge to the first group, who then looked at me in silent expectation.

Would this be any fun for them at all? "Now," I told the army of Saul, "you must choose a David."

The children looked at each other, then one of them stepped forward. He must have been about the age of the crown prince and was equally as tall.

"Good choice." I smiled in approval. "Now, David, you must run toward the line of Philistines as fast as you can. They will hold hands as you run, but if you break through the line, you may take a captive back to the army of Saul. If you can't break through their line, you become *their* captive."

A light appeared in the boy's eye as he grasped his objective. With his siblings around him, he crouched in a starting position, then raced toward the opposite line, choosing a weak spot between two of the younger ones. They released each other's hands as soon as it became apparent he was barreling toward them, and my young David burst through the line with a victorious shout.

His teammates cheered and chattered as I drew near. "Congratulations, David! Now you may take a captive back with you to the army of King Saul. And by the way—" I drew closer to hear him better—"what is your real name?"

"Pharnaces," he said, lowering his chin as he gave me a shy look. "Son of Malta."

"Congratulations, sweet Pharnaces." I reached for his hand and clasped it. "You are a fine player, and I'm sure you are a fine prince."

The charming child beamed at me, then snagged a little girl's hand and dragged her back to his group.

We played the game for over an hour, and at one point I joined a team and collapsed in delight when my gentle charge toward the enemy line resulted in my stumbling into a living net of arms and legs. I sank to the soft grass, breathed in the scent of warm, sweaty children, and decided I couldn't remember a happier moment.

Later, when the children had gone back to their mothers, I met Hatakh in the garden to inspect the battlefield for damage. "To my knowledge, no queen has ever done anything like this," the eunuch said, shaking his head. "I shall have to ask Harbonah if Vashti—"

"I care not what she did," I interrupted, taking pains to make sure my voice reflected the happiness I felt. "I am a different woman and a different queen. I want the king's sons and daughters to enjoy their station, but also to learn about the world outside Persia."

The eunuch blinked. "But there is no world outside Persia— nothing that matters, anyway. The king's empire stretches from horizon to horizon—"

I turned toward the southeast, toward the distant rubble that was Jerusalem. "Persia has not assimilated every people and culture, Hatakh."

The sound of leather slapping on marble diverted my attention. A servant stood on the portico, his face red and his eyes as wide as hibiscus blossoms. "My queen! The lady Vashti approaches." Remembering his manners, he was about to lower himself to the floor, but I waved him away with a flick of my hand. I struggled to remain calm before Hatakh, but my happiness vanished like morning fog.

What business did Vashti have with me? I had no wish to see her, and this ought to be the one place where I did not have to receive anyone I didn't want to encounter. . . .

A shadow fell across the lawn, forcing me to look up. Vashti waited on the portico, still far more regal and lovely than I could ever hope to be. She stood at least a hand's width taller than me, and though she had borne three children, she remained slender through the waist and richly endowed above.

Even Hatakh seemed stunned by her icy beauty.

Ignoring royal protocol, she did not bow or bend in my presence. Struck by her commanding personality, I resisted the urge to bow before her.

"You asked for my children," she said simply, her voice as cool as an evening breeze, "and you shall not have them. They are mine, they are the king's, they are Persia's. They are most definitely not yours." She arched a brow as her dark eyes bore into mine. "Nor do they belong to whatever people you come from, for you are most definitely *not* Persian nobility."

She turned, a majestic column pivoting in one graceful movement, and walked away, leaving a trail of awe in her wake. My handmaids had been struck speechless, Hatakh remained stunned, and I felt . . . cowed.

I had lived my entire life in Susa, yet I had never felt like a second-class citizen until that moment.

CHAPTER TWENTY-NINE

HARBONAH

I HAD JUST SENT ONE OF THE LESSER EUNUCHS to fetch the queen when I saw Biztha approaching, his face flushed and perspiring. I took a deep breath and braced myself, sensing the eunuch brought bad news. No one wore such a worried face at the end of the day unless he was burdened with a troubling report.

"Harbonah." Biztha whispered my name with a sigh of relief. "There is trouble in the harem and I don't know if we should tell the king. But Shaashgaz said I should tell you."

I lifted a brow. "What kind of trouble?"

"One of the young princes has gone missing. His nurse left him sleeping with the other boys, but when she went to check on them, he had disappeared. We have searched the nursery and the harem, but no one has seen him. None of the women has seen him, either."

I folded my arms. "That's a lie. No one goes in or out of the harem without one of the guards seeing something."

"They insist they didn't see the boy leave. That's why I suspect trouble is afoot. No child of the king's has ever gone missing from his bed."

I narrowed my gaze as I considered the implications. "Is it the crown prince?"

"No, Darius sleeps safely with his brothers. It's Pharnaces, son of the concubine Malta. He's a good boy who never causes trouble. His mother is hysterical, and his tutor is quite distraught."

I scratched my chin. Biztha had good instincts, and he was almost certainly correct to think that trouble stirred in the harem. But who would take one of the king's children? A rival for the throne would snatch the crown prince or his brothers, not one of the king's lesser sons.

"Are you sure the boy did not wander away? Could he be hiding? Did someone reprimand him?"

"No, and—"

Biztha fell silent as the sounds of sandals slapping against tile alerted us to the approach of the queen's escort. Two Immortals led her retinue, two walked at her sides, and two followed in the rear. The queen smiled when she caught my eye, but I must have been too distracted by the problem at hand to adequately smooth my expression. She halted at once.

"Harbonah—is all well with you, my friend?"

Biztha and I fell to the floor in obeisance. "Grace and peace to you, lady."

"Rise, please, and tell me what troubles you."

I stood. "Nothing that need concern you, my queen."

"If something concerns you, then it concerns me." A line occupied the space between her brows. "If it will trouble the king—"

"In truth, the king does not yet know, but one of the young princes has gone missing. Guards are searching the harem for him now."

The line between her brows deepened as her hand flew to the rising mound of her belly. I did not know if the king had discovered her secret, but I could not help noticing the change in her manner—of late Esther had been more quiet, more gentle, and more protective. She was undoubtedly in a most delicate condition, so news of a missing prince was bound to upset her.

"I'm sure it is nothing, my queen. The children often play hiding games—"

"Which child?" The eyes she lifted to mine had gone cloudy with worry. "How old?"

"He is called Pharnaces, my queen." Biztha answered for me. "You should not worry. He is a big boy and quite capable of handling himself."

"I know him well." The corners of the queen's mouth went tight with distress. "Please find him, and will you send word when you do?" Her gaze met mine again. "I'll let you tell the king when the time is right, but please—even if you must send a message secretly, do let me know when he is found. He has become quite precious to me."

Doubtless remembering that she was on her way to see the king, she drew her lips into a tight smile, then reached out to squeeze my arm. "Please, Harbonah, don't forget."

I promised her I would not.

CHAPTER THIRTY
HADASSAH

I TOLD HARBONAH THAT I WOULD NOT SPEAK to the king about the missing child, so I tried to put thoughts of Pharnaces out of my mind. But though I sat at dinner with my husband and smiled at his comments, I could not forget about the boy I had grown to love. Was he safe? Was he only hiding in some out of the way corner of the palace, or was he in the hands of someone who might hurt him?

Mordecai had warned me about the dangers of the palace, and I had heard enough stories to convince me that although threats might be silent and invisible, they were never too far away. Men with power attracted men who *wanted* power, and the axiom also held true for women. But who would be bold and heartless enough to involve an innocent child?

What if one day someone came for *my* child?

The king offered me a sprig laden with plump grapes. "You like these, my love, yet you have hardly eaten anything tonight. Has something upset you? Some problem with your maids?"

I looked up, grateful he'd noticed my preoccupation but determined not to break my promise to Harbonah. And I did have news to share with him.

"My king." I slipped from the small couch where I sat and went to kneel at his feet. Resting my head upon his muscular thigh, I held on to his leg and closed my eyes. "I am with child. In time, I hope to bear you a son or daughter."

I waited with my eyes tightly shut because I could not bear to be disappointed by his reaction. He didn't need another son or daughter, and as far as I knew he didn't want another child. But I would soon have a baby, his baby, and I desperately wanted him to be happy about the idea.

A Sabbath stillness reigned in the chamber, with nothing but the heavy sound of his breathing to disturb it. His broad hand fell upon my head, but I couldn't tell whether he wanted to caress me or crush me.

"My darling little queen," he finally said, his fingers finding my chin and lifting it upward, "are you happy about this?"

"Oh, yes." I looked into his eyes and gave him a heartfelt smile. "I've never been happier about anything."

"Then I am content." Something that looked like a smile twitched into existence and out again among the curls of his beard. Then he lifted me and held me on his lap. For a long while I sat within the circle of his arms, my face pressed into his neck, his hands on my belly where his child safely grew.

If HaShem would be merciful and grant me the blessing of a son, I silently told myself, I would name the child *Avraham, father of many.*

CHAPTER THIRTY-ONE

HADASSAH

I WAS STILL ABED THE NEXT MORNING when Hatakh pounded on my door. "I bring an urgent message," he told me when one of my maids let him in. "A man outside says he has important news for you."

I frowned, unable to imagine what the eunuch meant. "A man? I cannot have a man in my bedchamber—"

"The man says he walks outside the harem walls every day."

I closed my eyes as realization washed over me. I had abandoned Mordecai for far too long, and now he had urgent news. Was he ill? Had something happened to Binyamin or one of our other friends?

"Tell him—" I hesitated. Did I dare grant Mordecai an audience? If I ran to his arms and treated him like a father, anyone in the vicinity would know we were related. So if I saw him, I would have to pretend he was a stranger.

I sat up and smoothed my hair. "Tell him I will grant him an audience later today, after I have dressed and breakfasted."

Hatakh bowed and left to deliver his message.

As soon as the door closed behind him, I threw back the covers and gestured to my maids. "Quickly," I told them, not caring if they saw my haste and concern. "Dress me in royal attire. I do not want to keep this gentleman waiting."

Hulta raised a brow at this, but none of the other maids said anything as they hurried to prepare me for receiving guests. After the dressing ritual and a quick meal of bread and honey, all I could keep down, I entered the audience chamber and took a seat on the golden throne, a smaller version of my husband's. My maids sat in chairs to my right, ready to be of service, and a company of eunuch guards stood at my left. Hatakh stood behind me, where he could discreetly whisper the name or position of any petitioner who requested an audience with the queen.

At my signal, Hatakh nodded to the guards at the door, who opened it and allowed my petitioners to enter the chamber.

An elderly woman, the mother of a young girl, approached to ask that her daughter be presented to the crown prince at court. I smiled and pretended to listen to her long-winded request, nodding at what I hoped were the appropriate places. But while I smiled and nodded, my eyes roved over the waiting visitors, then focused on the dear figure who sat behind the bench the old woman had vacated.

Mordecai.

A sharp pang of nostalgia assailed me as I studied his weathered face. Passion had shoved thoughts of my cousin from my mind of late, but I had never stopped needing him. I ought to ask him about Vashti and how I should react to her challenges. I ought to ask about Binyamin and his father. I ought to ask what I could do to help the king's children. Pearls of wisdom continually dropped from Mordecai's lips, so he would be able to give me good advice.

If he could forgive me for neglecting him. I had conjured up dozens of reasons for not visiting the harem garden, but chief among them were my embarrassment and shame at my riotous feelings for my very handsome, very pagan husband. I loved my husband the king, I carried his child, and I knew Mordecai could not approve of either.

But at least he had come to see me. Perhaps he had invented a reason to come; maybe he only wanted to assure himself that I was alive and well. He would not reproach me in such a public place, nor would he reveal our kinship. Since he had taken great pains to preserve my reputation and my safety, I had to wonder what had lured him out of his office and into the queen's palace.

As the elderly mother droned on about her daughter's beauty and virtues, I clutched the armrest of my chair and tried to focus. Pregnancy had made me light-headed and queasy, and I dreaded the hot months ahead. I had heard women complain about the distress of carrying a child during the sweltering summer, and I wasn't looking forward to sweating through a hard labor. . . .

"My queen?"

My pulse stuttered at Hatakh's question. "Yes?"

"I have assured the lady that we will do all we can." Hatakh's eyes narrowed as he studied my face. "Are you well enough to hear a request from the next petitioner?"

"I am." I forced a smile and pinned it in place as I turned my gaze upon Mordecai.

"Grace and peace to you, my queen." My cousin stood, then prostrated himself on the floor. I looked away, biting back the protest that rose to my lips.

"Rise," I said, my voice strangled. "And please tell us what brings you here today."

Mordecai stood, his eyes meeting mine. "I have news of a situation of some delicacy. If I may approach, I would speak to you privately with your servant, the valiant Hatakh."

I turned to Hatakh, realizing Mordecai had said exactly the right thing. No man would have been allowed to approach the queen alone, but by inviting Hatakh to join him, Mordecai had shown respect to the king and to my chief eunuch.

I nodded. "You may approach."

From the corner of my eye, I saw movement among my maids as they jostled for better positions to observe the stranger who had appeared in my audience chamber. Hatakh and Mordecai approached simultaneously, until each stood close enough for me to touch them.

"Cousin." I smiled, freely, into his eyes. "I have so longed to talk to you."

"Are you well, child?"

"I am. I'm sorry I haven't attempted to contact you—"

"I know you have been . . . preoccupied. You are no longer a girl, and I respect your new position."

Hatakh observed our exchange with a speculative gaze, his eyes flitting to Mordecai's face, then mine, then back to Mordecai's. Harbonah might not have told him of the relationship between me and my visitor, but he was no fool.

"I am glad you have come." I smiled again, and might have reached for his hand if Hatakh had not been watching so closely. "What brings you to my chamber?"

"Before I speak, I have to know—how trustworthy is the eunuch who attends you here?" Mordecai glanced pointedly at Hatakh, who glared with indignation at the question.

My mouth quirked with a smile. "I assure you, cousin, Hatakh is quite trustworthy. He is in my service every hour of the day."

"You would trust him with your life?"

"I would. I do."

Mordecai breathed deeply, then gave the eunuch an apologetic glance. "Very well. In truth, if I had not been able to see you I would have sent a written message." He hesitated and stepped even closer,

his eyes glittering with purpose. "I have urgent news. It concerns—"
he lowered his voice—"the life of your husband and king."

The audience hall seemed to shift before my eyes. I reached
for the chair's armrest and felt the slickness of sweat beneath my
palm. "Surely you are mistaken." Despite my conviction, my voice
trembled. "The king is most safe; he is surrounded by guards at all
times. His devoted Immortals stand watch outside the door even
while he sleeps—"

My voice broke as I thought of the young prince who had gone
missing from his bedchamber. I had not heard anything from Harbonah, so I did not know if the child had been found.

"Two of those Immortals are not so devoted," Mordecai went
on, unaware of my troubling thoughts. "This morning I was at
the King's Gate and paused to rest in the shade. Hidden there, I
overheard two of the king's bodyguards plotting to assassinate their
master in his bedchamber. I waited until they stepped out of the
passageway where they plotted so I could identify them."

"Who?" My whisper scratched against my throat. "Did you
know them?"

"I didn't, but another guard told me their names: Bigtan and
Teresh. They are in charge of the entry to the king's private chambers."

A chill slithered up my backbone. I didn't know the name of every
guard in the king's palace, but I knew their faces. I could scarcely
believe that any of them would conspire to harm my beloved—

But had some of them conspired to abduct the little prince? And
were the two plots connected?

I closed my eyes. Harbonah might not have told the king about
the missing child, so I could not speak of the matter without risk-
ing the eunuch's life. No one wanted to upset the king if a problem
could be solved without confronting the royal temper, so Harbonah
and the other eunuchs were probably still searching for the boy.

Could the boy have overheard the two plotting guards as Mordecai had? I considered the question, then shook my head. The possibility was too terrible to think about.

"Why?" The question slipped from my lips. "Why would anyone want to harm the king?"

Mordecai glanced at Hatakh for a moment, then looked back at me. "Those two were devoted to Masistes, the king's brother. It is an old story, but many believe revenge is a dish best served cold."

My mind whirled at my cousin's brief response. "But that makes no sense; the king's brother is dead. He died months ago, or so I've been told—"

"Don't you understand, Hadassah?" Mordecai's eyes snapped with urgency. "You must get word to the king. Go to him immediately, speak directly to him and say nothing to anyone else. If you relay this message to any guard in league with these two, you will endanger your own life."

In the anguished rasp of Mordecai's voice I heard the reason he had hurried to protect a king he did not particularly admire. He knew that I might be in the king's bedchamber when an attack came, so I might be at risk as well . . .

Along with my unborn child.

"Why don't *you* go to the king?" I lifted my head and gripped my chair even more tightly. "You work at the King's Gate; you could probably get an audience with him. I can't go to him without being summoned, and if I wait until evening I might be too late."

"I might not get an audience at all." Mordecai relaxed as his voice settled back into his reasonable and patient tone. "You will not be refused. I have heard how the king adores you."

The king adored me. For that, I could only be grateful.

I released my grip on my chair, then stared at the reddened flesh of my palm and fingers. I could go to the king because he loved me. I could trust that love . . . couldn't I?

I could. I had been in the king's bed last night, and would be again tonight. Because he loved me.

"I will go," I whispered hoarsely. "I will go at once and will give him your message. And cousin?"

"Yes?"

"Thank you. I know you didn't have to do this."

I gazed at him, drinking in the sight of his precious face, and then I heard his soft benediction: "May Adonai bless you and keep you, daughter. Now go."

CHAPTER THIRTY-TWO
HADASSAH

THOUGH I KNEW I WAS FLYING IN THE FACE of Persian law and royal protocol, I dismissed the other waiting petitioners and asked Hatakh to accompany me as I went to the king. With a queasy stomach and trembling limbs, I approached the throne room without being summoned, an offense worthy of death. But I flew to my husband on wings of love and duty, fueled by an urgency that could not be denied. I knew I would be safe, for my husband would see the desperate look of love on my face and know my intentions were honorable. Though the Immortals would eye my approach with suspicion, though they might draw their swords as I crept toward the king, my royal husband would hold out his scepter and pardon me.

The scene played out just as I had imagined it. As I touched the tip of the golden rod, I fell to my knees before the throne and reached out to catch and hold his feet. "My king," I whispered, strengthening my voice, "I have received urgent news from a man who is honest and trustworthy. His message concerns your life, and love has compelled me to breach every prohibition and hurry to you."

I did not expect the king's reaction. Surrounded by his vice-regents, he laughed aloud and bent to help me to my feet. As his lips neared my ear, however, he lowered his voice to a pitch only I could hear. "What's this? Has someone made a threat?"

I wound my arm around his neck as if overwhelmed by the power of his presence—a gesture far more honest than the king realized. Leaning close, I spoke directly into his ear: "The two Immortals who guard the door of your bedchamber—Bigtan and Teresh. They plan to kill you while you sleep."

The king's hand closed on my wrist. "Your informant is certain of this? I know those two; they have been with me for years."

"Mordecai, an accountant at the King's Gate, heard them plotting, and he does not lie. He said they were devout friends of Masistes."

My husband lifted his head to look into my eyes. "You trust this Mordecai?"

"I would stake my life on the man's word."

The king kissed me on the forehead, the way a father kisses a dear daughter. He then looked around, caught Hatakh's gaze, and motioned for the eunuch to come forward. "The queen is not well; escort her back to her chambers immediately. And then have the guards Bigtan and Teresh meet the captain of my Immortals on the training field. A certain matter needs immediate investigation."

Hatakh nodded and extended his hand to support me. I accepted it gratefully.

As I walked out of the throne room, part of me yearned to linger and make certain my husband the king would be safe. But I was a woman, and I had done all I could do.

But it was enough for now. By working together, Mordecai and I had warned the king. I would leave the missing prince to Harbonah.

Chapter Thirty-Three

HARBONAH

WHEN I HEARD OF THE GUARDS' PLOT against the king, I almost hoped Bigtan and Teresh would confess to abducting the young prince. But they admitted their conspiracy and treason without mentioning the boy, and I realized I had been guilty of reckless hope.

Two more days passed with no sign of Pharnaces. The highest-ranking officers of the king's Immortals searched the entire palace for signs of the young prince; then they interviewed the other children, the concubines, and the eunuchs who guarded the harem.

Finally their captain approached the king and shared the tragic news—the prince Pharnaces had disappeared without a trace.

My master's fury thundered as I had known it would, but the mystery left him with no one to blame. He did not want to admit the child might be dead, so how could he execute someone for murder? He could hardly kill the captain of his guard, though I am certain the idea crossed his mind, nor could he condemn the child's mother.

"Mark my words," my frustrated king finally proclaimed before a crowd in the great hall. "When the prince Pharnaces again appears before his father, Xerxes the king, he shall declare the name of the person or persons who caused his disappearance, and those persons will be impaled on the mount at Susa. By the favor of Ahura Mazda, I will find the villain and have no mercy upon him."

That night, one of the king's bodyguards pulled me from sleep with a sharp jab from the blunt end of his spear. "Biztha summons you," the guard whispered. "He tells you to hurry."

My first thought, as always, was for the king, who snored loudly in his bed. Though he scarcely knew his missing son, the boy's loss had plunged him into melancholy and reminded him of the queen's delicate condition, so he slept alone. After making sure the king would rest unmolested during my absence, I followed the guard out of the royal bedchamber and went in search of Biztha.

I found him in the subterranean areas far below the rooms that housed the royal family, the guards, and the cooking areas. Only the lowliest slaves and eunuchs slept here, but when I found Biztha, he was not in his bed. Instead he was bent over a straw mattress where another man lay, a eunuch I recognized from the harem.

Blood streaked the man's round face; red tracks ran from the man's eyes, nose, and mouth. The arm he clutched was purple and so swollen that I feared the skin would tear.

"Jangi," Biztha said, informing me of the man's name. "He has a story to tell, and you should hear it now, before he dies."

The wretched man rolled onto his side, shuddered, and vomited his last meal in a slurry of blood. When he had finished, he rolled back onto his mattress, his eyes fixed on the ceiling. In truth, I thought I had come too late.

"Go on." Biztha jostled the man's shoulder. "The king's chamberlain is here. Tell him what you told me."

I sat cross-legged on the floor and leaned closer. "I will listen."

The man drew a gasping breath, then shook his head. "I cannot see you. How do I know it's you and not . . . her?"

I clasped his uninjured arm and leaned close enough to whisper in his ear. "It is I, Harbonah. Tell me what happened."

With great effort, the man swallowed. "She has killed me. She sent me to fetch a ball . . . for the crown prince . . . but when I put my hand in the box . . . an adder instead. She did it so the truth would die . . . with me."

I bit my tongue, knowing it would be useless to hurry him along. The man was dying. Since he had not been able to control the events of his life, the least I could do was let him control his death.

Biztha was not as patient. "Tell him who sent you."

"Vashti." The man shuddered again, and when I pressed my hand to his forehead, I realized that he burned with fever.

"She commanded me . . . to help her," the man continued. "I took young Pharnaces from his bed . . . put him in a cart . . . and told him we were playing a game. Then I took the cart from the harem . . . without anyone seeing."

I pressed my lips together, frustrated beyond the point of endurance. "Where did you take the boy?"

"Vashti . . . wanted a sacrifice for Ahura Mazda so . . . the new queen . . . would lose . . . her baby. She wanted . . . a nobleman's son, but what child could be more noble than . . . the son of a king?"

I glanced at Biztha. For the past few weeks Vashti had been a near continual presence in the harem; everyone had seen her. If she had only arranged the prince's abduction, perhaps there was still time to save his life.

"Tell us where you have hidden him," Biztha commanded. As the man spewed blood and foam from his lips, Biztha looked at me. "Before I sent for you, I knew only that Vashti had forced him to take the boy. I don't know what she did with him."

Terrified that the eunuch would die before finishing his confession, I grabbed the front of his robe and shook him. "Speak, man! Where is the boy now?"

Jangi's breathing grew still as his head lolled to the side. My heart rose to my throat as I considered the real possibility that I had killed him. Then he gasped another breath. "The tomb," he said, and the exhalation that escaped his lips was his last.

I released his robe, then scrambled backward, shaken by the man's death and the news I'd learned. Vashti was the queen of cunning, so I did not doubt that she had used this slave and killed him to ensure his silence. She must have had him take the prince away from the royal mount because she could not leave the palace without attracting attention.

"Did he say what I thought he said?" Biztha caught my gaze. "A tomb? Which tomb?"

I shook my head. My master's burial chamber was under construction in a cliff north of Persepolis, where his father had been buried. The distance was too great; Pharnaces could not possibly be there. As for other tombs—many noble families had tombs in rocky areas near the river. The boy could have been taken to any of them and placed inside. If he had been provided with ventilation, food, and water, he could still be alive, but if not, he was almost certainly dead.

Knowing Vashti as I did, Jangi's story made complete sense. The former queen had no tolerance for competition, and she had seen Esther in the sort of free-flowing gown favored by expectant women. Vashti had guessed at the truth and taken action to ensure that Esther's offspring would never usurp her own sons' positions.

And she'd been willing to sacrifice another woman's child to accomplish her goal.

I leaned against the uneven wall and propped my hands on my bent knees. Biztha looked at me, weariness evident in the lines on his face. "So what do we do now?"

What, indeed? Two eunuchs could not accuse one of the king's women of murder. With our only witness dead, providing information to the guards might only implicate us in the crime. If a search was conducted and the boy found, Vashti could always say that Biztha and I had concocted the plot, stolen the boy, and planned to demand our freedom and a ransom. After all, I was the king's chamberlain and in a position of some authority. Likewise, as one of the king's trusted attendants, Biztha could have easily snatched the boy while pretending to be on royal business.

If faced with that scenario and his shrewd former queen, I could not be certain that my master wouldn't believe her. . . .

Before I laid the bare truth before Biztha, one question demanded an answer.

"Do you believe it will happen?" I asked.

"What?"

"Do you believe Ahura Mazda will honor Vashti's sacrifice? That he will destroy the present queen's child?"

Biztha scowled. "Ahura Mazda honors men who are pure in heart." He lowered his voice, lest the shadows around us harbor a pair of listening ears. "Vashti's heart is not pure." He waited, then cocked his head at me. "Don't tell me you think Ahura Mazda will hear her."

I shrugged. "I have no doubt that *some* god rules this earth . . . but though my king honors Ahura Mazda with ceremonies, he does not seek the god's favor in his life. If Ahura Mazda honors sacrifices, I've seen no proof of it. And if a god does not answer the king of an empire, then who can hope to appeal to him?"

Biztha turned to stare at the body of the eunuch, then shook his head. "So we have no hope of justice. Will you tell Queen Esther about this?"

I hesitated, remembering the queen's earnest request that I tell her when the boy had been found. He hadn't exactly been found . . . and probably never would be.

I rose, slowly, and eased my tired bones back into an erect position. "We can do nothing to change the outcome of this misadventure, and the queen should not be at risk. So we should do what we have always done—remain silent and serve our master. Tomorrow will almost certainly be a better day."

I had no idea that an even greater evil awaited us.

CHAPTER THIRTY-FOUR

HADASSAH

LAST NIGHT, FOR THE FIRST TIME since our marriage, the king did not send for me at sunset.

Though I had risked my life to tell him about the conspiracy that threatened his life, he chose to sleep alone . . . or with someone else. Why? Had I offended him? Had Bigtan and Teresh involved someone else in their plot, someone who might still be planning to murder the king while he slept? Hatakh had no answers, and I did not want to cause a stir by making inquiries.

I endured an evening of fitful sleep and woke with pains in my abdomen and a queasy stomach, which emptied itself as soon as I got out of bed. I sank to the floor and gratefully accepted the wet cloth my quick-thinking handmaid offered, then mopped my mouth and perspiring brow. I hoped this horrible feeling was not a sign that something had happened to the king.

One of the maids hurried to tell Hatakh that I had awakened;

a few moments later the eunuch entered my bedchamber with a breakfast tray. I took one look at the fruit and bread, then shook my head and turned away. "I have no appetite," I told him truthfully. "But let the maids eat their fill. I will not feel better until I know the king is safe."

"But the king *is* safe," Hatakh replied, straightening. "After you left him yesterday, the king and his officers conducted a trial. Bigtan and Teresh were confronted with the charges and they confessed to their treasonous plan. They have been sentenced for their crime."

I turned bleary eyes toward the shuttered balcony, which overlooked the army's training field. "What will happen now?"

The eunuch shrugged. "Given time, they will die. You can see them, if you like."

Something warned me away from the sight, but desperation for the king's safety drove me forward. I had to know that justice had been done.

As I approached the balcony, two of my handmaids rose to pull the sliding doors aside. I glanced over the royal gardens and stared at the brown plateau outside the city walls. In the center of the warriors' encampment, I spotted two stick figures that looked like puppets. But they were seated on the ground and apparently tied to tall poles.

I glanced at Hatakh, then pointed toward the two men in the distance. "Are those the guilty ones?"

Hatakh looked out at the scene and nodded. "Yes, my queen."

"But they're simply sitting there."

"No, my lady." Hatakh's face paled slightly. "They have been impaled upon a sharpened stick. They will sit beneath the sun until the gods take pity on them and snuff out their lives."

For a moment his words hung in the air, making no sense, and then they clicked into place. My gorge rose, I vomited again, and the walls swirled around me.

I remember hearing my maids' frightened cries, along with
Hatakh's high-pitched wail before the room went dark.

When I woke, the royal physician told me I had lost my baby.

Hatakh said he should never have mentioned the condemned
guards; Harbonah said a pregnant woman who looked on death was
asking for trouble. I didn't care why I lost my baby; I only wanted
to be comforted in my husband's arms.

But the physicians told me to remain in my chamber for at least
a few days, and while I recovered I waited for some word from the
king. Surely he would send a message of condolence or caring . . .
but he did not. So every morning my maids dressed me and did
my hair, though I saw no one but my girls and Hatakh.

And while I convalesced, my husband plucked other girls from
the harem to fill his bed.

I wish I could write that the knowledge didn't twist in my heart
like a knife. I knew the king did not limit himself to one woman;
I knew that willing concubines crowded the harem, each of them
eager to be called for an hour with the king.

But the realization that my husband was finding pleasure in
others spawned a brooding sorrow that spread until it mingled
with dozens of other sorrows—the loss of my child, of Mordecai's
companionship, of Miriam, even my home. I had lost so much since
arriving at the palace, and what had I gained? For what possible
reason had Adonai brought me to this miserable place?

My husband did send for me after I regained my health, but
the bond between us had changed. I yearned for a word of understanding or compassion; I heard nothing. I might have dared
to broach the subject of the baby, but I remembered what Hatakh
had told me about Persian fathers: they did not want to be at-

tached to a child younger than five, lest they be "afflicted by its loss."

So I bore my grief silently, though my misery was often so overwhelming, so intrusive, it felt like another body in the bed, a dark and foreboding presence. My husband took me in his arms and I tried to respond, but grief had stolen the passion from my kiss.

I wasn't surprised when he stopped sending for me.

And so began a new chapter of my life in the palace, a phase a wiser woman might have foreseen. I was no longer new and exciting, and though I believe the king remained fond of me, he did not call for me more than once or twice a week. I tried my best to be pleasant and charming when I was with him, but the grief of loss clung to me like the smell of smoke from a blistering fire.

Days passed, like leaves from a sycamore tree, one after the other, virtually indistinguishable.

CHAPTER THIRTY-FIVE

HARBONAH

DID I BELIEVE THAT VASHTI successfully petitioned Ahura Mazda for the death of Esther's child? Only Biztha and I knew why the former queen had committed her terrible crime, and afterward, even as I heard the rumors about Queen Esther's tragic loss, I assured Biztha that I still did not believe in the power of Ahura Mazda.

But inwardly . . . I wondered.

Privately, I grieved for our queen. Despite her maturity, Esther still possessed the idealistic optimism of youth, so losing her baby left her devastated. During my time in the harem I had seen many young women lose their unborn children, but I had also seen them rally and become pregnant again.

Yet weeks later, Hatakh told me the queen had still not recovered, but frequently curled up on her bed and watered her pillow with tears.

I wanted to weep for her.

I wish my master had been more observant of his young bride. The king adored her above all the virgins who'd been brought to the palace, but he also adored his horses, his hunts, and his harem. After serving the man for so many years, I knew my master to be as fickle in his infatuations as in his hobbies.

Fortunately, he had chosen a worthy wife. Mordecai's lovely ward might quietly grieve over her husband's wandering eye, but she would be a dutiful and faithful consort. If only the king's heart could be as steadfast as his queen's.

Not long after the queen lost her baby, she summoned me to her chambers. After finding her in her garden, bowed low near a rose-bush, I pretended to be surprised at the shadow of grief on her face.

"I am fine," she said, her eyes damp with pain. "I have been ill, but I am better now."

"I am glad to hear it, my queen."

She pulled a small knife from the basket on her arm. "Harbonah," she said, cutting a single rose blossom, "did anyone ever find young Pharnaces?"

My bowels tumbled at the question, and I struggled to keep a blank face. "No, my queen. I would have told you if we had."

"I am sorry to hear that. I am . . . deeply saddened." Her words were lighter than air, though I knew they had come from a heavy heart.

"Harbonah, you have served the king for how long?"

"Twenty years, my queen. I hope to serve him the rest of my life."

"I hope you are together forever." She offered me a sincere smile that momentarily brightened her face. "Since you know him so well, and since you are a man of discretion, I wondered if you could answer a question for me."

"I will do my best."

"This question must not be repeated, do you understand? Not even to another eunuch, because I know how eunuchs love to gossip."

I smiled, acknowledging the truth in her statement. "I would die, my queen, before I would betray your confidence."

"I would not ask you to sacrifice yourself for me, not ever. After all, neither of us chose this life, did we?" She forced a quick smile, then looked away. "When I was younger, my friend and I used to look up at the palace and dream of living in such a grand place. We imagined royal life as an endless succession of banquets, dress fittings, and travel. I thought I would love living in the palace . . . but now I find that the queen lives a life of unbearable loneliness. I was far happier in the little house with Miriam and Mordecai. I think of how Miriam used to welcome Mordecai home with a hug, and I am envious of what they shared."

I waited, knowing she had not summoned me to talk about her life with her cousins. She looked down, her long lashes hiding her eyes, and hesitated. "I know the king has many children, including three sons from his former queen. But I also know that Persian men consider it their duty to father many sons. So what I need to know is this—do you think the king expects a child from me? How important is it that I present him with a son?"

Her voice softened as she spoke, and had dwindled to a mere whisper by the time she finished. Her face, which had been composed in regal lines, shifted to the sincere and frightened face of a teenaged girl.

I resisted an almost overwhelming impulse to run forward and enfold her in a comforting embrace. But because such an act would earn a death sentence, I stammered out an answer. "My king—your husband—adores you, my lady. And while I'm sure he would delight in a child from you, I do not think he married you to have more children. He married you because you were unlike anyone else. Of all the women in the harem, you were the one who caught his attention and held it. You were the only one to make him laugh."

She listened, a fine line between her brows, and her forehead relaxed as I finished. "I made him laugh. If only I could accomplish that feat now."

"My gentle lady—" I cleared my throat in order to stall and gather my thoughts—"you have been married only a few months. I think the king has enjoyed getting to know you as a woman, not a mother. If you were with child, your attention would naturally be divided between your baby and your husband the king. So why not enjoy these days when your thoughts can center on pleasing your husband?"

She closed her eyes, considering, and then nodded. "You are wise, Harbonah. I suppose one can find good in any situation, if one takes the time to look."

I bowed my head. "The queen is wise."

She smiled. "The queen has wise counselors. And since you are so astute, I wonder if you could help me with something else."

I waited, though I could almost see anxiety hanging above her like a dark cloud.

"I want to love the king," she said, moving to another rosebush, "but I find it difficult to understand him. He talks of trivial things, sometimes he asks about me, but he never tells me much about himself. And if I am to love him well, I must *know* him." She cut another rose, dropped it into her basket, and whirled to face me. "You know him better than anyone, Harbonah. Tell me what moves him. Tell me what frightens him. Tell me what he needs—and why he needs to love so many women."

Her blushing face was so open, so honest that I could see the hurt and pride warring inside. In asking these questions she was admitting that she was lost, a queen who did not have a firm grip on her husband's heart.

I hesitated, wavering between two loyalties. I had never exposed the secrets of my master's soul to anyone, not even Vashti, but never before had anyone wanted to care for him as much as

I did. And I wanted to help Hadassah; I wanted Queen Esther to be the salve for my king's deepest wounds. I sensed that she could help him, if only he would allow her to peer behind the mask he wore.

Still . . . he was my master and my king. And his wounds were not mine to share.

But perhaps they rightfully belonged to his wife.

"I . . . admire you," I began, "and I know the king does, too. Yes, you made him laugh, but it was the sincerity and compassion behind your laughter that touched his heart. He chose you because you remind him of the king he wants to be—wise, generous, compassionate, and courageous."

Her lip trembled as her eyes filled with tears, and she looked away as if embarrassed for me to see her emotion. "He . . . has never said anything like that to me."

"He wouldn't. I'm not sure he understands the man beneath the crown. Since I love my master I cannot speak ill of him, but you should know three things: first, he struggles to live up to his father's example. Second, the defeat at Greece haunts him still. And third, in bedding other women, for the space of an hour he sees himself as a conqueror."

I covered my mouth and turned away as my blood ran thick with guilt. If the king had heard me confess these things, he would have pronounced me guilty of treason and sent me to the executioner. I couldn't help feeling that I had transgressed against him and he would read my sin on my face.

But then Esther the queen broke every rule of protocol and placed her hand on my trembling arm. "Thank you, Harbonah. I will hold your words in my heart and consider them carefully. And I will never, ever speak of these things again."

I closed my eyes and exhaled in relief.

"Thank you for coming," the queen said, removing her hand.

She stepped back, reassuming her royal demeanor. "I appreciate your heartfelt advice."

I left her, grateful that I had been able to offer some measure of comfort. Aside from the king and her seven maids, to whom she had grown close, the queen was quite alone in the palace. Her position isolated her from her rivals in the harem, and she had no children to occupy her time.

I hoped she would not remain alone forever.

While working to serve my king and ensure my queen's happiness, I watched Mordecai's gentle ward grow into a beautiful woman. Over the course of the next five years, her oval face softened and became even more refined. She no longer exuded youthful enthusiasm, but radiated a refined, almost visible aura. The other eunuchs frequently questioned her handmaids to learn what lotions produced her haunting loveliness, but I knew the effect did not derive from any potion or oil. The delicacy and strength in her oval face were the result of loneliness, unspoken sorrow, and unfulfilled love.

I don't know how many times our queen found herself with child during those years, but I do know that for weeks she would beam with inexpressible joy and then, without explanation, her joy would be swallowed up by sorrow. Though Queen Esther appeared to be in perfect health, the royal physician visited her chambers regularly and her loyal handmaids could not be persuaded to speak of whatever ailed their mistress.

Every time I suspected Esther of being pregnant, I told the harem guards to keep a watchful eye on the king's children. Though Biztha and I did not speak again of what Vashti had done to Pharnaces, I wanted to be sure she did not attempt to sacrifice any of the other royal sons. I did not believe in Ahura Mazda's power, but I had no trouble believing in the former queen's ambition.

I did not worry so much about Esther. The queen's maids were the most tight-lipped crew ever to dwell in the palace, immune to bribery, flattery, and threats. They did not gossip, they did not slander, and they did not hobnob with the other servants, so most of the eunuchs knew practically nothing about their queen. Once Hegai made a wager with Hatakh, betting a cloak of fine wool that he could discover from which nation the queen had descended, but he finally had to pay, for no one who knew Esther wanted to break her confidence.

Our queen, so unlike all the king's other women, exuded mystery, which only added to her allure. The women of the court imitated her simple style of dress, her habit of shyly ducking her chin, and her modest posture when seated on the throne. Completely un-like Vashti, Esther's rare appearance in the king's audience hall introduced a pleasant atmosphere to a situation that had always been fraught with tension. The king remained unpredictable and impulsive, but he appeared to mellow in the queen's company.

My king and queen might have been supremely happy if not for the ghosts that haunted them. Esther mourned the children she could not seem to carry, and the king mourned the loss of his reputation as an invincible warrior. If they had been willing to confess these matters to each other, and if they had been honest, they might have comforted each other and eased their respective burdens.

But the king would never confess that he feared not measur-ing up to his father—in order to remain on the throne, he had to believe he deserved it. Esther might have been willing to open her heart about her grief over her unborn children, but I think she feared hearing that he didn't need a child from her because he had more than enough children from other women. If he had said those words—even if they were meant to comfort—she would hear that he didn't care about the thing she valued more than anything else.

Though neither of them spoke of the matters uppermost in their hearts, their hidden burdens built a wall between them. Perhaps the king sensed the queen's unhappiness; perhaps she sensed the king's dissatisfaction. In any case, they began to drift apart.

As the king and queen saw less and less of each other, the king sent for women from the harem, and Hegai was quick to supply. These females—dark, tall, short, fair, round, or willowy—would entertain the king for a night, but none of them captured his heart the way Esther had.

He missed her. She had made him laugh. She had gazed at him as though he could do anything he set his mind to. She had given herself completely, with no thought for her own advancement. She was unlike any of the other women, and he yearned for the heart of his queen.

If only he would realize it.

Chapter Thirty-Six
HADASSAH

AFTER FIVE YEARS OF MARRIAGE, my husband and I had developed a sweet and comfortable relationship. He did not send for me every night, but at least once a week I visited his chamber and slept in his arms. He visited me too, often dropping by when the royal children came to play in my garden; occasionally he would even join in their games. Watching him at play and seeing him smile warmed my heart. Perhaps, I told myself, this was why I became queen. If I could do even some small thing to help this father love his children better, then my life might accomplish something worthwhile.

But during the spring of our fifth year, our routine shifted and I rarely saw my husband the king. Whenever I sent one of my maids to ask how the king fared, I was told he was busy in his audience hall or he had gone hunting. As the weather grew warmer and the time came for our annual journey to Ecbatana, I expected to hear that we would soon be leaving, but no order came. The king seemed content to remain in Susa indefinitely, and I could not understand his reasoning.

One afternoon I was in the garden playing with the little dog the king had given me on his forty-fourth birthday. The dog was nothing like the big hunters the king kenneled or the massive canines used in bear baiting, but a creature so tiny it could curl up in my lap. At the birthday banquet my husband joked that he had no use for a dog so small it should really be a cat, but I wept tears of joy because the gift was evidence that my husband loved me and wanted to ease my loneliness.

I was almost embarrassed to admit how much the pup and I doted on each other. I cared for him with great tenderness, realizing he had taken the place of the child I had hoped to hold to my breast. The creature's furry face, button nose, and bright eyes never failed to comfort my aching heart. My little dog gave me a reason to get out of bed and renewed my determination to please my lord and king.

But one afternoon as I played in the garden with my dog, I was bending to pick up a ball when a shadow crossed mine. I straightened to find Vashti standing behind me with her arms crossed, her head held high, and a secure smile on her face. "Haven't seen much of your husband lately, have you?" she asked without preamble.

I blinked. How would she know anything about my visits with the king? She never saw him except on state occasions. She had even less access to the king than I did, so she should know less about him.

"He has a new favorite." Her red-painted lips curved in a smile. "I have seen them in the king's garden, on the archery field, and at private dinners when the king entertains in his bedchamber. His favorite joins him under the curtained canopy at banquets, a favor not even granted to me in my time—and, I suspect, never granted to you."

I swallowed hard. The woman had spies; that was how she knew so much. I had never stooped to spying because I didn't want to torture myself. I had always thought—hoped—the king loved me almost as much as I loved him, but if he didn't . . .

I looked away from the former queen's victorious smirk. "He is the king," I said simply, my voice sounding flat in the open air. "He can do as he pleases."

She laughed. "Oh, he does," she said, her gown rustling as she turned. Her sandals swished over the lush grass as she moved away. "He certainly does."

I sank to a marble bench as my knees turned to water. A new favorite? I knew the king had women, and I knew he felt a responsibility to produce many sons for the empire. Of course, he had dozens of concubines, as well as responsibilities to the governors and his nobles. . . .

But I had once been his favorite. I won the crown because I charmed him in a way no one else could.

Apparently I was no longer as charming as someone else.

I turned and leaned over the edge of an elaborate stone fountain. Water splashed noisily at the top, yet only small ripples moved in the large bottom bowl. I stared at my reflection and saw a woman barely in her twenties, a woman who no longer felt at all young.

Had the king transferred his affection because I had not given him a son? Or had I done something to cool his ardor? Perhaps he had grown weary of the nights when I mentioned not feeling well, or perhaps he had simply become bored with me. After all, I did not sing, I did not dance particularly well, and the only thing I had ever demonstrated a talent for was making him laugh.

Somewhere in the palace, someone else was with my king, flattering him, pleasing him. And dozens of servants were seeing this and realizing the truth: the king had grown tired of his second queen.

Was he planning on crowning a third?

CHAPTER THIRTY-SEVEN

HARBONAH

JUST WHEN I THOUGHT THE KING HAD DECIDED to be content with his queen, a new face appeared in the royal court, a face belonging not to a woman but to Haman, son of Hammedatha the Agagite.

I distrusted this Haman the moment I saw him, but I could not attribute my dislike to anything in his appearance. Of average height, he was swarthy and solid, while a soft paunch at his midsection testified to a life of luxury and sumptuous meals.

Dressed in clothing rich enough to rival the king's, he walked as though he were a prince in disguise or one favored by the gods. His plump hands glittered with jeweled rings; his robe and tunic, both constructed of expensive fabrics, shimmered with every movement. His belt had been woven with gold threads, and his shoes jingled as he walked. A turban of scarlet silk, held at the center with a golden brooch, capped his round head.

Haman, I learned from eunuchs who worked at various posts in the palace, had settled in Susa some months earlier. After building an impressive home in the Valley of the Artists, he arrived at the King's Gate bearing lavish gifts and demanded the right to personally deliver his tributes to the king. More than one Persian noble raised a brow as the upstart wandered into the royal court, and when pressed for information, Haman revealed that he had a wife, ten sons, and a fortune derived from trading and the gods' blessing. "I have come to Susa," he said, clutching the edge of his robe and casting a confident smile over the nobles, "to bless the king with my fortune and my friendship."

Several of the nobles snickered at Haman's arrogance, but others admired his boldness. Nothing about the man could be called understated. He spoke in a loud voice, even in close conversation, and commanded every chamber he entered. He exhibited a quick sense of humor, a sly smile that seemed to fascinate every woman in the room, and strong opinions, which he dispensed with confident authority.

Yet years in royal service had taught me that no one gives the king anything without expecting something in return, and what people usually want is position and the power that comes with it. Time proved me right—Haman had arrived in Susa with money alone, yet in only a few weeks he managed to elevate himself to a coveted position in the king's court. He gained this high status only a few days after being introduced to the king, and most of the eunuchs, including me, worried that he might one day gain real influence.

I would have paid the newcomer little attention, but my master developed an acute fascination with the man. Haman had a way of answering the king's questions with thoughtful ideas, then humbling himself and suggesting the solution had been lurking beneath the original question, and surely the king would have come up with the answer if only given another moment to consider the

problem. Haman's glib tongue always managed to utter exactly the
right response . . . an ability that had eluded me but that the gods
heaped upon Haman.

As the newcomer prospered at court, I began to wonder if I
alone found him arrogant. Everyone from the other eunuchs to
the noblemen's wives seemed charmed by the man. Even serving
girls twittered when he sauntered by. Once, when Haman stood
in the garden opining on a random topic, I found a pair of snob-
bish noblemen eavesdropping behind a hedge. When the Agagite
spoke, people listened.

Everyone in the royal court, it seemed, had been snagged in
Haman's web, but I did not trust him. I couldn't deny that the
man possessed many gifts, including a golden tongue, but as far
as I could tell, he used it only to benefit himself.

The king's fascination with Haman might have passed like his
other infatuations, but Memucan, the oldest and wisest of the king's
seven vice-regents, fell sick and died within a few days. The old
man's family had no sooner finished burying him than my master
announced that Haman, not Memucan's son, would take the vacant
position on the king's inner council.

Something in me shriveled at the news. Instead of waning, as a
vice-regent of Persia, Haman's influence could only grow.

Within a matter of months, the Agagite had wormed his way
into the king's innermost circle—and I daresay he would have
taken *my* position if it were possible to be a chamberlain without
also being castrated and a slave. The man began to show up at the
palace every morning and soon demanded entrance to the king's
residence as well as the throne room. Even more amazing, the king
granted Haman permission to come and go at will.

I watched with increasing amazement as Haman's authority
grew. The king consulted Haman on almost every topic, listening
to his advice and then parroting it back as if Haman's ideas were

his own. Haman advised the king on how to handle fallout from the debacle in Greece, on the administration of the satraps, and on handling a meddlesome royal brother, the governor of Babylon. Haman visited the harem to look over the concubines and suggest which of them might make the best entertainment for the king's evening. The Agagite even changed the royal diet, suggesting that wines from the southern provinces were fuller and more robust than those the king had been drinking.

I eyed Haman with increasing alarm and wondered if he might purposefully be trying to sabotage the king's relationship with the queen. I don't think Haman knew anything about the queen's history—as far as I could tell, only Hatakh and I knew of her relationship with Mordecai—but I sensed that Haman didn't want the king confiding in anyone but himself.

I believed that I alone disliked the Agagite, until the afternoon I left the palace to run an errand for my master. I was walking down the grand staircase when I saw Mordecai at his station outside the accounting office. I was about to shout for Mordecai's attention, but the rapid clip-clop of horse hooves warned me to halt where I stood.

I turned and saw Haman leaving the palace on a majestic white horse, undoubtedly a gift from the king. He held his reins loose and his chin high, and every man in the area stopped what they were doing to prostrate themselves as he passed by.

Then Haman rode by Mordecai's post. The Agagite glanced pointedly at my friend, but Mordecai bowed neither his head nor his body. He simply stood at his desk, an expression of profound indifference on his face as Haman moved by.

Even a fool would have noticed the way Haman's eyes narrowed, but the Agagite said nothing. He merely rode on, his chin higher than ever, as those who had prostrated themselves rose and dusted themselves off.

Amazed at my friend's audacity, I walked over to Mordecai.
"Well met, my friend."

"Harbonah!" All smiles now, Mordecai clasped my arm and
squeezed my shoulder. "How are you? And how is my cousin?"

"She is well, and so am I. But you, friend—you have given me
cause for concern."

Mordecai's brow crinkled. "Have I mismanaged some report?
Has my accounting proved faulty?"

I shook my head. "I know nothing about your work. But surely
you know the rider who just passed is a confidant of the king's.
Haman has risen to a position of great influence in only a few short
months. The king listens closely to everything the man says, so to
publicly snub him as you have—"

Mordecai shook off my words as if they were dust. "I have heard
about that son of Amalek. I would not bow to him if he were king."

I lowered my voice. "Why such animosity? Do you know of
some crime he has committed?"

The lines around Mordecai's mouth deepened in a look of firm
resolve. "I don't have to know of a crime. I know him and I know
his people."

I crossed my arms and pressed a finger to my lips, more confused
than ever. Apparently the accountant's dislike of Haman sprang
from tribal rivalries, not the personal aversion I felt toward the man.

"A son of Amalek?" I asked, lifting a brow. "I don't understand."

Mordecai sighed. "Amalek was a son of Esau, brother to Jacob,
later known as Israel. But though Amalek was also a grandson of
Isaac, son of Abraham, he did not worship the God of his fathers.
Years later, when the children of Israel were at their weakest after
leaving Egypt, the warriors of Amalek attacked them, striking at
the aged ones, women, and children who straggled behind. Later,
Adonai told our King Saul to strike Agag, the Amalekite king, and
to leave no one in his city alive. Saul disobeyed, sparing Agag, and

though that king was later put to death, the Agagites—a remnant of the Amalekites—survive today."

I remained silent as I sorted through the confusing history of Mordecai's people.

"Yet I do not refuse to bow purely for historical reasons," the accountant added, his voice softening as he peered down the road at Haman's retreating figure. "Look at the man. See how he sets himself above everyone else? He is filled with pride, and Adonai hates a proud look and a proud heart. A proud man will be set against all that is holy, for he is the god of his own world. Haman is evil, and you, Harbonah, would do well to guard the king's heart. Protect your master if you can."

I relaxed, grateful to discover that I wasn't the only person in the palace who hadn't been mesmerized by the newcomer. "I don't like Haman, either, but the king must be handled tactfully." I frowned. "I have always had a bad feeling about that interloper, but everyone around me praises him as if he were some kind of victorious warrior."

"He is a warrior, but that sort does not fight with spears and arrows. He will fight with words and ideas, and he will overpower the unwary. Watch him carefully."

"And you?" The corner of my mouth lifted in a wry smile. "Will you continue to watch him from your post? No bowing for you? Not even a bend of the knee?"

"Not even a twitch of the eye." Mordecai tipped back his head and met my gaze, a reluctant smile tugging at his lips. "Nebuchadnezzar took thousands of Jews captive and then commanded them to bow before his golden idol. Thousands of my people bowed, all but Shadrach, Meshach, and Abednego. By remaining erect, those three taught a pagan king that he didn't rule the universe." Mordecai's teeth showed through his beard in an expression that was not a smile. "Maybe this old man can teach a stubborn Amalekite that he doesn't rule the universe, either."

I exhaled a deep breath and hoped my friend would be proven right.

⊰⊱

The edict became official within the week, and no one was more surprised to learn of it than me.

In the throne room, with Haman standing by his side—head bowed, hands clasped, and expression appropriately sober—the king proclaimed a new law. "Haman, son of Hammedatha the Agagite, is hereby gifted with the honor of being the king's chief counselor," my master said, speaking slowly for the sake of the scribes, who were furiously translating his proclamation into each of the empire's many languages. "So as a measure of respect, whenever Haman approaches on foot, horseback, or some other conveyance, proper obeisance must be rendered. Throughout the empire, this shall be done to respect the man whom the king delights to honor. So shall it be, today and forever more."

I struggled to maintain a blank face as the other nobles murmured among themselves. Most of them seemed to like Haman, but never had such an honor been granted to anyone who had not emerged either from a noble family or the royal army. The king had a circle of faithful counselors, dozens of devoted military generals, and ten thousand brave Immortals, but never in the history of the empire had a Persian king selected a relative outsider to be his vizier.

I loitered in the shadows as the assembly dismissed for the midday meal. I was about to go seek Hegai's opinion of this latest development when I felt a hand touch my shoulder. I whirled around, expecting to find another slave, but Haman himself stood before me, his gleaming eyes dark and direct.

A cold panic started somewhere between my shoulder blades and shivered down my spine.

"Harbonah, isn't it?" Haman asked, his tone smooth and pleasing. "The king's chamberlain?"

I nodded, struck speechless. Not even my master called me by name.

"You and I have a great deal in common—" he lowered his tone—"as you are the king's chief attendant and I his chief friend. Because I am his friend, I count it my great honor and duty to learn all I can about the issues and situations that influence the king."

I nodded again, not trusting my voice. The hair on the back of my neck rose with premonition as my heart congealed into a small and terrified lump.

"Good, good." The Agagite smiled and smoothed the pointed end of his beard. "It has come to my attention that certain rebels reside in the empire; indeed a few of them even work within the king's court. You, for instance, were seen talking to such an upstart yesterday. Surely you know him—the man who stands at the King's Gate to collect tribute. I hear he has worked in the treasury a long time."

Panic welled in my throat. He meant Mordecai, of course, but how did he know these things? He had passed Mordecai's post by the time I spoke to my friend yesterday . . . which meant Haman had spies in the King's Gate and possibly on the streets of Susa.

Drawing on my years of experience as a slave, I decided to play dumb. "I did go out yesterday, sir, but I spoke to several people. And as one who has served the king for over twenty years, I know many people in the palace—"

"I'm referring to a most peculiar man." Haman's eyes narrowed. "He wears an untrimmed beard and dresses in a dark tunic with fringe at the hem of his robe. He lives alone in the eastern part of the city."

Haman had more than spies on the street—he had *moles* he'd bribed to dig up information. If he knew how and where Mordecai lived, he had to know my friend's name. He was searching now for confirmation.

So I could do no harm by replying.

"You must mean Mordecai." I smiled the carefree smile of an imbecile. "He has served the king faithfully for many years."

"He is a troublemaker." Haman spoke in a flat voice, then lifted a warning finger. "I have heard that he might associate with a most peculiar and troublesome people—"

"Accountants?" Again I flashed a wide smile. "I have known many accountants in my life, and while some of them are not very talkative, most of them are good company."

"Not accountants." He spat the words at me. "He lives near others of his kind. You must know the people I speak of. They are close-knit, they worship an invisible god, they intermarry and will not give their daughters to anyone outside their clans—"

I responded with a wide-eyed stare.

Haman drew an exasperated breath, then tried again. "Perhaps you have heard the word *Jew*? The people who came here from Judea?"

"Ah." I smiled even more broadly than before. "I have heard of them. They have never brought the king any trouble."

"They should be wiped off the face of the earth." Haman glowered at me, then tugged on the edges of his robe and rearranged his face into pleasant lines. "If you see your friend again, remind him of the king's latest edict. He must obey or accept the consequences. And those consequences, as you know, can be severe. I pity the man who breaks the king's laws."

I nodded, then stood by a column until the crowd dispersed and I alone remained in the polished stillness. Then I shook off my alarm and hurried out of the throne room.

Chapter Thirty-Eight
HADASSAH

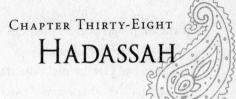

Since my husband began spending all his time with a new favorite, my life had fallen into a peaceful and largely pointless routine. I woke every morning and submitted to the ministrations of my handmaids. They drew my bath, rubbed my skin with salt and oil, rinsed me clean, washed my hair, and anointed me with perfume. After the bath, hairdressing, and application of cosmetics, they dressed me in garments I would have desperately coveted as a young girl. Now they seemed little more than an unnecessary extravagance.

After dressing, I ate a light meal with my little dog, then I played with the royal children in the queen's garden. Of all the hours in my day, I enjoyed this time most. The toddling boys I had met five years ago were now training with bows and arrows; the girls were learning to sing and dance. The crown prince and his two younger brothers were on their way to becoming young men. I watched them all, proud of their progress, and quietly missed Pharnaces, who had never been found.

I once had Hatakh make discreet inquiries about the boy's disappearance, but after a day or two of searching he appeared in my chambers and told me that the boy's disappearance would—and should—remain a mystery. "Some things," he said, lifting a brow as he peered into my eyes, "are better off left alone."

I had no idea what he meant, but accepted his response as a reminder that a queen's power was quite limited.

When we finished our games, the children and I would sit in the shade while I told stories I'd learned from Mordecai—tales of David and Solomon, of Gideon and Joshua. I told them about King Saul, who had been richly blessed until he disobeyed, causing Adonai to give the throne to another.

The story had already escaped my lips when I realized it could come back to haunt me. If the king heard that I had taught his children a story about a failed ruler who lost his throne . . .

I smiled around the circle of young faces, hoping to change the subject. "And how are all of you today? Have you heard any interesting stories lately?"

"I have." Darius, the crown prince, lifted his chin and boldly met my gaze. "I heard that you are a mere commoner and ashamed of your heritage. That is why you never talk about your father's family."

"An interesting rumor." I smiled without humor. "Unfortunately, it is not true. I am descended from a great king, but I never talk about my father's family because they are all gone. And I have learned that it is better to be concerned with the living than the dead."

"Which king?" several of the children chorused, but I shook my head. "What does it matter? Your father is the greatest king in the world, and I am his. I am yours too, so why shouldn't we live together in peace?"

My time with the children touched the barren place in my heart—

sometimes filling it, sometimes opening the wound that still ached every time I looked at those sweet little faces. But I had turned my yearning for babies into a desire to influence the king's children. Someone had to teach them as Mordecai and Miriam taught me. They needed to know that life consisted of more than jostling for power and destroying one's enemies. They ought to know that they'd been created for a purpose, and that purpose was to know the one true God.

The Persians knew gods, of course—a plethora of them. The king worshipped Ahura Mazda, in statuary inscriptions at least, and on every important feast day my king would meet a priest, travel to an outdoor altar, and sacrifice an ox to ensure prosperity in the coming season. In private, however, rarely did the king ever talk of his god as anything other than a distant entity who required seasonal acknowledgment in order to keep the annual cycles of harvest and reaping on course. The priest's prayers were more like ritual recitation than conversation, and if Ahura Mazda *had* ever performed a bona fide miracle, I was convinced no one would have been more astounded than my husband.

In truth, my years of marriage had convinced me that my husband was the god of his own life—he did what he wanted, when he wanted to do it. Only the great law of the Medes and the Persians constrained him, yet the king could amend those statutes so long as he did not change any decree that preceded his amendment.

Did I still love him? I did, but in a far different way than I had in our early months together. My giddy infatuation, born in the first blush of physical intimacy, had matured into something more compassionate, even maternal. As I shared weekly meals with my husband, I realized he was prone to extremes of light and darkness—he could be delighted with a new horse, a new treasure, or with me, and on those occasions he would laugh and talk as though shadows had never lain across his heart.

On other occasions, some dark memory or nightmare would

torment his mind, leaving him sleepless and irritable, desperate for surcease. When he was in the grip of such darkness, I couldn't help being relieved when he chose to leave me in my chambers . . . but then guilt would avalanche over me. What if I had the power to lighten his mood? Couldn't my love make a difference in his outlook? I contemplated going to him on my own, but I never carried through. No rational being would approach the king unannounced while darkness occupied his thoughts.

By the time my king prepared to enter the twelfth year of his reign, I knew my marriage would not be the romantic dream I had envisioned as a girl. But I had learned to adapt and was happy pouring my love into the royal children and my little dog. The situation might have continued for many more years, but then I met the interloper who had come between us.

One day the king asked me to join him in the audience hall. I did, and I was amazed to discover a stranger standing by my husband's side. "Haman," one of my maids whispered. "He has become . . . *close* to the king."

At our first meeting, I thought the new vizier charming. He was not a handsome man, nor unusually dignified, but he had a bright charisma that seemed to compel the other nobles to include him in their conversations. He also had obvious wealth, which he lavished on his wardrobe and on gifts for those in the royal circle.

I had no trouble understanding why the newcomer had become so popular. When he was presented to me, he knelt before my gilded chair and produced a necklace from a velvet bag—a gold chain featuring a pearl pendant. Pearls were a rare sight in our court, and Haman quickly explained that they were formed when a common sea creature discovered an irritating grain of sand inside its shell.

"The humble oyster wraps a material around the sand," he went on, peering at me through half-closed eyelids, "and from trouble comes beauty. Judging by the size of this pearl, this oyster was

troubled indeed." He then offered me the gift, along with a wish
that my troubles would always result in beauty like that of a pearl.

I accepted his gift with a polite smile, then handed it to one of
my maids. In truth, I wasn't sure I wanted to be indebted to this
stranger—he reminded me of the sort of man Mordecai referenced
when he warned about those who flatter with their lips.

But Haman paid only perfunctory attention to me, and before
I left the throne room I realized I'd been tricked. Despite what
Vashti wanted me to believe, my king wasn't in love with another
woman; he had become fascinated with this man. Still, I wasn't
terribly concerned about Haman until I learned that the man had
begun to eat late dinners with the king, often talking with him
well into the night . . . when the king could have been with me.

I might have borne my concerns privately, except for a chance
meeting with Harbonah in the king's garden. Harbonah bowed,
wished me life and good health, then lowered his voice and asked
what I thought about Haman the Agagite.

"I've only spent a few moments with him," I said truthfully.
"What do you think of the man?"

The eunuch's mouth curled as if he wanted to spit. "I don't like
him."

I lifted a brow, for Harbonah rarely spoke so bluntly. "What
has he done?"

"As far as I can tell, he has done nothing improper, but his talk is
so smooth and flattering I know he cannot be trusted. Worse still,
when the king is in a dark mood, Haman tells him not to worry,
for *he* will take care of everything. So the king takes the man at his
word, surrendering his authority and his position to that upstart."

I knew I shouldn't be listening to gossip from a slave, even one
I trusted as much as Harbonah. But he served the man I loved,
and he undoubtedly had a better understanding of the situation
than anyone else.

"That's not all." Harbonah took a half step closer and lowered his voice to a confidential note. "This Haman has been spying on your cousin. Mordecai has never prostrated himself before Haman, and he will not do so despite the king's edict. Every day Haman rides past Mordecai's post, and your cousin merely stares at him. Haman has not reacted yet, but I fear for your cousin and my friend. Haman has the king's ear—"

So do I. The words sprang to my lips, but I could not utter a lie. I shivered as my blood ran cold. "You must warn Mordecai."

"I've tried." The eunuch's voice cracked with desperation. "I've talked to him, but the man is as stubborn as a bloodstain. He won't lower himself to a creature such as Haman."

"Does he give a reason?"

Harbonah grunted. "He says something about his people and your people and ancient rivalries. And he doesn't like Haman's attitude."

"He must be more careful." I pressed my lips together as my thoughts raced. "Harbonah, you must take Mordecai a note from me. Maybe for my sake he will obey the law."

Harbonah drew a deep breath, then pressed the bridge of his nose as if his head ached. "I pray you are right. A sincere warning from the right person might break the man's will."

"Let us handle the matter at once." I walked toward the garden gate, quickening my pace as Harbonah followed the required distance behind me. Once we reached the queen's palace, the eunuch waited in the antechamber while I went to my desk and scratched out a note on a sheet of papyrus. I folded it, sealed it with wax and the imprint of my ring, then went into the antechamber to deliver the message.

"Hurry, Harbonah," I said, placing the letter in the eunuch's hand. "Take this to Mordecai before the king notices your absence. This foolish standoff must not continue for even one more day."

CHAPTER THIRTY-NINE
HARBONAH

BREATHLESS FROM CLIMBING THE KING'S STAIRCASE for the fourth time in a single day, I paused at the upper landing and braced my heaving body against a glazed portrait of minions offering treasures to King Darius. I was too old to play errand boy, even for the queen and her cousin. I had carried her warning to Mordecai; he sent back a terse reply: he would not bow to a son of Amalek. After delivering his message, I ran back down to the accounting office to whisper that the queen was upset to the point of tears; wouldn't her cousin capitulate and obey the king's law? Mordecai, as stubborn as a stuck door, again told his ward—his queen—that some things were more important than pleasing a king. He would not bow.

To make matters worse, Haman was now striding toward me, his strides long and his brow set in a straight line. He must have heard about my sprints up and down the grand staircase, and he would want to know why I had so many dealings with a Jewish accountant in the king's treasury.

"You! Eunuch!"

As I bent and prostrated myself on the cobbled pavement, I closed my eyes and drew a deep breath, overcoming an inexplicable urge to slap the vizier for ruining my afternoon. "Sir?"

"You are acquainted with the scribe called Mordecai, are you not?"

Too weary to play the idiot again, I looked up and nodded.

"Did you obey my order and visit him? Have you asked if he has a death wish? If he wants to be impaled? Or perhaps he would prefer to be tied between two stallions and pulled apart? Such are the penalties for those who break the king's laws."

I swallowed hard. "I'm sure you know the empire is made up of many different peoples."

"I do not need a lesson in Persian affairs."

"Well, then." I rose to my knees, and only with great difficulty did I manage to suppress a cocky smile. "Mordecai says he will not bow because he is a Jew."

Anger blossomed in the man's round face. "I knew it! That arrogant—"

"Excuse me, sir, but Mordecai is not arrogant. He has been humble and pleasant in all his dealings with the people."

"But he will not obey the king's law."

"Begging your pardon, sir, but the law of the Medes and the Persians allows Mordecai to uphold the traditions of his people. The older law supersedes the newer, and Mordecai is free *not* to bow before you. To do so would violate his sensibilities as a Jew."

Haman stiffened, then narrowed one eye in a squint. "You are much changed since our first meeting."

I shrugged. "Though I am a eunuch and a slave, I am not made of unthinking stone. I can reason as well as any man—and better than most."

"Then tell me, O reasoning eunuch, would this Mordecai not bow before the king? If he met the queen, would he not show any sort of obeisance?"

The insertion of my queen into the conversation set prickles of unease nipping at the back of my knees, but Haman had no reason to suspect any connection between Hadassah and Mordecai. Still, better to turn the subject away from Queen Esther.

I pressed my hand to my chest as a bead of perspiration snaked a path from my armpit to my lowest rib. "I am certain Mordecai would prostrate himself before the king and any other figure deserving of his respect. Mordecai's people fear the king and obey the law. The way my friend explained it, the only nobleman he will not bow before is you, because you are an Amalekite. Apparently the God of the Jews has cursed the people of Amalek for something that happened long ago."

Haman gritted his teeth and drew back his hand—and I knew only my relationship with the king saved me from a hard slap.

"I should have *smelled* him," Haman growled, lowering his arm. "No wonder that man torments me. His cursed race has afflicted my people ever since Saul decimated the city of Agag. . . ."

He stalked away, muttering under his breath, and I smiled as I watched him go.

⚜

During Nisan, the first month of the king's twelfth regal year, Haman gathered a group of toadies in the open area outside the entrance to the King's Gate. I had been out stretching my legs while the king breakfasted, but when I saw Haman holding court in such a public place, I slowed my step to see what he was about.

His minions had gathered around Haman and a priest of Ahura Mazda, who wore his traditional white robe. Haman's sons were among the crowd, but neither they nor the other onlookers appeared at all solemn. Indeed, after some unintelligible joke and the resultant burst of laughter, one of Haman's sons produced a pair of *puru*, or lots, and handed them to the priest. The smiling priest chanted something, sprinkled some sort of sand over the stones, and then tossed them against a carved rock on the ground.

The priest stood back to let the king's vizier read the outcome.

"Ah." Haman studied the stones with a smile. "A twelve and a thirteen—the thirteenth day of the twelfth month. They say the greatest Jew in the world died in the twelfth month, so perhaps the last month of the year is unlucky for the descendants of Jacob. Perhaps their God is tired, so he goes off to take a nap in the month of Adar."

As the vizier's sycophants laughed, Haman strolled away, heading toward the grand staircase and presumably on his way to visit the king. I caught my breath, about to run forward and cut him off lest he interrupt my master, then I thought the better of it. Why not let him disturb the king? Maybe Haman deserved to feel my master's undiluted irritation.

I found Mordecai working at his post. "Friend," I called, too preoccupied by what I had just witnessed to greet him properly, "who was the greatest Jew in the world?"

Mordecai looked up, his brows raised, then returned his gaze to a clay tablet filled with numbers. "Only HaShem knows the answer to such a question."

"But what would men say? Who do you think the greatest Jew in the world would be?"

Mordecai put down his stylus and studied me. "Some would say Abraham. Some would say Jacob. But I would say Moses. We have not had a tzaddik like him since." Mordecai's squint tightened. "Why do you ask?"

"When did this Moses die?"

"Before we crossed into the Promised Land."

"But when? Did he die in the month of Adar?"

A line appeared between the accountant's brows. "From the writings of Joshua, yes, we can deduce that Moses died in the last month of the year."

My jaw tightened as understanding dawned. "I don't know what Haman is up to, but he's planning something for Adar. Something that has to do with you, I'm sure. Maybe something that will affect all of your people."

Mordecai's mouth curved in a smirk. "What could Haman be planning? I have broken no law other than the king's edict. And if Haman wanted to have me arrested for not bowing, he could do it long before Adar. As far as punishing the Jews, the king has already halted work on our temple. What else could he do, impose a Jewish tax?"

"I don't think Haman would hire a professional diviner to choose a date for new taxes," I warned. "And you must not forget that he despises you. Every day you refuse to bow or even stand in his presence is another day his hatred grows. You must keep your wits about you."

"So the man hates one Jew." Mordecai shrugged and picked up his stylus. "I will be careful, but there are yet thousands of Jews scattered throughout the earth. Adonai has promised that we shall be as numerous as the sand of the sea."

"But his hatred—trust me, my friend—is as deep as the ocean. And it grows deeper every day."

I sank to a stool against the wall and crossed my legs. From what I'd seen and heard, Haman's animosity seemed to extend far beyond a feeling for one particular Jew. Yes, he hated Mordecai, but his comments about "those people" and "their God" seemed to indicate he hated the entire race.

"Why?" I looked up at the accountant. "Why would Haman

hate your people? Today he sneered as if he would wipe every Jew from the earth if he could."

"Then we should be grateful he is not all-powerful." Mordecai lowered his stylus again. "Some hatreds have roots far beyond the present generation, my friend. I have told you that the Jews are descended from Jacob; the Amalekites from Esau. Before those twins were born, Adonai revealed that they would produce two rival nations, and the older would serve the younger. As the Lord foretold, Jacob received the birthright and blessing from his father, Isaac. Esau's descendants have resented us ever since."

"So nothing can be done to heal the breach between your two tribes?"

"Jacob and Esau reconciled, though Jacob never fully trusted his brother," Mordecai answered. "And Adonai's promise cannot be denied. He builds up and He tears down, and no man can argue with His purposes."

The accountant studied me for a long moment, then smiled. "Do not worry about me. If Haman hasn't done anything by now, he won't." Mordecai picked up his stylus again and glanced at the scribblings on a nearby parchment. "And if he's planning mischief for Adar, that's nearly a year away. Today is much too early to worry about such a resentful little man."

⁓⁂⁓

What could Haman be planning?

I carried that unsettling question with me for a full twenty-four hours before I learned the answer. At the end of the following day, at the time the king used to send for the queen to join him for dinner, he summoned Haman instead. I gritted my teeth as the eunuchs left with the invitation, realizing the king was as enthralled by Haman as ever.

I helped the king dress in a comfortable cotton tunic, then arranged his couch the way he liked it, at an angle to his dining partner's. I had just placed a bowl of sliced apples, dates, and grapes on the king's tray when the eunuchs returned, Haman strolling casually in their midst.

The Agagite ignored me, of course, but lowered himself to the shining marble floor and shouted an enthusiastic greeting, "O king, most blessed of men, most glorious and magnificent, live forever and prosper!"

"Rise, Haman." The king smiled and gestured to the empty couch. "I hope you are hungry after our long day. This is the hour when we relax and think of more pleasant things than Babylon and taxes and famine. This is when we forget about troublemakers in Greece and your problems with that new stallion."

Walking backward, I left the open area and tucked myself into an alcove. Through the sheer curtain that hid me, I could watch and listen without being noticed.

"My king." With a frown on his brow, Haman pounded his chest and rose to one knee. "As much as I would enjoy relaxing with you, I fear I cannot abide talk of such trivial things as a stubborn stallion. Today I have learned of trouble in the empire, trouble that need not concern you but greatly distresses me."

The king froze, an apple in his hand. "Rise, friend, and tell me about this calamity."

Haman took a seat on his couch, his hands resting on his knees. "I'm concerned about a particular people who seem intent on fomenting rebellion in the empire."

The king reached for a grape and popped it into his mouth. "Forget your concern, friend Haman, for I have dealt with this before. I will simply appoint a new provincial governor and send my army to enforce his authority."

Haman's brows drew together in an agonized expression. "Therein lies the problem, for they don't dwell in a particular region. Like noxious weeds, they lie scattered among all the provinces of your empire. Yet they are clannish and keep to their own. They don't intermarry with other tribes, their ways differ from those of the king's other subjects, and they ignore the king's laws. Often they flaunt their disobedience, as though the law of the Medes and the Persians had no authority over them. They have been cheats and liars since the beginning of their lineage."

When a shadow fell over the king's face, I knew Haman had scored a direct hit. My master allowed his conquered territories a measure of freedom, but never were they free to ignore his edicts. Furthermore, Persian tutors stressed three important skills when they taught young princes: horsemanship, bowmanship, and virtue, or the necessity of telling the truth.

The Persian love for truth was nowhere as evident as on the lower epitaph of King Darius's tomb. Of his father, my master had written, *By the favor of Ahura Mazda I am of such a sort that I am a friend to right, I am not a friend to wrong. . . . What is right, that is my desire. I am not a friend to the man who is a lie-follower.*

"Go on," the king said, his eyes narrowing.

"These people concern me," Haman continued, "and I can't think of any reason for the king to tolerate them. So if it please the king—and know that I have given this a great deal of consideration—let it be written that they are designated for destruction."

My master looked up, his eyes mere slits in his face, and I knew what he was thinking—who would dare stir up trouble for him now? The royal treasury had yet to fully recover from the disastrous war against the Greeks, and though he would never admit it, the king's psyche still bore a deep wound from that loss.

"The king need not worry over the trouble or the expense," Haman went on, apparently oblivious to my master's troubled frown. "I will personally hand over three hundred thirty tons of silver to the officials in charge of the king's affairs to deposit in the royal treasury."

Behind the curtain, I nearly choked on my astonishment. Haman, who obviously loved his money and all that it could buy, wanted to donate a fortune to the royal treasury? And he had used the word *destruction*, though I doubt the king realized its full significance. My king was more focused on rebellion, liars, and a fortune for his treasury.

I was still reeling with disbelief when the king slipped his signet ring from his finger and dropped it into Haman's outstretched palm.

"If you are convinced that this group means trouble for the empire," the king said, his eyes closing, "then see to your plan. The money is given to you, and the people too—do with them as seems good to you."

I pressed my hand over my mouth to choke off a cry. A smile snaked over Haman's thin lips as he slipped the royal ring on his own hand. "I will see to it at once," he said, oil in his voice. "Letters written in your name will be distributed to all the royal provinces. And when the matter of this troublesome people is settled, all will be well in the empire."

Let it be written . . . what innocent words! Haman had not asked the king to murder or execute; he had cloaked his request in passive language that never quite penetrated my master's thoughts.

Then Haman lifted his silver goblet and offered a toast. "To the eternal health of the empire, its people, and its king!"

The king lifted his own goblet, touched it to Haman's, and drank deeply.

꧁꧂

On the thirteenth day of Nisan, Haman summoned the scribes to the royal audience hall—not to take transcription from the king, but from Haman himself. He stood in front of the throne, flashing the king's signet ring as he read notes from a parchment scroll. I held my breath, half expecting him to sit on my master's throne, but he had not yet reached that level of effrontery. When would he?

The scribes looked at each other, exchanging wordless expressions of alarm, but no one spoke as they wrote out Haman's orders to the army commanders and governors in all one hundred twenty-seven provinces, to each province in its own script and to each people in their own language. The edict was authorized in the name of King Xerxes and sealed with the signet ring in Haman's hand.

My blood still chills when I recall the wording of the edict:

> "Thus says Xerxes, King of Persia: all the kingdoms of the earth has Ahura Mazda given me, and he has charged me with ridding the empire of all who deal falsely, who follow lies and do not honor the truth. In order to preserve the peace of the empire, on the thirteenth day of the month of Adar, every person in the empire, young and old, is given the authority and command to destroy, kill, and exterminate all Jews, from young to old, including small children and women, and to seize their goods as plunder."

Something in me wanted to stand and protest this action, but such an act would mean almost certain death. And so it was that one of the world's greatest empires, one that tolerated diversity and respected the individuality of its subject peoples, prepared to annihilate one of those peoples because they were different.

Nothing about Haman's edict made sense, but my master had been so blinded by Haman's flattery, half-truths, and lies that he had not given serious thought to the matter. Haman had convinced my king that the Jews were traitors without offering any proof or testimony other than his own. The king had asked no questions and demanded no examples of the allegedly treasonous people. He had stupidly, foolishly played into Haman's hands.

The king's unthinking obedience worried me, but I did not dare confess my fears to anyone in the palace, for to doubt the king would be treasonous. His once-sharp mind had been dulled by depression, defeat, and disillusionment . . . or perhaps he had simply given up. Failing to live up to his father's example, he seemed content to hand over government to his vizier and take his pleasures in the harem and the hunt.

When the meeting adjourned, the scribes hurried to transcribe final copies of the inflammatory edict. When finished, they dispatched letters to the post, from where they would be carried by mounted couriers to all the royal provinces and distributed throughout the empire. Once received, a copy of the document would be publicly proclaimed to all the people in every province so they would be ready for the appointed day.

As riders raced out of the royal fortress and headed toward destinations in the north, south, east, and west, I knew the governor of Susa had to be reading the edict with great apprehension. He knew Susa had a thriving Jewish community; he probably had Jews working in his office. But he could not question the just-delivered document, nor could he refuse to proclaim it.

I left the palace as soon as I heard the trumpets. Every citizen of Susa knew the trumpets heralded an assembly, and so, like me, they left their work and headed toward the bazaar, where the governor waited to deliver his address.

I stood in the shadows with folded arms as the governor climbed the steps of a platform. Around him, a sea of residents, merchants, diplomats, artists, and farmers stood looking up at him with questions in their eyes.

With trembling hands he unrolled the scroll and read the edict. When he had finished, a heavy silence answered him, a silence that then erupted in cries of horror and confusion.

I did not linger. My master would be looking for me, so I ran up the grand staircase and hurried to the king's chamber, where I found him and Haman having another pleasant drink together.

Struggling to maintain my composure, I served the wine as my master and Haman banqueted and drank until dawn.

Then, knowing I would be beaten if my master woke and found me gone, I ran from the palace, flew down the grand staircase, and went in search of Mordecai, burdened with the details I had to share.

CHAPTER FORTY

HADASSAH

THE FOURTEENTH DAY OF NISAN began like any other. I woke, my maids brought me breakfast in bed, and we talked and laughed together while I ate and played with my little dog. Hulta had ordered a new tunic for me, so she slipped away to fetch it from a dressmaker in Susa.

She returned later that morning, her face flushed and her veil askew. "My queen," she said, falling before me with unusual clumsiness, "I bring news of your cousin."

My maids had known of my association with Mordecai for years, and had been faithful to join in the quiet conspiracy that allowed me to communicate with my cousin. But I had heard nothing from Mordecai the day before.

I lifted my hand to silence the harpist playing for my amusement. "Has something happened to Mordecai?"

When she lifted her head, I saw the tracks of tears on her cheeks. "He is not at his post, my queen."

I felt my stomach drop. "Is he ill?"

"He is in the city square, dressed in sackcloth and covered in ashes. He cannot enter the King's Gate dressed in mourning, so he kneels on the cobblestones and wails his lament. He would not leave, despite the urgings of many who have urged him to go home."

Mordecai in sackcloth? I pressed my hand to my mouth and let my mind run backward, sorting through names and faces of our friends and distant relatives. Had someone close to him died? Perhaps someone from the synagogue or one of the neighbors.

Surely not. Mordecai had met death before, and he had never carried on in the city square. He did not wear sackcloth even for Miriam.

I rose from my bed and hurried to the room we used as a wardrobe. The walls were covered with garments, fine tunics and cloaks, fine enough for a queen or her cousin.

"Here." I drew out a nondescript robe of dark linen. "Take this, and a gold belt, and find some decent sandals to fit a man. I don't know what ails my cousin, but I can't have him sitting in the square. Take a shawl, something to cover his head, and see if one of the eunuchs will go with you. He needs to go home, change his clothes, and compose himself."

My maids flew into action, knowing even better than I what a respectable older man should wear. Within minutes they had folded a stack of fine garments, a gift any man should be happy to receive.

Even Mordecai.

"Hulta and Rokita, please take these at once," I instructed. "Be firm with my cousin and see that he dresses properly and returns to his post. If he protests, remind him . . . remind him that he is cousin to the queen." I said these last words in a hoarse whisper, but my maids understood. They drew their veils over their faces and hurried away, intent on their errand.

I went to the balcony, mentally tracking their steps as I looked

over the garden and the river in the distance. Had age begun to
affect Mordecai's mind? Had some trivial loss sent him over the
edge and driven him to dress in burlap? He had always been the
most dignified of men, the most self-possessed. The thought of
him on his knees in the street, pouring ashes on his head while he
wailed in some imagined agony . . .

I shivered as a heavy weight settled in my stomach. I would
care for Mordecai no matter his condition, but how could I care
for him while I lived in the palace? For all the luxury around me,
I lived in a gilded cage. I could not go to Mordecai personally, nor
could I bring him to live with me. I could, perhaps, arrange for
someone to live with him, someone who would cook for him and
make certain he did not hurt himself. . . .

I gripped the edge of the balcony as an eerie howling rose from
the city beyond the royal fortress. Susa, it seemed, had either been
taken over by grief or my cousin had developed a hundred agonized
voices.

❧

Hulta and Rokita returned within the hour. Hulta still carried the
garments I had sent, and Rokita's eyes watered with unshed tears.

"Live forever, my lady," Rokita said, falling before me. "We found
your cousin, but he would not take the clothes."

"Nor would he be persuaded to leave," Hulta added. "He is
sound in mind and body, my queen, and he insisted that he has
reason to mourn."

"But why?" I looked from Hulta to Rokita for an answer, but
their faces remained blank. "What has happened to put him in
such a state?"

Hatakh, who had been silently waiting at the back of the chamber, stepped forward. "Shall I go to him, my queen?"

I blinked, stunned by a glimmer in my chief eunuch's eye. He knew something he was not willing to tell me.

"Hatakh, do you know why my cousin mourns in the city square?"

The eunuch met my gaze without flinching. "I have an idea."

"Will you tell me?"

His eyes remained deadly serious. "I dare not spread rumors, my queen. But I am willing to speak to your cousin and return to you. I will tell you everything he says."

I stared, probing his countenance for some clue, but Hatakh had not achieved his high position through transparency. "All right, go at once. And bring me the full story. I must know what has upset my cousin so."

I spent the rest of the morning pacing in my chamber. When I wasn't pacing, I stood outside on the balcony, listening for cries on the wind. Once or twice I thought I heard sustained wailing, but the sounds of music, workmen, and the harem children drowned out most of the city sounds.

Finally Hatakh returned, and not empty-handed. He carried a leather satchel, and from it he withdrew a parchment scroll. "The king's vizier," he said, not wasting time with formalities, "has written a decree in the king's name. According to the edict, on the thirteenth day of Adar, every Persian has the right to kill any Jew, young or old, and confiscate their belongings." He unfurled the scroll and handed it to me. "The edict has been published and proclaimed throughout the empire."

I skimmed the document and gasped as the words blurred before my eyes. "How can this be? How could the king allow something so senseless and cruel?"

Hatakh had a servant's face; almost anything could have been going on behind that blank facade, yet his eyes narrowed with dislike. "Mordecai knew more of the story, my queen. This is completely

Haman's doing. He persuaded the king with half-truths born out of hatred and personal animosity for your cousin. He also offered to deposit three hundred thirty tons of silver into the king's treasury in order to enact the decree."

"Surely the king refused!"

"He did, my lady, as one will when bargaining, but the money will still be paid and given back to Haman to pursue this evil end. And finally there is this: your cousin directs you to go to the king to beg for mercy and plead for your people."

Your cousin directs you . . .

The words hung in the air, dancing before my eyes. Mordecai had not commanded me in years, not since I left his house, yet now he was commanding me again. As my adoptive father, he had every right to do so, but did he realize what he was saying? Everyone knew that to boldly walk into the king's throne room meant instant death. I had done it once before to save the king's life, but his love had given me courage. Things were different now. Yet that's what Mordecai was asking . . . no, *commanding* me to do.

I turned to Hatakh. "Go to my cousin again," I said. "And remind him—pointedly—that he must know that for me to go to the king means death. He is not asking an easy thing."

Hatakh nodded, acknowledging my concern.

"Furthermore—" my voice broke—"tell him the king has not called for me in over a month. So—never mind. Just tell him; he'll understand."

He would understand that the king's love for me had grown cool. He'd understand that I was no longer the king's favorite, so I had no assurance that he'd look on me with favor. If he wanted to be rid of me as he had wanted to be rid of Vashti, it would be easy for him not to extend his scepter and grant me mercy.

"Go," I told Hatakh. "I will not move from this spot until I receive your reply."

Hatakh returned a short while later—so quickly, in fact, that I wondered if he had only pretended to speak to my cousin.

But his reply was pure Mordecai. "Your cousin," the eunuch began, "says you should not imagine that you will escape just because you live in the palace. You are hidden at the moment, but you will not always be secreted away. And do not trust in the king's protection—if you doubt his loyalty now, you will doubt it after the thirteenth of Adar. If you avoid approaching the king, you will still be in jeopardy. It is as dangerous for you to stay away from the king as it is for you to go to him.

"Mordecai," Hatakh went on, "says that if you keep quiet at this time, deliverance and relief for the Jews will come from some other place, but you and your relatives will die. And who knows if you were made queen for just such a time as this?"

I lifted my head, waiting for something else, but Hatakh had finished. I smiled my thanks, then gestured for him and all the maids to leave the room.

I needed to be alone. I needed time to think.

When the last servant had closed the door, I crawled onto my couch and buried my face in my hands. Who was I, and why had I been thrust into this place? I was no obedient Jewish girl; I had not yearned for martyrdom or a prophet's mantle. I was no brave soldier like Deborah, no prophetess like Miriam, no devoutly praying Hannah. I was a foolish girl who yearned for luxury and lovely dresses and social status. I had been so concerned with superficial things that my first thought today had been to get Mordecai out of embarrassing sackcloth and into a proper tunic. To get him out of the dust and back to the King's Gate.

And that, I now realized, was why he dressed in rags. He had not resorted to public mourning because he felt responsible for

Haman's edict, for who blames the victim for the injustice done to him? He could easily have sent me a message, so he had not poured ashes on his head merely to get my attention.

He had dressed in mourning because he knew a public display would spur me to action. That I would promise anything to get him off the street.

By dressing in sackcloth, Mordecai had held up a mirror, forcing me to see my own superficiality and self-centeredness. I didn't want to go to the king because I feared losing my life—how could I even utter those words when thousands of other Jews would lose their lives if I didn't go?

Moses, Gideon, and Saul, my own kinsmen, had expressed hesitation when Adonai asked them to accept a difficult task, but they had expressed their fears in terms of their unworthiness of HaShem's call. I had expressed mine as simple cowardice.

I was terrified. Of watching my husband reject me. Of seeing a hard, cold light in his eyes. Of hearing the swish of a swift sword as it curved toward my neck.

I paused to take a few deep breaths, to knit the raveled cloth of my courage.

As always, Mordecai had led me to see the truth, as unpleasant as it was. And since thousands of Persians called me queen, the time had come for me to act like royalty. But how did I do that?

I closed my eyes and heard Mordecai's voice on a wave of memory. *"HaShem has commanded us to fast on one day only, the Day of Atonement. On this day we consider our unworthiness and our sin, and we repent of our disobedience. We end our fast with thanksgiving and a commitment to live differently, so we will not fall into sin again."*

A fast? I had not fasted since coming to the palace.

As a child I had voluntarily fasted with Miriam and Mordecai on various ritual days. But for me the fast had been only a minor inconvenience, for I gorged myself before sunrise and stuffed my empty stomach as soon as the sun set.

This fast would be different. I would follow Mordecai's instruction, denying myself food so that I might think of the ways of Adonai and commit myself to His plan, no matter what it might be. I would repent of my shallow self-centeredness, and I would confess that my heart had been set on my pleasures and not His will. I would spend the days of my fast in prayer and contemplation, forgetting about food, cosmetics, frivolous pursuits, and the luxury of my bathing ritual.

I would send my little dog to stay with the harem children.

I would wear a simple linen gown and wait alone in my chamber, feeding my soul instead of my body. And when I felt Adonai's strength flowing through my veins, I would rise, dress, and do my duty.

I raised my voice and called for my servants. When they had all returned, I met Hatakh's gaze head on. "Give my cousin this message: Go and gather together all the Jews of Susa and fast for me. Do not eat or drink for three days, night or day. My maids and I will do the same. And then, though it is against the law, I will go to see the king. If I must die, I must die."

And that, Hatakh reported when he returned, was enough to persuade Mordecai to go home and change his clothes.

꙳

After explaining my plan to fast for three days, a horrified Hatakh protested that going so long without food or water would deprive me of my beauty, the thing I would need most to win mercy from the king.

Beauty? I wanted to laugh. As a child I had yearned for it, as a new bride I had been grateful for it, and as a queen I had realized its deficiencies. Solomon was right—beauty was fleeting, and now I wanted the king to love me for the woman I was beneath the cosmetics and perfumes. I wanted him to yearn for my company, my thoughts, and my soul. I did not want to be just another beauty from the harem.

After giving Hatakh a wan smile, I closed the doors to my chambers, locking myself and my maids inside. I didn't worry about the king sending for me—the last month had proved how completely I had been replaced in his thoughts and affections. Whether my rival was another woman or a vizier, what did it matter?

The king no longer loved me like he once did. And I could no longer make excuses for his inattention.

Thus began the darkest hours of my life. I walked through my rooms with the shutters drawn to block the sun. I did not want sunshine and brightness; I wanted no reminders of the beautiful plain beneath the palace mount. I did not want to look out upon the citizens of Susa, because I had to face a hard truth: over the years, I had insulated myself from reality. I had come to care for my sheltered self more than I cared for my own people.

By wearing torn burlap and ashes, my cousin had reminded me that we Jews were not like the rest of the world. We walked in it, traded in it, communicated in it, and did acts of kindness for it. To the casual observer, we might have looked like ordinary people, but we were not. About that, at least, Haman was right.

We were children of Abraham, Isaac, and Jacob, and we served an invisible God, who remained close to us no matter where we lived. But our hearts did not—should not—belong to this world.

Caught up in a flood of memory, I closed my eyes and heard Mordecai reading from Deuteronomy: *"What great nation is there that has God as close to them as Adonai our God is, whenever we call on him? What great nation is there that has laws and rulings as just as this entire Torah which I am setting before you today?"*

Though we had disobeyed HaShem's laws and rulings, and though He had scattered us throughout the world, preserving only a remnant in our beloved Jerusalem, still He had promised never to desert us. Never to abandon us. As long as we did not abandon Him.

I had done exactly what my people had done. I had grown up knowing about HaShem and His requirements of a holy people, but I had kept His precepts at arm's length, observing them in my head while my heart exulted in the world around me. I had refrained from work on the Sabbath while dreaming of a Persian boy; I had worn modest gowns while coveting the luxurious silks of the merchant's daughter. I had been reluctant to marry Binyamin, and I had secretly rejoiced to find myself living in the palace, where I could indulge every hidden yearning while affecting an air of quiet martyrdom when speaking to Mordecai.

Now my life hung in the balance, as did the lives of my people. And all I could do was pray.

I had no answers. I had no assurances. I had no children to guarantee my place in the harem. Even if the king chose to spare my life when I went to him, he could very well cast me away or sell me into slavery, and no one would protest.

But if I did not go to the king, thousands of Jews, possibly thousands of thousands, would not survive the year.

For two full days and nights my maids and I prayed for courage, for resolve, and for strength. I confessed my sins, my frailty, and my idol worship. Though I had never bowed before a graven image, I had worshipped my love the king, and for a while he had been my everything. And no one but Adonai should hold that place in my heart.

I wept and prayed, though prayer gave me no answers and no assurances.

What it gave me was the confidence that I would stand before my God and my king with a clear conscience.

CHAPTER FORTY-ONE

HARBONAH

WHEN YOU ARE A SERVANT—especially if you are a slave and have grown up in service—those who order you about and wait for you to provide food, clothing, and whatever else they may need, tend to forget that you have a mind and feelings of your own.

On the third morning of Queen Esther's fast, I stepped into the king's bedchamber and dragged a young concubine out of his bed. The girl was heavy-footed and sleepy, so it was with great difficulty that I managed to get her into a robe and send her back to the harem. I would let Hegai take care of the concubine; the king was my priority.

I crept around the room, cracking the shutters so that the morning light could gently wake my master. Haman had remained at the palace until late last night; he and the king had downed many cups of wine before Haman departed and the king sent for a woman. I went to bed after that. The king probably fell asleep before the girl arrived, but she had remained in his bed, undoubtedly to boast to her peers.

I set out the chamber pot and poured fresh water into a basin, then laid out a towel and a bottle of oil for his hair and beard. A servant brought a bowl of fresh fruit and bread; I set them on a tray near the window. Now all that remained was for the king to wake and begin his morning routine. As soon as he finished, I would be free to check on the queen.

My stomach twisted as I shooed flies away from the sliced fruit. I couldn't help thinking of Esther and her maids, who had not partaken of any food or liquid over the past two days. I had been so worried about them that I had found it difficult to eat, counting every hunger pang as commiseration for Esther's cause. My prayers would have reached no farther than the ceiling, for I was a man without gods, but at least the queen would face the king knowing she had my earnest support.

The king stirred in his bed, and I retreated into the shadows. Only when he sat up and looked about did I clear my throat, reminding him that I stood nearby if he needed anything.

"Eunuch—" his voice sounded tired—"do we have a banquet planned for this evening?"

"No, my king." I stepped out from behind the sheer curtain. "You may dine privately if you like."

"Make it so. I would like to enjoy a quiet night—no guests at all. I have begun to weary of people who hover like flies."

I could only hope he was referring to his vizier.

My sleepy master scrubbed his scalp with his knuckles. "Do I have a full day?"

"Emissaries from Babylon are coming to speak to you about water rights," I reminded him, "and three of your generals have petitioned for an audience. They want to discuss plans for establishing trade with a Grecian city."

The king sighed and threw back the silk coverlet. "Let's begin, then. Sounds like we won't have a spare minute until dark."

I smiled and gestured to the fruit on the stand.

CHAPTER FORTY-TWO

HADASSAH

I WOKE ON THE THIRD MORNING with a pounding drum at my temple and Miriam's voice in my head. *"You will love whomever you choose to make precious to you,"* she had told me when I fretted about marrying Binyamin. *"By taking care of your husband, praying for him, and putting his needs before your own, you will love him. I promise."*

I opened my eyes, half expecting to discover her lined face in the darkness, but all I could see was a faint gray line around the window, a precursor of dawn.

I rose in the semidarkness, not waking my maids, and dipped a cloth in a basin of cool water. Wringing it out quietly, I held it to my throbbing head and closed my eyes.

Did I love the king? I had strong feelings for him, but I had not loved him as Miriam loved Mordecai. I had not prayed for him, nor had I consciously put his needs before my own. And how could I take care of him when he had dozens of slaves to meet his needs? I had acquiesced and bowed and favored him because he was my king, but lately I had not done anything—not made even the smallest gesture—simply because I loved him.

If the king spared my life, I would try to love him better.

I dipped the cloth back into the cool water, then wrung it out and pressed it to my eyelids. My heart and mind had resigned themselves to the task ahead, but my body protested. I had starved it, dehydrated it, and worried it until I felt as insubstantial as air.

But I had never felt more convinced that I was about to do the right thing.

For five years I had lived as Queen Esther, but beneath the crown I had been, in turn, a naive girl, a love-struck fool, a barren woman, and an insecure wife.

Today, at last, I might be a queen.

I moved to the balcony and slid the wooden shutters aside, then stepped out to gaze at the blue-black dome of the predawn sky. The moon lingered over the northern horizon, silvering the mountains, and I smiled as I remembered how their beauty moved me on my first night in this chamber. I had been such a girl. I had believed that love required nothing but a man and a willing woman.

I drew a deep breath, relishing the silence, and felt an instant's disappointment when footsteps shuffled behind me. "My lady? Can I get you anything?"

"No, thank you, Hulta." No food, no juice, nothing this morning. None of the usual rituals, not even in my dressing room. Because today I would not clothe myself in hopes of catching the king's eye or stirring his heart. Today I would put on royalty.

I walked into the cedar-lined room where my garments were stored on shelves, and then I lifted the hinge of a giant trunk and sorted through a mountain of luxurious fabrics. I had worn a traditional gown the day the king announced my selection as queen and arranged a banquet in my honor. I would wear that dress, along with my crown and the heavy gold chain given to those who had earned the king's favor.

I had the garments set out by the time my maids rose and began their work. Speaking in quiet whispers, they pulled out the copper tub for my bath and hurried away for hot water.

I sat silently as they scrubbed my body in preparation for what I had to do. After the bath, I slipped into my dressing gown and sat before my bronze mirror, watching silently as Hurfita painted my lips and elongated my eyes with kohl. Regoita braided my hair and wrapped it around my head. As she pinned the last piece into place, I was surprised to see a touch of gray at my temples. Who went gray at twenty-two?

"I can paint over that, my queen." Regoita picked up the kohl pot. "With just a touch of my brush here and there—"

"No." I caught her gaze and smiled. "Let it remain."

I stared at my bronze reflection and remembered the dark day when the king's nephew had done what I was about to do. The memory shivered my skin, chilling me despite the warmth of my crowded dressing room.

The man who would be seated on the throne was not the man who invited me into his bed. And no matter where I met him, my husband's nature was both malleable and mercurial. Only Adonai knew how he would respond to my premeditated offense.

Vashti had been deposed because she did not come when called. I might be executed because I came when *not* called. Both of us, the people would say, should have learned that not even a queen could safely ignore the king's wishes.

I motioned for Genunita, who held my royal tunic—a silk gown embroidered with the gold of Ophir and encrusted with precious stones and African pearls. Genunita helped me into the garment, then clicked her tongue as she tied the belt—I was noticeably thinner than I had been five years ago.

I did not want her sympathy. "I think," I said, "that the belt might have stretched a bit."

When Genunita had finished, Regoita stepped forward and placed the crown on my head. I turned to face my maids, and in their expressions I saw that I had succeeded—they gazed upon me with awe and a trace of wonder.

Hatakh, who had entered at the back of the room, nodded with solemn approval. "I have come," he said simply, "to escort you to the throne room. Whenever you are ready, my queen."

I looked at Hurfita and Ruhshita, who had been busy preparing for a banquet. "Is everything ready?"

"Yes, my queen."

I gripped the back of a chair for support, lifted my chin, and met Hatakh's gaze. "Then let us go."

⤖

A tremor of mingled fear and anticipation rippled through me as I left the queen's palace and walked with Hatakh, my maids, and several other eunuchs to the throne room. With no fanfare, we slipped into the great entry hall. Beyond it, in the inner chamber, I could see my husband sitting on his throne, his forehead creased with deep thought.

"Are you sure you want to do this?" Hatakh whispered.

I wiped my damp palms on my gown, then reached for the solidity of his arm. "I'm a little wobbly, dear friend."

"You should have eaten something," he said, wringing his hands like a nervous mother. "Pinch your cheeks, you're far too pale. Hulta, straighten the hem of her gown. Regoita, secure the crown; I think it might be slipping."

My maids hurried to obey, supposedly repairing my appearance, but I knew no real damage had been done on the walk from my chambers. Hatakh was only trying to postpone the inevitable.

If only he could command strength to my spine as easily as he commanded my maids.

"Leave me now." The words sprang unbidden to my lips, urged there by my desperate wish to have the ordeal finished. I took a step forward, moving closer to the shimmering veil that marked the boundary of the inner chamber, the place no one could enter without a royal summons. Beyond the veil, I saw my husband on the throne and Harbonah standing behind the gilded seat. I could not see Haman.

I drew a deep breath and stepped forward, aware that my gold-encrusted sandals made a faintly metallic sound on the gleaming tiles. The guards stiffened, and Harbonah's head turned in my direction. The king looked up, a frown darkening his countenance.

My knees trembled, but I had committed myself. I continued on, moving forward so resolutely that the heavy dress seemed to move with an energy all its own. Encased in pearls, gold, and precious stones, my body felt numb. I tried to smile at the man I loved, but I am not sure what emotions flashed across my face. I only knew that my husband was unhappy at the disturbance. Soon he would prove himself every inch a king and condemn me to a messy and violent death. . . .

But his face cleared, as if he had suddenly recognized me, and he reached for his golden scepter, extending it to me over a space that felt like a thousand paces away.

Still on my feet, I reached out and touched the corporeal symbol of my king's authority and power.

Relief, combined with physical weakness, merged in a wave so strong that the room went black for an instant. But I would not faint. I closed my eyes, forcing myself to remain upright, then lifted my eyelids and smiled at my husband.

"What troubles you, Queen Esther?" the king asked, clearly recognizing that I would not risk my life on a whim. Genuine concern shone in his eyes, along with something that looked like respect. "What brings you to me? Whatever your request, up to half the kingdom, it will be given to you."

I took comfort from the fact that the king had spoken of me as his queen. And his extravagant offer bode well for my petition.

But I could not lay out my case before these nobles. I knew my husband's nature and I knew my enemy. If I explained my situation now, Haman would have time to conspire against me. He would have opportunity to renew his efforts and persuade the king to honor his edict, and my people and I would be doomed.

So I could not afford to be open with my request. My husband had looked on me with generosity, but his was a changeable nature. Tomorrow he might not look on me with such favor, but I would have to face that risk.

I bowed my head in a gracious gesture. "If it is all right with the king," I answered in a strong voice I barely recognized as my own, "let the king and Haman come today to the banquet I have prepared for him."

The king did not even take the time to consider, but immediately glanced at Harbonah. "Bring Haman quickly, so what Esther has asked can be done."

I closed my eyes, well aware of the irony. Once before, a king asked a queen to attend a banquet and she refused, with disastrous results. But a queen had just asked a king to attend a banquet, and he had accepted.

My beloved husband smiled at me. "I will be with you soon."

CHAPTER FORTY-THREE

HARBONAH

THE KING DID NOT NEED ME to accompany him to the queen's banquet, but I wouldn't have missed it for all the gold in the treasury. I walked behind the king and Haman, then stood out of the way as the queen welcomed her husband and the fiend. "Everything has been arranged in the garden pavilion," she said, her smile only slightly frayed. "I am honored, my king, that you would grant me this wish."

The king looked at her, obviously bemused, but he didn't question her further until all three of them had finished eating. As they reclined on their couches and Hatakh poured a dessert wine, the king leaned toward his queen and repeated his question. "What is your wish? It shall be granted you. And what is your request? Be it as great as half the kingdom, it shall be fulfilled."

My thoughts flitted to another occasion when he had uttered those same words—the day when he had promised Artaynta up to half the kingdom. She had only asked for his robe, but oh, what dire consequences resulted from her entreaty.

My queen would face dire consequences if she didn't summon the courage to ask for her life.

The king studied his queen intently, and I saw her bosom rise as she drew a breath to answer. But she did not unmask her identity, nor did she reveal the plot against her.

"My request, what I want, is this," she said, lowering her head as though she knew she might be testing the king's patience. "If I have won the king's favor, if it pleases the king to grant my request and do what I want, let the king and Haman come to the banquet I will prepare for them tomorrow. Then I will do as the king has said."

"A woman of mystery," my master answered, a half smile brightening his face. "The orphan star fallen from the sky to grace my throne room—yes, Haman and I will come. We will not fail you."

I blinked in bafflement when the king and his vizier rose and left the queen's palace.

Feigning some business with Hatakh, I waited until they had departed, then turned to Esther. "My queen, do you think it wise to toy with the king in this way? You know his nature—you know how changeable he is."

"I do," she said, her voice pitched for my ears alone. "And I know I must use his impulsiveness in my cause. I must defeat Haman quickly, so I cannot allow him time to parley with the king behind my back. If I had spoken out today, the king might have gone to his advisors as he did with Vashti. The advisors would remind him that the law of the Medes and Persians cannot be changed. Then Haman and his silver tongue would convince the king that he would do well to be rid of a Jewish queen and her people."

I stared at her, amazed that Mordecai's little Hadassah had become wiser than many of the king's vice-regents—indeed, wiser than the king himself. She had reasoned carefully, and she understood the king better than Haman could ever hope to.

She knew him nearly as well as I did.

"May your God bless your undertaking," I told her, meaning every word. "I must return to my master."

Later that afternoon, while the king rested and Haman took his leave, I stood at the king's balcony and watched the vizier descend the grand staircase. The man practically skipped down the steps, so pleased was he by the queen's special attention, and as he entered the court of the king's treasury his heart must have been buoyed by the sight of so many falling prostrate before him.

Except for one rogue accountant. Even from where I stood, I could see Mordecai at his post, dignified and solidly upright. He did not bend, he did not tremble, he did not even look up as Haman strutted by. This complete lack of respect could only inflame Haman's overly inflated sense of importance, so I reminded myself to speak sense to my friend. If Mordecai didn't at least stay out of Haman's sight, he might find himself meeting the executioner before the thirteenth day of Adar.

I was napping in my alcove when a loud and rhythmic banging rose from the plain. I went in search of the sound and found Hatakh standing by the balcony that overlooked the Valley of the Artists, where the sound seemed to originate. "What is that noise?" I peered at the area below, home to many of the noble families. "And why must they work at night?"

Hatakh gave me a sour look. "Have you not heard? The workmen have not ceased to talk about it. Susa has never seen the like."

I searched the rooftops and grounds of the nearby homes. "The like of what?"

"A pike," Hatakh answered, his face grim. "Earlier this afternoon, Haman ordered workmen to erect a seventy-five-foot pike in his courtyard. Apparently he plans to execute someone and hoist the body for all the city to see."

A subterranean chill ran through me. Without being told, I knew who Haman planned to impale.

◦◦◦

That night I put the king to bed at the usual hour, but apparently he had much on his mind. I sat in my alcove, waiting for the steady sounds of his breathing, but sleep eluded him. Clearly, something troubled my master, for he tossed and turned, fitful in his restlessness yet unwilling to talk about whatever weighed on his mind. I had an idea of what vexed him, but a slave dared not broach a personal subject without the king's invitation.

After a long while, he sat up and called out for me. "A light, eunuch. I can't sleep."

I hurried into his chamber and lit the oil lamp by the bed. "Is something troubling my master?"

"My thoughts are too heavy for sleep. I need a distraction."

I folded my hands. "Would the king like me to summon a harpist?"

"Too entertaining. I need something dull." He thought a moment, then settled back on his pillows. "Summon one of the court scribes. I will review the daily record."

"Any particular year, my king?"

A thoughtful look flitted over the king's face. "The seventh year of my reign."

I smothered a smile as I sent for a scribe. The king might not want to admit it, but I knew why he yearned to hear records from that particular time. That was the year he met and crowned Queen Esther.

◦◦◦

Arsames, the scribe who arrived to read the court chronicles, had one of the most unpleasant and monotonous voices in the palace. I sat in my curtained alcove, out of sight but not out of hearing, and in no time at all the scribe's thin voice put me to sleep. I was drifting in a shallow doze, my head bobbing, when the king's voice abruptly brought me awake.

"Read that again!"

I lifted my head and blinked to focus my eyes. Still in bed, my master sat upright and stared at the startled scribe.

Arsames lowered the scroll and peered over the top. "My king?"

"Read that part again—how the queen came to me with news of a plot."

With shaking fingers, the scribe searched the leather scroll while his servant held an oil lamp closer to the text.

"'Queen Esther approached the inner throne room,'" the scribe read, "'with urgent news from a man called Mordecai, who works in the treasury at the King's Gate. Being skilled with languages, this Mordecai overheard a plot by two of the king's guards, Bigtan and Teresh, who planned to assassinate the king. The men were summoned immediately and sent away for trial.'"

"I remember." The king smiled, his eyes alight. "Continue."

Arsames searched the scroll again, then read, "'Bigtan and Teresh confessed and were executed for daring to plot against the king.'"

"Read on," the king urged. "What was done for this Mordecai? Was he promoted? How was he rewarded?"

The scribe searched the scroll, then finally lowered it. "I can find no record of any reward, promotion, or honor." He cringed as though he was afraid the king would punish him for the omission. "Apparently nothing was done."

The king looked at me. "What was done for this Mordecai? Was he granted honor or promotion?"

I stepped forward, honored to point out the oversight. "Nothing was done for him, my king. Nothing at all."

The king pressed his lips together, then pointed at the scribe, who quaked beneath the long shadow of the royal finger. "That is not acceptable. But you may go."

The scribe gathered his scrolls and hurried for the door while the king got out of bed. "Who is in the courtyard, Harbonah? Find someone and bring him to me."

I ignored a lifetime of protocol and left the room without a proper bow. I flew down the corridor and into the open courtyard, where one or two of the royal counselors usually arrived early in case the king had some urgent need. Dawn had barely pinked the eastern sky, but I sensed movement in the courtyard. I saw the shadow before I saw the man.

"My lord," I called, walking around a column that obscured the early riser. "The king has need of you."

I startled when I saw who I had hailed: Haman. The man must have truly important business to appear at this hour; we usually didn't see him until midmorning.

"Eunuch." Haman stepped toward me, his face a study in eagerness. "Is the king awake? I must speak to him as soon as possible."

I tilted my head, surprised by his request. Apparently he'd been so lost in his own thoughts that he hadn't heard my greeting.

I bowed. "The king is awake. And—"

"I'm sure he'll see me."

Haman rushed ahead, moving confidently down the hallway and pausing only when the guards blocked his advance. "My king!" he called, lifting his voice to be heard through the door. "I must see you at once!"

I blanched at the man's impertinence, but on this occasion, at least, the king wanted to see him. "Enter!" my master called. The guards lowered their swords and allowed Haman to pass.

I followed, desperately curious about what had kept the vizier awake last night. Had it anything to do with the gigantic pike he had erected in the courtyard?

The king, who was sitting on the edge of his bed when Haman entered, was in such a jovial mood that he rose and clapped his vizier on both shoulders before turning to snatch a hunk of bread from his breakfast tray. "Haman, my friend and counselor," the king mumbled over his food, "I am glad you have arrived early, for I have something of great importance to ask. I have been remiss in something, and I would know what you think. What should be done for a man who the king desires to honor?"

Haman remained blank-faced, but I saw thought working in his eyes. Then he blinked, his face glowing as though a candle inside him had just been lit.

"What should be done for a man the king desires to honor?" he repeated. "For a man the king wants to honor, have royal robes the king has worn brought out, and bring out the horse the king usually rides, with a royal crown on its head. The robes and the horse should be handed over to one of the king's most respected officials, and they should put the robes on the man the king wants to honor. Then they should lead him on horseback through the streets of the capital city, proclaiming ahead of him, 'This is what is done for a man whom the king desires to honor!'"

Only with great difficulty did I manage to keep my mouth closed, for I wanted to gape in delighted astonishment. Haman, the egotistical fool, had just described what he wanted the king to do for *him*. He had repeated the phrase "a man the king desires to honor" like a song, emphasizing the syllables in loving tones. He had not asked for wealth or power because he already possessed those; he asked for what he craved most: honor and recognition. The man had an insatiable appetite for public praise.

More significant, he had asked for the king's garment. Artaynta had come to rue the day she asked for the king's robe, but Haman was not shy about wanting to wear a garment that might confer royalty upon its wearer. And even the horse should wear a crown! The man's craven desire for kingship was so obvious, I marveled that my master could not see it. Haman would never be content being the king's second-in-command. He wanted the throne.

"Haman, as always, you have spoken well." Smiling, my master clapped to summon the guards waiting outside his chamber, then pressed his hands to the vizier's round shoulders. Haman flushed, lowered his gaze, and looked as though he were about to melt from the fervent heat of his own humility.

The king beamed at him. "My friend Haman, hurry and do just as you have said. Take my robe and my horse, and adorn the horse with royalty. Do not leave out anything you mentioned. Do all this for Mordecai the Jew who works at the King's Gate."

I bit my tongue just in time to stifle a squeal of pure pleasure, but thankfully the king didn't seem to notice.

The flush receded from Haman's face, leaving him pale and tottering beneath the king's broad hands. But my master didn't seem to notice. He turned and approached me, for I stood near the king's wardrobe.

"What about that one?" He pulled out his coronation robe, the gold and pearl-encrusted tunic he had worn when he first claimed his father's throne. "I can imagine nothing finer." He tossed the tunic to me. "Eunuch, you will assist Haman in this. Make sure the horse is regally dressed. And make certain that all the city hears of this long-overdue honor."

Struggling to keep a triumphant grin from my face, I bowed. "I will assist him with the greatest of pleasure, my king."

CHAPTER FORTY-FOUR

HADASSAH

ON THE DAY OF MY SECOND BANQUET, I woke with the sun to oversee the preparations. I could not invite the king for a third banquet—his patience would not endure further testing—nor could I stand another meal in the company of that horrible Haman.

I was about to undress for my bath when the sound of a shout broke the morning stillness. Two of my maids flew to the window and peered at something below, then looked at me with bewilderment on their faces.

My stomach twisted. In my experience, any shout emanating from the palace signaled bad news, and I did not need bad news today.

Hulta called from the window: "Do not worry, my queen, all is well. But Haman—perhaps you should see this for yourself."

What trouble could the man be stirring up now? I flew to the window and peered out at the palace courtyard beyond my garden.

I saw two mounted Immortals in full armor, followed by a bearded man on the king's black stallion. A man in fine attire led the horse, which wore its royal trappings, complete with a gold crown tied to its forehead.

Shock flew through me when I recognized the jeweled garment the rider wore. Had Haman finally coerced his way into the king's wardrobe? No, the man's beard was too long and unkempt to be the vizier's, and his figure too portly.

"Haman?" I asked.

"Walking," Hulta said. "He's leading the king's horse."

I looked down again and saw that Hulta was correct. "Then who—?"

The rider shifted to look over his shoulder, and I gasped. *Mordecai* sat astride the horse, while Haman struggled to control the skittish beast.

I felt the world shift around me as my head spun. "Who has wrought this?" I murmured, staring at the incredible scene. "Is Haman up to some sort of trickery?"

None of my maids could explain the situation, but Nehorita volunteered to find Harbonah, who would surely be able to explain the odd sight. I considered sending her, then thought the better of it. We had a banquet to plan, and the meal had to be perfect. Nothing could irritate my husband or darken his mood.

"We will hear details soon enough." I stepped away from the window. "But now I have to prepare for another meeting with the king and his vizier." I couldn't stop a wry smile as I gestured to Hurfita, who had readied my bath. "I only hope this morning's activity doesn't completely spoil the vizier's appetite."

CHAPTER FORTY-FIVE

HARBONAH

"IF THOU ART A MASTER," a wise man once said, "be sometimes blind. If thou art a servant, be sometimes deaf."

Years of serving my king had proved this adage many times. My master often overlooked my faults, and I kept his secrets. Though I was as devoted as a eunuch could be, I was not above taking an hour or two to find pleasure for myself.

I stole one of those hours the afternoon of my queen's second banquet. Haman had hurried from the palace immediately after returning from leading Mordecai through the streets of Susa, but he had to return for the queen's feast. A company of guards would be dispatched to escort him to meet the king and queen, so I decided to be part of that company.

I donned a head covering and exchanged my white tunic for the simple kilt of a litter-bearer. I told the astonished slave that I would take his place on this errand. He was only too happy to relax in the barn while I picked up a pole at the back of the litter.

Our company arrived at Haman's house well before the appointed time. While the guards lingered in the vast courtyard and speculated about the tall pike standing amid lush gardens and beautiful statuary, I sidled toward the doorway and hid myself behind a stone outcropping.

From where I stood, I could hear Haman's angry voice, accompanied by the treble tones of a woman—presumably his wife.

"I shall never get over the humiliation," Haman said, anguish in his voice. "The man I hate most in all the world, seated upon the king's stallion! That should have been *my* seat! I should have been wearing the king's robe."

I expected his wife to comfort him, but Haman's woman answered sharply, "If this Mordecai before whom you have begun to fall is a Jew, you will not get the better of him. On the contrary, your downfall before him is certain."

I winced as a hard slap cracked through the silence. I caught the captain of the guard's attention and gestured toward the house. "Hurry," I mouthed. He nodded and pounded on the door.

A moment later, Haman stalked out and climbed into the litter, never even glancing at the slaves who had come to transport him. My tender hands developed blisters as I carried his substantial weight, but seeing his slumped posture and furrowed brow made the pain worthwhile. Yesterday the vizier had fizzed with glee at the thought of dining with the queen; tonight he rode to the palace like a man who had been condemned to dine in the dungeon. Before this morning he had run to and fro arranging for the destruction of the Jews, but now he was being carried toward an event my queen had arranged. He did not realize it, but he was no longer in control.

Yet I did not underestimate him. He was a changeling, able to rearrange his countenance and amend his approach as easily as he might change his cloak. Within a very short time he would be charming and witty, though the man beneath the facade would not change.

Following the queen's explicit directions, we brought Haman to the palace by way of the grand staircase, the one Darius had designed to intimidate visitors with glory and grandeur. Haman barely seemed to notice the gleaming pillars, the glazed tiles and artistic mosaics, even the fountains that bubbled with colored waters. Not until we reached the arched entrance to the queen's palace did he look up, climb out of the litter, and paste a pleasant expression on his face. Suitably composed, he left us behind and proceeded into the royal couple's presence.

The guards and litter-bearers dispersed while I slipped into the queen's garden and hid myself behind the diaphanous curtains hanging from the framework of the garden pavilion. Torches had been planted into the ground outside, giving light to the guards who would be stationed there and lighting the dining area with a soft glow. On the hexagonal platform, three couches—two gold and one silver—had been arranged in a triangular pattern. With one glance I saw that the king and queen would dine head to head, while Haman occupied a couch near their feet.

I couldn't stop a smile. My queen had arranged everything perfectly.

CHAPTER FORTY-SIX

HADASSAH

I WELCOMED MY KING AND HIS VIZIER with a warm smile, then led them to the garden pavilion where everything had been arranged. I greeted my husband with reverent kindness and asked him to sit near me, close enough that I could look into his eyes and read his mood with one glance.

I kept Haman at a distance, where he should be, and was pleased to see that my husband did not object to the arrangement.

The servants brought heaping trays of the king's favorite roasted meats, prepared the way he liked them. No sooner had one tray emptied than another arrived, venison and beef and pork surrounded with heaps of figs and dates, mulberries, plums, apples, pears and quinces, raw almonds, walnuts, and pistachios. The bread was soft and the beer stout. The cooks had done a wonderful job with the meal.

Yet I ate very little. I was sure the king noticed my lack of appetite, and I thought I saw concern in his eyes. But he said nothing, and I appreciated his discretion. I did not want to share anything personal in front of Haman, even if it were a matter so trivial as to why I only picked at the food.

I also said little during the meal, for my stomach had clenched so tightly I could barely draw breath. But Haman made up for my reticence, babbling about his handsome sons, his beautiful wife, and his fine house. Once I gave him a sidelong glance and wondered if I should ask how he enjoyed his morning with Mordecai the Jew . . . then I thought the better of it. The less Haman knew of my relationship with my cousin, the better. I could not give him even the slightest advantage.

At the end of the meal, Hatakh brought us a fine wine and a pudding of blended pomegranates and peaches. After one bite, I knew the moment had arrived. Any time now, the king would turn and ask why I had risked my life to see him, and this time I would have to answer.

When the trays had been taken away and nothing remained but our golden goblets, the king sat upright and looked at me. "What is your wish, Queen Esther?" he said, speaking formally. "It shall be granted you. And what is your request? Be it as great as half the kingdom, it shall be fulfilled."

I slipped from my couch and fell to the floor before my startled husband. I knew I had to be careful in what I said, for he was as involved in the threat to my people as Haman. I had to move him to action without accusing him or threatening his honor.

"If I have won your favor, my king—" I dared to reach out and touch the top of his foot—"and if it pleases the king, then what I ask be given me is my own life and the lives of my people. For we have been sold, I and my people, to be destroyed, killed, exterminated."

I looked up, but my husband's eyes had filled, not with rage but with confusion. He had no idea what I meant or who my people were. If I said nothing more, he might save me, but he would do nothing to prevent the destruction of the Jews in Persia.

And there was still the matter of money. The king cared a great deal for the health of his treasury.

"If we had only been sold as slaves," I continued, "I would have remained quiet; for then the misery we would suffer would not have been severe enough to justify causing loss to the king."

My husband, my king, stared at me as if I had begun to babble in a foreign tongue. "Who is the one, and where is he, who had the audacity to do this?"

I did not shift my gaze from my husband's. "A man hateful and hostile—this wicked Haman."

I heard a noise behind me and knew Haman had leapt to his feet, probably realizing for the first time that I could be dangerous, too.

The king's eyes glittered with rage. He glowered at his vizier, then stood and stalked out of the pavilion, ripping aside a curtain before heading into the quiet coolness of the garden.

I did not know what he was thinking, but I had an idea. He had to be wondering how he could punish Haman for a plot he had approved. He had issued an irrevocable law that could not be rescinded. So how could he rescue his honor and his queen from a threat he had never realized?

Trembling, I lifted myself from the floor and sank onto my couch, drawing deep breaths to calm my pounding heart. My thoughts remained with the king, but suddenly Haman was on top of me, having thrown himself on my couch in desperation. He must have glimpsed the rage in the king's face and knew his hours were numbered.

I stared at him, felt his breath on my face, and realized the man who had demanded everyone prostrate themselves before him was now groveling before a Jew.

"My queen, I didn't know. No one told me, no one ever said—"

He had barely begun to babble when my husband appeared in the opening between the curtains, his hands on his hips and his face livid. "Is he going to rape the queen here in the palace, before my very eyes?!"

The moment the words left his mouth, two of the ever-present Immortals stepped up and grasped Haman's arms. They pulled the blubbering vizier from me, and then one of them tied Haman's hands behind his back while the other tossed a cloth over his head, sparing me the sight of a condemned man.

Before the guards dragged the former vizier away, the king stepped behind Haman and pulled the royal signet ring from the man's fat finger.

I breathed easier than I had in days, but the victory had not yet been won. The king had dealt with the personal insult to his honor and his queen, but the edict still stood. My people remained in danger.

Then my silent friend Harbonah, who missed nothing, stepped forward to direct my husband's frustrated rage. "Look! A seventy-five-foot pike has been erected at Haman's house. The vizier made it for Mordecai, who has only done good for the king."

That was enough. A Persian king could not execute a man for a single offense, but Harbonah had just supplied a second one. Not only had Haman dared to throw himself upon the queen's person in the king's presence, but he had planned to attack one of the king's benefactors, an act commensurate with an attack on the king himself.

My husband's mouth flattened into a thin line. "Impale this traitor on his own pike."

Haman screamed at the prospect of Persian justice as the guards led him away.

My king sank down onto his couch, then leaned against the curving support. He dropped his head to his hand and gazed at me in a posture of weariness and disbelief.

Then, without speaking, he reached across the chasm between us and took my hand.

"I have been blind," he said simply. "I cannot believe he would threaten my queen."

My queen? Not *the Jews*, not *you, my beloved wife*. But *my queen.*

What could I say? Clearly, the king cared more for his honor than for me or my people. His anger would be appeased by Haman's death, but millions of my people still lived under an irrevocable death sentence.

The thirteenth of Adar loomed before us.

CHAPTER FORTY-SEVEN

HARBONAH

MY HEART SANG WITH RELIEF to see our good queen justified and Haman dispatched. I was also glad to see the king use his forceful personality for good. Before the day ended, my master had presented the queen with Haman's estate and sent for Mordecai.

The accountant arrived at the palace before moonrise. The man looked older than when I had last seen him; clearly, the extermination order had grieved him. But he greeted his cousin warmly and then prostrated himself before the king in the royal audience hall.

"A man the king delights to honor," my master said, looking upon Mordecai with appreciation.

Esther spoke up, finally explaining how she and Mordecai were related. Upon learning that the man who had once saved his life was Esther's adoptive father, the king removed his signet ring and gave it to Mordecai. "You shall be my second-in-command, my vizier and chief counselor. For you have wisdom in abundance, and a heart more righteous than Haman's."

Mordecai bowed again, obviously moved, yet shadows lingered in his eyes. "I shall serve you, my king, throughout my remaining days."

Esther then placed the management of Haman's vast estate into Mordecai's capable hands.

I stood to the side and watched these developments with an approving and wistful heart. Hadassah was no longer a young and inexperienced girl. In the space of a few days she had become a courageous, powerful, and wealthy woman, though she had not yet completed her task. She had toppled her formidable enemy, but his evil machinations would still result in the murder of untold thousands.

I looked at her, tilting my head to study her lovely face. Though she kept her eyes downcast as the king talked with Mordecai, a line had crept between her brows. The woman was thinking, and thinking hard. Her most difficult challenge still lay ahead, for my master clearly considered the matter settled. He had defended his queen, executed her enemy, and elevated her cousin. What else could she possibly expect him to do?

I looked at Mordecai, whose face remained smooth and passionless; he was not trying to solve this conundrum. He was no longer Hadassah's counselor, but her co-worker, and he was trusting her to handle the situation.

Queen Esther lifted her chin, squared her shoulders, and again stepped toward the king's throne. His brow rose, probably curious as to why she was formally approaching yet again, but then she surprised all of us by falling at his feet, tears streaming down her face. "Please," she said, her voice breaking, "save my people."

My master extended his golden scepter, awarding her mercy, and the queen struggled to her feet. "If it please the king," she said, strengthening her voice, "and if I have found favor with him, and if he thinks it is right, and if I am pleasing to him, let there be a decree that reverses the orders of Haman, son of Hammedatha the Agagite, who ordered that Jews throughout all the king's provinces should be destroyed. For how can I endure to see my people and my family slaughtered?"

I covered my mouth, amazed at the queen's persistence. She used a Persian word meaning *to make pass away* in regard to Haman's edict, but Persian law most emphatically did *not* pass away. She knew she was asking the impossible, so she had appealed to my master's nobility, his affection for her, his legal authority, and his commitment as her husband. She knew her request could not be granted under a royally authorized decree, but instead of blaming the king for his role in the edict, she was petitioning everything that was good and reasonable within him.

I frowned. I admired the queen, but she was putting the king in an impossible position. He could do nothing, yet she still begged him to undo what Haman had done. How could she expect him to do the impossible?

I drew a deep breath and struggled to think.

Though the king had foolishly handed his authority over to Haman, Esther had not uttered a single accusation against her husband. She blamed Haman alone, probably hoping to give the king a legal reason to nullify a decree that had been the work of one evil man.

Then she had reminded him that even though he might protect her, she would feel unimaginable pain if she had to witness the slaughter of her people.

My master considered her request, a vein in his forehead swelling like a snake. I had seen that vein bulge before and knew it indicated his rising irritation. The king was feeling trapped between his queen on one side and an irreversible law on the other.

"I have given you the property of Haman, and he has been impaled on a pike because he tried to destroy the Jews," he said, his voice sharper than it had been a moment before. But his eyes softened as his gaze fell upon the anguished woman before him, and when I saw that softening, I knew he would surrender.

"You go ahead," he said, "and send a message to the Jews in the king's name, telling them whatever you want, and seal it with the king's signet ring. But remember—whatever has already been written in the king's name and sealed with his ring can never be revoked."

Unable to rescind his own edict, the king had just given two Jews permission and the authority to issue their own royal decrees, commands that would effectively constrain the king himself.

Then, in an obvious attempt to escape a situation he found uncomfortable, my master rose and left the room, his guards following him. I should have gone too, but I decided to linger a moment more.

Esther turned, looked at her cousin with relief and gratitude in her eyes, and stepped forward to clasp his hands.

～❈～

On the twenty-third day of the Jewish month of Sivan, two months and ten days after the publication of Haman's decree, the palace issued another edict, this one penned by Mordecai. The first royal decree had come from the king's vizier, so the second decree was issued by the *new* vizier, a very different man. Mordecai wrote the edict in my master's own name, so that no one would doubt or deny it, and unlike Haman's proclamation, this decree mentioned that the law had the full backing of the king.

Haman's decree had gone out urgently, but Mordecai's counter-decree went out with urgency and great haste, for the Jews would need time to prepare to defend themselves.

"The king has permitted the Jews in each and every city to gather
and to make a stand for their lives: to slaughter, slay, and destroy
the forces of every people and province who afflict them, together
with children and women, with their property as spoil, on a single
day, in all the provinces of King Xerxes, on the thirteenth day of
the twelfth month, the month of Adar."

A copy of the edict was issued as law in each province and made
public to all the people, so the Jews could be ready to take vengeance
on those who afflicted them on the assigned day.

I had been a party to the writing of the document, placing myself at Mordecai's service whenever the king had no need of me. I
watched and listened as the new vizier and the queen debated how to
best answer Haman's edict, and I agreed when they finally decided
that the best approach was to take Haman's words and turn them
around. "Unlike Haman, we do not want to kill peaceful people,"
Esther told me, "but we will not surrender to those who would take
our lives and destroy our children."

Copies of the letter were quickly dispatched throughout the
empire, so that the Jews would have months to prepare to defend
themselves against their enemies.

That night Mordecai set aside his somber garments and left the
king's presence wearing violet and white, a heavy gold crown, and
a linen robe of fine purple. At the sight of his success, the city of
Susa shouted for joy.

For the Jews, Esther's people, all was light, gladness, joy and
honor, for Mordecai and Queen Esther had reacted to Haman's evil
with courage and justice. The Jews feasted and celebrated this good
news, and many people of Susa observed the rising tide of Jewish
prosperity and began to worship the God of Abraham.

But though the Jews had received the power and the right to
defend themselves, the battle had not yet begun.

CHAPTER FORTY-EIGHT

HADASSAH

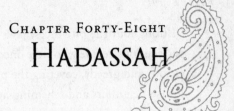

NINE MONTHS PASSED, the remainder of a year that had begun in horror and might end on the same note. As time pushed us into the month of Adar, Mordecai assured me that the Jews in all the provinces were well prepared for any attacks that might come against them, but I couldn't help being concerned. I had risked my life for my people, and I could not forget about them as the day of reckoning approached.

During the two months we debated how to answer the problem of Haman's edict, I wondered if an answer would even be necessary. Our family had lived in Susa for years without facing any significant oppression, so perhaps people would simply forget about Haman's decree and ignore the appointed day.

I voiced this thought to Mordecai, but he laughed and told me I was being too optimistic. "Reports have already begun to reach me," he said, turning to accept a scroll from one of the servants.

"Throughout the provinces, Jews have begun to feel the sting of persecution. People who were once kind and tolerant have become vicious and greedy, coveting the property and possessions of their Jewish neighbors and scheming how best to get them. Evil is like a potent dye, Hadassah—once it is spilt on linen, the stain must be cut out of the fabric. And if the garment must be sacrificed—" he shook his head—"so be it."

Fortunately, Mordecai's edict seemed to stop the most brazen episodes of intimidation, though I doubted it quelled the hate-filled hearts of the most greedy. Haman had taught me that some men were inspired by the evil of pride and would not hesitate to do anything necessary to further their selfish intentions.

Harbonah, ever a friend to me and my cousin, reported that members of the imperial army had also expressed their gratitude for our intervention. If Mordecai had not countermanded Haman's edict, the king's army would have been required to enforce the law. On the thirteenth day of Adar, they would have been dispersed through the empire, charged with entering every city, village, and synagogue to murder every Jew they could find, even the very young and very old.

After the appointed day passed, I hoped my king and his empire would settle down to peace and safety. I did not think my husband would mount any other military campaigns, for he had lost the zeal for battle. He was still a strong man, but he had aged over the past year.

Some nights when we dined together in his chamber, I looked across the space between us and saw that his eyes were as wide and blank as windows, as though the soul they harbored had long since flown away.

Did he realize how badly he had erred? Did he wake in the night burdened with the realization that he had nearly caused the deaths of millions of innocents?

Perhaps he had, but I would never accuse him, for I had never forgotten Humusi's advice: *"Listen, little Esther, and hear what is on his heart. Hold it securely and do not share it with anyone. And then, if you can find it in your heart to do so, love him for the man he is and the man he could be. Expect greatness of him. And then, perhaps, he will find it in himself."*

Xerxes, son of Darius and king of Persia, was my husband, and 'twas not my duty to rebuke him. I was to respect him, honor him, and obey him. And through it all, to love him.

CHAPTER FORTY-NINE

HARBONAH

WHEN THE SUN ROSE ON THE THIRTEENTH DAY of the twelfth
month, Jews throughout the provinces assembled outside their
homes and synagogues to defend themselves against anyone who
tried to do them harm. I wish I could write that no one attempted
such a rash act, but the world has never experienced a shortage of
fools. Coveting the property and businesses of their Jewish neighbors, some citizens of the empire attempted to cut the Jews down,
but the children of Israel fought back with vigor and skill.

In the royal fortress of Susa, where Haman's hostility had spread
like a fungus, the Jews killed five hundred soldiers and noblemen
who were bent on slaughtering them. And—most significantly—
when the ten sons of Haman attempted to lead an attack on a Jewish
business at the bazaar, they were captured and killed. But no one
touched any property that had belonged to them.

I wondered why Mordecai's edict had expressly stated that the

Jews could take the property of any aggressor and yet no one did. When I asked the vizier about it later, Mordecai smiled and said that he'd written that the Jews *could* take property in order to emphasize that they *wouldn't*.

"And there is yet another, more important reason," he added. "The Jews who defeated the Amalekites under King Saul disobeyed the word of Adonai by taking spoil from the defeated. By sacrificing our lawful right to take goods and property now, we are demonstrating our repentance before HaShem."

I didn't understand why Mordecai thought it so important to settle an issue from an ancient battle, but Haman had been right about one thing—the Jews were a peculiar people. I lived for each day, with little thought to what lay ahead or behind, but the Jews spoke of their distant forefathers and their future descendants as if they were bound together by a single cord.

"I am confident," Mordecai told me, a light glowing in the depths of his eyes, "that no matter how dark our present despair, Israel is the hope of the world. Adonai has promised that all nations will be blessed through the children of Abraham, Isaac, and Jacob. Of the coming one, the prophet Isaiah wrote:

'I, the LORD, have called you to demonstrate my righteousness.
I will take you by the hand and guard you,
and I will give you to my people, Israel,
as a symbol of my covenant with them.
And you will be a light to guide the nations.
You will open the eyes of the blind.
You will free the captives from prison,
releasing those who sit in dark dungeons. . . .
You will do more than restore the people of Israel to me.
I will make you a light to the Gentiles,
and you will bring my salvation to the ends of the earth.'"

"Who?" I asked, intrigued by the words Mordecai had quoted. "Who was the prophet talking about?"

Mordecai's squint tightened. "Adonai's servant. The one who will restore justice to all who have been wronged. The chosen one."

"And who is that?" I insisted.

Mordecai looked at me with a smile hidden in his eyes. "The Messiah, and may He come quickly."

I had other questions, but just then one of the eunuchs ran toward me with a summons from my master, so I had to take my leave.

As the thirteenth of Adar drew to a close, the king sent for the queen and told her of the battle's results in his royal fortress. "Now," he added, his voice low and conciliatory, "whatever your request, you will be granted it; whatever more you want, it will be done."

The offer came out of nowhere; the queen had done nothing to elicit it. But Esther did not hesitate to answer. "If it please the king," she said, her voice calm and clear, "let the Jews in all of Susa act again tomorrow in accordance with today's decree—and have Haman's ten dead sons impaled for all to see."

All of Susa—not the fortress only.

I saw determination in her eyes and heard steel in her voice. No longer a sheltered, pretty pet, she had met evil and learned that it could not be vanquished in a single day. Families who had lost loved ones at the fortress would be bent on vengeance, and the Jews in the city might need to defend themselves against another attack.

Recognizing the wisdom in his queen's request, the king agreed. Warriors hoisted the bodies of Haman's dead sons on poles as a grim reminder that the tide had turned; the God of the Jews had protected His people. Yet the next day, another three hundred died in attacks upon Jewish families and neighborhoods. Word arrived from the other provinces, informing us that over seventy-five thousand had died because they attempted to destroy their Jewish neighbors.

In the end, Haman's edict resulted in the opposite of what the

Agagite had intended. Instead of eradicating the Jews, Esther's courage and Mordecai's wisdom worked to purge the empire of those who hated the children of Israel.

When the bloody work was finished, Mordecai recorded the events. Queen Esther, the daughter of Abihail, wrote another letter, putting her full authority behind Mordecai's missive to establish the annual Festival of Purim—an annual celebration to commemorate the days on which the Jews obtained rest from their enemies. So the command of Esther confirmed the practices of Purim, and it was all written down in the records.

Mordecai became very great among the Jews, who held him in high esteem because he continued to work for the good of his people and to speak up for the welfare of all their descendants.

Best of all, he continued to call me *friend*.

HARBONAH

THOUGH THE DAYS OF PURIM have faithfully been celebrated by Queen Esther's people ever since that first amazing victory, the fate of my master and his empire has been largely forgotten. I was fond of my king, devoted to him and his charming queen, but not everyone in the empire saw his tender side or knew of his weaknesses.

Seven years after the events of that first Purim, when Queen Esther was but thirty years old, my master returned his attention to what he had always considered his greatest failing: the conquest of Greece. Like a man who cannot ignore a phantom itch, he mounted yet another campaign, traveled to Greece with his armies, and was soundly defeated again.

But not all his enemies were found on foreign soil. Though I cannot prove my suspicions, I am convinced that Vashti, the former queen, devised the tragic events that occurred next.

After my master's return to Persia, on a night when illness prevented me from occupying my post, Artabanus, the captain of the king's bodyguard, assassinated my king as he slept. Crown Prince Darius claimed the throne, but a few months later, in an attempt to avenge his father, eighteen-year-old Artaxerxes killed his murderous older brother and Artabanus, the conspirator.

If only he'd thought to kill his mother, as well. For though Vashti had a son on the throne, noble Artaxerxes was not the son of her choosing. In time she goaded her second son, Hystaspes, into attacking the king. Alert guards foiled the evil plot, and Artaxerxes was forced to execute his only surviving brother.

Twenty-one years after his father had assumed the crown, Artaxerxes moved into the palace at Susa and claimed his father's throne. He was nothing like Vashti, his mother, and resembled his father in form only. I believe he modeled his nature after the kind and gentle Esther, who spent many afternoons with him and the other children in her garden. Artaxerxes proved to have a quiet and noble spirit, much like Esther's, and he was king over the empire when Nehemiah the Jew served as the king's cupbearer. Artaxerxes thought so highly of the children of Israel that he willingly dispatched Nehemiah to Jerusalem to oversee the rebuilding of the ruined city walls.

After the king's death, my beloved friend Queen Esther and her maids left the queen's palace and retired to quiet rooms in the harem. Vashti clung to her authority as the queen mother, and Damaspia, Artaxerxes's wife, became queen.

But Esther would forever be loved and admired by her people, by both the Jews and the Persians. She died while the royal household was dwelling at the palace in Ecbatana, and now she rests in her tomb there.

As for me, when I am able to stand, I work in the kitchen. The king has graciously allowed me to remain in the palace for as long as I live. I am no longer able to run up and down the grand staircase as I did in his father's day, but I still count it a joy to be able to serve. I spend my hours roasting meat, polishing silver goblets, and overseeing the details of royal banquets—*small* royal banquets.

When my little room is quiet, I lie down, breathe deeply, and remember. Because my weary eyes have witnessed greatness, and my heart has been stirred by love. My spirit too has been touched by men and women who placed their trust in a God they could not see.

Unlike Ahura Mazda, this God did not delight in murder, destruction, and lies. This God cared for His people, imparted wisdom and courage, and encouraged His people to love one another.

When I die, I hope to meet Hadassah and Mordecai again . . . so that we may worship that God together.

DISCUSSION QUESTIONS

1. Angela Hunt has said that she tries to invent as little as possible when writing about historical characters. Assuming that her historical sources are correct and much of this novel is based on actual facts, what surprised you about the story of this biblical heroine?

2. The biblical book of Esther tends to give us only the facts, a spare canvas on which the story plays out. Theologians and storytellers have interpreted the story in various ways, painting Esther either as a beautiful girl who won an ancient beauty pageant or as a girl who was taken by force and raped by a lascivious king. What was your impression of Esther before you read this novel? What was your impression after reading it?

3. Many religious people, Jewish and Christian, have considered Esther an almost perfect person. Some rabbis believe that Esther was married to Mordecai, and she remained righteous, even though she had to sleep with the king, because a heavenly being "filled in" for her when she had to perform her conjugal duty. Some Christians tend to think of Esther as almost

without sin and completely heroic in her actions. But Esther was human, and some of her recorded actions—her insistence that Mordecai remove his sackcloth, for instance—seem to reveal a superficial mind-set. Has this novel influenced your ideas and thoughts about Esther's nature? About her actions?

4. Angela Hunt writes from a Christian perspective, and she has said that she sees parallels between her place in today's American society and Esther's place in Persian society. In one scene, Esther ruminates about her world:

> We walked in it, traded in it, communicated in it, and did acts of kindness for it. To the casual observer, we might have looked like ordinary people, but we were not. About that, at least, Haman was right.
>
> We were children of Abraham, Isaac, and Jacob, and we served an invisible God, who remained close to us no matter where we lived. But our hearts did not—should not—belong to this world.

What parallels do you see between these two worlds?

5. Hunt chose to tell this story from only two character viewpoints: Hadassah's and Harbonah's. Do you think the story should have been told from another point of view? What other character would you like to hear from?

6. Is this story similar to other biblical historical fiction you have read? How was it similar or different? Do you prefer historical fiction or contemporary fiction? Why?

7. Hunt has said she never knowingly contradicts the biblical or historical record—unless historical records disagree, then she chooses the view she believes is the most logical. Prior to reading this novel, had you read much about ancient Persia? Were you aware of how advanced their culture was? In what ways is ancient Persia similar to the United States?

8. What lessons or ideas will you take away from the novel? If you read the biblical book of Esther again, how will the story be different for you?

9. Who was your favorite character? Who was your least favorite?

10. Would you recommend this novel to a friend? Why or why not?

AUTHOR'S NOTE

Whenever I write a historical novel, I am always asked how much of the tale is fact and how much fiction. I hope you will be pleased to know that nearly every event in this novel comes from the historical record. The biblical account is accurately represented here, and I have supplemented that story with writings from the Greek chronicler Herodotus. He wrote extensively of the Persian court and its kings, particularly of Xerxes and his Queen Amestris (Vashti). He did not mention a queen called Esther, but just because he didn't mention her doesn't mean she didn't exist.

The casual reader can be easily confused, because anyone researching this period will have to deal with at least four different languages: the Greek version of names, which were applied later and would never have been used by the actual people, the Persian name, and, to those familiar with the biblical account, the Hebrew name as well as the Anglicized version of the Hebrew name. The king represented in the story of Esther, for example, is Xerxes (Greek), Khshayarshan (Persian), Achashverosh (Hebrew), and Ahasuerus (Anglicized Hebrew).

Which is why I often referred to him as "the king."

I carefully considered which names to use in this novel. The Greek names are the easiest to read and pronounce, but something in me resists referring to characters by names they would never have used themselves. The Persian names are obscure and hard to track down, as well as hard to pronounce. Anglicized Hebrew is more familiar and easier for the average reader to understand, but the Hebrew is the closest thing to what the characters themselves would have experienced. But since most people are familiar with the English Bible, I have chosen to use the Anglicized Hebrew names.

Other details:

Theologians believe that Amestris (Greek) is Vashti (Hebrew) of the biblical account. And while the Bible is silent about what happened to Vashti after her demotion, Herodotus relates the story of how she mutilated the mother of one of the king's lovers. He also tells us that she was alive and well during the reign of Artaxerxes, her son, and as late as 454 BC she had one of his political enemies impaled. She is also rumored to have buried alive fourteen noblemen's children as a sacrifice to Ahura Mazda.

We have no record of Esther ever being pregnant. But the three sons in line for the king's throne were his children by Amestris, so if Esther did have children, they would have been far down the line of succession unless Xerxes had elevated them.

Herodotus tells us that the provinces of Babylonia and Assyria sent King Darius five hundred boys to be made into eunuchs, along with a thousand talents of silver. According to another source, this was an *annual* payment, but I sincerely hope it was a one-time event. So from that fact I fleshed out the character of Harbonah, whose existence is biblical.

Scripture does not tell us that Mordecai had a wife, but since the first of the Torah's 613 commandments is to have children, devout Jewish men would have felt responsible to marry and raise a family. Furthermore, society would have considered it improper for a single man to raise a young girl without a wife's help, so I invented Miriam.

The Scripture does not tell us that Esther was betrothed, yet most Jewish children were betrothed by their parents at an early age, so it seemed natural and logical for Esther to have a fiancé. And theologians are divided about the king's call for beautiful virgins. Did he ask for virgins as in "young women" or did he want young, *sexually pure* women? The Hebrew word could mean either (see Isaiah 7:14: "virgin" meant *young woman* when applied to Isaiah 8:3–4, and *sexually pure* when applied to Luke 1:34. This is an example of the "law of double reference," where one Scripture is applicable to two situations).

Some of the Jewish sages believe Esther was actually married to Mordecai and was still taken up by the king's men; in that case the former use would apply. But since the Bible stresses the fact that Esther was as a daughter to Mordecai, I don't believe they were married.

Would a king want a potential bride who'd been married to another man? I doubt it. And since in many Eastern cultures tradition still demands the "blood on the sheets" proof of virginity, I believe it's reasonable to assume that the king wanted young, unmarried women—their youth alone would help explain the year-long preparation before they were allowed to go into the king's bedchamber. On the other hand, if a man brought a stunningly beautiful woman to the palace or gave her to the king as a gift, I doubt she'd be turned away.

Given all of the above, I believe Esther must have been a teenager when she entered the king's palace, and therefore not much older than many of his children. Her cousin Mordecai loved her like a father and, because he'd lost his wife, invested his life in his work and in his young ward. Because he worked "at the King's Gate," or in the courtyard of the palace complex, he undoubtedly heard palace rumors and knew of the many dangers lurking behind the smiling faces belonging to other royal concubines, eunuchs, politically ambitious nobles, and dissatisfied soldiers.

Seen in this light, and supported by the writings of Herodotus and others, we have a thoroughly fascinating story of how God worked within a pagan culture to sustain His people . . . and drew the heart of a distracted daughter back to himself.

REFERENCES

———. Vol. 137, *Bibliotheca Sacra Volume* 137:548 (October 1980). Dallas, TX: Dallas Theological Seminary, 1980.

Allen, Lindsay. *The Persian Empire*. Chicago: The University of Chicago Press, 2005.

Bell, Albert A. *Exploring the New Testament World*. Nashville: Thomas Nelson Publishers, 1998.

Berlin, Adele. *The JPS Bible Commentary Esther*. Philadelphia: The Jewish Publication Society, 2001.

Boucher, Francois. *20,000 Years of Fashion: The History of Costume and Personal Adornment*. New York: Harry N. Abrams, Inc. 1962.

Breneman, Mervin. "Ezra, Nehemiah, Esther," electronic ed., *The New American Commentary*, 327–33. Nashville: Broadman & Holman Publishers, 1993.

Brosius, Maria. *The Persians: An Introduction*. New York: Routledge, 2008.

Brosius, Maria. *Women in Ancient Persia*. Oxford: Clarendon Press, 1996.

Bush, Fredric W. Vol. 9, *Word Biblical Commentary: Ruth, Esther*. Dallas: Word, Incorporated, 2002.

Chrastina, Paul. "King Xerxes Invades Greece." http://www.old newspublishing.com/xerxes.htm.

Curtis, John, and Nigel Tallis, editors. *Forgotten Empire: The World of Ancient Persia.* Los Angeles: University of California Press, 2005.

Davis, William Stearns. *Readings in Ancient History: Illustrative Extracts from the Sources, vol. 2: Greece and the East.* Boston: Allyn and Bacon, 1912.

Elwell, Walter, and Philip Wesley Comfort. *Tyndale Bible Dictionary.* Wheaton, IL: Tyndale House Publishers, 2001.

Fox, Michael V. *Character and Ideology in the Book of Esther.* 2nd ed. Grand Rapids, MI: William B. Eerdmans Publishing Company, 1991.

Gerig, Bruce L. "Eunuchs in the OT, Part 1." http://epistle.us /hbarticles/eunuchs1.html, 2010.

Ginzberg, Louis, Henrietta Szold, and Paul Radin. *Legends of the Jews.* 2nd ed. Philadelphia: Jewish Publication Society, 2003.

Harvey, Charles D. "Probing Moral Ambiguity: Grappling with Ethical Portraits in the Hebrew Story of Esther." *Southern Baptist Journal of Theology,* Fall 1998.

Knowles, Andres. *The Bible Guide.* 1st Augsburg Books. Minneapolis, MN: Augsburg, 2001.

Matthews, Kenneth A. "The Historical Books," in *Holman Concise Bible Commentary.* Nashville: Broadman & Holman Publishers, 1998.

Meir, Tamar. "Esther: Midrash and Aggadah." Jewish Women: A Comprehensive Historical Encyclopedia. 20 March 2009. *Jewish Women's Archive.* August 14, 2012. http://jwa.org/encyclopedia /article/esther-midrash-and-aggadah.

Neuffer. "The Accession of Artaxerxes I," *Andrews University Seminary Studies 6* (1968):81.

Radmacher, Earl D., Ronald Barclay Allen, and H. Wayne House. *Nelson's New Illustrated Bible Commentary.* Nashville: Thomas Nelson Publishers, 1999.

Severy, Merle, Seymour L. Fishbein, and Edwards Park, eds. *Everyday Life in Bible Times.* National Geographic Society, 1967.

Smith, James E. *The Books of History, Old Testament Survey Series.* Joplin, MO: College Press, 1995.

Spence-Jones, H.D.M., ed. *The Pulpit Commentary: Esther.* Bellingham, WA: Logos Research Systems, Inc., 2004.

Stortz, Rodney, and R. Kent Hughes. *Daniel: The Triumph of God's Kingdom*, Preaching the Word. Wheaton, IL: Crossway Books, 2004.

Utley, Robert James. *Old Testament Survey: Genesis–Malachi,* 117–22. Marshall, TX: Bible Lessons International, 2000.

Vos, Howard Frederic. *Nelson's New Illustrated Bible Manners & Customs: How the People of the Bible Really Lived.* Nashville: Thomas Nelson Publishers, 1999.

Weinbach, Mendel. *127 Insights into Megillas Esther.* Southfield, MI: Targum Press, 1990.

Wiesehofer, Josef. *Ancient Persia.* New York: I.B. Tauris Publishers, 2011.

Angela Hunt has published more than one hundred books, with sales nearing five million copies worldwide. She's the *New York Times*-bestselling author of *The Tale of Three Trees*, *The Note*, and *The Nativity Story*. Angela's novels have won or been nominated for several prestigious industry awards, such as the RITA Award, the Christy Award, the ECPA Christian Book Award, and the HOLT Medallion Award. Romantic Times Book Club presented her with a Lifetime Achievement Award in 2006. In 2008, she completed her doctorate in Biblical Studies and is currently completing her Th.D. Angela and her husband live in Florida, along with their mastiffs. For a complete list of the author's books, visit angelahuntbooks.com.

More Fiction
You May Enjoy

You May Also Like . . .

Shipwrecked and stranded, Emma Chambers is in need of a home. Could the widowed local lighthouse keeper and his young son be an answer to her prayer?

Love Unexpected by Jody Hedlund
BEACONS OF HOPE #1
jodyhedlund.com

To fulfill a soldier's dying wish, nurse Abigail Stuart marries him and promises to look after his sister. But when the *real* Jeremiah Calhoun appears alive, can she provide the healing his entire family needs?

A Most Inconvenient Marriage by Regina Jennings
reginajennings.com

Ewan came to West Virginia to help his uncle Hugh start a brickmaking operation. But when Hugh makes an ill-advised deal, the foundation he's built begins to crumble. Can the former owner's daughter help Ewan save the brickworks—and his future?

The Brickmaker's Bride by Judith Miller
REFINED BY LOVE
judithmccoymiller.com

⬥ BETHANYHOUSE

Stay up-to-date on your favorite books and authors with our free e-newsletters. Sign up today at bethanyhouse.com.

Find us on Facebook. facebook.com/bethanyhousepublishers

Free exclusive resources for your book group! bethanyhouse.com/anopenbook

anopenbook